ALAN CHIN

SURVIVING IMMORTALITY

DSP PUBLICATIONS

Published by

DSP PUBLICATIONS

5032 Capital Circle SW, Suite 2, PMB# 279, Tallahassee, FL 32305-7886 USA
www.dsppublications.com

Trade Paperback ISBN: 978-1-64080-545-3
Digital ISBN: 978-1-64080-544-6
Library of Congress Control Number: 2017919630
Trade Paperback published June 2018
v. 1.0

Printed in the United States of America
∞
This paper meets the requirements of
ANSI/NISO Z39.48-1992 (Permanence of Paper).

Readers love *The Lonely War*
by ALAN CHIN

"This is the most beautiful book I've read in a very long time. It is magnificent."

—The Book Breeze

"…a modern classic. … While *The Lonely War* is not always an easy read, it is most definitely worth your time and I highly recommend it."

—Joyfully Jay

"*The Lonely War* simply exemplifies Chin's superb writing!"

—Paddylast Inc

"Chin's writing is often literary, sometimes poetic, and in keeping with the broad sweep of the story, it illustrates the intensity of the love, relationships, and the coarseness of an all-male crew and prison camp."

—Historical Novel Society

By ALAN CHIN

The Lonely War
Surviving Immortality

Published by DSP PUBLICATIONS
www.dsppublications.com

SURVIVING IMMORTALITY

PROLOGUE

THROUGHOUT RECORDED history, many humans were labeled monsters. Some were born physically misshapen, no legs or arms, enormous heads and spindly bodies, crooked backs, joined twins, no sexual organs, or both sexual organs. The list is endless. These corporeal abnormalities were once considered God's retribution for the sins of the parents, but now they are thought of as nature's accidents, an unlucky roll of the dice, no one's fault.

There is, however, a different breed of monster, where the deformity is hidden from the eye. The face and body may be faultless, yet a twisted gene or benevolent drug with devilish side effects taken during pregnancy results in a malformed psyche.

Monsters are deviations from the traditional norms. As one child is born without legs, another can be born lacking empathy and a conscience. The child born without legs eventually learns he is handicapped and struggles to overcome his physical abnormality. But the child born with no compassion goes through life unaware of his defect, because he has nothing visible to compare with others. He wrongly assumes everyone is like him, cold-blooded, calculating, unfeeling, self-absorbed. To this kind of fiend, a soul-stricken man seems weak, even comical, in the same way that to a criminal, honesty seems pathetically ludicrous.

This means, of course, that to an inner fiend, integrity and simple human kindness seems abnormal, dishonest, and perhaps even monstrous. They will, therefore, do everything possible to expose the monster in everyone around them, and they will interpret that as an act of righteousness.

PART ONE
ESCAPE

The birth of a man is the birth of his sorrow. The longer he lives, the more stupid he becomes, because his anxiety to avoid unavoidable death becomes more and more acute. What bitterness! He lives for what is always out of his reach! His thirst for survival in the future makes him incapable of living in the present.
—Chuang Tzu

CHAPTER ONE

Matt Reece Connors straddled his Appaloosa stallion, Comet, loping along a ridge at the eastern foothills of the White Mountains. Bitter cold air kept him anxious for the sunrise, which, if nothing else, would warm horse and rider a few degrees.

Minutes later, winter curled into an early spring. With a single spectacular dawn, the season changed. A rush of amethyst and gold flooded the sky as the sun inched above the horizon, and the Nevada desert awakened with a new and inexplicable hope. Wind rushed down the mountain carrying the crisp scent of snow, and it sweetened the sunrays tumbling over the scrublands, lifting Matt Reece's spirits to the point he forgot about the sorrow that awaited him back at the ranch house.

To the unpracticed eye, this land seemed a place of absence, but Matt Reece saw carved gorges and wind-sharpened peaks and undulating mounds spread over the sprawling panorama. To the west, the mountains rose and rose, smoky blue and snowcapped. To the south, they grew tamer, the colors muted, and the edges faded into the prairie where the land seemed as endless as time. To the east lay the Promesa Rota, which is Spanish for Broken Promise. But this landscape's promises were never broken; how could they be? These clattering streams and sculpted canyons swallowed him whole with their fathomless, uncomplicated beauty.

It was impossible to wallow in sadness on such a morning. His life seemed one with all creation, and he took no more heed of death than he did the dormant dogwood trees or fading stars. *This daybreak feels like freedom*, he thought, *a glimpse of immortality*.

The moment came, however, while scuttling by rock formations heavy with history, when an icy hush at his core told him a long-awaited death had occurred. It could be Grandpa Blake, or it could be his dog, Groucho. Both had weltered on the threshold for weeks. In this country, you trusted your instincts, and so he turned Comet east and prodded him into a gallop. He was near the Promesa Rota's western property line, with twenty miles of raw country between him and the ranch house. He had over an hour of hard riding before he faced the inevitable heartbreak.

Once he reached the lower pastures skirting the river, he heard a rumbling. He glanced north and saw a bay stallion, six mares, and four colts thundering in a tight group, heads and tails held high and proud. He admired the movement of shoulders and flanks. When the stallion veered east and the herd followed in a sweeping arc, Matt Reece noticed Kenji riding Pepper, a black Arabian saddle horse. Kenji's shoulders were straight, chin tucked in, and his Stetson sat square on his head. He held himself in flawless dignity. Even Pepper was curried and gleaming.

Kenji drove the herd toward the corrals.

A stab of shame rose up in Matt Reece. Kenji rounded up a herd, and he hadn't. Spring was branding time, and his job was to find mustangs in the hills and ravines and deliver them to the holding pens. It didn't matter that he was only eighteen years old while Kenji was a middle-aged man. On the ranch, he needed to pull his weight. He figured he could ride and rope as well as anyone, and he hated being bested.

He leaned forward and gave Comet a spiteful kick, as if coming up short was his fault. Comet jolted into a run. Matt Reece pressed the horse's flanks between his boot heels. They blue-streaked toward the herd, and the hard-packed ground careened under them. He urged Comet on until they were flat out. He held the reins with his right hand and held his hat on his head with his left. From his perspective, Comet flew like a mythical figure, legs outstretched, mane streaming, tail billowing behind. Horse and rider became a force rocketing through space. Matt Reece knew that a misstep or a prairie-dog hole would put their chance of survival a notch below none. Electric waves sizzled his head, but he kept Comet redlining; the thrill of running down Kenji proved too great for caution.

When he caught up with the bay stallion, he reined Comet into a lope. He and Kenji flanked the herd, Kenji north, he on the south.

He saw disapproval etched on Kenji's face. Yes, he was reckless, endangering a beautiful animal, not to mention himself. He didn't care. He experienced a last burst of elation before they reached the ranch house, and perhaps he could cling to that feeling over the next few weeks, a spark of candlelight in a world gone dark.

They rode over a rise, and the Promesa Rota came into view. The compound crouched at the end of a dirt road, two miles off County Road 124, near an area the locals called Dead Bull Butte. Named after the river that flowed through the property, the Promesa Rota had ten sections of grazing pastures bordering each side of the stream. The rest was desert scrub populated by rattlesnakes, coyotes, and mountain lions.

A putty-colored barn dominated the work yard, and an assortment of corrals, sheds, and a windmill over a water tank hovered around it like moons around Jupiter. A two-story Victorian house nestled within a grove of cottonwoods. Farther south stood a dozen pippin and Red Delicious apple trees, the fruit from which Matt Reece's great-grandmother, Audrey Connors, had made the best cider in the county.

Knowing what awaited him there, a bizarre feeling came over him: that he was, and always had been, too fragile for this lonely landscape. As they rode nearer, he tried to imagine how life would be if he had never been born into this desolate place. He wondered what he would be like if he had not spent the last eighteen years absorbing the silent vistas, the river's hypnotic pull, the meadow lark's ascending three-note song. Until his older brother, Patrick, went off to college, he'd been happy enough, but over the last two years, loneliness weighed on his shoulders to the point where any kind of life somewhere else seemed an improvement.

Kenji spurred Pepper into a run, and they dashed ahead to open the corral gates. When Matt Reece reached the compound, a sour taste worked its way up his throat, and he swallowed it down.

He drove the mustangs into the main holding pen to join a dozen horses grouped at the far end. They were a mixed lot, duns and roans and bays and paints. They varied in size, sex, age, and conformation. Kenji closed the gate after them.

Kenji and Matt Reece dismounted and led their horses into the barn without a word. Matt Reece pulled his Hamley saddle and blanket from Comet and sat them over a sawhorse. He lifted the bridle off Comet, haltered him, and led him into his stall. He gave the horse's damp coat a rubdown with a gunnysack before he closed and latched the gate, and then hung the bridle on a peg on the wall.

The lecture he was expecting never came. Instead, Kenji wrapped an arm over his shoulders and said, "Go start on breakfast. I'll feed and water the stock and milk Lucy."

His offer to do the chores convinced Matt Reece that he also had an inkling of what awaited them in the house.

"If you say so, sir." Matt Reece leaned into Kenji, finding the warmth he searched for. Kenji Hiroshige was his stepfather, a Japanese man in his forties who looked younger than any thirty-year-old, which was an impressive feat in this godless territory. He was strong yet lissome, with a stomach as flat as Matt Reece's. The only things that showed his age were his eyes. Beneath his Zen-like gaze lurked something wounded, ancient… and untouchable.

Feeling that reassuring heat, he thought of how admirable Kenji was, a Buddhist, a vegetarian, and a veterinarian working at Golden Eagle Industries, a research firm studying the aging process and age-related illnesses. The company experimented on a variety of animals, and Kenji helped with the research while caring for the livestock. He was a scientist, for God's sake, working with Consuela Rocha y Villareal, one of the most celebrated minds in the scientific world, and a household name, like Einstein and Stephen Hawking. That alone made Kenji everything Matt Reece longed for, but he held no illusions that he would ever rise so high in life. He seemed destined to be stuck on this ranch, where it was impossible to become anything more interesting or useful than a cowboy.

Like Matt Reece's paternal father, Jessup Connors, Kenji had made something of himself before coming to the ranch. That was the key, Matt Reece knew. Try as he might, he couldn't make something of his life without abandoning this ranch and the people he loved.

He shucked off his canvas chore coat and draped it over the top rail, then pulled off his rawhide gloves and stuffed them in his hip pocket. Kenji squeezed Matt Reece's neck and nudged him in the direction of the house. Matt Reece picked up a pail by the barn door, swung by the chicken coop, and gathered seven eggs before climbing the steps to the mudroom. Slipping inside confirmed his suspicions. Under the sink where the men washed up before entering the house, Groucho lay on his patch of carpet, too weak to even lift his head.

A wirehaired pointer with blue roan coloration, Groucho owned a face only his mother—and Matt Reece—could love. The dog was bloated and wheezing.

He was relieved that it was Groucho—not Grandpa Blake—who was near dead, but that did little to lessen his heartbreak.

He set his pail on the floor, knelt, and scooped Groucho into his arms. One bleary red eye showed like a signal in a fog; the cold and dripping nose pressed to his neck. The dog broke wind, and his face pulled into what looked like an apology. Matt Reece knew it was cruel to prolong what must be done, but after Patrick moved away to attend UC Berkeley, Groucho became his only friend. Clutching that head to his chest, he tried to will energy back into the limp body that held no warmth. What little life remaining had retreated to the dog's core, leaving the extremities cold.

Matt Reece's heart felt like it squeezed up into his throat, his typical reaction to death or violence or abandonment. A harsh pressure in the back of his esophagus tugged at his solar plexus, pitching him into a coughing fit. Each coughing rasp clogged his windpipe with mucus until he couldn't take in enough air. A suffocating, nervy rush drove him to his feet.

"Oh—" He drew in a painful breath. "—shit." He stared at Groucho's peaceful face. *Can I live here without him?* Doubt settled over him, which gave birth to despair.

He thought of Patrick, visualizing his smooth face, thin lips, black hair, and fatally blue eyes. They'd slept in the same bed until Matt Reece became a teen, their heads angled toward each other, their legs and torsos touching. Patrick outgrew that intimacy, but Matt Reece still longed for it, still hankered to wake with the feel of his brother's breath on his neck. He thought about his mother, Gail, now living in Long Beach with Lester. All the people who abandoned him. And now Groucho. He felt sorry for them. He imagined walking to the barn, saddling Comet, and riding away. He could, for the first time, forsake them instead. He could reach the foothills by noon and be lost in the mountains by dark. It would take them weeks to find him. But the need for air spurred him into a different direction.

With his heart racing, he rushed through the kitchen and into the living room. Jessup had fallen asleep on the sofa the night before and was still there, snoring, his red shirt unbuttoned, his jeans fly open. A near-empty glass of rye sat on the coffee table. Jessup drank lately because his father, Blake Connors, was in the same condition as Groucho. They had been a reasonably happy family until six months ago when Blake became bedridden. In Hawthorn, the doctors did biopsies, and the news was as bad as it gets, well into stage four. All the doctors could do was administer drugs to keep him comfortable. He had, however, wanted to die at home, so Jessup and Kenji packed him up and brought his sorrow to the ranch.

That's when Jessup's deterioration kicked into high gear. Each night at sunset, in the name of unwinding, Jessup threw back a glass of rye, and another, and so on, until he couldn't keep his eyes open. He often passed out before he made it to the bedroom.

The two bedrooms on the first floor were down the hall from the living room. Jessup and Kenji shared one, and across the hall Blake lay dying. Matt Reece's bedroom, his sanctuary, was upstairs.

Matt Reece's lungs were clinching, and he didn't have much time. He tugged on Jessup's elbow with no effect and then slapped his face hard enough to rattle teeth. Jessup opened one eye. The act of focusing proved too much for him, and he mumbled, "Leave me be, dammit."

For a moment, still, it seemed like nothing too serious—another desertion, the loss of one more loved one. He was used to that, right? But anxiety wrapped itself around his chest and squeezed, taking him with such force that it felt like being squashed by a python.

Matt Reece tried to speak, but his lungs refused to draw air. He shook Jessup harder. He believed in Jessup, trusted his strength; his touch was nourishment from a realm beyond normal human interaction. Jessup had never let him down. He slapped his face again, harder. This time Jessup opened both eyes.

"Is Grandpa dead?" Jessup asked.

"Grou—*hee*—cho."

Jessup's eyes registered nothing. He sat up, took Matt Reece's arm, and drew him onto the couch. He tugged Matt Reece's Stetson off his head and dropped it on the easy chair, then wrapped his arms around Matt Reece and held him. "Okay, son. It's just another anxiety attack. Close your eyes, and breathe with me. Deep as you can. We'll work through this. You and me."

This close, Matt Reece smelled the sour whiskey tainting Jessup's breath. That didn't matter. He closed his eyes and felt Jessup's empathy flowing into him. He knew Jessup's strength could protect him from everything except loneliness. He let that body heat and sour breath carry him to a gentler place. His lungs slowly unclenched. Jessup could do this, only him, because of the trust they shared.

They stayed nailed together with Matt Reece gazing out the front window at the unpeopled vastness of the Promesa Rota, until Kenji ambled across the work yard carrying a pail of milk.

"I know what Groucho means to you, son," Jessup said, his voice low and soothing, "but we have to face it; everything that lives will eventually die—you and me and Kenji and Patrick and Grandpa, everyone. It's how nature works. We can't change that."

"He's all I've got, sir."

"You have me and Kenji and Comet, and for a short time we have Grandpa. Old Groucho had about the best damn life a dog could want. Maybe it's time we gave another dog an opportunity. There's bound to be a litter of pups somewhere in the county."

He looked down, not wanting to think about a replacement. There was, however, no denying the mention of a puppy lit a spark of yearning in his heart. He could even name it Harpo, as a way to honor the memory of his greatest friend.

"Tell you what, sport," Jessup said. "You put the coffee on while I clean up. After breakfast I'll dig a grave, we'll say goodbye to him, and I'll make a few phone calls to see what's available." He loosened his arms, and Matt Reece stood. Jessup pushed himself off the couch and had trouble balancing. Matt Reece held his arm to keep him from falling backward.

"I'm okay," Jessup said, but his face winced. Jessup shared those same features that Patrick had—high cheekbones and thin lips, black hair, and sapphire-blue eyes—only nineteen years older. Before Blake got sick, Jessup had a youthful appearance and strong physique. But over these last months, Jessup's face lost its vitality. The effects of drink and depression spread over his features, making fine lines appear around the mouth. His cheeks grew flush and more pronounced, the eyelids sagged, and deep lines etched across his forehead. At forty-three, he had a sixty-year-old face, and the slight drooping across his features gave the impression of profound grief.

Looking into those bloodshot eyes, Matt Reece figured this was how he would end up, not a scientist or even veterinarian, but rather, he would stay on the ranch living a small, dull life, and when everyone abandoned him, he would let whiskey beat him down to nothing.

As Matt Reece grabbed the coffeepot, a noise came from the mudroom. He crossed the kitchen to the doorway and saw Kenji leaning over Groucho, using a stethoscope to listen to the dog's chest. His vet-medical bag was open and within easy reach. There was an assortment of futuristic-looking devices in it, the kind of equipment one would expect to find only in scientific laboratories.

"Don't let him die, sir," Matt Reece said with a low voice so Jessup couldn't hear.

Kenji looked up. "Must be hard never leaving the ranch. A boy needs friends."

For the last two years, Matt Reece had been homeschooled to protect him from bullies at school. Jessup and Kenji assumed he was picked on because they were a gay couple, but Matt Reece knew better. The other boys had rightly guessed he was also gay. This was a tough country, and the boys were coarse. When Patrick was no longer there to protect him, they picked fights with him. Once they realized he couldn't fight back because of his phobia with violence, the persecution intensified. After months of black eyes and broken teeth, Jessup put his foot down. Matt Reece hadn't left the ranch since.

Kenji seemed to turn inward, as if analyzing himself, rather than Groucho's condition. After a moment, he nodded. "Maybe there's something I can try."

Jessup passed behind Matt Reece and eased himself into the mudroom. Kenji stood, and they embraced and kissed as Matt Reece looked on. Their intimacy was a reminder that they had each other while he had only Groucho. He felt his heart free-falling.

There was nothing to do but start on breakfast. He grabbed the bucket of eggs and the pail of milk Kenji had carried in. He set them on the counter next to the stove, rolled up his shirtsleeves, and washed his hands in the sink. Jessup walked to the bathroom, but Kenji stayed in the mudroom, which seemed somewhat suspicious. Matt Reece tiptoed back to the doorway and leaned his head inside. Kenji was again stooped over Groucho, but this time he held a gadget in his hand. It looked surprisingly similar to a *Star Trek* medical tricorder that Dr. McCoy used to diagnose patients. It didn't make a sound, but it did emit an aura of purplish light that engulfed both dog and man.

Matt Reece eased back into the kitchen, his hopes raising the width of an eyelash. He knew the *Star Trek* tricorder was used to gather and interpret data, but he couldn't remember if it actually cured anything. But of course, that was a TV show, purely fiction. No telling what Kenji was doing, if anything.

Matt Reece poured coffee beans into a hand grinder and pulverized them. As Jessup hauled himself to the dining table, Matt Reece measured out water and coffee into the percolator, set it on the stove, lit the burner with a match, and turned up an inch of flame.

"Fried or scrambled?" Matt Reece asked.

"Over easy will do."

Kenji joined Jessup at the table.

Jessup said, "After breakfast, I'll dig a grave."

Kenji shot Matt Reece a glance and told Jessup there was still hope. Before Jessup could argue, Matt Reece turned on them. "After we bury Groucho, I want to go live with Patrick and enroll in college. I love you both, but I'm done here."

He wanted to tell them it was time for them to man up and take care of Grandpa Blake themselves, but that sounded too confrontational. Why state the obvious? And he was hoping they wouldn't ask what he wanted to study in college, because he wasn't sure yet. He just wanted a different life than this, something like being a marine biologist. His favorite TV shows were the Jacques Cousteau documentaries. He often pictured himself living on the *Calypso* as part of Cousteau's red-capped crew, studying climate change and making a positive difference in the world. His favorite one was about sharks, and he longed to swim alongside a hammerhead or mako. They claimed that sharks have to keep moving in order to breathe—constant forward motion to force water through their gills. That's what he felt like, that the ranch was stagnation, and he needed forward motion to someplace else so he could finally breathe.

Jessup shook his head. "Son, I know the ranch is lonely and the work is hard, but it's also safe. You know how you respond to violence. Patrick lives in Berkeley, which borders Oakland, one of the most dangerous cities on the planet. I'm talkin' gang wars, innocent people shot down in the streets, and thugs willing to kill you for the change in your pocket."

"I need to be more than a cowboy."

"Son, we're all sad about Groucho. Kenji and I will help you through this. On the ranch we stick together and live the way nature intended, no matter what. Here we're safe, and we live a fine life."

"Fine for you, sir. You have your writing and a husband. I've got nothing."

"You have us. Funny thing about people, they're like coins. Holding four quarters is far better than lugging around a hundred pennies."

"Give it a rest," Kenji said. "Groucho ain't dead, so let's wait to see what happens."

"All's I'm saying is: it's foolish to rush headlong toward danger," Jessup said. "When it comes to courage, better than passing the test is not being put to the test."

Matt Reece turned his back on them and clamped his jaw so tight it could crack his teeth. His mind was set. His ass was Berkeley-bound an hour after they lay Groucho to rest. He would ride his thumb, and if nobody stopped to lend a ride, he would walk there. He imagined himself hoofing it along the highway, head held toward a new future, as dignified and lonely as an asteroid hurtling through space.

Chapter Two

Matt Reece prided himself on his ability to make a first-rate cup of coffee—he only used Arabica beans from Columbia and knew the exact measurements and brewing time—but today he was not himself. After setting a frying pan on a burner, putting a pot of pinto beans on to heat, mixing up ground masa and hand patting a tortilla, he dropped it on the hot frying pan. But by that time, he forgot about brewing coffee. It boiled over. When he heard the sizzle, he panicked and grabbed the pot, burning his hand. Coffee spilled. Jessup leaped up and snatched a dish towel to wipe up the stove. "You sit, and I'll clean this up."

"No, sir, I'm fine." Matt Reece seized the dishrag. But of course, he was light-years from fine. His hand stung, and his palm would no doubt blister, but he wasn't about to let Jessup baby him. "I can do this." It was only then he smelled smoke. He caught the tortilla just in time to keep it from catching fire. He slid it from pan to counter. It was charred on one side.

"Don't let it upset you," Jessup said. "This'll be a shit day for all of us."

Matt Reece wrapped the dishrag around the coffeepot handle, poured two mugs, and carried them to the table. The room smelled of burned corn. He withdrew into a vacuum of silent churlishness. He busied himself with frying eggs and potatoes shiny with grease. He transferred them to china plates and added pinto beans and tortillas slathered in butter. He poured milk into odd-sized mason jars and served the men at the table. Rather than eat with them—he knew eating would make him sick—he prepared a breakfast tray and carried it down the hall to Grandpa Blake's room.

Blake didn't respond to his knock. He knocked again, harder, and opened the door. A sickroom smell greeted him, something akin to a short-circuited electrical device.

The curtains were drawn with the windows wide open. Although the room was filled with nothing more than the ordinary light of a country morning, it seemed luminous. An empty bed was revealed in that luster, and Matt Reece glanced around, searching for Blake. Before coming to the ranch, Blake was a country music musician, playing guitar in honky-tonks and barrooms from Nashville to Lodi. He lived out of suitcases, always poised to go someplace else. But once installed in this room, for the first time in his life, he built a nest and feathered it with a La-Z-Boy recliner, shelves of hardbound books, Navajo rugs, Indian pottery, and paintings involving cowboys on horses.

"Grandpa?" Matt Reece called.

"Help me up."

Matt Reece focused on a naked figure sprawled on the floor beside the bed. He set his tray on the dresser and knelt beside Blake.

"What are you doing on the floor?" he asked, but it was obvious from the pool of piss around Blake that he had fallen while trying to get himself to the bathroom.

"Been up all night, staring at the moon, trying to figure out how my life slipped by in the time it took to wink. The cold floorboards help me think."

"Sure, and I'll bet the smell of piss helps stimulate your brain cells."

Blake's face showed a venerable yet childlike wonder. A sparse pelt of gray hairs covered the meager mass of muscles stubbornly clinging to his skeleton. His blue-white skin shimmered in the light.

A coughing fit racked Blake's body.

Matt Reece pulled the shirt off his back and wiped off the piss still clinging to Blake. He flung his shirt onto the puddle to soak up the remaining urine and muscled Blake onto the bed. He would wait until after breakfast to give Blake a sponge bath.

With nothing covering his torso, he felt a chill. He closed the windows and was about to give the old man a lecture on the dangers of catching pneumonia, but Blake said, "It's terrifying to think that a person is just a collection of cells that you drop into a hole in the ground and there's nothing left. But it's so comforting to know that the agony will soon end."

Blake raised his legs and swung them onto the mattress. His scrawny back pressed into the pillow that Matt Reece propped against the headboard. Matt Reece held the coffee mug to Blake's lips. The old man sipped while scratching his gray wedge of pubic hair.

"Comforting for you, maybe."

Blake's face scrunched up in thought, as if Matt Reece proposed a difficult algebraic question, finding the hidden value of x and y. He drew an audible breath, and another. It seemed as if the dazzling light penetrated his skull. His eyes pooled with water, and he mumbled a barely audible, "Yes, son. I'm sorry to bring this on you."

A series of watery coughs shook Blake's body and left his eyes streaming.

Blake snatched the bottle of painkillers at his bedside and popped three Vicodin. Matt Reece held the mug to his lips again so he could wash them down. He sat the mug on the nightstand beside an aromatic candle, which had burned down to a half inch from extinction.

"The pain bad?"

"Like a nagging wife; it never leaves me in peace. The pills only turn down the volume." His voice was a wheeze.

Matt Reece thought about taking one of those pills to ease the pain in his blistered hand. The sting had grown sharper.

"Hungry?"

"Just coffee."

"Eat," Matt Reece said, using his most authoritative tone. He pulled the sheet over Blake's legs and carried the tray over and sat it on the bed. "I'll clean up this mess while you eat and then give you a bath. Can you handle the fork, or should I feed you?"

"Up yours, you cocky little bastard!" Blake lifted the coffee mug and sipped.

"That Vicodin must be some kickass stuff."

"Take this away. I'm done eating, done prolonging this shitty existence. I'm sorry you'll be hurt by it, but there's no point in dragging it out." He leaned over the nightstand and lifted his silver pocket watch on a chain. It was something Blake cherished. He held it out to Matt Reece.

"You're the timekeeper now. Don't let me down."

Matt Reece was startled. Blake watched him with the strained grim look that had become habitual to him, the look of someone with an utterly regrettable past and no future.

On the ranch, the men told the passage of time by the position of the sun and moon and the movement of shadows across the walls. There were two clocks on the ranch: Blake's pocket watch and an antique, nickel-plated alarm clock that always ran a bit erratic. Both clocks were the property of Grandpa Blake, and he considered himself the custodian of time on the ranch. It was his only responsibility since becoming bedridden, and being the authority on time grew into his passion. Whenever asked the time, he would answer down to the second, as if lives depended on him being exact. Everyone except Blake knew that Kenji's iPhone gave the time, but nobody had the heart to tell Blake. They let him believe he contributed something useful.

Earlier in the month, while Blake napped, Matt Reece noticed the watch's black hands stuck on quarter after one. Blake forgot to wind it, and it ran down. He couldn't let Blake see it; it would have robbed him of the one purpose his life still held. Matt Reece snatched up the watch and raced to the living room to get the correct time from the iPhone. He reset the timepiece and slipped it back on the nightstand before Blake woke. After that, he reminded Blake twice a day to wind the watch, at which point Blake always snarled at him to mind his own damned business.

Matt Reece took the watch, which had a winged boy engraved on it and had originally come from Switzerland, carried by Blake's grandfather. It was heavy, solid, and slightly tarnished. He flipped it open and checked it was set to the proper time, the second hand moving with a delicate jerking motion.

"You're quitting?"

Blake closed and reopened his eyelids. His face had a peculiar tightness about it. "You say that like I have some chance of improvement. If being fed like an infant is all I have left, then I want no part of it. You have another bottle of this?" He pointed at the Vicodin. "A full bottle? Bring it here. And take this food away. The smell is making me nauseous."

"What do I tell Jessup?"

Blake was breathing hard and with effort. "Tell him to pack a suitcase and drag your skinny ass off this ranch. Tell him to let you see some of this old world while you're still young. You deserve that. Now leave me be, and fetch me those pills." He closed his eyes, gasping for air, until he no longer struggled, lying there peacefully.

Matt Reece slipped the watch into his pocket. Feeding, bathing, and administering medications to Blake fell solely on him. He did it willingly and had done everything short of reaching inside Blake's flesh and scraping out the cancer with his fingernails. But all his effort had been futile. He felt that he only accomplished two things in his short life: one was becoming a superb horseman, and the other was to love this cantankerous old man. Caring for Blake taught him to love unconditionally, to give all and expect nothing back. And Blake's gift for that life lesson was infinitely more valuable than a silver pocket watch.

Now he had no reason to stay on. He could finally and thankfully leave without guilt.

Still, it felt like another betrayal.

He dropped his urine-soaked shirt on the breakfast tray and carried it to the kitchen. He saw Jessup through the front window, hauling a pick and shovel up the road toward the family burial plot. Kenji paced back and forth in the living room, talking on his iPhone. His voice grew harsh. His anger permeated the house. He was scolding someone that the timing was too early, that there were more experiments to analyze before the announcement could be issued.

Matt Reece paid him no mind. He didn't need any more drama heaped on his shoulders. He thought about Blake, all those bouts of black diarrhea and vomiting and scrubbing the sheets and washing the body, and now the upcoming burial. He felt profound sadness, but mostly he admired the man's courage. Blake was giving him one more gift before checking out.

He's teaching me how to die. He stares death in the eye with his head held high, without speaking the name of God or using any other crutch.

He set the tray on the counter and glanced at the Vicodin bottle sitting in the cupboard. That could wait, he thought. He dropped his shirt in the sink and cranked the tap, wanting to rinse it before tossing it into the laundry hamper. As the sink filled, he cleared the dishes from the table and stacked them on the counter. He turned off the faucet, and as he wrung out the shirt, something nudged his leg. He looked down and found Groucho standing beside him. The dog's eyes were clear, and he was doing a full-body wag. He hadn't looked this animated in months. Matt Reece dropped the shirt and knelt on one knee, hugging the dog. Indeed, he looked years younger, in the prime of life. Matt Reece placed Blake's untouched plate of food on the floor. Groucho wolfed it all down.

Matt Reece glanced at Kenji's medical bag still sitting in the mudroom. *If Kenji could bring Groucho back from the brink of death, why didn't he use that power to help Grandpa?* In the living room, Kenji's voice rose to a furious shout. This was no time to question him.

He tiptoed to the mudroom and searched the medical bag until he found a box holding the tricorder device. It had only one switch, and when he clicked it on, it gave off the same purplish light as before. A minute later his hand stopped hurting, and the blister melted.

He switched it off, hustled back to Blake's bedroom, and stood over the old man. He switched on the tricorder and waved it up and down the length of Blake's sleeping body, moving his arm in measured passes. The light engulfed them both. Blake seemed to breathe easier. That, however, could have been from the Vicodin he'd swallowed earlier.

He heard footsteps. He turned to find Kenji standing in the doorway, red-faced, too livid to speak.

CHAPTER THREE

HOURS EARLIER that same day, Pedro crowed in the gray predawn, drawing Jessup from a turbulent sleep. Jessup rolled over and sank back into slumber, searching for that splendid sleep which comes from being at peace with the world. But he had not found that serenity at any time in the last six months, and he didn't find it this morning either.

Later, a few hard slaps to his face brought him fully awake. Buttery light poured through the front windows, burning his eyes. It took only a moment to realize Matt Reece was having an anxiety attack. He rose up and held Matt Reece, massaging those clenched chest muscles, gentling him like an unbroken colt. Once their breathing merged into a single, composed cadence, he continued to embrace the boy, like he used to do when Matt Reece was a child and fell asleep on his lap. At eighteen, Matt Reece still carried that musty smell that kids have, something akin to fresh-baked bread. He had brown hair as fine as corn silk, an oval face, and his hazel eyes held both the rough-puppy innocence of youth and the despair of middle age.

When Matt Reece began breathing normally, he felt his own pain, a soul-crushing headache.

He pulled himself off the couch and stumbled toward the mudroom, where Kenji was examining Groucho. He was aware of his disheveled shirt and hair. As he passed the oval mirror in the living room, he was tempted to look at his reflection, but he forced himself not to. Kenji's reaction would tell all, because they hid nothing from each other.

He and Kenji married eleven years ago. Some days it felt like eleven weeks, other days, this one for example, it felt like eleven well-lived lives.

In the mudroom, the dog was now as ugly a crow bait as ever Jessup saw. Surely this day was Groucho's last. It was time to end the dog's suffering. Kenji rose and kissed Jessup, making him feel relieved that he somehow passed muster.

Jessup lurched to the bathroom while Matt Reece prepared breakfast. He turned on the faucet and splashed water on his face, pulled the aspirin bottle from the medicine cabinet, and downed four pills. He needed more, but not on an empty stomach.

He stood stock-still, wanting to postpone all the trappings of a sorrowful day. He needed to drive Matt Reece into town to round up a replacement pup, and he hated the thought of going out into that hostile world where anything could happen.

The moment came when he could wait no longer. He hauled himself to the dining table and stared out the window, across the enormous sweep of silent space to the amber light on the distant mountain peaks. He heard the ice-blue river tumble over smooth stones, accompanied by chickens scratching the hard-packed work yard. Much as he loved those sounds, loved the ranch, all he felt was dead tired. The three of them worked for five days with their growing cattle herd, branding, earmarking, castrating, dehorning, and inoculating. On the fifth day they switched to horses, driving mustangs down from the mesas. Now they would work their butts to the bone branding the yearlings. Ranch life was never easy, except when it rained. He glanced up at the unblemished blue dome and sighed.

Kenji sat at the opposite end of the walnut table. "You look done in already."

"Thanks. You look just dandy yourself."

"No rest for the wicked."

That word "wicked" stung like an accusation. It was Kenji, Jessup thought, who brought home an enormous mirror three weeks ago and hung it over their bed. They both drank whiskey (so unusual for Kenji) that night and had sex under it. There was something tragic and desperate about the way they made love, more like gladiators fighting to the death. What started as intimate fun evolved into playful slaps and then grew into rage vented on each other. They had gone at it without the slightest sentiment. Pure animal lust. It proved a delightful escape from this house shrouded with impending death. As salacious as it still seemed, it was the last time they'd made love.

Jessup said, "I'll dig a grave after breakfast."

"Hold off; he might pull through. He's a tough old mutt."

Jessup looked up to see the hope in Matt Reece's eyes. He hated giving the boy optimism when there wasn't any. *It's easy for Kenji; his beliefs teach him that life is suffering and relishing that anguish brings one closer to Enlightenment. He sees misery as a sacred lesson, but that's no reason to drag Matt Reece through the mud.*

At one point the coffee boiled over, and Jessup grew angry at himself when Matt Reece refused his help. It was then that he saw something different about the boy, who wore his normal jeans, snap-button shirt, and cowboy boots. Jessup admired how manly he looked—short for his age, just shy of five foot seven, slender, his brown hair needing a cut. He was serious—like his older brother—and he often demonstrated a high intelligence. Jessup realized his boy stood on the threshold of manhood. He couldn't put his finger on what made him see the boy in a new light, but something did. He thought about something his grandmother once said: "A boy grows into a man when more is expected of him." Indeed, every child believes his family is immortal, and when death shatters that illusion, he has to ask that tortured question: "Why?" And when acceptance comes, the child becomes a man. That told Jessup his son had accepted Blake's passing before even he did.

Jessup believed the boy was as fragile as a May butterfly, but there was also a core of tough self-determination in him, a quality Jessup thought of as "cowboy spirit." There was a fair amount of that attribute in his father, Blake, and also Audrey, his grandmother. And that spirit shone crystal clear when the boy announced he was quitting the ranch to live in Berkeley.

Six months back the boy insisted they stop calling him by his pet name, Mattie, and start using his middle name, Reece. It was a sign he was maturing, but Jessup had made little of it. *At least the boy kept something of his childhood*, he thought, *by using a double name. Now he's a man.* Pride rose up in Jessup's throat, and he swallowed it down with overcooked coffee.

Nobody spoke again until Matt Reece set food on the table. While eating, they kept the conversation on the roundup and branding. Jessup wanted to talk about the dog, but not with Matt Reece listening. He assumed Kenji would inject Groucho with something that would gently pull him into death. Jessup hated the thought of using a bullet.

Matt Reece took a tray of food to Blake's room. Jessup reached for a tortilla and took his time eating. There was no need to hurry into a day that had already turned bad and would no doubt get worse. He sopped up the last of his egg yolks with a final bit of tortilla, sighing.

He pushed back his chair, feeling subdued by a sense of loss, and said he'd go dig the grave. Kenji scowled but didn't try to stop him. Jessup knew he would soon dig a second grave, but he recoiled from thinking of that hardship now. He instinctively knew that it needed to happen, and the sooner the better. They all needed to move past this darkness so they could grieve and mend. That thought brought him to his real problem, perhaps the only one he had the power to influence. He glanced at Kenji. "The agency sent me another contract. They need three more scripts."

"Perfect timing," Kenji said. "Taxes are owed midmonth, and Patrick's tuition for the summer semester is due in May."

Jessup prided himself on being a graduate of the Cornell University writing program. He had the ability to compose any kind of fiction—short stories, novels, screenplays. His real passion, however, was poetry. Whenever he wrote, his prose propelled him past the concerns of his life. He felt a mysterious inner faculty push aside his intellect and emotions and pour from his diaphragm onto the page. Most people called this inner force a soul, but being an atheist, Jessup thought of it as creativity channeling through him—a crystalline stream gurgling through a forest. He had no words to describe what he felt while it happened. Something took him over, reducing him to a state of transcendental perception, bodiless.

In that state, his writing often—for short periods—touched genius.

But it was a long dry spell since the last time he had experienced that feeling. To earn money to keep the ranch going and put Patrick through college, he contracted with a Los Angeles advertising agency, writing scripts for television commercials.

"I know we need the money, but I'm having second thoughts."

"You love your writing," Kenji said.

"One-minute screenplays for Cap'n Crunch or Dawn dish soap or Crest toothpaste is as satisfying as a low-carb, low-fat, gluten-free diet. These days, I hate to even sit at the computer, let alone attempt serious work."

"But it's not just the writing. The reason the agency keeps coming back to you is your creative imagination. Nobody dreams up shit like you can."

"Let's tone down the BS, okay? I'm not one of your 160-IQ science nerds who doesn't have enough common sense to tell fiction from fantasy."

Kenji laughed. "Just trying to cheer you up. It seems obscene to waste your gift simply to make money for people already richer than God. Write whatever you want. We'll get by on my salary. And in a pinch, we'll sell some mustang stock."

Jessup nodded, making no commitment either way.

He poured another cup of joe on his way to the back door. In the mudroom, he pulled on work boots, pushed his Stetson on his head, stuffed rawhide gloves into his hip pocket, and stepped outside. He finished his coffee as he crossed the work yard. He slung the dregs into the dirt and entered the toolshed, leaving his mug on a shelf. He balanced a pick and shovel on one shoulder and moseyed back out, heading for the patch of earth near the top of the hill where his ancestors rested.

A silence lay on the land. No animals moved about, and the air was so still that the leaves of the oak stood unmoving. In that silence, and combined with the relief of having Kenji's support for his writing, he could feel his heart pumping in smooth gushes.

Glancing northwest, he noticed a black stone spire not as high as the crests around it. It reminded him of something his grandmother told him: spirits reside in sacred sites—mountain summits, rocky outcrops, groves of trees, waterfalls—and if you damage the natural world or upset the earth's flow of energy, you anger these spirits, and then you suffer the consequences. He thought of Kenji's resistance to Groucho's looming death. On the Promesa Rota, things aged, deteriorated, and died. The old and the new grew out of each other. To resist that balance of life and death was to oppose nature, and that would surely piss off those spirits.

He reached the handful of gravestones and began to dig next to the one marked Patch. He worked up a sweat. It felt good doing something purely physical, if only to sweat last night's alcohol out of his system. Over time his hangover retreated and he thought more clearly, and as with most people dealing with death, he took stock of his own life.

He gazed down at the valley where pastures glistened with waving grass. Wildflowers were in bloom—purple and blue and gold. The range cattle staggered under their fat, and their coats looked tight and sleek. Even the mustangs looked sturdy. Yes, the ranch was healthy, an island safe from the world. He loved it as much as he loved the people who lived here. But loving something doesn't necessarily make one happy.

As he gouged the earth with his pick, he realized that he desperately needed to feel joy again. But happiness didn't just fall out of the sky and hit you on the head. It had to be fashioned over time. And only one person could make that happen.

The moment transformed into a life-changing decision. He would make Groucho's death the starting point of rebuilding. He was done with commercials. This afternoon he would begin something that would challenge his talent. *A novel based on the theme of passing the torch from one generation to the next, something simple and direct. The first two acts will build using playful humor to draw the reader in, bridging into a third where death is confronted—ending with a jolt of gravitas. The third act will contrast the first two upbeat acts and expose the underlying darkness of the theme that was there, hidden all along.*

He smiled. *Who knows, perhaps this time next year I'll be working on a full-length screenplay of the same story.*

As he swung that pick, every deep-drawn breath became sweeter. The pleasure of working his muscles became as satisfying as a great, stretching yawn. He dug until the grave was three feet wide, four feet long, and four feet deep. The rocky soil made for tough work, but hard toil had never bothered him.

A clattering of hooves lifted his head. Below in the work yard, Kenji and Matt Reece were mounted, urging their horses away from the barn at a run. "What the…."

He thumbed his hat higher on his forehead. He assumed they were riding out to gather more mustangs, but a third horse trailed them, a packhorse loaded with supplies. And Jessup noticed a dog running with them. From that distance it looked like Groucho, but the old mutt hadn't displayed that kind of pep in months. Still, what other dog could it be? It was more startling than if his grandmother's ghost rose up from her grave and demanded a cup of ginger tea.

Jessup left the pick and shovel at the gravesite and walked back to the house. In the mudroom, there was no trace of Groucho. He hung his hat on a peg. On the kitchen table lay a yellow envelope holding a handwritten note and a computer flash-drive device. He hesitated, knowing this could only spell trouble.

Jessup,

We are about to suffer violent times. I must go into hiding to protect myself from those who will no doubt come looking for me.

I've taken Matt Reece because he exposed himself to an experimental treatment I've been researching. He needs constant monitoring, and rest assured I'll do everything possible to keep him healthy and safe.

Don't try to find us. Once things settle, we'll contact you.

What I've done will spoil the quiet life you've tried so hard to maintain, and I'm sorry to put you through this ordeal, but I have no choice. Nothing less than the future of our world depends on what I've put into play. Stay on the ranch, hidden, because the meek are about to inherit the earth, and I want you included in that assembly.

Please know that I'm taking Matt Reece to the one place that is perfectly safe, because lightning never strikes the same spot twice.

Over the years, you've given me the greatest possible joy. I don't think two people could have been happier, and I pray that when we reunite, we will have a rewarding life together, well into the future.

For your protection and ours, stash this flash drive in a secret place and never tell anyone you have it. It holds mysteries both wondrous and terrifying. Trust no one. If something happens to me, give it only to someone calling himself God.

I will love you through eternity.

Farewell.

K.

Never before had Jessup felt so unexpectedly gut-shot. He reread the note, lingering over the "farewell" and the fact that Kenji couldn't be bothered to sign his full name. All Jessup rated was a single initial.

He struck a matchstick, set the note on fire, and dropped it in the sink. He felt as if the world had folded in on itself, and everything was now rushing backward.

After hearing his father's prognosis six months back, Jessup did his best to remain upbeat and to keep his family together. Sure, they had problems—didn't everyone?—and he knew Kenji disapproved of his drinking, but there never was any sign of them separating. During their first three years, they suffered a score of shouting matches, weeks at a time without talking to each other, and even came to blows once. But their relationship matured. These days they talked through their differences, handling each other in a supportive way.

Jessup glared at the flash drive with cold fury. He detested this experimental treatment that drove his son and lover away. He was a writer and rancher, and like his grandmother, he mistrusted anything that claimed to make life easier, because there was always a price to pay for every convenience. And what really burned his butt was now he had to cope with a dying father alone.

Jessup dropped the flash drive into his shirt pocket.

The handwritten note stung as much as the hasty departure. They sat in this kitchen not two hours ago. Why couldn't they have talked it out? Why didn't Kenji trust him enough to explain face-to-face? Nothing more than scribbled lines from the man whom for eleven years had shared his home, bed, food, tears, and laughter. A man who wrote, "I will love you through eternity."

The day's gone from me standing up to my belly in a tub of shit, to being immersed in it, and it's not even noon. At least things can't get any worse, he thought, but he wasn't altogether sure.

CHAPTER FOUR

JESSUP HUNG his head, not from shame but weariness.

He heard a faint noise, a mechanical thumping. As he watched Kenji's note turn to ash, the thumping grew loud. He glanced out the window over the sink and saw a helicopter hovering just beyond the holding pens.

The horses spooked, galloping along the fence in all directions. Their panic turned to terror as the copter drew close. Dust thrown up by their hooves and by the copter's rotor blades turned the corral into a brown tempest. By the time Jessup raced out the back door, the horses crashed through the corral rails, bursting into the work yard. In a single body, they tore across the yard hell-bent for the foothills.

Jessup leaped for his life and landed only a few feet from flashing hooves. He rolled under the porch and waited until the last of them sped by. He stood, squaring his shoulders, preparing for a fight. The herd was almost out of sight by the time the copter touched earth and the blades slowed. As soon as the air cleared, a man and a woman crawled from the cockpit, leaving the pilot in the plastic bubble.

The man was meticulously groomed, wearing Dockers, a polo shirt, and aviator sunglasses. He looked to be in his midfifties, sporting a full head of salt-and-pepper hair and a salon tan. He cradled a bottle of champagne in his left arm and held out his manicured right hand to shake Jessup's rough paw. The woman wore her brown hair in a tight bun on the back of her head, and her stylish navy blue silk suit and heels made her seem as if she'd just stepped from a boardroom rather than a helicopter. Her skirt showed off a great pair of athletic legs. She was seductive and seemed cheerily aware of it. She carried champagne flutes in one hand and a briefcase in the other. She walked several feet behind her male companion, letting Jessup know who was in charge.

Jessup pointed after the herd. "Do you halfwits have any idea what you did?"

"All too sorry," the gentleman said with a slight Scottish brogue, "but there was no time to waste with airports and rental cars. I wanted to be the first to congratulate our rising star." He flashed a billion-dollar smile. When Jessup didn't answer, he added, "Fear not. I'll buy you a new herd of thoroughbreds. Any breed you'd like."

"Who the hell are you?"

"Declan Hughes, at your service. I'm the founder and chairman of the board of Golden Eagle Industries, parent company to Golden Eagle Pharmaceuticals." He turned to the woman. "And this is Miz Diane McCarthy, Golden Eagle's CEO."

She lifted her hand to shake, but it was holding four wine flutes, one stem between each finger. She shrugged, and her cheeks blushed a lovely peach color. "Pleased to meet you. I assume you're Mr. Connors?"

Even Jessup, tucked away on this ranch for the last dozen years, knew plenty about Declan Hughes. A 2004 *Time* magazine article listed twenty people under the age of forty who were shaping the new century. Declan Hughes was fifth on that list. A multibillionaire physicist and businessman, he was the Steve Jobs of the US defense industry. He made a killing in the decade-long Iraq war. In addition to owning Golden Eagle Applied Avionics, the premier corporation developing drone-aircraft weaponry for the US military, he also owned the pharmacological research company that employed Kenji.

Jessup had also read his name online and in the society columns of the *LA Times*, enough to know that Declan had a penchant for sexy women, vintage cars, and Cambodian art, and his charity functions drew most of Hollywood's A-list to his Holmby Hills mansion, yet his politics were surprisingly liberal. He reportedly abhorred war, even though that's what earned the lion's share of his billions, and he sat on the board of advisors of the Audubon Society, the Sierra Club, and the Wilderness Society.

Jessup's anger imploded. This grand entrance, no doubt, had something to do with Kenji's hasty exit just a half hour before. Jessup waved an arm toward the back door, and Declan brushed past him, as cheerful and confident as British royalty.

In the kitchen, Declan unwired the cork on his champagne bottle, and Diane McCarthy lined up flutes on the counter. The cork came out with a festive pop.

"Pernod Ricard Perrier-Jouët, two-thousand-four," Declan said, holding up the bottle. "It's not quite as expensive as the Dom Pérignon

Oenotheque Rose, two-thousand-six, but I think it tastes as exquisite, and I love the flowers on the bottle." He poured the slightly golden liquid into flutes. "Please invite Kenji to join our celebration. We have much to talk about."

Diane handed Jessup a glass of bubbly.

"He's not here."

"When will he return?"

Jessup shrugged.

Declan glanced around the kitchen, lingering on the two things that were unusual: the ashes in the sink and the envelope on the counter. "I see you're a man of few words, Mr. Connors. Would you tell me where I might find him? I'm sure his letter gave his destination, or you wouldn't have destroyed it."

"We're just simple ranch people here. We don't like folks butting in, and we don't give out information until we know why someone is asking questions."

Declan's smile broadened as he held up his flute in a toast. "Mr. Connors, cheers." He swallowed a thimbleful and seemed to roll it on his tongue. "Superlative."

Diane also sipped. Jessup drained his flute in one swallow. Declan refilled his glass.

"As to the why, we want to congratulate him and his research partner, Miss Consuela Rocha y Villareal, for their discovery of the greatest scientific breakthrough in the history of mankind." He took another sip, but his eyes never left Jessup's face. Jessup felt like he was being dissected like a lab rat.

He shook his head. "Kenji never mentioned any breakthrough."

"Mr. Connors," Diane said, "Kenji and Consuela are leading authorities in the field of regenerative medicine. Let me show you something that will explain everything." She set her flute on the counter and placed her briefcase on the walnut table. She sat before the case, popped open the latches, and removed a laptop.

Jessup drained his second glass while she brought the computer to life and clicked an avatar. The monitor filled with a video of Kenji and Consuela in a lab setting. As he listened to Consuela spout off a lot of scientific jargon about altering human DNA, he felt the blood drain from his face. They claimed their breakthrough regenerated human tissue so effectively that a body could remain healthy for thousands of years. And with this ability to mass generate healthy cells, the body could reverse many forms of cancer, AIDS, heart disease, and even Alzheimer's. Kenji made the outrageous claim that he was born during World War II, which would make him over seventy years old. Absurd, of course, because he looked not a day over thirty. Jessup had to admit, however, that during the last eleven years of living with him, Kenji had not aged, not a day.

To prove their assertion, they showed an elderly Asian patient who they claimed had been treated moments before. The old man looked wrinkled and sickly. A clock on the bottom corner of the screen showed the passage of time. He went from looking ninety years old to a healthy forty years old in five hours, and with the aid of time-lapse photography, those hours sped by in three minutes.

Then came the kicker. Consuela announced they would not share their research findings with anyone until every gun, bullet, bomb, tank, battleship, and nuclear warhead had been destroyed. "When the world is wholly disarmed, when there are no armies, when war and mass killing are no longer possible, then we will end disease and aging. Everyone will live for several thousand years. Nobody will suffer old age."

On screen, Kenji added, "We can wait centuries for you to de-arm. You, unfortunately, have little time if you wish to live." He smiled, and the screen went dark.

"Oh shit," Jessup mumbled.

"Spot-on, Mr. Connors," Declan said. "You Americans have such clever slang."

Diane closed her laptop. "Consuela posted this video on YouTube this morning at 6:00 a.m. Eastern time. Because of Consuela's considerable fame and reputation as an exemplary scientist, nobody is doubting its authenticity. It scored a hundred and sixty million hits before YouTube crashed. The world is going crazy over it."

"You see, old boy," Declan said, "Consuela disappeared after she made that post. We want to tether Kenji before he vanishes as well. They're hiding because they're in severe peril."

Jessup grabbed the champagne bottle, pressed it to his lips, and upended it. He emptied the bottle and wiped his mouth on his shirtsleeve.

"You're not as simple as you would have us think, Mr. Connors," Declan said. "You see the gravity of this situation. They've engineered a formula worth several trillion dollars, over time, perhaps a hundred trillion.

Everybody on the planet will pursue them—every government, every drug company, every bounty hunter. No telling what will happen if the KGB or the CIA get to them first. I have the resources to protect them. I can safeguard them and the formula, but we need to find them in a hurry."

Jessup's head spun from the champagne. He sat at the table. It was all too preposterous. He thought of Kenji's note, telling him to trust no one. These people had, no doubt, concocted this harebrained story to get information from him, information he didn't have. But no—he had a flash drive in his shirt pocket. He cupped his hand over his heart.

Diane said, "The research facility where they worked burned to the ground last night. We suspect Kenji and Consuela set off firebombs to destroy any trace of their research. We have our best and brightest sifting through the ashes for any documentation. So far we've found nothing. I think they truly mean to stay hidden until the world de-arms."

Jessup didn't know what to think or who to believe.

Declan said, "It might help to search his belongings here. Perhaps we'll find clues as to what they discovered or where to find them."

Jessup rose and squared his shoulders. "You have no right to make demands. This is my ranch." His confusion morphed into anger, and he made no attempt to hide it.

"We have every right," Declan said, his voice rising. "They worked for my company, using my equipment and my money. That formula belongs to Golden Eagle Industries!"

Ordering them to leave was on the tip of Jessup's tongue when he caught movement out of the corner of his eye. He turned to see his father standing at the doorway to the living room. Blake stood erect, his cheeks rosy, eyes clear, and his now darkened hair jutting out at rakish angles. He wore a threadbare blue robe adorned with Mickey Mouse and Pluto. Jessup didn't recognize him; he seemed years younger, and the scar on his jaw was missing. To Jessup, it was like looking in the mirror.

Blake cleared his throat. "Why don't you all quit jabbering and fix some lunch. I'm so damned hungry I could eat a bear."

"Oh shit," Jessup mumbled through his third shock of the day.

Chapter Five

THE FLIGHT from the Promesa Rota to LAX took forty minutes. The drive into downtown Los Angeles took two hours, and they still had miles to go. Stopped traffic clogged the freeway. Far ahead in a brown haze of exhaust fumes, an 18-wheeler rested, jackknifed across all but one lane. Cars trickled through the open lane like sand through an hourglass. Much as Declan Hughes loved cruising in his Rolls-Royce Silver Wraith, he fidgeted. "Damn this traffic! A fifty-dollar bill waiting on a pocket full of nickels. This is precisely why we need a helipad on the Golden Eagle headquarters building."

Diane McCarthy placed a hand on his. "Another twenty minutes won't matter."

"Every second they're getting farther away and harder to find." Declan pulled the notes from his briefcase, the only research documentation they were able to find at the charred lab where Kenji and Consuela worked. A series of firebombs detonated in all areas of the research center— just hours before Consuela posted her video on YouTube—incinerated everything of importance. He reread the references to "back translation from proteins" to determine the RNA, "hence to the DNA transcription." Nothing extraordinary about that. Farther down, however, it referenced using sterioisomers in translating the enhanced RNA sequences in protein molecules.

The documents, what little there were, gave enough information to convince Declan the research team had a full understanding of DNA purification and restructuring subunit composition techniques, yet it fell short of revealing any of the key facts. It did, however, lead up to those facts with chilling accuracy.

"They've done it. They've really done it, and that makes them the most dangerous people in history. They've not only mapped out the whole DNA chain, they know how to restructure it to make humans virtually immortal."

He thought about his next move, reached for his phone, and called the president's science advisor, Jeffery Wolfe. Wolfe's official handle in Washington, DC, was "Secretary to the President for Science and Technology, and also Educational Liaison." Secretaries to the president, Declan knew, were thick as fleas on a Bangkok street dog. The job was a real one, of sorts. He sat on several advisory boards and met with delegations of teachers and members of the scientific community who descended on Washington; he documented their problems and got them passes for White House tours.

It took fifteen minutes to bulldoze his way through a barrier of secretaries just to talk with Wolfe's personal assistant.

"Mr. Hughes, we've been calling you all morning." Her voice held a tone of relief.

"You couldn't have tried very damned hard. I've had my cell with me the whole time. Patch me through, and tell him this is the most important call he'll ever take."

"Yes, sir. I'm forwarding you to Secretary Wolfe."

Declan took deep breaths to calm himself. His fingers still trembled, and he couldn't decide if that was from nervousness or elation.

Jeffery Wolfe's voice burst through the phone. "My God, Declan, is it true?"

"I believe it is, but we've encountered a snag. I need your help."

"Anything. The president is adamant we secure this as soon as possible." His tone was professional. "She also wants a face-to-face with you at Camp David five minutes ago. I've got a jet waiting for you at LAX. How soon can you get there?"

"In this traffic, two hours. Hold a second." Declan turned to Diane. "We're going back to the airport to catch a plane to Camp David. Call my personal assistant, and tell him to pack a bag for each of us and drive them to the airport ASAP."

"I'm going with you?"

He nodded as he lifted the phone again. "My two key scientists have disappeared with all the research data. You need to organize a nationwide manhunt. I'll have my secretary email you all their personal information. Use the CIA, FBI, military, local police, and the Boy Scouts if you have to. There's no time to lose."

"The FBI's already on it," Wolfe said. "We got them involved as soon as we heard about the death threats."

"Death threats?"

"The ayatollah of Iran ordered a fatwa on both your scientists. We have hard evidence that the pope has joined forces with them and is funding them. We suspect Israel is in on it too. So you see, there's already a manhunt going on. We're moving as fast as we can with everything we've got."

"What the hell is a fatwa?" Declan asked, knowing it couldn't be good.

"An assassination contract. It's now the holy duty of every Muslim to kill your scientists. Iran put a ten-million-dollar bounty on each head. I'm arranging a Secret Service security team to protect you, in case your name pops up on that list."

"I can't believe the pope would do that, even behind the scenes."

"Really? Any idea how many billions of dollars flow into the Vatican every year?"

"But why, Jeff, would anything change for them?"

The expression on Diane's face turned from concern to shock.

"Religions have a love-hate relationship with death," Wolfe said. "Fear of dying is the source of their power, not to mention their income. I mean, if everyone lives forever, who the hell cares about an afterlife? So nobody'll drop money in the collection plates."

"Okay, I get it. Goddamn that YouTube video."

Diane touched his arm, obviously trying to calm him.

Declan continued without looking at her, "That's the price we pay for allowing people to wallow in religious ignorance. It's high time we sweep the myth of a God into the cosmic dustbin, as we did with a flat earth, babies delivered by storks, and the GOP concerned about the middle class."

"Right, well, let's hope we find your people long before that happens. The FBI is swarming the airports, shipping ports, and border inspection units. Our first priority is to contain them in this country."

"Thanks for your help, Jeff. I'm feeling better already."

"Declan, if it were anybody other than Consuela Rocha y Villareal making these claims…. I mean, changing a person's DNA to cure cancer, AIDS, Alzheimer's, and heart disease, I'd be treating this as some crank stunt."

"Jeff, can we shut down all flights in and out of the country?"

"That would cause a panic, so that's a presidential call. Believe me, we understand this situation is vital. We'll do everything possible."

"Okay, I'll call again when I get to the airport."

Declan switched off his phone and bounced it off the car seat. "Dammit!"

Diane picked up the phone and placed it on the seat between them. "This means I'll finally meet Madam President?"

Chapter Six

Their rode side by side with their packhorse, T-Bone, trailing. Groucho roamed within calling distance. They cantered through open country among scrub mesquite, piñon trees, and nopal. The day warmed beautifully, and lupine, growing in rocky crevasses, bloomed fragile lavender stalks. By midafternoon, they came upon Cash Creek in the hills below the White Mountains. The water had green trailing moss threaded over granite boulders. They followed the creek south as it cut its way through the broken hills.

They scarcely spoke all day.

Matt Reece rode leaning forward in the saddle, his right hand resting on the rope tied to his saddle horn that drew T-Bone. They rode beyond the boundaries of the Promesa Rota into hilly country he roamed often. This land, however, seemed altered, made suspect by the miracle that happened at the ranch. Everything held a hidden possibility; nothing could be taken at face value. The world felt different, and so did his body. His flesh tingled, as if the tissue clinging to his bones was buzzing like a swarm of bees; only instead of hearing it, he felt it rolling through his core in waves. It set him trembling at odd moments, his heart pounding, sweat pouring. He wondered if he was experiencing the hot flashes that women in menopause speak of. At times he thought about the possibility of possession. It felt like that—a demon invading his flesh.

The bottom line was, the tricorder set something in motion within him, like the slow beginning of an avalanche. He was frightened by it, but it happened while trying to save Grandpa Blake, so whatever price he must pay was okay by him.

Kenji, so silent and self-assured, now seemed a god who had supremacy over life or death. Matt Reece didn't know if he should be scared or comforted. The thing he knew with certainty was that Groucho was now running through the brush with the pep of a dog half his age. He prayed the tricorder did something similar to Grandpa Blake. He saw little improvement before their hasty departure, but hope was burning a hole in his gut.

They came upon an abandoned cabin on the slope of a stony mesa. Timbers of a collapsed windmill were heaped nearby. The place held a forlorn air, so isolated in this hard country. Matt Reece imagined the Promesa Rota looking like this someday, and the thought saddened him. They climbed a rise and dismounted, staring to the east, at the trail they traveled so far. They stood silent, like men who came to the end of something.

Melancholy descended upon Matt Reece. He looked at the mountain peaks where the sun flashed on jagged teeth. He listened to the wind croon. When he mounted Comet again, he knew he could never lose his feeling for this land. The creak of his saddle, the jingle of his spur chains, the rasping of the horse's tongue over the bit-roller all merged with the land's melody. He felt suddenly sensitized, as if awakening from a deep slumber. And in a corner of his heart, he knew he was turning his back on his family, his home, his childhood. He'd wanted to leave the ranch even before the miracle, but now he felt he was abandoning everything he owed a duty to.

To combat losing those beautiful memories of ranch life, he thought of the calm and peaceful strength, and eternal rightness of his father, for Jessup and this land were one. Matt Reece glanced at the shambled windmill again and shuddered.

He dug Blake's silver pocket watch from his pocket and checked the time. The hands had stopped at 8:15, which was about the time he had held the tricorder over Blake. He twisted the nob to rewind it, but it did no good. Busted. He clicked the lid closed and repocketed it. *Some "Keeper of Time" I am*, he thought.

They rode on.

Riding through a ravine, Matt Reece heard the shrill yelp of a coyote in distress. They halted the horses when they saw three coyotes near an outcrop of manzanita. Two reddish-brown beasts held a third coyote down. One had his jaws locked on the victim's neck while the other sat on its haunches, tearing and eating the victim's belly.

The largest attacker pulled up and stared when he caught the horses' scent. It growled and returned to ripping the victim's flesh. "Damn you," Matt Reece shouted. He slipped his carbine from its scabbard under his leg and aimed at the largest coyote. The prey was near dead, he knew, because its cries went silent. Above, a dozen buzzards swept across a circular sky, waiting their turn.

Matt Reece lowered the barrel and thumbed the hammer down. "I just hate cannibals," he told Kenji. But he knew that when these animals saw a helpless creature, even one of their own, they ripped it to bits. They were predators, after all, unfamiliar with mercy.

They skirted around the beasts.

Once they reached the tree line, they slowed to a leisurely pace, staying under the cover of evergreens as much as possible, and whenever they heard the drone of a plane or helicopter, they halted under cover until the sound died away.

Kenji finally spoke. "There should be more game, considering the time of year."

Matt Reece nodded. All day he saw birds, and now and then he caught sight of a jackrabbit, but no sign of deer. He felt grateful that Kenji broke the silence. Now maybe he could ask a few of the million questions bombarding his skull.

"You have the power to save Grandpa, just like Groucho, and you were letting him die." He didn't mean it to be an indictment, but there was no softer way to state it.

"Maybe you should wait until you know the facts before you start accusing?"

"Where're we headed?"

"A spread thirty miles south of Bishop. We'll be plenty safe there for the time being."

"Who we running from?"

"Everybody and his dog will kill to get their hands on what's in here." He patted his saddlebag. "From now on it's just you and me, kiddo. We trust nobody."

Matt Reece didn't have to be told who to trust. That became evident when they lit out without so much as a wave goodbye to Jessup. If they couldn't trust him, then the entire world was against them.

They rode under a stand of pines beside the creek and dismounted. "Water the stock while I round up some protein for dinner."

Kenji pulled the .30-30 carbine from Comet's saddle scabbard. The rifle belonged to Patrick, but Kenji brought it along, almost as an afterthought. Matt Reece never saw Kenji eat meat, so the idea of him hunting seemed as bizarre as everything else that had happened that day. Matt Reece led the horses to the creek and let them drink while Groucho splashed around in the shallows. A shot rang out, and the horses reared and kicked out. He held the reins and spoke to them in a mollifying voice, telling them it was nothing more than a distant lightning strike. He walked the horses back up the slope.

By the time he'd tied the horses to a pine limb, Kenji came through the trees carrying a jackrabbit with a bloody head and one ear shot off. Matt Reece's stomach lurched when he saw the mutilated skull, but he looked away and quelled his nerves. Kenji reholstered the rifle and removed a hunting knife from his saddlebag.

Kenji nodded at the stream. "Why don't you cool off?"

He knew the water was icy, but that seemed a better option than watching Kenji gut that poor creature. He shucked off his clothes. It felt delightful to be naked with the sun on his skin, and yet, his feet stung as he stepped into the stream. Every nerve ending howled as cold bit his ankles. He waded out up to his knees and sat with his back to the current, spreading his arms out and leaning into the flow until only his face was above the surface. The cold grew excruciating, to the point he couldn't draw air. His reflexes demanded that he leap up and away from the torment. Yet, in a surprising display of will over instincts, he forced himself to endure that soul-consuming sting until he felt nothing.

The need to fill his lungs finally forced him to stand. He pushed his hair back and wiped his eyes. His body trembled violently. On shore, Kenji squatted several feet from the horses, gutting the rabbit. He called Groucho over and fed him the organs. He rose, wiped the blade on the rabbit pelt, and placed the knife back in his saddlebag before tying the rabbit by its hind legs to his saddle horn. He pulled a notebook and a pen from the saddlebag and walked to the boulder where Matt Reece had piled his clothes.

Kenji washed his hands in the stream and said, "I need to assess any changes in your body." He motioned for Matt Reece to come ashore. "I don't have lab equipment, so I can't do a proper examination, but I can take measurements to see if there are any outward changes over the next several days."

Matt Reece splashed to the bank and stood warming in the sun while Kenji scrutinized every inch of him. Blackbirds in the trees sat squawking, as if he were one of them newly emerged from his baptism. He felt a twinge of satisfaction that he had endured nature's stinging assault.

Kenji asked how he felt and took pages of notes. By the time he was done, Matt Reece was dry enough to climb back into his clothes.

Kenji opened the canvas camp bag strapped to T-Bone and pulled out a loaf of bread, a block of cheddar, and a bag of oats. While Matt Reece prepared cheese sandwiches, Kenji poured oats into his upturned Stetson and fed the horses one by one.

They ate the sandwiches quickly, swung into their saddles, left the creek, and climbed a ridge. They followed a valley southwest, still keeping to the trees. A cool wind rushed down the slopes, and Matt Reece wondered if they would find shelter for the night.

Late afternoon brought arrowheads of geese speeding north, no doubt searching for the shine of water where they could rest the night.

By the time the sun coppered the landscape, they'd covered over fifty miles. They now rode in unfamiliar country, rolling hills with grassy meadows and streams rushing off the mountain. Fading light fanned upon the plains below and withdrew along the edges of the world, leaving a blue shadow that crept toward them. They dismounted in a clearing beside a pool surrounded by pines as abundant as blades of grass. Matt Reece unsaddled and brushed Comet and Pepper. Kenji unloaded T-Bone. Matt Reece hobbled the horses and turned them out to graze while he gathered firewood. It seemed dangerous to build a fire, but he sure as hell wasn't going to eat that rabbit raw.

He built up a flame. The wind made the fire squirm and scuffle as if ill at ease, even though it was sheltered by heavy stones. But the resiny branches of the dwarf pines couldn't be blown out, and a blaze soon rushed up in long yellow spirals.

Kenji skinned the rabbit, skewered it on a green limb, and propped it over the flames to broil. Matt Reece pulled the coffeepot from the camp bag and filled it with water from the pool, measured out grounds, and set it on the coals. He also set up a flatiron over the fire, and while the coffee brewed, he mixed masa with water in a bowl and patted out tortillas, dropping them on the flatiron.

Kenji laid out the bedrolls and placed the saddles at the ends for pillows. He leaned back into his saddle and watched the fire. His face grew mysterious with the gentle play of firelight and shadows. "How's that food coming?"

Matt Reece used his fingers to flip tortillas. "The caviar and pheasant under glass are ready. The white peaches in champagne will take a few more minutes."

"I guess it's time we talked," Kenji said.

"Yessir."

Kenji propped the heel of his right boot on top of the toe of his left, as if he were about to pace off the distance between the ground and the stars. "I guess you figured I've discovered a way to make people younger. Oddly enough, it all started before I was born. You see, my family lived in Hiroshima during the Pacific War. My mother was eight months pregnant with me when the Enola Gay dropped the A-bomb. It killed a hundred and forty thousand people, including my mother. Radiation poisoning killed or disfigured tens of thousands more. But it had an opposite effect on me and a few other fetuses who were exposed to the emissions in utero."

"In what?"

"Unborn babies. Radiation caused nightmarish birth defects, but there were exceptions."

"Jesus, sir, that would make you old as Grandpa. What was it like growing up there after the bomb?"

"They are pure torment, my memories—an exquisite torture."

Matt Reece turned the spit holding the rabbit, trying to absorb his shock.

"That radiation altered an enzyme in my system, and that changed my DNA, which makes my body produce masses of highly charged human growth cells. Those cells rapidly destroy and replace old cells and keep my organs and tissue healthy."

The last of the sunlight bled from the sky. The temperature fell. It would no doubt be a cold night. Sparks rising from the fire raced red through the tree branches.

Matt Reece took the last tortilla off the griddle, laid it on a stack of others, and set the griddle on a rock to cool. He wrapped a rag around the coffeepot handle, filled two tin cups, and carried one to Kenji. He walked back to the fire and knelt, sipping his coffee while staying within the circle of warmth. He threw more logs on the flames, hoping he'd gathered enough firewood to get them through the night.

"Because of the radiation, I aged slowly until I grew to where I am now, and then I stopped aging altogether. Thirty years ago I hooked up with Consuela, and we've been researching how radiation changed me. Six years ago we discovered how to reproduce it, and now we can virtually reverse aging. It's partly because of me that they built our research lab out in the middle of nowhere. Consuela didn't want anyone discovering what we were up to, or noticing that I wasn't aging."

Kenji talked about the impressive list of diseases this treatment cured. "This will eliminate the medical industry."

What could Matt Reece say? Outlandish? Yes, but he'd never known Kenji to lie, and hell, he could see for himself; Groucho lay by the fire after a hard day's run.

It grew so quiet that he could hear the faint sound of big rigs rolling along Highway 168, ten miles to the south.

"What will happen to Grandpa?"

"Barring murder or accidents, and with regular inoculations from the tricorder, he'll live four, maybe five thousand years. Maybe forever. We just don't know."

Kenji went on to tell how Matt Reece exposed himself while treating Blake.

"Does this mean I'll be eighteen forever?"

Kenji explained that he had never experimented on non-Asian humans, and never on anyone younger than sixty years old. All his human experiments had been on elder Japanese men like himself, so he wasn't sure what side effects would occur with non-Japanese DNA. That's why he brought Matt Reece into hiding with him, to study the effects and to protect him.

"Protect?"

Kenji described Consuela's and his intentions of keeping the findings to themselves for as long as there were weapons on earth. He told of the YouTube video that went viral and the fact that the whole world was now, no doubt, searching for them. "Scientists will want to dissect you in order to find out this secret. No telling what they'll do."

"Is Grandpa Blake in danger?"

"Hopefully he'll have enough sense to keep his mouth shut."

Matt Reece spat into the fire. He'd been reasonably calm all day, and often happy to be on what seemed a grand adventure, but all this talk terrified him. He wished he could back up time by thirty minutes to a point before Kenji unloaded all this information. Being a dumb kid, he reckoned, had its advantages.

"How long do we need to hide out?"

"We're headed to a place where it'll be safe to be ourselves."

"Where?"

"The last place on earth they'll look for us."

"Jesus, sir, you're making my goddamn head hurt."

"Sorry, but you're the one who opened Pandora's box."

"And you built the fuckin' box!"

Matt Reece turned his back on Kenji, wanting to quit this talk. He lifted the rabbit off the flame and set it on the flatiron. It didn't look appetizing, and he wasn't sure Kenji would eat it, but screw him. He could starve. Matt Reece pulled the meat from the bones with his fingers and piled it onto two tin plates. He peppered them with bottled hot sauce and carried the food to the blankets. They rolled stringy meat in tortillas and chewed while staring at the fire.

"It's not all that bad," Kenji said.

"The hell it's not! I'll never see Jessup or Patrick or Grandpa again. And I'm stuck in puberty forever."

"I was talking about the rabbit."

Matt Reece scowled at him while he ripped off another bite and chewed.

When they wiped their plates with the last of the tortillas, Matt Reece moved back to the fire. He cleaned the plates with a rag and held them close to the flames to kill any bacteria. He wrapped the rag around the coffeepot handle, poured two more cups, and carried them back to the blankets. Kenji pulled two wool serapes from the camp bag. Matt Reece set the cups between them and draped the blue serape over his shoulders, leaving the dirt-brown one for Kenji.

He felt lost in such a large serape, but it would keep him warm. He pulled off his boots and stood them beside his bedroll, but he left his socks on. "It'll take decades to destroy all the bombs and battleships. Maybe hundreds of years. If this cures cancer and AIDS and heart disease, what about the people who are sick now? How many will die before they dearm the world?"

"What's the good of saving their lives if someone blows them up or shoots them in the streets? We have an opportunity to eliminate all weapons by dangling a golden carrot, otherwise it'll never happen. It's the only way to defeat war and gun violence, forever."

Matt Reece shook his head. "I can't stomach so many good people dying when you can save them."

"Being a human being doesn't make you 'good,' just like being a dog turd doesn't make you anything but a pile of shit. You are one or you're not—nothing good or bad about either one. And let's not forget that as many people die at the hands of 'good people' with guns as die from any other group."

Matt Reece ran a warp-speed mind search for an effective counterargument, but he came up empty. He tossed the rest of his coffee on the ground, rested his head on the saddle, and looked up through pine branches at the sky. It was one of those nights when the sky rioted with stars and the earth seemed doubly black because of it.

He suddenly felt the burden of gratitude. Having been granted this impossible gift, he felt he should do something meaningful with it. Before today, he'd lived a smallish existence, cooking and cleaning, learning his lessons, caring for Blake, riding through canyons and over buttes, and on Sundays baking something sugary. Now he expected more of himself, although what that could be he hadn't a clue, yet. Perhaps helping to purge the world of arms was the most significant thing he could accomplish. He tried to envision the planet with no guns, no violence, no war, but it was too bizarre to imagine.

He held his breath, waiting for a shooting star to wish on.

DEEP INTO the night, howls of coyotes woke him. He lifted his head and saw glowing spots on the far side of the fire, firelight reflected in several sets of eyes.

The horses twisted their heads against the halter ropes, sniffing for danger. They nickered and stamped their hooves. Groucho leaped up and growled.

Matt Reece lurched wide-awake. He shouted for Groucho to stay. Those glittering eyes sunk back into the darkness. He felt movement all around the camp, beyond the fringe of light. He sensed them waiting. He reached for the rifle but remembered the coyotes he saw that morning, ripping their own kind to death. The idea of killing turned his stomach to ice.

He walked to the fire instead and built it into a blaze. He drew a flaming branch and waved the torch over his head to scatter the pack. He shouted, and only silence answered.

By the time he was back with his head on his saddle, they were howling again. Those earlier feelings of doing something important fled. Now it felt like the world was waiting for its chance to pounce, and all his energy needed to focus on staying alive.

Chapter Seven

In a pale dawn, Matt Reece woke to snowflakes swirling about his head and warm breath on the back of his neck. He closed his eyes, wanting to crawl back into his dream of lying on a tropical beach. Who knew, another interlude of sleep might let him wake in a warm, happy place where he was not a hunted man. But try as he might, his shivering kept him awake. He craned his neck and saw the trees were dusted with white. The campsite resembled a Hallmark Christmas card.

More surprising, he found himself encircled by Kenji's arms, cuddling for warmth while both their heads rested in the same saddle.

He disengaged himself without waking Kenji. He pulled on his boots and hurried to the fire pit, hugging his serape. He used a stick to dig into the still-hot coals and sprinkled dry pine needles onto them. He blew a flame to life and piled on more needles, followed by twigs, and then branches. When he had a blaze going, he cleaned out the coffeepot, refilled it, and set it into the fire.

He glanced at Kenji, who seemed uncannily at peace in the snow-blown dawn. Sunrays made his skin seem as luminous as the snowflakes caught in his eyelashes. Matt Reece thought about all they discussed last night. He didn't know if he was blessed or cursed. Whatever came, he thought, they were now bound to each other for perhaps a thousand years. Much as he revered this man, that didn't feel like a blessing.

On the other hand, if Matt Reece had to spend a millennium with someone, why not him? He was as beautiful and graceful and inscrutable as a mortal could aspire to, and he was nearly immortal. And now Matt Reece was too. He hated the idea of being trapped in a teen's body forever, but he would never suffer old age and disease like Grandpa Blake.

Kenji's eyes twitched over a dream. Matt Reece imagined those dreams as a bright and serene time when the world forgot all it ever knew of violence and disease and even death. Yes, those imaginings must be of an idyllic future devoid of suffering. He hoped with burning optimism that it would evolve quickly.

He pulled his silver watch from his pocket and clicked open the lid. The hands were still frozen at 8:15. He snapped the lid closed and tucked it away just as Kenji lifted his head off the saddle and asked how soon the coffee would be ready.

They were fed, packed, and on the move an hour after sunup. The saddle leather creaked from the cold. They kicked the horses into a lope and rode to a lower elevation where there was less cover but warmer temperatures. Once they reached the high prairie, with the sun warming their backs, they slowed the horses to a walk and became cheerful again. Even Groucho seemed happy to leave the cold behind.

They traveled for three days through barren hill country of the Waucoba Mountain range and then along the western slopes of the White Mountains. The country's stark splendor and vast openness reminded Matt Reece of home. They ate tortillas and cheese and whatever game Kenji could shoot.

The afternoon of the third day, a towering cloudbank swept south across the land with long tendrils of trailing rain. At first the clouds didn't seem to move, and yet forty minutes later, they caught and consumed the sun. The day turned to dusk, and the mountains radiated a pewtery light, hard and dull. A white lance of lightning shot downward. Thunder rolled like caissons over the land. Matt Reece trembled with pleasure in the promised turmoil. What began as startling detonations—metallic, clashing notes—faded into low bass rolling in the distance. The first fat raindrops thudded up dust in spurts. The sharp smell of dampened earth saturated the air. Then lazy drops peppered the brim of his Stetson. He lifted his face to the sky. Droplets beat his cheeks, and water trickled down his neck.

He glanced at Kenji.

"Looks like we're in for it," Kenji said. "Sorry you came?"

"Not yet."

"We're in luck, because we're almost there." They galloped over a rise and spotted a cabin tucked into a stand of cottonwoods, with smoke funneling from the chimney. It looked inviting, but it was still a half hour's ride away. The rain abruptly turned to hail—hailstones a half inch in diameter beating on them with stinging force. Minutes later it settled into a heavy rainfall, streaming down as if the heavens were dissolving, turning earth to mud, dry gullies to torrents. They spurred their mounts into a run, but they were soaked to the skin by the time they reached their destination.

The cabin was rustic, made of horizontal timbers, a shingle roof, and a covered porch. The windows had drawn curtains of dark cloth that let no light escape. Beside it stood a shed with a compact car parked inside.

They dismounted. Matt Reece called Groucho to his side and held the horses' reins. Kenji climbed into the car and backed it into the rain so Matt Reece could lead the horses into the shed.

Kenji walked up, untied his saddlebags, and slung them over his shoulder. "You look done in."

"'Done in' came and went three hours ago. Now I'm a zombie."

"Cheer up. We'll sleep in warm beds tonight. You tend the livestock while I announce our arrival."

Matt Reece unsaddled the horses and rubbed them down with a towel from the camp pack. He watered and fed them the last of the oats and closed the shed doors to lock them in for the night. Groucho followed him to the front door and sat beside him. He wasn't sure Groucho would be welcome inside. Hell, he wasn't even sure he was welcome.

He stood with hat in hand, listening to what sounded like an argument. It didn't take much imagination to understand it was about him. He knocked, opened the door, scraped his boots on the doormat, and stepped into an area that was a living room on one side, a kitchen on the other. Groucho followed him in. As he closed the door, the only sounds were a crackling fire, a ticking clock, and rain swishing the roof.

Consuela Rocha y Villareal stood at the sink. Matt Reece had met her. She came to the ranch for dinner several times, and he talked to her at Golden Eagle's company picnics. She turned to him gracefully, smiling an empty smile.

In the orange light from the fireplace, she looked oddly theatrical, passing the back of one hand across her brow to brush back some loose strands of hair. She stared at him, and her face was pale and austere, with that hint of red from the firelight.

"*Buenas tardes, señora,*" he said, nodding to her.

"*Hola*, Matt Reece, *¿cómo estás?*"

"*Estoy bien, pero un poco mojado.*"

She nodded. "*Sí, eso veo.*"

Kenji sat at a table, drinking tea with both hands cupping the mug. Before him was a sizable tower of money, crisp bills bound by white strips of paper into inch-high bundles. Matt Reece was staring at a fortune. It took his breath away. A MacBook Pro perched on top of the money, and also a flash drive, a half-dozen credit cards, and what looked like two US passports.

He gasped. "Holy shit! Did you rob a bank?"

Kenji chuckled. "You're looking at seven hundred grand. I funneled the lion's share of my salary into a brokerage account for over twenty years. My investments did well once the country dumped Bush. On top of that, Consuela sold her house."

"I also sold several fine paintings, some valuable books, and antique furniture I inherited from my parents," she said. "Those raised over fifty thousand."

Consuela wiped her hands on her apron and poured another mug of tea. She had a sturdy body—not fat, but stout as a Shetland pony—with a head of lovely silver-streaked hair. She wore jeans and a white blouse, with turquoise Native American jewelry on her neck and arms. Her face was wrinkled, telling him that she never exposed herself to the radiation treatment.

When she glanced his way again, he noted a flash of anger—no, fury—directed at him. She was, he could tell, trying to conceal that rage. Her eyes were birdlike, sharp and fierce. She conveyed a raptor's deft awareness. No part of her seemed fragile.

She carried the mug to Matt Reece and held it out. "*Es bueno verte de nuevo*, Matt Reece. *Esto te va a ayudar a calentarte.*"

"*Gracias, señora. Y gracias por recibirme. Siento ser un invitado sin invitación, pero creo que no me di cuenta de las consecuencias.*" She didn't seem to mind a wet dog in the cabin, so he decided not to ask permission. Better to not mention it.

"I see you still have your lovely manners," she said, switching the conversation to English. "How delightful. You must be having quite an escapade so far."

"Yes, ma'am. Beyond anything I bargained for."

"Brace yourself, honey. You've only seen the tip of this iceberg. Are you hungry?"

"Starving, ma'am." He took the mug, blew over the rim, and sipped. The heat scalded his mouth, but he took a second sip.

"Good. I've had my dinner, but there's plenty of cabbage soup left over, and a loaf of sourdough bread. Shuck off those wet clothes, and stand by the fire to warm yourselves. I'll bring blankets to wrap around you while your clothes dry. Then you can eat."

"Much obliged, ma'am." He thought it best not to mention that cabbage soup gave him gas.

Kenji joined him at the fireplace as Consuela disappeared into a room at the back of the cabin. He didn't feel cold, but the heat on his wet legs felt divine. He pulled off his serape, laid it on the stone hearth, and dropped his Stetson and rawhide gloves on top of it. He took off his boots and stood them near the fire and draped his socks over the boots. He pulled his shirt and T-shirt over his head and arranged them over a rocking chair.

His jeans began to steam. He peeled them off and stood in his sopping underwear, absorbing all that delicious heat. He slipped his silver watch from the jeans pocket, checked the time—8:15—and set it on a table beside the rocking chair.

He took in the room. The walls were neatly fitted horizontal timbers stacked to the pitched roof. A calf hide was nailed to one wall, and an elk head hung over the fireplace. An oxblood-colored Naugahyde sofa and matching armchair faced the hearth. This seemed more a hunting cabin than a ranch house, a place where hunters huddled before the fireplace waiting for the dawn when they would go out to kill. He looked back at the elk head. Yes, the air had a slight stench of death, giving the impression that this was a site where life could not succeed for long.

Consuela returned holding two patch quilts. She handed one to each of them, and then gave Matt Reece's body a critical stare. *"¿Cuántos años tienes?, Matt Reece?"*

"Dieciocho, señora."

"Que no se ven más de catorce."

Kenji cupped Matt Reece's shoulder with a gentle hand. "Relax. He's eighteen but small for his age, a bit of a runt. You should see him handle a working horse. You'd swear he was twenty-five."

She walked to the stove and stirred the soup.

Matt Reece wrapped a quilt over his shoulders and shimmied out of his underwear. By the time he arranged his clothes in front of the fire to dry, Consuela had served two bowls of soup. Matt Reece joined

Kenji at the table. He slathered butter on a slab of bread and dug in. He tried not to wolf his food, but he never knew such a consuming hunger. He occasionally tore off a hunk of bread and tossed it to Groucho.

When he glanced up, she was staring at him with a predator's scrutiny. The clock on the mantle ticked, and the burning logs crackled. Even the sound of the rain swishing the roof had softened to a murmur.

Matt Reece sopped up the remains of his soup with the last of the bread and ate it with relish. He wanted more but was too shy to ask.

The clock's ticking became loud.

"I will not support this," she finally said. "We must get him to a lab. We have to—"

"There is no longer a lab. We can't go back." Kenji's tone was adamant. "You flushed that option when you blew the lab and posted the video two weeks early."

"Don't make this about me. We were ready, and you got careless."

"Ready? Obviously not. But I'll grant you we are both at fault."

"We've never experimented on someone so young. We can't be sure how his cells are responding. Our first priority is to safeguard his health. I know people at UCLA Medical Center who will help us and who we can trust to keep this quiet. It will only take a few days. We can be in and out of there before anyone recognizes us."

"We can't reverse this even if it's raging havoc. It'll play its course no matter what we do now. Look, it's been four days with no visible effects. We made a plan." Kenji's voice rose. "Even though you, yes you, jumped the gun, we'll stick to the plan."

"How can you be so callous toward your own son?"

Kenji's lips pressed together. He would not answer her.

The air grew humid from the steam rising off wet clothes. A rank smell, mindful of damp horses, permeated the room.

She gathered the dishes from the table. "The bottom line is this: tomorrow I take him to UCLA Medical Center for a full regimen of tests. That is not negotiable."

Kenji glanced at Matt Reece. "She's got brass-ball opinions. Always did." Matt Reece and Kenji stared at each other. Kenji said, "What do you want?"

She set dishes in the sink. "He doesn't get a say, and neither do you."

Kenji winked at Matt Reece. "I guess we'll have to shoot her."

Matt Reece grinned. "Then we can take all this money for ourselves."

"We'll split it fifty-fifty. We can even take her car."

"Yeah," Matt Reece said, "but I'm not digging a grave in the mud like I did last time."

"No problem, kiddo. We'll just drag her outside and let the coyotes have her."

Matt Reece smiled, nodding. "You want to flip to see who goes to get the rifle?"

"I didn't bring any change. Did you?"

"Nope," Matt Reece said.

Consuela carried the teapot to the table and refilled their mugs without saying a word. Her face grew as emotionless as a clenched fist.

Kenji said, "Seems our hostess doesn't appreciate irony or wit. It's a vernacular little known in the scientific community."

"This is no joking matter," she said. "I've made up my mind."

Kenji sipped more tea. "I'm too tired to argue. Let's sleep on it and see how we feel in the morning."

Matt Reece could only agree. He longed for a bath and to sink his head into a pillow. He led Groucho into a bedroom and trotted off to the bathroom. He mixed the bath water as hot as he could stand it and took his time soaking. He could hear them arguing still, but he tuned it out. Right then he was beyond caring. He simply wanted to be clean and warm and in bed so that he could crawl into his dreams. That sunny beach was calling to him.

The voices hushed, and a door slammed. Kenji stepped into the bathroom. "I guess that tub is too small for both of us?"

"I'm getting out now." He opened the drain and grabbed a towel. He stood and gave himself a brisk rub, wrapped his quilt around him, and slipped out the door. The bedroom had two twin beds, the covers neatly laid back. Groucho was snoozing on an oval hooked rug between the beds. Matt Reece spread his quilt over a bed and crawled in. The sheets felt clammy. He heard the sound of water running in the bathroom as he closed his eyes and drifted into sleep.

What seemed only moments later, he felt a shaking. He opened his eyes. Kenji knelt beside his bed, his black hair still damp.

"Even though Consuela is upset, I'm glad you came. You're a good kid, a handsome kid, and I don't feel so lonely with you here."

Matt Reece's sleep-drenched mind struggled to understand. "Thanks, but I ain't so good or handsome."

"You took care of Blake," Kenji said. "That demonstrates your character more than anything."

"I only did what anyone would."

Kenji caressed Matt Reece's cheek. "Much as you hate death and violence, you didn't recoil when you saw cancer eating up that old man. You gave him every comfort."

This conversation came out of left field. The room was so still and silent that he heard his own heart beating in even gushes.

"I need comforting too," Kenji said.

Matt Reece stared at him, fully awake now.

"Let's share the same bed?" Kenji said. "I'm not putting moves on you. I'm just lonely."

Matt Reece grew acutely aware that they were both naked, and his heart rate doubled. He shook his head no.

"It'd be nice just to hold each other. Could we do that?"

He shook his head again.

"We'll be together a long time, kiddo. Sooner or later, we'll stop seeing each other as father and son. I mean, hell, I'm only your stepfather. We're not real flesh and blood. There's no harm in comforting each other."

"Let's shoot for later, rather than sooner." Matt Reece turned to the wall. A minute of silence passed before the light clicked off and he heard Kenji climbing into the other bed. He was now too wired to sleep. Kenji being his stepfather had nothing to do with anything. He felt that need for intimacy, but he needed the right person to give it.

His eyes stung as he closed them, trying to picture this mysterious person who could give the intimacy he craved. He knew that their paths would eventually cross, because he couldn't bear the thought of it not happening.

MATT REECE woke alone. He sat up and swept the drapes back from the window. The day was bright with a fresh blue sky. He slipped from the covers, draped his quilt over his shoulders, and walked into the living room. He found Kenji fully dressed, stuffing that pile of money into a canvas traveling bag.

Kenji brought his finger to his lips to quiet Matt Reece. Kenji pointed to the clothes draped over the furniture. "Get dressed," he whispered.

"Where's Groucho?"

"Outside, taking care of nature's call."

"And Consuela?"

"Let's hit the road before she wakes. We'll grab breakfast at the first café we see."

Matt Reece dressed quickly. He picked up his silver pocket watch. The timepiece was useless, yet he couldn't stop himself from sliding it into his pocket. He was still, after all, the new custodian of time, even if time was stuck on 8:15.

At the kitchen sink he turned on the faucet, cupped his hands, and flung water on his face. He slurped a handful to rinse his mouth. Kenji carried the money sack outside, and Matt Reece followed, closing the door softly behind him. They marched to the car, which turned out to be a Prius. Matt Reece popped the trunk lid. Kenji dropped the sack in the trunk. "I'll load up what we'll need. You turn the livestock free. We'll leave the saddles and bridles here."

Matt Reece flinched. It had not occurred to him before now that they would abandon the horses, but of course now that they had a car, it made perfect sense.

"Can't we leave them with Consuela?"

"She doesn't have any feed, and who knows how long she'll stay here once we leave. Cut them loose, and let's get."

What did I expect? He knew it was a question he would return to many times, and he doubted he would ever answer it. His grand departure occurred so quickly that he had no time to think it through. Now the regrets were piling up.

He swung open the shed doors. The horses craned their necks toward him, no doubt expecting some oats. He had nothing but his sorrow to give them—sorrow and freedom. Comet walked to him and nudged him. Matt Reece laid his forehead to Comet's and hugged that long beautiful head. Comet was a light gray color with a spotted rump, stood sixteen hands high, and he was well muscled and built for speed. Matt Reece loved this horse for as long as he could remember. To him,

Comet embodied liberation, his magic carpet to lose himself while riding the scrublands and canyons.

"You take care, ol' boy. Find yourself a mustang filly and make some colts."

Kenji went through the packs, tossing aside the camping gear. He didn't seem to mind how much noise he made with clattering pots and dishes, so not waking Consuela no longer seemed a priority. He carried the lightened pack to the car, dumped it into the trunk, and herded Groucho into the back seat.

Matt Reece felt himself at a crossroad. If he crawled into that car, he would lose Comet. If he stayed with Consuela, he assumed he would eventually go back to the Promesa Rota, but at least he could still ride the range with Comet and Groucho. He thought about Kenji's plan to rid the world of violence, and how he could help bring that about. His decision flickered before him like a candle flame held close to the eyes.

Kenji called from the driver's seat. "Get it in gear. We're burnin' daylight."

Matt Reece took off his hat and swatted Comet's flank with it. The horse took off at a gallop. Matt Reece raised his arms and shrieked, and Pepper and T-Bone raced after Comet.

Walking to the car, he felt like this was karmic punishment for not letting Kenji into his bed last night. He knew it was good that he would live for five thousand years, because it would take that long before he forgave Kenji for this loss.

They headed due west on Country Road 32, blowing up dust the whole way. The clicking of gravel on the undercarriage transported Matt Reece into a taking-stock mood. Something felt amiss. It didn't make sense to leave Consuela behind and yet take her money and her car. He couldn't bring himself to confront Kenji, because it was still just an odd feeling. He was now hurtling into a world where he knew no one except his stepfather, and he admitted he didn't know him as well as he'd thought. With the loss of Comet, his only remaining friend was Groucho, who sat in the back seat whining to have the window put down. Right then he felt as alone as a man could get.

Twenty minutes later, they came to a paved road that led them to Highway 395, which they took north, following the signs for San Francisco.

Chapter Eight

Jessup slouched in a chair beside a hospital bed where his father lay. Aftershock biochemicals still raced through Jessup's arteries, making his head a vacuum devoid of thoughts. He took in the room for the thousandth time, the crack in the green tile floor, television hanging from the ceiling, window blinds drawn, shadows moving in the corridor.

Dr. Katherine Hitchens stood beside him, reading Blake's charts. "It's vanished."

"Impossible," Blake said through a full mouth of scrambled eggs while layering four strips of bacon atop his third english muffin.

"We repeated the tests three times," she said, "and found no trace of cancer. None, zilch, nada. It's not in remission; it's gone. Even the lesions on your liver. It's the first true medical phenomenon I've ever witnessed."

"Will it come back?" Blake asked.

"Not for a few thousand years or so," Jessup mumbled. They ignored him. His mind began to engage this parallel universe that he somehow plunged into three days ago. He had no idea how to deal with these new developments or even how to plan for a future. He focused only on the immediate, which was caring for his father.

"A month ago your body was replicating cancer cells at an alarming rate," Dr. Hitchens said. "Now you're producing healthy cells by the millions in every organ, muscle, and bone. You've somehow exchanged the rampancy of bad cells for good."

"So I can two-step my way out of this damned hospital?"

"Don't open the champagne yet. I'm worried about your color. We need more tests."

Jessup eyed his father. Blake grew healthier and younger by the day, yet he was still mentally shaky, like a punch-drunk fighter groggily declaring that he'll fight again. That instability was more disturbing than the greenish hue his skin took on. The color was hardly noticeable, but as his body flourished, the color became more pronounced.

"You've poked and jabbed and MRIed me nonstop. How many more tests could there be?"

"What's happened to you is monumental, Mr. Connors. Surely you can tolerate a few more days in order for us to understand what caused this astounding turnaround. We're flying in specialists from Johns Hopkins and scientists from Golden Eagle Labs."

"You can't keep me here."

He was about to say more, but Dr. Hitchens popped a thermometer in his mouth. For as long as he lived, Jessup would remember the anguished look Dr. Hitchens turned on him. Her eyes were intense, fraught with hope, and as profound as the silence that accompanied them. She would not, however, get his help in persuading Blake.

"Actually, Mr. Connors," she said, "FBI agents are investigating a crime they think you might be involved with. If they arrest you on suspicion, you'll stay here indefinitely. But I will need your approval to perform these tests. Please don't make me take extreme measures." She extracted the thermometer and noted the results on the chart.

Jessup was now out from under the shadow of Blake's impending death, yet in this parallel world, he didn't know if he felt relieved or simply confused. It was too new to wrap his head around. But her term "extreme measures" struck a note of alarm in him.

Jessup saw two men in the corridor who looked like a cliché detective duo—older/younger, dark suits, and the leisure of movement evocative of a monarch. Their footsteps resounded as they walked closer. The older one had thinning white hair and wore spectacles on his sage-like face; the other was about Jessup's age with a middleweight-boxer's build and the distinct look of Middle Eastern ancestry.

Two nurses soft-shoed past them, pushing an empty gurney.

"Well, dammit," Blake said, raising his voice, "if I'm a prisoner, at least bring me another Dr. Pepper. And I want pizza for lunch."

When she nodded, he added, "Large pepperoni, extra cheese and meat, and plenty of jalapeños. I like my pizzas like I like my women: so spicy they bring tears to my eyes."

Dr. Hitchens smiled for the first time. "Looks like we have something in common."

"Your women or your pizza?" Blake asked, now full-on flirting.

"I never eat pizza."

Blake laughed and turned to Jessup. "I'm beginning to like her."

The two suits invaded the room, looking stern and unflappable. As soon as they entered, Dr. Hitchens retreated out the doorway. They seemed to fill every cubic inch of empty space. They both reached inside their jackets and drew out badges, holding them out for Jessup to see.

"Jessup Connors, I'm Senior Special Agent Salman Landau," the older man said, "and this is Special Agent Ahmed Souad. We're with the Federal Bureau of Investigation, and we've been assigned the Golden Eagle case. We need to question both of you."

Jessup stood. "I doubt we can help, but you have our full cooperation."

Both agents pocketed their badges.

"Bullshit," Blake said. "All you're getting from me is name, rank, and serial number."

Jessup smiled at his father. "You won't talk because you don't know anything. Don't act like you've got something to hide just to inflate your importance."

Agent Landau brandished a document, holding it out for Jessup to read. "This is a search warrant, Mr. Connors, issued by a federal judge. I have a team at your ranch now, combing your house."

"Just what the hell do you expect to find?" Jessup's hand slid into his jeans pocket and fingered the flash drive Kenji left him.

Landau folded the document and tucked it into the inside pocket of his jacket. "Mr. Connors, someone incinerated an eighty-million-dollar research facility, which injured three security guards and killed hundreds of animals. Those same people stole the documentation for a trillion-dollar medical discovery. All indications point to Kenji Hiroshige and Consuela Rocha y Villareal. We hope to uncover clues as to their whereabouts."

"Someone firebombed Kenji's lab?" He realized that if a judge granted a search warrant, then he might be considered an accessory. That meant these men most likely had authority to wiretap his phone, keep him under surveillance, even arrest him.

Landau nodded. "All the security data was destroyed, but we know from interviewing security guards that Kenji and Consuela were alone until two in the morning, three nights earlier. We believe they blew it up to destroy all evidence of their discovery. We intend to find them and determine if they had any accomplices."

The floor shifted under Jessup's feet, but he didn't crumble. Rage braced him up. He didn't know if his sudden anger was directed at these agents or at Kenji or simply at this alien universe that seemed to change shape every time he blinked.

"If you don't mind, Mr. Connors," Landau said, "I need you to accompany me to the police station for questioning. We'll leave Agent Souad here to interview your father."

"And if I do mind?"

"Believe it or not, Mr. Connors, we're the good guys here. Kenji is in serious, if not life-threatening danger. Any information you give us only helps him."

The sincerity in Landau's voice left Jessup indefensible.

Landau escorted Jessup to the front of the hospital, where a throng of reporters shifted anxiously and a line of policemen held them behind a tape barrier. The press swarmed forward, cameras clicking like machine guns. A dozen officers gathered around him like vultures over roadkill. Jessup followed Landau to an unmarked police car. They climbed into the back seat behind two men dressed in sheriff uniforms, who were glaring at Jessup through protective wire mesh.

The engine roared to life, and the car lurched forward. Minutes later, Landau led Jessup into the Hawthorn sheriff station and to a room with no windows and furnished with an oak table and four metal chairs. Two sets of fluorescent tubes inside a wire cage recessed into the ceiling gave off a buzzing sound, and weak yellow light made the room even gloomier. A four-by-six mirror dominated the far wall; Jessup assumed it was two-way and people were watching from the other side.

The place seemed like a one-way conveyer belt for felons, drug addicts, and murders, a way station where one landed but nobody stayed for long, a place for those whom the final hope is wrung out and flushed down the drain. Jessup assumed these gray walls were the very ones people spoke of when they talked about having their backs against the wall. Indeed, he thought, this place was where men were brought to their deepest confessions. The more false and far-fetched their beginning lies, the truer their final admissions. It was here a man found his limits, and thus, came to know himself.

Landau guided him to a chair at the head of the table, facing the mirror.

"Coffee?" Landau asked.

"Black will do."

Landau opened the door and spoke to a secretary passing in the corridor. "Excuse me, Miss. Could you have someone bring in two coffees?" He returned to the table, sat to Jessup's right, and removed a notebook and pen from his jacket. "Our conversation is being recorded. We have no reason to suspect you of any wrongdoings, however, since any statements you make may be used later as evidence in a court of law, I need to read you your rights before we begin. This is just a formality, nothing to be frightened of. Anything you say may be held against you in a court of law. You have the right to have an attorney present."

As Landau droned on, a chill ran along Jessup's spine. *Why am I being treated like a criminal?* He was frightened of being arrested, which would result in emptying his pockets and them discovering the flash drive. He sized up the unimposing detective, who didn't seem hostile. He decided to cooperate fully and hope for the best.

He acknowledged that he understood his rights and waived the right to an attorney. Landau asked several mundane questions—name, occupation, who lived on the ranch, how long had he lived there, how long he'd known Kenji Hiroshige, etc.

"Let's focus on Kenji. When did you see him last, and what were the circumstances?"

Jessup described waking up three days ago to Matt Reece's anxiety attack and the conversation with Kenji about burying Groucho. He left out nothing, and Landau took copious notes. During his account of the breakfast banter, a deputy delivered two paper cups of coffee. He sipped the bitter liquid, which was easily an hour old.

Jessup recounted his trek up the hill to dig a grave and his returning to find Kenji, Matt Reece, and the dog missing. Jessup skipped over the facts that they left on horseback and Kenji left a letter and the flash drive. He launched into the arrival of Declan Hughes and the bombshell Declan dropped about living forever.

During his narration, Landau asked many pointed questions. Jessup found him a shrewd and efficient listener, and he came to trust the man, but not enough to disclose what he'd skipped over. For all of Landau's professionalism, he reminded Jessup of an overconfident predator, sure of his tactics now that his prey was isolated.

By the time Jessup finished his narrative, which took the better part of an hour, he was soaked in sweat and exuded a faint smell reminiscent of rotten eggs. He realized for the first time that there was no ventilation in the room. Was that some trick to make him even more uncomfortable, more susceptible?

"Kenji amazed you, didn't he?" Landau said.

"Beg your pardon?"

"This story is pretty shocking no matter how you look at it."

Landau glanced at his coffee that had gone cold. He lifted the cup and drank half of it with one swallow. "Christ, this sludge could dissolve fillings. Where the hell is a Starbucks when you need one?"

Landau leveled his stare back on Jessup. "I don't understand why he'd give up such a sweet life—important job, lovely ranch, good family."

"Isn't it obvious?" Jessup said.

"No, I don't believe it is. It's all so bizarre that it doesn't add up. Does he really think he can de-arm the world? Was there a chance of dissuading him? Did you even try?"

Jessup propped his elbows on the table and cupped his head in his hands, gathering his wits. "Your question is an accusation that I had prior knowledge."

"Pleading ignorance won't fly with me, Mr. Connors." Landau removed his spectacles and rubbed his nose. "I've read your police record, and I found no incidence of gun violence. What exactly turned you against firearms?"

"I've always been a pacifist. I've hated guns all of my life."

"Aha! So you approve of Kenji's plot."

"Every time I try to wrap my mind around it, something new hits me in the gut. But I do know he couldn't have injured security guards and killed lab animals. He's a devout Buddhist who reveres all living creatures."

"Why would someone else have done such a thing?"

Jessup cleared his throat and spoke hoarsely. "I have no idea. But Kenji didn't blow up that building. This is all a dreadful misunderstanding."

Landau fished a bottle of pills from his jacket, popped three into his mouth, and washed them down with his remaining coffee.

Jessup reached over, lifted the plastic bottle, and read the prescription. "You take Oxycontin on an empty stomach? Are you trying to induce a coma? No way in hell a practicing physician prescribed these to a relatively healthy man like you."

"I told him I was having severe migraines. What do doctors know anyway?"

"I won't ask who you obtained this prescription from."

Landau took the bottle from him, slipped it back in his pocket, stood, and paced the room lengthwise. "You're stalling."

"Stalling?"

"Buying them time to go deeper into hiding," Landau said.

"They've had three days, for God sakes. They could be at the South Pole by now."

Souad sauntered into the room. He removed his jacket and draped it over the back of a chair. Jessup noted his handsome face and virile allure, and the snug-fitting shirt that accentuated his physique. Landau shot Souad a questioning look, and he shook his head.

Landau continued to pace while Souad sat to Jessup's left.

"You haven't seen Kenji or Matt Reece in the last three days?" Landau asked.

"No."

"You saw them drive away?"

"No."

"How can that be? There's only one road in and out of the ranch."

"I told you, I was waist-deep in a grave a half mile from the house."

"The Jeep at the ranch is the only car registered in Kenji's name. Does he have access to another?"

"Not that I know of."

"So we're forced to assume Consuela picked them up while you dug that grave?"

Jessup shrugged.

"But you've spoken to them on the telephone?"

"No. I haven't been home since that morning, and I don't own a cell phone."

Landau glanced at Souad. "We've already checked the DMV database and issued an APB on her car. When we take a break, check with the office to see if anything turned up."

Souad removed a pen and notebook from his jacket and scribbled notes.

Landau stood before a starburst of cracks on the wall. He flipped through his notes, studying each page. "One thing still baffles me. Why did he take the boy?"

To answer that question, Jessup knew he would have to confess about the letter where Kenji explained why. He stared at Landau, silent.

"What kind of bullshit question is that?" Souad asked.

Landau closed his notebook. "Is there a problem here?" he asked.

Souad said, "You always do this; everyone says so. Obsessing over questions that go nowhere."

"Well, excuse me for trying to do my job." He turned to Jessup. "This is our first case we've partnered on. He's unfamiliar with my methods."

"A rocky honeymoon, eh?"

Souad waved an arm to silence him. "Look, we know they were at the lab by themselves with plenty of time to set the charges three nights earlier. We know the lab burned down at about the same time Consuela posted the YouTube video. Now we know she drove to the ranch, picked them up, and they disappeared together. Those are the facts. Who the fuck cares why they took the boy? They did, so deal with it, and stop wasting time. We need to know where, not why."

Jessup half smiled. "Do you two need a minute?"

"Okay, hotshot," Landau said to Souad. "He's all yours. I'll be at the nearest Starbucks." Landau tucked his notebook into his jacket pocket and left the room.

Souad leveled his sexy eyes on Jessup. "Let's start at the point you last saw Kenji."

Jessup pounded a fist on the table. "I've gone over that with your sidekick. If you clowns can't compare notes, that's your problem. Just know that if Kenji took that formula, it's because he created it. It's his baby. As for blowing up buildings and killing animals, he's not wired like that. He's incapable of taking a life."

Souad nodded. "When did you last see Kenji?"

LANDAU AND Souad took turns questioning Jessup for twenty-four consecutive hours, spelling each other in that squalid room with no windows and no ventilation. Every four or five hours they brought in burgers and soft drinks, and they were generous with bathroom breaks. It was nothing like the third-degree treatment beloved of the movies. Rather, they relied on repetition and asking questions about very specific details to break him down. What kind of jeans was Kenji wearing? Did he take his wallet? What pictures did he carry in his wallet? Which credit cards does he use? How much cash did he have? What were Matt Reece's last words to you? Was Matt Reece wearing sneakers or boots? We found ashes in the kitchen sink. What did you burn? How old was Groucho? How deep did you dig the grave? How long did it take to dig?

The questions were accompanied by fists striking the table anytime his eyes closed.

The agents were a formidable team because they were such an odd couple: the tall, languid, deep-voiced older man and the aggressive, buff, Middle-Eastern stud with his laser-beam eyes. They were the classic good cop/bad cop duo, and they were effective because Jessup made the mistake of first assuming that Souad was the dangerous one. He later realized that Souad was driven by volatile passion, while Landau was a calculating, cold-blooded killer type.

The continuous buzz of the light bulbs grew louder and louder, nearly to the point of driving Jessup mad. The questions resounded in his head like muffled incantations. His muscles ached and his sweat-soaked shirt reeked. He would have told them any secret in exchange for a few hours' sleep. In a moment of lucid thought, he became confident that what they were doing to him was tantamount to torture, and that it was illegal. It was high time to stop this abuse.

Landau repeated his last question. "Why did Kenji take the boy, and what is Matt Reece's role in all of this?"

Jessup lifted his head with effort. He swallowed. "I'm not saying any more until I have legal representation."

Landau closed his notebook. "That won't be necessary, Mr. Connors. We're done."

Jessup shook his head to clear his mind of this surprise.

Landau laughed a dry old man's laugh, almost a cough, his shoulders shaking. "You passed with flying colors, Mr. Connors. Congratulations."

Jessup failed to see any humor in anything.

"You see," Landau said, "we made you repeat your story many, many times. Whenever there are no variations in a story, we're 100 percent certain it's fake, something rehearsed. Human beings telling the truth never tell a story quite the same way twice."

Souad said, "Since your storyline stayed consistent but details varied, we're convinced you're telling the truth, that you had no prior knowledge and you're hiding nothing."

Landau stood and laid a comforting hand on Jessup's shoulder. "We've arranged some decent food and a bed. Get some rest. In a few hours, we'll escort you to your ranch."

"Take me home, now."

Landau squeezed his shoulder. "A hundred reporters are camped on your doorstep, waiting to sink their teeth into you. You better rest here before facing that mob."

They lifted Jessup from under his armpits and half carried him to a toilet where he relieved himself, and then helped him to a cell with a table and chair and a plate of bacon and scrambled eggs and toast. Beside the table stood a cot with a pillow and blanket.

Jessup was so tired he almost collapsed on the cot without eating, but hunger drove him to the table. He wolfed down the food before he sank his head into that gloriously soft pillow.

Chapter Nine

Declan Hughes sat for three rainy days in a cabin at Camp David, waiting for the president to fit him into her schedule. After it became evident he was not her top priority, Declan flew Diane McCarthy back to Nevada to gather more information from the scientists who worked with Consuela and Kenji. Jeffery Wolfe, the president's science advisor, weaved back and forth between Declan and Madam President with questions and responses. On Declan's arrival at Camp David, he considered himself a patriot, but now he felt like a prisoner.

On the first face-to-face with Wolfe, Declan removed a file from his briefcase. "We recovered some notes from the lab wreckage." He opened the file and read from the paper on top. "The people of the United States and other Western nations created tremendous agony in my country, crushing our collective soul, and then washed their hands with our blood in their false patriotism. The West's true desire was, and still is, absolute power. Most Western nations are tyrants, indifferent to the suffering of underdeveloped, weaker countries. Now I have power over death, I am the tyrant, and I am indifferent to your misery. It matters little to me how many people die, for you will all die if I keep the formula to myself. There is only one way to acquire immortality, and that is to de-arm the world."

"A diatribe," Wolfe said. "He's raging against our victory over Japan."

"Yes," Declan said, "but it sheds light on who we're dealing with. He's suffered great spiritual anguish, a wrenching of his soul. Perhaps he has a madman's impulse to make others share his anguish."

"So you think this demand of de-arming is a red herring?" Wolfe asked.

"I think it smells fishy. I mean, even if we de-arm, we can rebuild our arsenals once we have the formula. He's shrewd enough to know that."

Wolfe nodded at Declan. "It's interesting his note uses the singular 'I' and not the plural 'we.' Could it be a case of male chauvinism, or is he thinking of shedding his partner now that he has what he needs? I dare say he wouldn't be the first man to play that card."

Declan had no idea how to respond.

After Wolfe left, he thought for the millionth time that his long-held dream was now within his grasp. The one roadblock holding back drone weapons from the next major advancement was the size and heat of the computers needed to control a network of drones, both onboard and at the command centers. For years, computers became faster by cramming components closer together on chips, which in turn generated greater heat. Computer chips had reached an upper limit, becoming so densely packed that any more speed would melt the circuit boards. Having anticipated this a decade earlier, Declan created a subsidiary company to develop a computer using the quantum attributes of atoms. In the eighties, physicist Richard Feynman speculated that such a "quantum computer" would be a million times faster than any current technology. IBM, Sony, and HP were also working on prototypes.

Declan was confident that with so much raw computational power, he could link a network of drone aircraft, all coordinated by an artificially intelligent system. His dream was to replace a human army with advanced machines capable of defending America against any threat. The idea was made popular by the *Terminator* movies that labeled it Cyberdyne Systems Skynet, a functional, self-aware, synthetic defense system. Only to Declan it wasn't fictional; it was simply yet to be built. Research and development outlays had already run into the tens of billions, nearly bankrupting him, and the finish line was still beyond the horizon. He needed a cash cow to continue the research, and Kenji's trillion-dollar formula was precisely the golden heifer he craved.

Emails from Diane McCarthy held little information. Consuela and Kenji shared nothing with their peers. Still, Diane pieced together enough data to make some knowledgeable guesses.

After a pulled-pork sandwich and a green salad lunch on day four, Jeff Wolfe escorted him to an unobtrusive neoclassical building set away from the other cabins.

Upon entering the foyer, Secret Service agents patted them down so thoroughly that to Declan, it felt like a sexual assault. They checked his briefcase with the same diligence. "Gentlemen," a female receptionist greeted them, "this way, please."

She led them along a corridor to a double door flanked by two armed Marines. She knocked as she opened it and motioned them into a conference room that seemed too small for its massive oak table and two dozen straight-back chairs. A team of top-ranking military men and politicians stood around the table with their iPads and briefcases.

Wolfe made no effort to introduce Declan to the others, although Declan recognized four senators on the Homeland Security Committee he worked with in the past, two generals from the Joint Chiefs of Staff, the foreign relations secretary, Bernie Hurlburt, and the superstar national security advisor, Herman Chan.

Declan sensed a testosterone-rich aura saturating the room. These men were the puppeteers who manipulated the strings to make the world dance. He smiled. These were his kind of people.

The double doors reopened, and President Harrington marched in and cut a beeline for the head of the table. Her back was ramrod straight, and she walked with purpose; her blonde hair pulled away from her face in a simple ponytail; her impeccably tailored blue pantsuit broadcasted her brusque professionalism, and the magenta blouse and pink rose pinned to her lapel affirmed her feminine qualities; yet she was not as attractive as she always seemed on television. Without makeup her puffy face and bags beneath her eyes made her look like she was recovering from a three-day binge.

She said, "Gentlemen, my apologies for keeping everyone waiting for so many days. I assure you it was not by choice. This YouTube video has caused a shitstorm across the globe. The Joint Chiefs and I have tried to contain the panic, both here and abroad. So far, we've been unsuccessful." She shot an accusatory glance at Declan. "Mr. Hughes's scientists claim to possess the greatest godsend in human history, but the price they demand for this boon is astronomical. Let me remind everyone that the lion's share of our economy is based on military spending and selling arms to the world. Without it, we would suffer the deepest and longest depression in our history. That, gentlemen, is intolerable. We need a strategy to retrieve this formula without affecting America's ability to defend herself, both militarily and economically."

She sat, and the men followed her lead. Declan and Jeffery sat on her left, across the table from Gerry Chalmers, the head of the World Health Organization.

"Mr. Gonzales," the president said, "please enlighten us with your findings."

The director of Homeland Security stood before a stack of blue folders. He rose and passed one to each attendee. "This is everything we have so far."

She raised an eyebrow at the thinness of the folder and murmured, "Everything?"

Gonzales held up three fingers. "We're attacking this problem on three fronts. First, we've thrown a military cordon around every airport, harbor, and border crossing to contain the fugitives and keep known assassins out. Obviously we need to keep these scientists within our reach. If they slip beyond our borders, it will be impossible to protect them. We've deployed the bulk of our resources on containment. That leaves us shorthanded to deal with our second objective: controlling the rising internal strife. We are now shipping all of our overseas troops home to help with this effort."

The president opened Gonzales's file and skimmed the documents. She gave the impression she already knew everything it offered.

Gonzales adjusted his glasses and leaned forward, as if to give his words more weight. "A number of townships in the Midwest and South have cut themselves off, claiming that they will never surrender their weapons. Armed vigilantes have supplanted local governments. The media is all over it, which has spurred a panic that is spreading exponentially. Vigilantes are using social media to organize resistance to any disarming."

General Henry Pollard waved a hand. "Fragmentation left unchecked leads to revolution. If this situation deteriorates, we'll need to declare martial law in several states. I've put the entire National Guard on alert."

The president glanced at General Pollard, an obese, florid-faced man with cold blue eyes and thinning hair. She nodded her approval. "Let's be candid about this, gentlemen. It's not only a few dozen towns scattered across red states. Unrest now spans coast to coast. The nation is polarized, thanks to the NRA's fanning the flames of fear and distrust and resentment. Everyone on Capitol Hill has the NRA breathing down our necks. We're holding a political bomb set with a hair trigger."

Gonzales nodded. "Our third objective is to find the fugitives and recover the formula. The FBI is using every resource available to accomplish this. The file I've given you, Madam President, includes a profile for both scientists. There isn't much we don't already know from the tabloids about Consuela Rocha y Villareal."

Declan scanned her profile: Fifty-five years old, IQ above 180, a graduate of Northwestern, published several scientific volumes on anatomy, physiology, and genetics. An LA street gang gunned down her parents when she was an undergraduate. Also, her only child, a son, was killed while serving in Iraq, and because of that her husband drank himself to death. She now had no living relatives. Declan mumbled to himself, "No surprise she's on a mission to rid the world of guns."

Gonzales continued, "She recently cashed out a sizable portfolio of stocks and bonds and sold her house in Nevada, giving her over five hundred thousand dollars in cash. With that kind of money, they can stay hidden indefinitely."

"How could a researcher accumulate so much liquidity?" General Pollard asked.

"Obviously," the president said, "we are not dealing with country bumpkins."

Declan flipped the page to a picture of Kenji. It was a recent photo, taken at Golden Eagle Industries for a security clearance, yet the accompanying documentation supported the claim he was born in Hiroshima soon after the US dropped the bomb. *If this information is indeed true*, Declan thought, *he is living proof.*

"You're convinced this is no hoax?" the president asked.

Gonzales said in a tone of dismissal, "We must assume the formula is legit."

A jolt of electricity blistered the air. Something Declan had felt for days, and now the others felt it as well. The excitement became palpable.

Harrington closed the file and stared at the cover with a look of distaste, a folder labeled Homeland Security Council. "This is direfully inadequate. You've had days and days to prepare something meaningful, and you've failed to impress." She picked up the file, tore it in half, and tossed it back to Gonzales.

That was precisely the tone Declan sought. He knew from experience that bureaucrats did nothing unless you waved cash under their noses, publicly humiliated them, or both.

She turned on Declan. "Mr. Hughes, what can you tell us about this formula? And their fellow scientists, surely they didn't discover this on their own. Others must have assisted with their research?"

Declan said, "We have a man in custody who we believe was treated with the formula. We're running tests now to determine what's happening at his sub-cell level. What we've seen so far is remarkable, but true understanding could take months, perhaps years. As for the other scientists, they're as shocked as we are. We have a list of equipment the lab purchased over the last dozen years, which includes everything you'd expect from a first-rate DNA research center."

"Why will it may take years to understand?" she asked.

"We believe it intervenes in the body's enzyme system. We're seeing a radically different ammonia in the bacterial cultures. Amino acids are used for structure and energy—but this energy is being bound up in, profoundly altering, or somehow supercharging the enzyme system. Enzymes can change the body's RNA structure, and the RNA structure determines the DNA structure. The question is which elements of the DNA is augmented to mass produce cells that amplify the body's regenerative systems."

He pictured a double strand RNA/DNA molecule, one chain twined around the other in helical form, one chain fitted to the other, the adenine, guanine, cytosine, and thymine each determining a link on the opposite chain. It looked like an elegant spiral staircase.

"You haven't answered my question. Why so long?"

"We simply don't know enough about the DNA structure to know what's altered or even how it changed."

"Can you reproduce this 'different ammonia' and introduce it into an organism?"

"The problem lies in the fact that our genetic makeup is a seemingly limitless warren of chemical permutations, rather like a house of cards—each component is connected to and supported by countless other elements, most of which we little understand. The smallest mutation in a single gene could cause these links to shift or alter, causing a chain reaction and possibly resulting in catastrophic effects—cancers, organ failures, blood disorders, the whole menu. The human DNA structure took eons to evolve, and we don't want to simply tinker with it without knowing more."

"So, gentlemen," the president said, "it sounds like we're on a tediously long track to solve the lesser problem of reproducing the formula without de-arming. Now, I want everyone to understand the greater problem and why it is critical that we apprehend the fugitives and their work before someone else gets to them first. Dr. Chalmers—"

Dr. Chalmers stood. "The problem we face is called geometric progression, which sounds harmless, but it has a terrifying potential to destroy the human race. Consider this. It took two and a half million years, from the dawn of man until the 1800s, to grow the human population to one billion souls. It took only another hundred years to reach two billion in 1920. Fifty years later, it had doubled to four billion. We are now nearing eight billion mouths to feed, and adding a quarter million per day, two million per week. For those of us lucky enough to live for the next twenty years, under the current scenario, we'll see the population triple to twenty-four billion souls."

Dr. Chalmers let that number sink in a moment before continuing.

"Think of the implications. The demand for dwindling resources—clean air, pure water, nourishing food, fossil fuel—is already skyrocketing. The globe is warming, and oceans are rising. We have far exceeded our sustainable numbers, which experts agree is four billion humans. Even without this formula, population growth is the foremost catastrophe waiting to tear apart the world. Now think of the consequences if all these people, who are reproducing at this geometric rate, all live thousands of years. It will become, literally, a dog-eat-dog world within the next decade or two. Wars fought over water, neighbors killing neighbors for food, gangs taking what they need at gunpoint."

Everyone reproducing like rabbits, Declan thought, *and nobody dying to make room for the next generation.* He remembered a quote from Machiavelli: *When every province of the world so teems with inhabitants that they can neither subsist where they are nor remove themselves elsewhere… the world will purge itself.*

The president motioned for Dr. Chalmers to sit. "What our esteemed director of the WHO is saying, gentlemen, is that we cannot, under any circumstances, allow the blueprint of this formula to become public knowledge. It would exacerbate the overpopulation crisis tenfold. The mathematics are undisputable. This treatment can only be given to civilization's elite: the government and business leaders who shape the world. If it becomes common knowledge, we will likely see the apocalyptic collapse of society."

Declan glanced around the room. That excitement earlier turned to silent terror etched on each face, which, he thought, was the only suitable response. He should have realized it himself, but in his enthusiasm, he considered only the benefits, not the consequences.

But Harrington proposed that genetic enhancements be administered to the 1 percent only, creating a culture of haves and have-nots, a race of superhumans and subhumans. *That's a condition ripe for slavery or ethnic cleansing.*

The president motioned to Declan. "I need some fresh air. Walk with me." She stood and marched to the doorway. Declan followed.

Once outside, they meandered along a path that cut through a wooded area.

"I love to walk here," Harrington said. "I think better with my feet moving."

The rain tapered to a drizzle, not heavy enough for an umbrella. The temperature remained cold enough that their exhaled breaths were visible. Declan counted ten Secret Service agents surrounding them, all just out of earshot.

"Tell me honestly," she said, "what have you discovered with this man in custody?"

"Next to nothing. We're trying to form a precise biochemical description of this ammonia, but it's so unique, so extraordinary, that my people are baffled."

"I can give you any research team in the country to help."

"We have the right people and a comprehensive research facility."

"Good. This work is classified. Nobody sees any findings that haven't been cleared by Homeland Security. But there's more you're not telling me," she said.

"We're confident this is not a viral genome. It can't be transmitted, and it's something that nature could not have produced without human intervention."

"How can DNA be altered? Explain it to me as if I were a child."

Declan felt the cold seeping into his shoes. He pulled his coat more snugly to his body, wishing he'd had the good sense to wear a wool hat and muffler.

"Do you know anything about general recombinant DNA procedure?"

"Those are big words to a child."

Declan's frustration rose. There were plenty of people who could explain this, yet she was wasting his time. "It's a cut-and-paste procedure using enzymes. You cut something we all have within our plasmid DNA, introduce foreign DNA to the strand, and reinsert the plasmid to the host body. A plasmid is like a miniature chromosome, a circlet of double-stranded DNA present in bacteria, in addition to the bacteria's main, single chromosome. The plasmid replicates with the altered DNA, each time the cell divides."

"The children you know must be terrifying."

"Each time the cell divides, more cells carry this altered DNA, which permits that cell to do new things. In this case, things we've never seen before."

Declan felt the president trying her damnedest to be comfortable with him, but he also had the distinct feeling that she was never really comfortable with anyone, not even her own husband and daughter. She seemed to dwell in a dark hole somewhere deep inside herself, and all the world really saw, if anything, was the faint gleam under Maybelline-shadowed eyes peering from that hole.

They turned and walked toward the building they came from. She dropped her head, as if making sure of each step to avoid any mud. "You lost me back at plasmids. Regardless, let me explain why it's so important to know how close we are to replicating this discovery. During the last three days, I've been in constant contact with the heads of state in China and Russia. We all concur that this formula must not go public, and also, we must not allow the Vatican, the Iranians, or the Israelis to capture the formula."

"I understand," Declan said.

"I doubt that. You haven't the vaguest idea of what this government is primed to do to suppress this. I am prepared to protect this formula at any cost. If this manhunt goes on long enough for assassins to reach their target, we are willing to initiate action against Jerusalem, Tel Aviv, the Vatican, and Tehran to keep them from obtaining the formula."

"Initiate action?"

"Anyone intelligent enough to describe the inner workings of plasmids should know exactly what I'm talking about, Mr. Hughes. We assume if we cut off the monsters' heads, the assassins will give up. We are applying, of course, immense political pressure, but these talks are going nowhere, and we're running out of time. This is vital to our national security. We already have congressional approval, and we have a tentative partnership with China and Russia."

Declan assumed she was joking, but the look on her face told otherwise. He could easily imagine those decrepit fuddy-duddies on Capital Hill foaming at the mouth to become young again, no matter who they had to vaporize to get it. The cold in Declan's feet moved up his legs. He wanted to debate, to become a calming voice of reason, but he was afraid anything he might say would sound treasonous.

"We have so little time, Mr. Hughes. Your researchers need to move expeditiously."

Got it.

CHAPTER TEN

J ESSUP DRIFTED in a dreamless sleep until two uniformed officers shook him awake and led him back to the interrogation room. He cringed at seeing the low ceiling and dully painted walls.

Landau and Souad waited for him. Both wore slacks and white shirts with the sleeves rolled up. No ties, no jackets, and they both needed a shave.

Souad's eyes narrowed to slits. "You sorry bastard, you've been holding out on us." He held a look of precise malice that hadn't been there the day before. Today he looked ten years older and twenty years nastier. The breath going through his nose was faintly audible from across the room. It was obvious that Souad wanted, more than anything, to kick his teeth in.

Jessup said, "I'm guessing this is were I say, 'What's all this about?' and you say, 'We ask the questions.'" A beat of stunned silence. "If you're already calling me names, then I want some coffee. Fresh, not that shit you served yesterday. And some doughnuts. I like the ones with white powdered sugar."

Landau paced in front of the two-way mirror. "While investigating Consuela Rocha y Villareal's background, our team discovered she owned a cabin not far from Bishop, California. We sent agents there this morning. They found a dead body. We also found two sets of fingerprints inside her cabin that match prints taken from your ranch house. We believe Kenji and Matt Reece stayed overnight there. We also now believe you knew about the cabin and that they were going there. Don't look so surprised, Mr. Connors. Did you really think you could keep us from finding that out?"

Jessup could only stare. His mind went blank.

Landau pivoted to face Jessup. He removed his spectacles and wiped them with his handkerchief. "You said you've met Consuela Rocha y Villareal on many occasions?"

Jessup nodded.

After a brief meditation, Landau set his glasses back on his nose and nodded. "Whether or not that body in the cabin is Consuela, this is now a murder investigation, and guess who's topping our suspect list?" His voice held composed tones, as if he said things like that every day.

Jessup took this news like a bullet, jaw rigid and chest out, smack through his divided heart. He was sitting, so there was no fear of his legs giving way. He barked the words, "Don't be ridiculous," his voice breaking like an adolescent going through puberty. He knew beyond doubt that Kenji and Matt Reece could not have harmed anyone, let alone a friend and coworker. Still, from now until the end of his days, there would be before this moment and after it, and he would always regret the after because the dividing line was the point at which the last remnants of his hopeful youth drained out of him, leaving only a hard, bitter shell.

Landau said, "I'm going to suggest something that is unheard of in law enforcement. In fact, it's so contrary to standard procedures that it might get me fired. But we don't have even a minute to lose. We need to know for certain if that body is Consuela, and you're the only one we've got who can positively identify her." Souad shook his head, but Landau ignored him. "I want to take you directly to the murder scene."

When Jessup nodded, both agents folded down the sleeves of their shirts. Landau lifted his jacket from the back of his chair and pulled it on. He raised his cell phone from his pocket, punched a number, and said, "Ready the copter. We're on our way."

THE HELICOPTER landed three hundred yards from a cabin. Landau opened the passenger door and stepped out. While holding a handkerchief to his face to prevent breathing the dust being kicked up, he hurried toward the cluster of cars parked by the cabin's front porch. Agent Souad and Jessup followed him.

As they passed the marked and unmarked cars, Landau stuffed his handkerchief into his back pocket. He told Jessup to stay behind him and to not touch anything once they were beyond the yellow tape. Jessup followed him through the cabin's open front door.

Landau removed a notebook and pen from his jacket as he scanned the room. Two agents, one male and one female, were dusting for fingerprints, one at the fireplace and the other in the kitchen. Light from a camera flash spilled from a doorway off the living room every few seconds. Landau said, "No sign of a struggle, nothing out of place."

An agent walked into the living room from one of the bedrooms. A lit cigarette dangled from his mouth. The wrinkles across his forehead were deeply etched from many years of grim work. Like the male fingerprint duster, he wore black slacks, white short-sleeve shirt, and conservative tie. "Everything is the way we found it, Sal."

Landau shook his hand. "Hey, Fred. Do we know the time of death?"

"We're still waiting for the medical examiner, but judging from the amount of rigor mortis, I'd guess roughly six o'clock this morning."

"Fred," Souad said, "didn't they teach you never to smoke at a crime scene?"

Fred pulled the cigarette from his lips, bumped the ashes into the empty Coke can he carried, and said, "They taught me a lot of things about a hundred years ago, sonny. Like never bring a civilian onto a crime scene." He pressed the cigarette to his lips and walked toward the front door.

"The point is—" Souad said, but was cut off by Landau waving his arm.

"Thanks, Fred," Landau said. "Let's compare notes after I've examined the body."

Jessup followed Landau and Souad into a dim bedroom where everything was neatly in place. A body lay on the bed with the covers pulled up to her chin. Her eyes were open, peering at the ceiling with a shocked expression. A wound to the left temple looked like a blunt weapon struck her with moderate force.

A man crouched on the floor, stuffing a camera into a shoulder bag. He wore a surgical mask, even though the room held only a faint odor of decay. He stood and swung the bag strap over his shoulder. "How soon do you need these, Sal?"

"The usual, Eddie."

"You got it, boss." He gave Landau a salute as he left the room.

Landau locked eyes with Souad. He said in a low voice, "Tell me, what was the point you were about to make with Fred?"

"I wonder how many crime scenes he's contaminated with—"

"Drop it," Landau said. "One, he's our elite forensics investigator, and we're lucky to have him. Two, he's on our team, so we show him the utmost respect, rather than berate him in front of the others. We're a team here, and we support each other."

"But...."

Landau ignored him, turning to Jessup. Landau laid a hand on Jessup's shoulder. "Sure you're up for this? You never emerge unscathed from seeing a murdered body."

Jessup swallowed the lump in his throat. "I've seen this sort of thing before." He shot Landau a look that felt as immense and profound as the silence that accompanied it. A moment later, however, he lost confidence and became afraid—not of viewing a body, but because of what must have taken place in this cabin.

"I hate to put you through this," Landau said, "but whoever did this swept the cabin clean of identification. We need to verify that this is Consuela."

It occurred to Jessup that they could take the fingerprints and have a match within hours. Hell, they had likely done that already. And even without prints, she was famous, a household name. Half the country could identify her. So why bring him here? To shake him up?

Landau slipped his notepad and pen into his pocket, pulled latex gloves from his hip pocket, and slipped them on. He kneeled and looked under the mattress, pulled a pen flashlight from his shirt pocket, and shined it into the darkness.

Souad leaned over the bed, studying the body's face. "You called her a victim. What makes you think she was murdered? She might have bumped her head while having a coronary."

Landau rose and lifted the blanket, exposing her neck, which was sliced open.

"Or not," Souad said.

Landau shined his penlight on every area of the head and neck wounds. He drew the blanket all the way back and inspected the body, checking for other injuries. She was clean below the neck. Blood saturated the mattress but nothing else, so there was no mess on the floor or the body. Landau moved back so Jessup had a clear view of the face, neck, and shoulders.

Jessup felt his legs liquefy. Landau and Souad seized his arms, holding him up.

Consuela's face was yellow and waxy, hair plastered to her head, her eyes open. Her lips were nearly colorless, mouth jarred open in lolling disbelief. Her right temple had a sizable gash, and her severed throat yawned bloodlessly.

Landau told him, "My guess is, someone bludgeoned her with a thin, round object—a club or iron pipe. It stunned her, and loss of blood from the slashed throat killed her."

Jessup raised his hand and laid it across his eyes, gripping his skull with force, as if to squeeze out the image now burned on his retinas. "That's her." He took deep breaths to settle the sudden fear in his chest. "She's unmarried, an only child, with no living children or parents. Who will bury her?"

"The agency will keep her on ice until we know who killed her. There's plenty of time to think about funerals."

Souad said, "They left the ranch together. You think Kenji killed her?"

"Guessing at this point is no help. But look at her hands." Landau shined his light on two diamond rings on her fingers. "This is no break-in and robbery." He lowered the blanket and stepped to the nightstand where an overnight case sat with the lid unlocked. He opened the case and shined his light on the contents. Besides makeup there was a compartment holding jewelry—a white gold bracelet, strands of pearls, a diamond watch, and several broaches of silver and gold. "Definitely not a robbery."

A knock at the door turned all their heads. A man stood in the doorway. "I'm Clifford Baldridge, the medical examiner," he said. He flicked the light switch, and two lamps, one on each nightstand, came on. "No need to work in the dark, I always say."

"She's all yours, Doc," Landau said. "We'll step outside and get out of your way."

Baldridge dropped his medical bag on the only chair. Landau and Souad half carried Jessup back outside and leaned him against the cabin wall. Fred joined them on the porch.

Fred held a fresh cigarette in his lips. The smell made Jessup's mouth water. He was tempted to bum one but knew that was a bad idea.

"Paint me a picture, Fred?" Landau said.

"Photo ID in her purse confirms the victim is Consuela Rocha y Villareal. No forced entry, so I assume she knew the perpetrators. We found over three hundred dollars and some expensive jewelry in her overnight case, so this was no robbery. Judging by the leftover food in the fridge, food scraps in the garbage can under the sink, and dishes in the drying rack, three people ate cabbage soup for dinner here last night, but nobody had breakfast. Also, we found only one set of car tracks in the mud."

Landau nodded. "Anything yet on the other two?"

"This is your lucky day, Sal. I lifted three different sets of hairs from the other bedroom—two human, one dog. Judging by the length, they were both males, and you already know the prints match your suspects. No murder weapon yet, but the crown jewels of this murder scene are in that shed. The tracks in the mud and riding gear convinced me that three horses spent the night in there. Two saddle horses and one packhorse. We found all three not far from here."

Jessup followed the agents to the shed, and Fred swung open the door. Jessup saw at once they were his horses. He stepped aside, making room for Souad to stand beside Landau.

"That's fine horse flesh," Landau said. "Souad, find out which ranch uses that brand."

Fred held up his iPhone. "I googled it. They're from the Promesa Rota."

"Fred, I could kiss you." Landau turned to Souad. "Didn't I tell you he was good?"

Souad nodded. "Nice work, Fred. I apologize for earlier."

"No hard feelings, kid."

Landau laid a friendly arm across Souad's shoulder and said, "Impress me with your assessment so far?"

"They rode cross-country from the Promesa Rota, spent last night yucking it up with her—" He pointed over his shoulder, using his thumb. "—murdered her at first light, and drove off in her car. We assume it was her car because there is only one set of tracks."

"Bingo," Landau said. "That explains everything except the key question."

"Motive?"

"Double bingo. They were partners, doing this together. It doesn't add up."

"Maybe she got cold feet?" Fred said.

"Or maybe," Landau said, "there's a lot more to this case than we realize. We have an all-points bulletin watch for her Prius in all Western states. Now that they're moving on the highways, let's hope lady luck smiles our way."

Landau said to Souad, "Fred said they didn't have breakfast. That means they probably ate in Bishop or along the highway. Take copies of the pictures we took from the Connors ranch and canvass all the waitresses in the cafés north and south. Maybe someone will remember. That will tell us which direction they drove."

"I'm on it," Souad said with so much enthusiasm that Landau patted his shoulder.

"Also, copy all our files and send them to the Behavioral Science Unit in Quantico, for evaluation. Have them work up a psychological profile of Kenji. It might help us establish a motive."

Landau and Souad turned on Jessup.

"You lied to us," Souad hissed.

A different Landau now, hackles up, nerves extended, cleared his throat. "You knew they left on horseback. That's why you were stalling, to buy them five days to get away. When people lie to me, I come down on them with both my size-twelve's kicking."

Jessup swallowed. "You asked if I saw them drive away. I didn't."

Souad muttered a curse.

"I'd like you to take a polygraph test," Landau said.

"I've told the truth," Jessup said, panicking. "I didn't know where they were going."

"It's also true you haven't told us everything you know. Polygraph tests are not admissible in criminal cases, except in rare cases where the prosecution and defense stipulate an agreement in advance of taking the test. If you have nothing to hide, there is no reason not to cooperate. You'll see the questions before the test begins."

"And if I refuse?"

Souad said, "Then I get the pleasure of charging you with accessory to murder."

Landau leaned forward. "It will clear you of any suspicion and let us narrow our focus. This benefits both of us. Will you do it?"

"Yes, but I'm such an emotional wreck, I'll doubtlessly fail."

HOURS LATER a helicopter landed on the outskirts of Hawthorn. Jessup sat with Landau and Souad in the rear seat. On the flight, Souad explained about the death fatwas being waged against Consuela and Kenji by world powers, fatwas that could include Jessup, Blake, and

Jessup's eldest son, Patrick. "Your family needs government protection until we apprehend Kenji."

Jessup remembered every word of the letter Kenji left, searching for clues that might help him find Kenji. He had to put a stop to this madness.

They transferred to a sedan and sped two miles to the police station.

Inside, they led Jessup into another room, where he met George Graves, who worked for the Bureau of Investigation in Sacramento. He told Jessup he had nine years of testing experience and a three-year stint supervising other examiners. Before that he was a criminal investigator in the US Army.

Landau had Jessup sign a statement that he was taking the test "not under duress."

"What a joke, Agent Landau," he said.

While Graves attached two electrodes to his left-hand fingers, a blood pressure cuff on his right arm, and rubber straps around his chest to monitor breathing patterns, Landau read Jessup his rights again and informed him that although the lie detector test was inadmissible as evidence in court, if he confessed to any element of a crime during the polygraph or subsequent interrogation, his statements could be used against him independent of the test.

George Graves asked him about his knowledge of Consuela's cabin. Jessup said he had never seen the cabin and didn't know she owned one. Graves then asked personal questions concerning Jessup's boys, birthplace, education, job, and the like.

"When we start, I want you to answer each question with only a yes or no. I'll administer five different tests, each one about five minutes long. You can move about between tests, but please remain still during each test."

Jessup was shown a list of questions. He confirmed that he understood each one.

Graves reminded him to stay still and began. "Did you know that Kenji Hiroshige was traveling to meet Consuela Rocha y Villareal?"

"No," said Jessup. Tears pooled in his eyes thinking of her.

"Did you know that Kenji Hiroshige planned to murder Consuela Rocha y Villareal?"

"No."

"Did you conspire with anyone to cause Consuela Rocha y Villareal's death?"

"No."

Jessup began to cry. Mucus from his nose dripped into his mouth and down his chin. He couldn't wipe his face because the test didn't allow him to move. He became embarrassed because Landau and Souad were watching him suffer.

"Do you know who caused Miss Villareal's death?"

"No."

"Did you ever seriously want to kill or severely injure another person?"

"No."

Next, Graves administered a series of control questions, including questions on which Jessup was told to lie. He then repeated the first set of questions in a different order. After five exams, Graves unhooked the electrodes, arm cuff, and chest bands.

Landau said, "Congratulations. You're cleared."

Souad handed him a handkerchief.

Jessup wiped his face and handed the cloth back. "Thanks. Can I go home now?"

"Time of death was about five hours before our agents found her," Landau said.

"Had you told us they were on horseback," Souad said, "we could have found them before this happened. You share some responsibility for her death, Mr. Connors."

Landau nodded. "If we prove that Kenji murdered her, which all the evidence points to, then you could be named as an accessory for not being upfront in the questioning."

Jessup shook his head. "I admit I was protecting them, but they didn't do this. Even if Kenji is capable of murder, which is unthinkable, Matt Reece would never…." He couldn't finish the thought. It was too absurd. But he felt guilty, regardless, knowing he might have saved Consuela's life had he spoken out.

"There's something else," Jessup said, and both agents leaned forward.

"Kenji left a letter, which I burned."

Landau slipped his notebook and pen from his jacket pocket. "Go on."

Jessup recited the letter as close to word for word as memory allowed, leaving out only the part about the flash drive, which was still in his jeans pocket.

Landau scribbled notes and leaned back in his chair. "Well, that explains why he took the boy. It makes perfect sense. But what could he mean that the meek are about to inherit the earth? And also this business about taking Matt Reece to the one place that is safe because lightning never strikes the same spot twice?"

"Are you going to arrest me?"

Landau frowned. "To arrest you we would have to prove intent. In this case, that means knowledge a crime had been committed and Kenji was a fugitive, which any lawyer can prove you didn't have. I'm convinced you didn't know anything. What you are is a material witness, but we can't hold you for that without a court order. The chances of attaining that are as slim as finding a five-hundred-pound marathon runner. And if it makes Consuela's death any easier to swallow, I'd have done the same thing in your shoes. You had no reason to believe anybody was in danger."

That's the trouble with cops. Just when you've made up your mind they're all condescending assholes, you meet one that goes all human on you.

"Thanks. So I'm free to go?"

Landau raised an eyebrow. "There's death warrants on Kenji's head. Assassins will assume they can use you as leverage to get to him. Nobody in your family is safe."

"You mean I can't go home?"

"If you want to stay alive, I wouldn't recommend it."

"What do you suggest I do?"

"Help us find the spot where lightning has already struck and won't strike again."

CHAPTER ELEVEN

Matt Reece stared into a mirror in a tiny bathroom where an ancient toilet, a claw-foot tub, and a pedestal sink seemed to fight each other for space. Mold flourished in the tile grout. Rust stains decorated the tub. His reflection in the mirror showed the same familiar nose, large eyes, and wisps of brown hair framing his forehead, but his skin held the color of polished malachite. He wore only his briefs, and he saw his entire body swathed in the same green hue.

He first noticed a slight olive tint on his arms while they were riding cross-country, but he assumed it was from the scant diet. But each day he felt worse, his fever climbed, and his skin turned a deeper green. On top of that his throat hurt, like the time he suffered from tonsillitis. Kenji examined him and declared that his tonsils were growing back.

Kenji rented this four-room shithole above a head shop on Haight Street in San Francisco. Matt Reece was excited last night driving into the city, seeing all the people and lights and storefronts and restaurants. It lifted his spirits even though his body ached. They ate at a Chinese joint that had roasted ducks hanging in the window. It was the first time he had tasted Asian food or eaten with chopsticks. He gorged himself on shrimp chow fun and pork dumplings. He loved the food, but people stared at him as if he were some alien newly arrived from Mars.

Overnight his skin turned much greener. As bad as he felt physically, his spirits were free-falling. He couldn't go out in public without calling attention to himself. It slowly sunk in; this apartment had become a prison. It took an effort to hold back the tears. He turned away from the mirror because he felt the urge to put his fist through it. He knew he was running a temperature because his body was drenched in perspiration. His stomach began what felt like a slow roll, and he sensed his gorge rising. He slipped to his knees beside the toilet and vomited with great force into the bowl, as if turning himself inside out. He heaved and heaved.

A minute passed, and another. He climbed to his feet, washed out his mouth, and flushed the toilet. *Why did I choose Kenji over Consuela, when she was clearly the voice of reason? If I call her, will she come pick me up?* But he didn't have her cell number and had little idea about how to obtain it.

He grabbed the doorknob and twisted it, but it snapped and came away from the door. He held it at eye level as his anger detonated. He leaned sideways and hit the door with his shoulder, busting it open in a vicious assault.

He lurched into the living room, a place of mismatched garage-sale furniture trying to find its place. The walls were covered with drab brown-and-gray floral wallpaper, broken by two tall windows that overlooked the street. An ancient vacuum stood in one corner. He didn't know if it was some kind of retro decoration or something the cleaning lady left. Noting the general grime inundating the room, he decided this place hadn't seen a cleaning lady since before that vacuum came off the assembly line.

He paused before the doorway of the only bedroom. Kenji lay sleeping on a waterbed that had made Matt Reece feel even more nauseous. He crossed the living room and sat in an armchair beside a window. Groucho lifted himself off the shag carpet in the bedroom and walked over and sat at his feet. The look on the dog's face told him Groucho felt as bad as he did, but at least his coat was the same blue roan coloration that it had always been. He hugged the dog a long time.

Out the window, Haight Street was awake and vibrant. It was lined with shops and restaurants. Kenji told him about this area on the drive up the Central Valley. Home to Graham Nash, the Grateful Dead, and was the epicenter for the Summer of Love, the street went through decades of yuppification; it now seemed a mecca for the homeless, drug dealers, and tourists—the kind of tourists who were desperate to reach back in time to recapture a youthful atmosphere that couldn't be recaptured.

He opened the window and leaned his head against the cool wood of the frame. He became a video camera, recording every movement, every face, every detail. Cars and trucks and buses were loud and jangling, forming a wall of sound. The shops were embossed with Victorian scrollwork and detailing, all crammed right up against each other, consuming every available space. For a young man used to high-desert vistas and open space stretching to eternity, this city seemed more alien than Pluto.

He closed his eyelids, but that did nothing to stop his general awareness of the swift movement along the street and sidewalks. His need to merge with that humanity below became overwhelming. He pulled his head back inside and focused on the black bag on the kitchen table. He crossed the room, unzipped the bag, and spread open the flaps. Kenji's two passports—one American and one Japanese—sat atop that impressive stack of cash. Beside them lay a wallet. He lifted the US passport and opened the cover to reveal the picture page. It showed Kenji's face, but all the information was fabricated—name: Yukio Toranaga; date of birth: September, 1975; occupation: Bartender. *Bartender? That's rich. But why a Japanese passport as well?*

He thumbed through the wallet. All the information in it—driver's license, credit cards, business cards, Social Security card—agreed with the passport information. Kenji even had checks from a San Francisco bank under this new name. Yukio Toranaga would stand up to any casual scrutiny, and no doubt had Custom's database entries confirming the information. Kenji had everything he needed to board a jet at any airport, and by this time tomorrow, be lost forever. Kenji had planned his escape perfectly until a little green spanner got thrown into the works.

They rented this apartment, Kenji explained, because they needed time to get traveling papers for Matt Reece. "Four days," Kenji said. "A week at the most. I know where to get it. It won't be cheap, but we're covered."

What good were papers if his skin glowed green? He couldn't even walk outside, let alone board a plane. *He'll leave me here and run for it.*

He became keenly aware of his aloneness. He drew in, hunched his shoulders, raised his arms with fists clinched, and shut his eyes tight.

Matt Reece dropped the passport, remembering the conversation over dinner where Kenji told him about the fire at the lab—multiple thermite charges, exploding drums of ether-ammonium hydroxide. Nothing would survive that consuming heat. The authorities would assume arson, of course, but investigators would focus on raking through the ashes, giving them time to slip away.

That Kenji destroyed his lab was frightening, but that seemed a trifling price to pay for abolishing the world's weapons and restoring peace to the planet. Yet anyone who dared to incinerate an eighty-million-dollar lab would think nothing of leaving Matt Reece high and dry, or perhaps even dead? This man who he had known and loved for most of his life was now seemingly capable of anything.

He felt something delightfully cool touch his forehead. He opened his eyes to see Kenji standing beside him. Kenji wore only Jockey shorts, which did little to hide his morning erection. Matt Reece tried to step back, but arms held him by his waist.

Matt Reece lost himself in the feel of firm, bare skin. It awakened his senses, aroused every nerve ending. His body seemed to merge with Kenji's, and for a moment, he didn't feel so alone.

"Your fever's higher." Kenji's voice was a sensual whisper.

"I'm afraid."

"It'll pass. We can't risk seeing a doctor, so you'll have to tough it out." Kenji released his grip, and his hand rose to pat his shoulder. "We ate rich food last night. I should have known better. What you need is something bland and easy to digest."

Food was the last thing Matt Reece wanted. He told himself to cover his own erection by turning away from Kenji, but his body longed for another hug.

Kenji guided him to the chair by the window. He closed his eyelids, listening to the street noise and feeling the morning breeze on his face. He did not sense Kenji's departure, but after a long spell he was there beside him again, fully dressed, with a Styrofoam cup of rice porridge, something he called *jook*. It smelled like chicken and rice soup but was thick and meaty.

"You need baby food, but the grocery stores aren't open yet."

Matt Reece shot him a look. The baby food comment was startling on its own, but what caught him off guard was Kenji dressed as a priest— black suit and shirt, white collar, wraparound sunglasses that hid his eyes. Kenji got more than jook. He'd found a clothing store and bought himself a disguise.

"Baby food is nutritious and the easiest food to digest. I'll bring some for lunch. And applesauce, which is high in sugar to keep your energy up."

Matt Reece took the jook and a plastic spoon. It burned his tongue but soothed his stomach. He ate it all before sinking back into the chair.

"Sir, you turning religious on me?"

"No one will suspect a man of the cloth."

Kenji walked to the bedroom, brought back a pillow, and placed it behind Matt Reece's head. He snuggled into it, and the pillowcase felt cool against his cheek.

Kenji knelt before him and rested both hands on his thighs, squeezing tenderly. "I need to go out to get the ball rolling on your passport. You can't leave this room."

Matt Reece nodded.

"I'll bring back food and antibiotics to reduce your fever. I'll pick up some clothes and shoes too. Western duds and cowboy boots are too conspicuous. And I'll need a picture for the passport."

He pulled his iPhone from his pocket. "Stand here and try to look cheerful."

Matt Reece stood where Kenji pointed. Kenji snapped five pictures.

"But what about my green skin?" Matt Reece asked.

"They can photoshop that."

Matt Reece dropped back in his chair. "What's happening to me?"

"Your body is going through changes, things I've seen before. I'm sure you'll be fine once your body acclimates. You should be back to normal by the time we leave."

And if I'm not?

Kenji knelt before him again. "What name do you want?"

"What?"

"You need a new identity. We should make it Canadian, rather than American, unless you can fake a British accent. Foreign passports cost more, but they're safer."

Being asked to give up your name is no small thing. Neither is the notion of forsaking your nationality. He had already abandoned his home and family, his horse, and now he needed to lose his clothes. To give up more meant losing all his personal history. What was left? Combined with Kenji's suggestion of baby food, he felt newly born, a mound of clay waiting for the sculptor's hand. He tried to think of a suitable name, one that might bolster his courage. He thought of Cain, whom God marked with a different color skin and chased from the Garden of Eden. As appropriate as that seemed, it didn't sound suitable for a first name. He glanced around the room, groping for inspiration. His eyes passed over the vacuum cleaner standing in the corner and moved back to it. He focused on the name in red letters.

"Kirby," he said. "Kirby Cain, from Saskatchewan, Canada."

Kenji turned to follow Matt Reece's gaze. "It's lucky that vacuum isn't a Hoover." He smiled. "Okay, if you can say that fast ten times, then we'll go with it."

Matt Reece stared at him, not caring if they used that name or another.

"I'm kidding," Kenji said. "Kirby it is. And from now on, I'm Yukio Toranaga." He stepped to the traveling bag, lifted his wallet and American passport, and tucked them into his pocket. He also pocketed a packet of hundreds. A moment later he was gone, leaving only a whisper of the door closing.

Matt Reece leaned out the window. He watched Kenji cross the street and hold out his hand for a taxi. He wondered why Kenji didn't use Consuela's car. It was parked on a side street four blocks away. But he recalled Kenji saying they needed to abandon it. Being on the run was a constant burning of bridges, leaving no link from past to present.

A cab pulled to the curb, and Kenji sped off into the morning traffic.

Matt Reece pulled back into the room. On the table between him and the television sat a stack of magazines—*Vanity Fair, Architectural Digest, Travel + Leisure.* He snatched up the *T+L* and flipped through the pages. He stopped at a picture of a tropical beach with a Speedo-clad man walking out of the water, still glistening with drops of the sea. He admired both the man and the beach. He tore the picture from the magazine, folded it twice, and carried it to his pile of clothes in the bedroom. He slipped the picture into his jeans rear pocket and fished his grandfather's watch from the front pocket. The hands had not moved.

It crossed his mind he might feel better if he dressed. He slipped into his T-shirt, socks, and jeans and stepped into his boots. He did feel better, so much so that he lifted his Stetson off the back of the chair and placed it on his head. Standing in his hat and boots, he almost felt himself again.

He shuffled back to the living room and switched on the TV. The screen showed a demonstration in Washington, DC, people holding signs saying Death Before Disarmament and Kill the Infidels under pictures of Kenji and Consuela. People shouted threats. The CNN coverage switched to a mob at Vatican City setting fire to a large devil—with horns, a tail, and a picture of Kenji's face plastered over the head.

Matt Reece couldn't sit down. It seemed impossible to relax in the midst of all that hostility. The faces were livid and hate-filled. He wondered if this was how people looked at men being taken to the gallows or electric chair. A minute later he realized he was not half-wrong. Anderson Cooper described the fatwa placed on Kenji and Consuela by the Iranians, and their suspected alliance with the Vatican.

Cooper turned to interview a stock-market analyst about the nine-hundred-point drop that morning at the New York Stock Exchange. An upbeat expert urged investors to buy into this temporary dip in the market. Cooper cut him off in midsentence. "And just in," Cooper said, putting his hand to his earpiece, and spoke with a note of drama. "CNN now has substantiated evidence that the prime minister of Israel has placed a thirty-million-dollar bounty on the heads of Kenji Hiroshige and Consuela Rocha y Villareal."

It was the holy mission of the faithful—Muslims, Christians, Jews—to destroy them.

The search would, no doubt, be massive and move quickly. The life he had led to this point was of no use. Knowledge of raising animals and riding the range wouldn't help. To survive, he needed new knowledge and fresh skills. He and Kenji were caught in the eye of a hate storm, the focal point of the world's collective rage. Kenji had transformed into a priest to protect himself. Who could he become?

The screen showed mob violence breaking out in several cities—Islamabad, Paris, New York, Oslo, Beijing, Moscow, Delhi, Tehran, and Sydney, Australia. The toll of injuries and deaths was shocking. In Houston, police had fired on a crowd, leaving fifty-three dead and more than two hundred injured.

Britain and Israel had severed diplomatic relations with the United States. "Curiously," Cooper said, "the White House confirmed rumors that it was not President Harrington who broke off these associations."

Being raised on a ranch, he never knew until now that the world could rest so squarely on the acts of a single individual. The sheer weight of public opinion began to crush him.

He heard children yelling on the street below, and it somehow merged with the mob on the tube. It seemed like the throngs were downstairs ready to set fire to the building.

He punched the remote, and the TV switched to CNBC. It showed a mountain cabin that he recognized, Consuela's cabin, only it had yellow barricade tape over the front door. A reporter was saying the body had been found only hours after the grisly murder.

"Consuela," he whispered. His memory replayed their departure yesterday morning, how odd it seemed to leave without saying goodbye, taking her car, and leaving her stranded.

Consuela was dead. It was a fact, a simple truth connecting other truths. All he had to do was follow the facts backward and see where they led. He consulted his inner reserves and realized he had taken part in murder. He was a teenager, who believed all life was sacred, now as guilty as biblical Cain, and how ironic his choice of new names.

He avoided consciously blaming Kenji, but in the same heartbeat he knew he had to get the hell out of there before Kenji returned. He needed a plan, to change whatever lay in front of him. He tried to take a calming breath but came up short.

He leaned forward, planted his hands on his knees, and sucked air into unyielding lungs. He felt a familiar pressure in the back of his esophagus, and he coughed, long rasping coughs that clogged his windpipe with mucus.

"Oh"—he drew a shallow breath—"fuck." He dropped the remote as a nervy rush pushed him into a survival response. He had to find a place with enough air, and quickly.

He ripped open the front door and ran for the stairs, already dizzy from lack of oxygen. He flew down to the first floor, unaware Groucho was following him.

He dashed into sunshine. Several people on the street backed away. Groucho whimpered at his side. Heads turned in unison to stare at him. It was alarming to be so intensely visible at the moment he felt most vulnerable.

A homeless person crouched on the pavement a few feet away, scratching distractedly at whatever was crawling in his beard. He shouted, "Praise the Lord. The little green men have landed. Take me to your leader!"

CHAPTER TWELVE

THROUGH HIS panic he saw a door, the closest one, and he dashed for it, ripped it open, and lunged through. A bell over the door chimed as he pitched forward and fell to his knees on a black-and-white checkered tile floor. He struggled to suck air into his lungs. His head spun. He knew he was moments away from blacking out.

Arms hugged him from behind. A voice said, "Relax, cowboy. Breathe with me, nice and easy." Someone removed his Stetson and set it on the floor beside him.

He could do nothing beyond trying to draw air. Someone laid him out flat on his back, and lifted his head. He opened his eyes, and a flash of overhead lighting distorted everything into a Magoo-like blur. As his vision cleared, he saw a dark-hooded figure hovering over him, and he could feel an icy touch on the back of his neck. Within the recesses of that shadowy hood hovered a red, mutilated face surrounding gentle smoke-colored eyes under silky lashes.

Is this the Grim Reaper?

Fear caused a sick shrinking in his heart from the knowledge that he was dying.

That face lowered until those marred lips touched his and air pushed past the blockage in his throat. Oxygen inflated his lungs. As if standing at the edge of a cliff preparing to plunge, his mind delayed, struggling with the shock of coming back alive.

That face breathed more life into him a second and third time. He coughed, spitting phlegm, and inhaled on his own. He stared into that face, noting the black hair across the forehead, the coppery skin on one side, the rough, ugly, plum-colored scars on the other, and the wispy facial hair that was still a week's growth away from being considered a beard. Matt Reece was caught in that chemic gaze as the Grim Reaper cradled his head like a newborn, smiling down with such tenderness that it loosened the muscles clinching his chest. Time stopped. Nothing else existed.

"You're the cowboy everybody's looking for." His voice was soft with an Indian lilt to its American accent, slightly melodious, sounding like a flute that could form words.

"How… did you…?"

"It's all over Twitter, cowboy, how your grandpa turned green as an avocado, and how you and your stepdad are the new Osama bin Ladens. You're like, infamous."

"I'm someone else. I'm Kirby. Kirby Cain."

A dimple appeared on the coppery side of the Grim Reaper's face. "Who'd have guessed such an unobtrusive-looking boy could be public enemy number one?"

"Who are you?"

"Vishal Mandial."

"From India? Man, that's cool."

"My parents immigrated from India. But I was born here. And people don't say 'cool' even on Haight Street. You say 'beautiful,' or if it's something really spectacular you say 'sick.' Coming from Mumbai only merits a shrug of the shoulders."

Matt Reece glanced around the shop, a patchouli-oil-scented space heavy with sitar music. He saw racks of clothing, shelves holding pipes and other drug paraphernalia, posters of Jimi Hendrix and Janis Joplin, and statues of Ganesh, the elephant with many arms. Groucho lay by the door, inching toward him. He brought his gaze back to Vishal, who seemed Patrick's age, and wore a coal-gray hoody sweatshirt with the words "Sinner's Gin" stenciled across the front.

"Your face?" Matt Reece said, reaching up and touching the mesh of scars.

"My father fell asleep on the couch with a lit cigarette. I tried to put him out."

Now that he was breathing normally, he detected Vishal's scent— clean and carnal, with the hint of some exotic spice Matt Reece imagined as curry. Matt Reece wanted to ask if he had saved his father but thought that seemed too personal a question.

"You kissed me."

"Yeah, well, that's how I roll. Give me a pretty-faced cowboy and I lose control and snog the hell out of him." He laughed, again sounding like a living flute. "Is that your dog?"

Matt Reece nodded. "His name is Groucho."

Vishal helped Matt Reece to his feet and placed the Stetson on his head. His legs felt rubbery, but Vishal wrapped an arm around his waist to help him stand. Now Matt Reece saw much more than his face—the compact V of his torso, the hip clothes, the casual grace with which he moved. His hands, like his face, were red scars, as if coming forth from a furnace. The young prince deformed, seemingly incapable of cruelty or love.

"There's a kitchen in the back. I can make you some tea?" Vishal made a graceful curve of his arm toward a doorway leading to a back room. He turned to a man who seemed more like an ethereal presence sitting behind the counter by a cash register. "Mamaji, watch the front for a few?"

The man wore acid-washed jeans, a tie-dyed T-shirt, and several strings of beads around his neck. No doubt he was also wearing Birkenstocks to complete the '60s hippie look. He smiled under a bushy mustache. "What's with the green skin? Hey, kid, you sick or something?"

A brooding silence settled between the two men while Vishal awaited permission.

The old man nodded. "Take your time. Nobody's beating down the door."

These two men seemed alike. Each had a large nose and high, soft-rounded cheekbones; both faces seemed made of some material more durable than flesh, a flinty substance that didn't easily change. Vishal's facial hair was silky and so thin that it was scarcely visible. The old man's mustache was thick and silver, like the streaks in his hair. He touched it at the corner of his mouth, turning the end into a point.

As they walked to the back, Vishal said, "That hippie drag goes with the job, kinda like being a circus clown. The tourists eat it up."

"You called him Mama?"

"*Mamaji*. It's the Tamil word for uncle, and *ji* is a suffix that indicates respect. He's my father's older brother and now my only relative here in the States."

In the back room they passed what looked like a dentist chair, but it was surrounded by the paraphernalia of a tattoo artist.

Matt Reece sat at a table, and Groucho placed his head on his lap. He scratched behind the dog's ears while Vishal walked behind a counter separating a tiny kitchen from the rest of the room. Vishal poured water into a Mr. Coffee machine and tossed a Lipton tea bag into the glass pot. He stood loosely, nicely balanced. There was a sweet sheen in his eyes. After he turned on the Brew switch, he said, "I'll bet Groucho's hungry." From a small refrigerator under the counter, he removed two hot-dog links and tossed one to the dog, who snatched it out of the air and wolfed it down. Vishal tossed him the other as he came back to sit across the table from Matt Reece.

Matt Reece pointed to the dentist's chair. "You the artist?"

"Pays the bills."

He pointed to several photographs on the wall. "Those your designs?" When Vishal nodded, he said, "Man, you're better than Picasso and van Gogh rolled together."

Vishal shrugged. "So, Kirby, how can I help you?"

"You shouldn't get mixed up with a hunted man."

Vishal sighed. "I know what it means to be an outcast. And I saw the video. You're trying to rid the world of guns and bombs and shit. I'm all for that."

The room now smelled of brewed tea. Matt Reece still felt nauseous and was more than a little scared, but he craved something to drink. He read about these situations in dozens of mystery novels, but they never rang true. Now that it was happening to him, now that he was cornered in a grimy hotel in a strange city, with the world hunting him and no way out, there was nothing elevating or dramatic about it. It felt nasty and sordid and gray and dirty. Tea could only help.

"I have a brother, Patrick Connors, attending UC Berkeley. I need to find him."

Vishal opened a cupboard, removed two mugs, set them beside the coffee maker, and snatched a carton of soy milk from the refrigerator.

A clock above a sink made a distinctive tick. Matt Reece noticed each movement, each sound. The atmosphere made every little thing stand out as a performance, each movement distinct and vastly important. He had morphed into a hypersensitive time dimension where every element, no matter how mundane, became separate acts of will. It felt like learning to live again after being struck by lightning.

Vishal poured two cups of tea and added soy milk.

"No milk for me."

"Trust me, a shot of almond soy makes all the difference."

Yes, I do trust you.

Vishal carried the mugs to the table. Matt Reece sipped the brew, softened by sweet almonds, while Vishal drew a cell phone from his hip pocket. "What's his number?"

"All I know is he lives in the Alpha Chi Omega fraternity house at UC Berkeley."

Vishal used his phone to check the web for the number and placed a call. When someone answered, Vishal asked for Patrick Connors. He listened and switched off his phone. "Patrick moved out last semester but still hangs out on campus. If we find him, we're to remind him that he still owes some dude named Joseph eighty bucks."

Matt Reece sat his mug on the table. "He's my only hope."

Vishal looked blank-eyed at the wall. He had pulled back his hood while making the call, so now his face was in full view. The left side of his head was livid with scars that seemed to shine like the tracks on Mars.

A male voice in the other room followed the tinkle of a bell. Vishal rushed to the doorway and peeked around the doorframe. He pointed to the kitchen. "Hide," he hissed.

Matt Reece grabbed Groucho by the scruff of the neck and rushed behind the counter, ducking down, trying to be as small as possible. As he crouched, listening, he realized the man who entered the shop was a policeman. People on the street had called 911 about seeing a green-skinned kid. Vishal was doing his best to convince the man those callers must have mistaken his scarred face for the wanted man. A sense of deep shame flooded Matt Reece. To hide like a criminal was humiliating enough, but for his new friend to shift the blame to his disfigurement made it worse. Perhaps he should simply give himself up?

He started to rise when something on a shelf in front of him caught his attention. A stack of photographs stood in a neat pile, and the one on top was of a fetching Indian man with a delicious smile. He picked it up and studied the man's features. A heartbeat later, he recognized Vishal, a photo taken before being burned. Same smoky eyes, same dimple, Matt Reece was certain.

He drew the picture of the Speedo-clad hunk from his back pocket, the one torn from the magazine earlier. He compared the two photos, side by side. There was a trash can under the sink, and he slipped Speedo-guy into the trash and the picture of Vishal into his hip pocket. He managed a smile, realizing that his new dream guy was more than some makeup-wearing gym-queen posing for a magazine layout.

He heard the bell again, and Vishal said, "The coast is clear. To find your brother, we need to go to Berkeley and scour the campus, but you can't go out in public with green skin."

Matt Reece rose and faced his new friend. "What choice do I have?"

Vishal rummaged through drawers by the tattooing chair. "The gods are smiling on you, Kirby Cain." Vishal held up two packages of henna dye, one brown and one black. "Don't worry, it'll fade in a week or two. You wanna be a cholo boy or a brother?"

CHAPTER THIRTEEN

DECLAN HAD made it halfway to LA, flying on a commercial airliner, when a pilot broadcasted a message over the intercom: "Ladies and gentlemen, I'm sorry to announce that we have received FAA orders to turn back and land at Reagan National Airport in Washington, DC. Let me assure you there is nothing wrong with the aircraft, and there is no threat to the passengers or crew. We estimate cruising time back to Reagan National to be one hour, fifty-three minutes."

A chorus of groans rose from the economy section.

Once the plane landed, it taxied to an isolated part of the tarmac where a ground crew and a line of black SUVs waited. A portable staircase wheeled into place, and a steward opened the door in the first-class cabin. Two men in gray suits entered the plane and made a beeline for Declan. They flashed badges. "Sir, please collect your carry-on luggage and follow us. The president is waiting to see you."

On the tarmac, Declan crawled into the third SUV in a line of seven. On the ride into the city, he sat beside Captain Herbert Franks, an officer assigned to Naval Intelligence.

Declan counted twelve police motorbikes, all with sirens and lights blazing. "Captain," he said, "why all the fuss? Why not just escort me in a nondescript Escalade?"

Captain Franks glared at him with the pitying look people reserve for the chronically stupid or certifiably insane. "Sir, we've confirmed you've been placed on the Vatican's assassination hit list."

"I still can't believe, Captain, that the Vatican is capable of murder. Islamic extremists, perhaps, but Catholics?"

"Sir," Franks said, "the Vatican has a lengthy history of bloody warfare to protect its financial interests."

Being a target didn't bother him. His wealth could insulate him from danger, and besides, he'd been expecting this news. He assumed it would come from the Middle East, not Rome. It simply meant beefing up his personal security team and avoiding public transportation, like the plane he had moments before abandoned.

"Who else would you do something on this scale for, Captain?"

"Sir, we do this for heads of state of all countries in the G20." It was something of a shock to be bracketed with Vladimir Putin.

"How much more would you do for President Harrington?"

"Sir, with the president, we'd close down all the side streets intersecting this avenue, and we'd have snipers on the rooftops along the route. But in your case we thought it would draw too much attention."

Right, the inconspicuous seven-vehicle motorcade screaming down Pennsylvania Avenue with sirens blaring and lights flashing attracts no attention at all....

Jeffery Wolfe stood waiting on the White House steps. Jeffery waved for him to follow. "You can't believe what's gone on these last few hours. Inside the beltway is a free-for-all of finger-pointing. The House and Senate are like overturned anthills."

They moved through the halls of the West Wing and entered the Oval Office.

Declan sat next to Jeffery on a couch to the right of the president's desk. They waited along with three other men for the president to conclude her phone conversation with the secretary of state. He tried to concentrate on the briefing notes he was given, but his attention focused on the room—a symbol of the power and prestige, not only for Americans but for leaders across the globe.

He had attended many meetings with senators and military leaders. This, however, was his first time in the White House, and he couldn't beat down feelings of reverence.

The architectural features drew from baroque, neoclassical, and Georgian traditions. Three south-facing windows stood floor to ceiling behind the president's desk. The ceiling was adorned with elaborate molding around the edge, which contained elements of the Seal of the President. Two flags stood behind Harrington—the Stars and Stripes and the president's flag.

Of the three men on the sofa facing him, he only recognized Bernie Hurlburt, the foreign relations secretary. Declan arrived late to the meeting, and no one bothered with introductions. The mood was deadly serious. He felt the urge to lighten the atmosphere with a joke, but he didn't want to seem flippant.

A door opened, and a steward wearing a mauve jacket rolled in a tray with coffee and tea service. He pampered the meeting attendees with beverages and finger sandwiches.

Declan refused refreshments. He was too nervous to swallow. As the others munched and sipped, he scanned his briefing notes. His eyes widened when he read the laws Harrington proposed to Congress. It outlined a four-step procedure to de-arming the American public. One: an immediate halt to the manufacturing of all handguns, rifles, automatic weapons, and small arms ammunition. Two: halt all sales of firearms to the public. Three: issue a general order that all citizens other than law enforcement officers surrender any and all weapons they currently own, making it a felony for anyone who refused to surrender their weapons. Four: grant state and local officials authorization to search civilian homes and confiscate all weapons.

The powers that be were conceding that Kenji would likely not be found, he thought, and to gain access to the formula they must submit to his demands. Did they really have so little faith in the FBI? "This is crazy," he mumbled to himself. There was no way Congress would pass such laws. Not only did they fly in the face of the Second Amendment, they were political suicide. The NRA, one of the most influential political lobbying organizations in the world, would turn into an attack dog, inflaming their gun-toting supporters, causing riots in every city in North America. On the other hand, Harrington was too good a politician to ask for something she knew she couldn't get.

The briefing notes also detailed Harrington's plans on a global level. She was asking Congress for authorization to declare war on any government that refused to destroy their civilian and military weapons.

Sheer madness.

The president replaced the receiver on her telephone. At the same time, the president's personal aide entered the room and strolled to Harrington's desk. He held out a sheet of paper, which she took and read.

The room grew uncomfortably silent, not even the sound of someone typing on a keyboard in the outer offices. Jeffery explained about the no typing before entering the Oval Office; most everything was being communicated in direct conversations so there was little or no paper trail for the investigations that would surely follow at some point in time. Even the briefing notes in his hands had been typed on a manual typewriter so that nothing could be found after the paper had been shredded and incinerated.

Harrington had the look of a benevolent grandmother, but when she spoke, her voice carried an edge. "Gentlemen, the director of the FBI has informed me that we are now searching for only one fugitive. Miss Consuela Rocha y Villareal has been murdered near Bishop, California. Although the evidence is inconclusive, we cannot rule out the possibility that foreign entities are responsible for her murder, and the formula may now be in foreign hands."

"At least she died young," Secretary Hurlburt said. "They say lust makes a man old but keeps a woman young."

Jeffery said, "They say a lot of nonsense. They say the rich can protect themselves and that in their world it is a vacation in Wonderland. I've known rich people all my life, and they are mostly bored, lonely, and scared to death of losing what they have."

What the hell brought that on? Is he talking about me?

Harrington raised a hand for silence. When she had everyone's attention, she continued. "I have authorized a shutdown of commercial airline and train and bus arrivals and departures in all states west of Colorado, and we're setting up roadblock check stations on all highways. Only military flights are authorized until Kenji Hiroshige is in custody."

"Madam President," Declan said, "placing the country in lockdown will cause panic."

Harrington folded her hands on her desk, giving the impression of a governess preparing to deliver a lesson to an unruly child. "Mr. Hughes, once Congress sanctions the laws outlined in your briefing notes, which should happen by the end of the week, I fear all hell will break loose. I am prepared to declare martial law, that is, put the entire country on lockdown, as you call it, until the panic subsides and we are in possession of the formula. I'm deploying National Guard units in all major cities to quell the rioting."

Declan raised his briefing notes. "Approving these laws would be political suicide. The NRA and weapons manufacturers will fight this to the death. What makes you think you can push this through?"

"It's called greed, Mr. Hughes. All human beings dream of life everlasting, and the smart ones want it on earth and not in heaven. There is a small list of families who will receive the treatment, and there is everyone else. Only those who cooperate get included on the list, and let me assure you, nobody in a position of power wants to be excluded, no matter what the financial or political risk."

Of course, Declan thought, *quid pro quo is the universal language in Washington.* Senators, congressmen, state officials, and arms manufacturers would crawl over broken glass to cooperate. Declan was a fool not to see that coming. And she was right about the riots. When they closed the weapons factories and gun stores, thousands upon thousands of workers would lose their jobs. Gun owners would take to the streets, while hoarding their weapons. A black market would pop up, and people would rob their neighbors, even kill, for guns and ammunition. Gangs of vigilantes had already taken over towns. That would spread once troops begin confiscating firearms.

"Pardon my slow uptake. It's been a long few days. But even with congressional approval, the task of disarming three hundred and fifty million people will be monumental, even if the carrot you're dangling is life eternal."

She swiveled her chair around so that her back was to the men. She remained silent, staring out the windows. A strained silence settled over the room, and Declan knew she was giving her staff the opportunity to answer for her.

Bernie Hurlburt took the bait, saying, "The crises we face is not on US soil. Americans, for the most part, are sheep, willing to do whatever we tell them as long as we don't take away their McDonald's burgers, iPhones, and cable TV. I'm confident we'll de-arm the United States in a year, two at most. It's the rest of the world that presents precarious problems. First and foremost, we must demolish all arms manufacturers across the globe. Secondly, we must destroy all existing weapons on foreign soil. Both of those tasks could lead to thermonuclear war."

Harrington swiveled back around to face Secretary Hurlburt. "How are the negotiations coming with Tehran, Rome, and Jerusalem?"

Hurlburt rose and placed a folder on Harrington's desk. The label on the folder read Division of the New Power Axis. He stepped back one pace. "We're pressuring O'Neill, the secretary-general of the United Nations, but the talks have reached a crisis point."

"How so?" Declan asked.

Hurlburt kept his eyes on Harrington. "You know it's a crisis when the volume of encrypted communications between the capitals and the embassies of each country suddenly stops altogether. This is the fateful moment when a decision has been made. There is to be no more compromise, so embassies stop asking for more instructions. We reached that point with all three yesterday."

"At the same time," Wolfe added, "we are using global media to create, by displays of mutual vituperation, a state of mind in the populations of America and the G20 countries, where the public will acquiesce in targeted, small-scale nuclear strikes."

Declan glanced out the windows behind the president, where gardeners were turning the soil in the flowerbeds. It seemed too inexplicable that people were keeping their surroundings alive and beautiful while a handful of leaders a few dozen yards away plotted to unleash thermonuclear missiles on an unsuspecting world.

"Large-scale nuclear war with Russia or China," Wolfe continued, "as all experts agree, means not only the extermination of nine-tenths of the population of our three countries, but also the complete extermination of the populations of Europe and Britain. That, of course, is out of the question, but small strikes on rogue states...."

Secretary Hurlburt pointed to the folder he had laid on Harrington's desk. "Military Intelligence has compiled a list of all weapons-manufacturing plants outside the US, Russia, and China. Once the new power axis has flexed their muscles, taking out those targets and, of course, Rome, Jerusalem, and Tehran, we feel that the rest of the world will comply with our demands."

Harrington nodded. "Moscow and Beijing agree?"

"This was Putin's idea, Madam President, and Beijing is resolute."

Hurlburt's creamy voice annoyed Declan. This went against everything he stood for.

"We need to ensure that responsibility for an initial strike is shared equally and completely," Harrington said. "Also, our target is Tehran, not Jerusalem or Rome."

"It's all in the report," Hurlburt said.

"Have we heard from the American cardinals and bishops?"

Hurlburt nodded. "They are prepared to elect Cardinal McDonald as the new pope and rebuild the Vatican outside of Boston."

"McDonald?" Wolfe said. "Well, I suppose beggars can't be choosers."

Declan couldn't believe that the government could go raving mad in only a week. "Once we disarm the planet, who's to bell the cats?"

Harrington lifted an eyebrow. "Bell the cats?"

"The mice of the house all got together and decided it would be a great idea to strap a bell around the cat's neck so that they would all hear him coming. They all agreed, but then it came down to who would volunteer to strap the bell to its neck. My point is: Who will disarm Russia and China, and indeed, the American military, once the rest of the world is powerless?"

The president glanced at the unopened folder. Her lips shaped her words soundlessly, and she took a calming breath and tried again. "Keeping reins on the balance of power is dependent on one thing and one thing only, and that is capturing that formula. Once we are the only ones in possession of it, all other governments must comply with our demands or be excluded from eternity. Don't you see? We really can rid the world of weapons, of war, for all time. But to do that we need the trump card, that formula."

"And if we fail?" Declan said, his voice dropped to a whisper.

"You think I don't know the stakes?" she snapped. "I'm a devout Catholic. I curse the day I ever ran for office, but now that I'm here, I need to make the tough decisions."

"I'm sorry," Declan said. "I didn't mean to—"

"The reason you were included in this meeting, Mr. Hughes, is so that you understand the stakes. The longer your mad scientist stays hidden, the greater the risk some other government will attain the formula. We are out of time. Get back to your team, and kick them in the ass."

It all made terrifying sense. He knew that in time, she would be judged as either a lunatic or a genius, and he was thankful that the verdict would not be left up to him.

Chapter Fourteen

Landau and Souad sat with Jessup in the interrogation room in the Hawthorn police station. Souad asked him questions about Kenji's habits. Jessup strained to understand the questions and answer them accurately.

"I appreciate that they are trying to rid the world of violence," Souad said. "What I don't understand is how a man with so much going for him—intelligent, well respected, pampered by his family—would use a friend and colleague to blow up a multimillion-dollar lab, and in the next breath kill her."

Jessup's back stiffened, and he responded with a blank stare.

"And the riots, it's like he set off a powder keg. If he's so damned smart, why didn't he realize that he would cause exactly the kind of violence he wants to end? We've picked over every bit of information we could about him—his connections, his habits, everything. After all that I'm stumped. It doesn't add up."

"Agent Souad." Jessup found his voice. "Don't take advantage of my mental state. Kenji is innocent of murder. They may have spent the night in that cabin, but they didn't murder anyone. They couldn't have. You said yourself assassins are out to kill them. Now, please stop. I'm wiped out and confused and way too emotional for this shit. Right now, I want to see my father."

The agents didn't argue or try to question him more. The three men walked outside, slipped into a car, and drove to the clinic holding Blake. On the short ride, Landau told Jessup he had arranged entry into the witness protection program for Jessup and a military hospital for Blake. Jessup could go underground until Kenji and Matt Reece were apprehended, and the doctors could continue their tests on Blake at a secure facility. That surprised Jessup, but the next bit of information shocked him: the FBI had tried to locate Patrick at UC Berkeley and found that he dropped out of school and disappeared months ago.

Jessup stared out the window. The news kept getting worse, and all he could think to do was find a way to wake up from this nightmare. But it was a fine day with an immense sun hammering them.

He tried not to worry about Patrick, who could take care of himself. He focused on his surroundings, gazing at the other vehicles in their unhurried ballet and the pedestrians shuffling along the sidewalks, who seemed as sad as their shadows. He never liked this damn town, and he felt the hard need to be back on his ranch, the one place he felt safe.

They parked in the clinic lot, walked through the corridors, and rode an elevator car to the third floor. Two policemen stood guard outside of Blake's room. Jessup brushed past them to find his father sitting up in bed, devouring a cheeseburger and fries. Blake's skin showed a darker green tint, but he looked younger than before. In fact, they looked as if they were twin brothers, rather than father and son.

"What the hell took so long?" Blake said.

Jessup said, "Ready to fly this coop?"

"Toss me my pants."

Jessup stepped to the closet and removed a hanger holding a pair of jeans. He pitched them on the bed and reached for the shirt.

"Where do you think you're going?" Souad asked.

"Agent Landau said you can't hold us without a court order, and we're free to do whatever we damn well please," Jessup said. "We're going home."

"You look like shit," Blake said. "Did they rough you up?"

"All I need is a bath, something to eat, and a week of sleep."

Blake didn't seem at all convinced.

"You'll likely be taken hostage or killed," Souad said, his voice rising.

"We're done here, done with you," Jessup snapped.

Landau laid a hand on his shoulder. "I'll drive you, but you're in for a surprise."

Jessup backed away to avoid his hand. "Right now, nothing would surprise me."

They stopped at a KFC for a bucket with all the trimmings and drove to the ranch. When they came over the rise that looked down onto the ranch, Jessup saw a mob of reporters and television camera trucks in the work yard. Vehicles were parked on both sides of the dirt road as far as halfway up the hill. As for the house, the curtains were drawn and the front door hung open. It was dark inside.

Landau stopped the car in front of the house. Hundreds of reporters and camera crew personnel rushed them, swarming like drones in pursuit of their queen. Photographers climbed onto one another's backs for a clear picture. Jessup stepped from the car. He stood blinking and directionless, momentarily bewildered. There was no escaping this throng. With Landau and Souad's help, Jessup and Blake squeezed through the press of bodies and onto the front porch. Blake slipped into the house, taking the KFC bucket with him. Jessup turned to the crowd and held up his arms, asking for silence. The voices grew quiet; the cameras rolled.

"This is private property," Jessup said while flanked by Landau and Souad. "You are not welcome here. Please leave as quickly as possible, and don't come back."

The reporters surged forward. The cameras lit up Jessup's face, and the overlapping questions being shouted became a wall. He pressed his hands to his ears. A moment later, a blast to his left had reporters jumping back. A second blast had them running for cover. He turned to see Blake, shotgun to shoulder, fire another round over their heads. People scrambled into their trucks.

"Now get! All of you bastards," Blake shouted.

Souad moved to grab the rifle, but Blake turned the barrel on him, chest high. "That goes for you too, stud."

One camera crew was recording all the drama on the porch, but the others were fleeing. Cars kicked up dust as they sped away. Landau said, "Souad, wait for me in the car. Mr. Connors, please lower your weapon. There's no need for violence. The damage is already done here."

Blake lowered the shotgun barrel as Souad moved off the porch and opened the passenger door of their vehicle.

"Shall we go inside to see what these vultures did?" Landau said.

Jessup stepped into a living room that had been turned upside down. The same disorder reigned in the rest of the house. Lamps smashed, furniture ripped apart. In the corner, his roll-top desk was now a pile of rubble. A few days ago, he'd made a commitment to write serious stories, something that might lead to a novel. Now his dream was as dead as that heap of wood.

In his bedroom the mattress was flipped over, the bedding knotted in the corner, the dresser drawers spilled out onto the hardwood floor. Someone took the two family photos he had kept on the bedside table—one of Kenji and one of the boys. Most of the clothes in the armoire were missing. Only one change of clean clothing remained.

A bone-crushing weariness came over him, and all he wanted to do was to set the mattress back on the box springs and sleep for a month, but he didn't have the strength. He also didn't have the nerve to walk through the rest of the house to inspect the damage.

Landau came up behind him. "I'm so sorry. My search team left this house exactly the way they found it. The cyclone that hit these rooms came from those reporters looking for dirty little secrets to write about."

Jessup stared into the mirror on the armoire. His reflection was unrecognizable. Disheveled, wild-eyed, unshaven.

"There's not much left for you here," Landau said. "Let me set you up with a house in the witness protection program."

He shook his head.

"Suit yourself."

He found Blake in the kitchen dishing out chicken and biscuits and mashed potatoes.

"Eat, you'll feel better," Blake said. He had set up the table and chairs and laid out plates and cups. "I'll go feed the stock and milk Lucy." He grabbed his shotgun. "And I'll chase off any sons of bitches that are still nosing around."

The livestock! In the commotion, Jessup forgot there were animals depending on him.

"Be damned careful, Mr. Connors," Landau said. "Some of those people could be NRA zealots spoiling for a fight."

Blake pumped a round into the chamber. His coat pocket bulged with more shells. "Then they've come to the right place." He bolted through the mudroom and out to the work yard. The trucks were leaving. Blake let go with another blast to hurry them along.

Landau stepped closer to Jessup, holding out a cell phone and a charger. "You don't have a phone, so please take my spare, and call me twice a day. Once in the morning and once at night at a minimum."

"And if I don't?"

"If you don't I'll suspect the worst and come looking for you. Please cooperate so I can focus on finding Kenji and Matt Reece instead of chasing after you."

"On one condition."

"Shoot."

"That when I call, you tell me all the updated information about the investigation."

"You still don't believe it was Kenji?" He paused, and when Jessup didn't answer, he said, "Okay. I'll give you everything I can."

Jessup took the phone and charger.

"Jessup, believe me when I say that everything I'm doing is in your best interest. I want to protect your family, especially Matt Reece. But I need your help." Jessup started to protest, but Landau held up a hand to silence him. "I've been at this game a long time, so I know you're still withholding information. Please don't wait until someone else dies before you tell me the rest of what you know. Call me anytime, night or day."

"I will."

"And another thing: rest assured, those reporters will be back. The longer this drags on, the bigger the story will grow, and the more they'll hound you. You'll find no peace here. But I'll asked the sheriff to make daily patrols out this way."

As Landau drove away, Jessup sat and ate. He felt an appalling loneliness, a need for Kenji that felt primal. *This illustrates the disparity between different sorts of relationships*, he thought. Some people you miss instantly after parting, and then gradually less and less; and some—a few in a lifetime—you become increasingly aware of missing them. At first it's a discomfort and then misery and then pure agony. It wouldn't be so heartbreaking if there was some way they could eventually reunite, as Kenji's note implied. But he saw no hope of that. His future held only a question mark.

He cleaned his plate before Blake returned. He dropped his dishes into the sink, walked into the bathroom, and turned on the faucets in the tub. He mixed the water as hot as he could stand it. He didn't merely want to wash the last few days off his skin; he wanted to boil it out of his blood, to purge it by fire so he wouldn't need to think about it again, ever.

He stripped and inched into the water. The burn was consuming, but it felt better than the mental torture he'd been wrestling with. He clamped his jaw shut and endured until he was submerged to his neck. For the first time in days, he felt warm to his core. He closed his eyes and let himself dissolve in the hot torpor.

He lay dreaming, floating through some bomb-gutted city, nothing left but smoldering rubble. Hiroshima, perhaps Dresden, or maybe Tokyo after the firestorms? He heard the grumble of death wagons and a voice calling, "Bring me your dead...."

Another sound superimposed itself. Jessup awoke to pounding on a door. He opened his eyes as Blake stepped into the bathroom and switched on the light.

"What the fuck? You want to sleep, do it in a bed like a civilized person."

Jessup became aware that he was freezing. The bathwater had chilled. His teeth chattered, and his arms and legs were stiff as tree limbs.

Blake snatched a terry cloth towel from the closet. He hauled Jessup to his feet, draped the towel over Jessup's shoulders, and rubbed vigorously.

"The last goddamned thing we need," Blake said, "is you catching pneumonia."

"What time is it?"

"Just past ten."

He'd been soaking for five hours.

"Hell," Blake said, "all this time I thought you were in your bedroom, sleeping. I checked on you before going to bed, and you weren't there."

Blake rubbed him dry. They stood there, father and son, like many decades ago, Blake drying his son after a bath. Yet it felt freaky, now that they were physically about the same age. As Blake led him back through the kitchen and living room, the house seemed to be back in some kind of order. Blake had spent the last five hours trying to reconstruct their lives. Blake led him into his bedroom, placed the mattress on the box springs, and spread a sheet over it. Jessup crawled onto the bed and curled into a fetal position. Blake spread a quilt over him.

"I'll fix up a shot or two of something that will warm you up."

Blake came back a few minutes later holding out a mug of aromatic bourbon. He helped Jessup to sit up and almost poured the liquid down his throat. Again, Jessup was thrust back into childhood, with his father taking charge and administering care to his sick child. There seemed no way to pull himself out of this alternative universe, which seemed hell-bent on driving him mad.

The drink warmed his gut. Delicious. Heat spread into his chest and limbs. He laid his head to the pillow and was back floating through that city a moment after the door closed.

A SCREECH of rusty hinges woke Jessup. He lifted his head, listening. There it was again, and this time he recognized it as the barn door opening and closing. He threw off his cover and stumbled to the window overlooking the work yard. The moon was nearly full, pouring down bushels of light onto the yard. He saw two men skulking in the shadows.

He opened the window and leaned out. "Get the hell off my ranch."

One man raised a finger.

Jessup climbed into the pair of jeans hanging in the closet and rushed through the house and out the back door. The men jogged toward the road.

Barefoot, his head boiling, Jessup chased after them. But he noticed movement in the shadows by the barn, and more by the tack shed.

"You want my rifle, motherfucker, come take it, you terrorist bitch!"

The invectives stopped him cold. Before he could react, five men cradling assault weapons surrounded him. He raised his hands to show he was unarmed.

"Keep your guns. I just want you off my land."

He smelled smoke and heard the bray of frightened horses coming from the barn. In a flash of perception, he knew they had come to torch the ranch. They intended to obliterate the one place on earth he loved.

He raised his fists as they closed in on him. A jet of saliva struck his face, and a rifle butt slammed into his abdomen. He dropped to his knees in a shock of pain. An instant later, a boot kicked him in the middle of his back, sending him facedown in the dirt.

"You tell that fucking Jap son of a bitch that we ain't giving up our weapons, no how. And if you want to live another week, he had damned well better turn his self in."

A kick to his face split his nose and lips open. He curled into a ball as a storm of blows fell from above. Then a blast from a shotgun rang out. One of the attackers fell screaming, while covering his face with his hands. In the moonlight, Jessup saw blood pouring from between the man's clinched fingers. The others dropped to their knees, raised their weapons, and opened fire on Blake.

Blake jumped back into the house. Four attackers emptied their clips, shattering the windows, knocking holes in the walls. Jessup tried to rise, but a kick to the head dropped him again. From the barrage that hit the house, he was confident Blake was dead or seriously wounded.

Flames roared from the barn's hayloft. The stock screamed in terror.

When the bombardment stopped, it was clear the attackers were out of ammo. Shots rang out from the house again. Buckshot whizzed over Jessup. Groans and curses erupted from his assailants. They had no cover, and Blake cut them to ribbons in quick order.

Moments later, the men grabbed hold of their fallen buddy and hobbled up the road, leaving an impressive trail of blood. But once they were out of range, a voice came sailing back at him. "Don't think this is over, bitch. We'll be back."

Jessup lay in the hard, cold stillness of the night.

Blake ran from the house, letting go with two more rounds. He knelt over Jessup, lifting him to a sitting position. "Save the stock," Jessup mumbled.

Blake dropped his rifle, ran to the barn, and dashed in. Moments later, two horses and the milk cow ran out. Blake leaped into Kenji's Jeep and backed it into the work yard where the flames couldn't reach it.

There was no saving the barn.

Blake bent over Jessup again. "Five armed men against one unarmed man," Blake said, and he spit. "Those redneck pussies turn my stomach."

Blake brought his hand to Jessup's chin, turning his face this way and that. "They got you pretty good, but hell, I've come out of barroom brawls looking worse than this."

"Stop yappin,' and help me to bed."

"I'll help you into the Jeep and drive you to the hospital. Your face needs stitches."

"Hell no."

"Son, we gotta go into town anyway. I'm out of shells."

Jessup nodded. His thoughts became clear, and anger surged through him like lightning. "Okay, but we don't come back. We'll stop at the Bar-J ranch and get old man Hawkins to look after our stock. Once they sew me up, we head for Berkeley to find Patrick. After that, we go after Matt Reece."

"Now you're talking sense. First priority is family. How much money we got?"

Jessup had no idea. "Whatever's in the petty-cash drawer. All the rest is in Kenji's bank account. Fat chance they'll let us touch that."

"If it's in the cash drawer, those media bastards probably stole it."

Blake hauled Jessup to his feet, wrapped an arm over his shoulder, and they limped to the house. Once inside, Blake made a beeline for the cash drawer in the destroyed roll-top desk. Jessup stumbled into the bathroom, where he had left his old jeans before climbing into the tub. He retrieved Kenji's flash drive and Landau's phone and charger from the pockets, and slipped them into the jeans he now wore. He washed the blood from his face and pressed a towel to the gashes. He could feel the extensive trauma across his torso, arms, and right knee. Those areas were swelling and turning color.

The barn roared, and the sound detonated as the roof collapsed. It was a heartbreaking clamor. He tottered to the bedroom and dressed in the clothes hanging in the armoire.

By the time he was ready, Blake had the Jeep parked at the back door with the engine running. Blake helped him into the passenger seat and climbed behind the wheel. "Hard to believe those bastards overlooked it, but I found two hundred and thirty dollars in the cash drawer. That'll get us to Berkeley, but not much farther."

Jessup glanced at the house, the work yard, and the burning pile of lumber that had been the barn. Heat radiated from the fire like a blowtorch. This had been his island of safety from an unkind world, the one place he loved. He presumed those men would be back to finish the job. There would be nothing to come back to. For the first time, and for only a fleeting moment, he hated Kenji. He wanted to rip his guts out so that Kenji would know what he was feeling.

As if reading his thoughts, Blake said, "We lost the barn, and we may lose the house, but I'd be dead by now if it weren't for him. I gotta be grateful as hell to him."

"There is that blessing. But he destroyed my family, the ranch, everything my life was built on. Nothing can ever be the way it was. I want justice for my losses."

"You sound like a victim, blaming someone else for the fix you're in. Once you fall into that hole, you never climb out. It changes you forever."

It's true, Jessup thought. He had reached the most hideous state a man can sink to, that black space where the fear grows and hope fades. That place of confusion and helplessness, where it's impossible to find even a glint of light.

The Jeep pulled away from the house and sped up the road. Before they reached the top of the hill, still holding the towel to his face, his mood changed. He had lost nearly everything dear—his boys, his ranch, his writing, his lover. This alternative universe now seemed an empty void, but a determination began to germinate. He instinctively knew this was the point—now or never—to fight.

I'll get it back, he promised himself, *or die trying*.

Chapter Fifteen

DECLAN HUGHES glared across his desk, a wide expanse of polished mahogany. A failure of the ventilation system raised beads of sweat across his forehead. He tossed the file Salman Landau had presented to him on his desk. That file was scientifically precise, with footnotes, quotations, and source references. Much of it focused on Kenji Hiroshige, giving the subject's background, education, career, and financial situation. It was not until page thirty-five that Consuela was mentioned, at which point she was given an equally exhaustive analysis. The file also had a fifteen-page appendix, complete with recently taken pictures of Kenji, Consuela, and Matt Reece.

Landau was thirty minutes into a presentation of all the evidence his team had pulled together. They had labored round the clock doing a more thorough investigation than Declan thought possible, making use of all the archives and public and classified documents that were available, expanding the investigation to Kenji and Consuela's relatives and friends, scrutinizing their finances, and illuminating details of each upbringing and career.

The lack of information on Kenji was, nevertheless, discouraging. He was a noted veterinarian, graduating first in his class at UC Davis, a member of the American Medical Association, and author of a respectably long-winded, exceptionally tedious dissertation on regenerative systems in the salamander. His professional reputation was spotless. No criminal or medical histories. His finances were in good order. He was a member of Greenpeace and Amnesty International. He lived a quiet life, until now, never appearing in the media. And he was legally married to a man, Jessup Connors, and lived on the Promesa Rota ranch in Nevada.

"Okay, I'm convinced," Declan said, "that Kenji Hiroshige killed Consuela and went into hiding with her life savings." He raised his eyebrows as both Landau and Ahmed Souad nodded. They sat across that desk in straight-back chairs, and the heat had them sweating too. The only one not perspiring was FBI Assistant Director Dr. Rachael Laughton, who stood casually in a corner behind Landau. She wore a two-piece skirt suit, smartly tailored, pale red blouse, and a silk scarf arranged over one shoulder. Declan thought she looked like a million bucks.

"The only relevant question," Declan said with a slow, icy calm, "is why isn't he in custody? Landau, the president herself told me the reason they brought a retread onto this case was that you're Einstein reincarnated. Thus far, I ain't seeing it."

Declan's judgment of "retread" elicited a scowl from Rachael. To Declan, Landau looked like a wretched old mongrel, teeth worn, hardly a bark in him. A sad-faced fellow wearing a badly laundered shirt and worn brown suit. His pouched eyes and yellowish pallor probably came from generous amounts of scotch every night in order to unwind. Even old dogs knew a few tricks, but this man was a worn-out mutt.

Landau managed a smirk, a smirk of pure, exuberant fuck you. He said, "We have definite suspects, and thanks to Souad's canvassing of restaurants along the highways, we know they drove north from Bishop. We've focused our search from there to the Canadian border, but it could take weeks to comb every city, and that's assuming they're hiding in an urban area."

"I need results," Declan said, "not defensive posturing. Hell, the kid is supposed to be green as crème de menthe. How hard could it be to find him?" Declan knew he was being harsh, but he had learned in the business world that with some people the way to be subtle was to plow a Patton tank up their butthole.

Declan assumed Landau's modus operandi was easy to figure; thirty years at the agency turned him into a political machine. Whatever view held out his next advance was the view he clung to, and scuttlebutt said that if he captured the formula intact, President Harrington would hold out the Presidential Medal of Freedom, the nation's highest civilian honor. That recognition alone would bump Landau well up the ladder, perhaps as high as chief of the nation's intelligence agencies.

Landau cleared his throat. "In a manhunt, there's a time to demand action and a time to let things play out. It's like a boxing match—you sometimes crowd your opponent to keep him off balance, and sometimes you dance around letting him beat himself. This is tango time, in my opinion, and a time for you to keep your 'retread' comments to yourself."

Souad said, "We've plastered their picture on every TV news broadcast and newspaper front page. We're checking each border crossing, train station, bus terminal, and airport. But we can't assume they're still together and in a location people will see them. They could be at a remote farmhouse or camping in the mountains. Hell, the kid could be dead and buried by now. Every law enforcement agency has their photos and the license plate number of the car. If they're on the move, something should turn up soon."

Declan slammed his fist on the desk. "Soon isn't good enough. I'm being pressured from the president. Do you people know who I am?"

Landau said, "Sure, you're one of those three-comma jerkoffs that are sodomizing the middle class."

"Three comma?"

"You know, multibillion dollars, one comma, two comma, three...."

"I'm the CEO of a formidable corporation that pulls a shitload of political strings, and I'm yanking every damned string there is because I can taste that fourth comma."

Declan glanced out the sixteenth-story window, watching traffic clogging the Santa Monica Freeway. He clenched his left hand into a fist, relaxed it, and clenched it again.

Landau held up a file. "Our Behavioral Science Unit delivered their psychological profile of Consuela's killer. It describes Consuela as being a low risk for a violent crime that soon after she posted the video. Whoever murdered her knew about her cabin, went there to meet her, and probably planned to kill her before arriving. She knew the assailant. We know this because there was no sign of struggle. The throat cutting looked like a clean surgical incision, not something hurried by someone in a panic. The killer was cold, calculating, and deliberate. The report suggests the assailant's motive was not emotionally based, and this is most likely not his first murder."

Declan nodded. "Did he kill her for the money?"

Landau shook his head. "Remember, they were partners. They'd planned this over years, perhaps decades. She gathered that money for both of them to go into hiding. Which means she was already on board. No, there was another motive."

"Okay, Einstein, enlighten me."

"Matt Reece. He was the only parameter outside the established plan, the fly in the ointment. I'm guessing because he was exposed to the formula, she demanded they alter the plan in some way. Kenji had other ideas."

Declan clinched his jaw. "Speculation. But even if it's true, what does that tell us?"

"The other interesting deduction," Landau said, "is that because they made no attempt to cover up the evidence, Kenji doesn't care that we know it's him. He thinks he's invincible. We're searching for a man who is shrewd yet foolishly arrogant."

Souad nodded. "He might be playing us, waging a game of cat and mouse to show us his superiority."

"The report also suggests," Landau said as he tossed the report on the desk, "that he feels no remorse or guilt."

Declan rose and paced behind his desk. "You wasted a lot of effort on a report that tells us nothing important."

Landau took a slow breath before speaking. "We now know that Kenji Hiroshige doesn't have a conscience. He's a man who makes lists and checks everything off them to the letter—iron a shirt, pack a bag, cut your partner's throat, turn the horses loose. It's a premeditated puzzle conceived by someone with a God complex, and I fear it's only the beginning. I have a feeling something cyclonic is coming at us."

"You've got that whopping brain boiling up quite a little scenario," Declan said, "but you're asking the wrong questions. You want to analyze him, understand him. I want him behind bars and that formula in my safe. The only important question is how the hell to capture him."

This time Landau took several breaths before answering. The traffic outside the office became loud. "We're trailing his husband, Jessup Connors. We believe Jessup is withholding information. We've placed GPS transmitters in his clothes and the cell phone I gave him, and we're hoping he'll lead us to Kenji. We're keeping twenty-four seven surveillance on him. Right now he's in Oakland."

Declan waved a hand at the reports on his desk. "That's the best you can do?"

Landau stood, giving him an elevation advantage over Declan, and fixed the man with his stare. "We are giving you this briefing as a courtesy to the president, but don't push your luck any further if you want to stay in the loop. And just so you know, I didn't ask for this case. I was selected to lead it. If you've got someone who can bring in faster results, I'll gladly step back into oblivion. In fact, if you can pull your lips away from the president's asshole, perhaps you'd like to run the ground game, instead of being an armchair quarterback?"

"You'd better rein in that attitude, Agent Landau," Declan barked.

"Or what? You'll get me fired?" Landau reached for his briefcase and turned to leave. "This meeting has been a long, tedious stroll down Bullshit Boulevard."

"Why do men always feel the need for these pissing matches?" Rachael asked. The note of amusement in her voice stopped Landau halfway to the door. As he turned to her, she continued, "I'm not saying women are any better. Lord knows we have our own games we play to compete with each other, but why must men always fight to see who's alpha, especially when there is a female present? I can assure you it fails to impress any woman who has at least a double-digit IQ."

Declan's anger drained away. He smiled. He couldn't tell if Landau was stunned or angry, because the big man sat stock-still, waiting for the next shoe to drop. "Okay. I'll tone it down, but from now on, I want a steady stream of up-to-date, pertinent data. So stop jerking me off with all these bullshit analysis reports."

Souad rose just as Landau's phone beeped. He drew the phone from his pocket and read a text message. "We got lucky. Consuela's car was spotted ten minutes ago in San Francisco."

Declan waved his arms, motioning them to get going.

Landau and Souad rushed to the door, but Landau stopped and turned on his way out. "Mr. Hughes, I'll give you up-to-date status. However—" He paused to clear his throat. "No matter how much you plead… jerking you off is not in my job description. You'll have to manage that on your own."

Souad was visibly thrown, as if he had no idea Landau had a sense of humor. He let go with a tense laugh.

Declan laughed too. "Whatever you say, Landau."

Chapter Sixteen

Shirtless, Matt Reece stood before a mirror near the tattoo chair, staring at his reflection. His face, neck, hands, and even his eyelids were now a burnt-coffee hue. Vishal had also shaved his head to dye his scalp. There was a line across his chest and up over both collarbones where green skin clashed with black. Up close, he could tell it was a dye job, but from a few yards back, he looked African American—with hazel eyes. He was most upset over his hair. He had relinquished so much, losing his hair had nearly taken him over the edge.

A knock at the door turned his head. Vishal walked into the room carrying an armload of clothes and a pair of sneakers. "You're still dressed? Get it in gear, cowboy."

Groucho lifted himself off the floor and sniffed at the outfit draped over Vishal's arm.

"What's wrong with my clothes?"

Vishal tossed his bundle on the tattoo chair and dropped the sneakers on the floor. "Earth to Kirby. Those threads are perfect if we're planning to mosey down Main Street in Little Rock or San Antonio. But we're not, darlin'. We're going to Berkeley, and the last thing we need is for you to draw attention to yourself. Or we could stay here until your father gets back."

Matt Reece stepped out of his boots and unbuttoned his fly. "He's not my father. He's no longer my anything." He dropped his jeans to his ankles and stepped free of them, feeling self-conscious in his JC Penney's cotton briefs.

"Those too," Vishal said, pointing to his underwear.

Matt Reece shook his head no.

"Okay, but you'll be missing out on these." Vishal held up a pair of red silk panties, glossy and tantalizing. They seemed impossibly small, hardly the size of Vishal's palm. Matt Reece felt his pulse leap. He snatched them up and brought them to his cheek to test their softness. He inhaled, luxuriating in the scent of pure sex. "These are for women?"

"Kirby, those will feel so sensual you'll be walking around all day with a hard-on, and they'll look so good on you I'll be stiff thinking about them."

Matt Reece had never wanted to be girlish. To him, being gay was about cowboys rutting around with each other, but there was something enticing about the feel of underwear so soft and voluptuous. He decided to wear everything Vishal offered. He would let Vishal mold him into someone new, but he wouldn't rush this makeover. *Make a show of it,* he thought, a performance to tantalize Vishal, whose remarks showed he had some sexual interest. He turned his back to Vishal and slipped out of his briefs. He turned his head to see Vishal's eyes holding his gaze, making him feel, momentarily, the absolute center of Vishal's universe.

He stepped into the panties and shimmied them up over his knees, thighs, ass. They stretched, straining to cover him. The press of silk brought a delicious heat to his face. He turned to the mirror and realized that the flash of red covering his genitals had transformed him. He seemed more supple than the scrawny teen of moments ago. Also in the glass, he saw Vishal staring—mouth slightly open, a look of raw desire.

Matt Reece grinned. "What's next?"

Vishal scooped Matt Reece into his arms and kissed him. When he pulled away, Matt Reece still tasted Vishal on his tongue. "I meant, what's next to wear?"

Vishal held up a sleeveless potato-brown T-shirt with tiny sequins on the front that spelled out "Gay By Nature, Proud By Choice." Matt Reece slipped it over his head, pulled his arms through the holes, and smoothed it over his torso. It held a faint curry odor, Vishal's scent.

Vishal reached for the black jeans.

Item by item, Matt Reece watched his metamorphosis in the mirror, and also on Vishal's face. With his dyed skin and trendy clothes, his thin, awkward, inadequate shape blossomed into something sexy and deliberate—a young, bald, hip-hop celebrity. He saw a person with new possibilities. He could hardly contain his astonishment.

He moved in slow motion, taking his time slipping on the Skechers sneakers. He was beginning to realize from Vishal's reaction that the glamour of dressing is the first step in arousal. Each article of clothing, each pose in front of the mirror heightened the anticipation of taking it all off again for this appreciating man, and right then, Vishal looked very appreciative. Matt Reece visualized the striptease he would perform later, with the emphasis on tease.

The tight shirt sculpted his torso; his jeans were loose and sagging. Vishal pulled his Sinner's Gin hoody over his head and held it out. When Matt Reece drew it over his body, the transfiguration felt complete. With the hood concealing his head and much of his face, no one would mistake him for anything other than a brother.

Vishal, however, had one more surprise. He drew a pair of Ray-Ban sunglasses from his pocket and slipped them over Matt Reece's eyes.

Matt Reece's insides crystallized, becoming hard, formidable, and his body took on a swagger common with many African American males. It would take a lot of pluck to walk in public as a brother, and he took his time before the mirror, letting the illusion build his courage.

Vishal wrapped a collar around Groucho's neck and attached a leash.

"Hey," Matt Reece said, "what gives?"

"This town has a leash law, cowboy. Okay, let's vamoose."

Matt Reece lifted his old Wrangler jeans from the chair. He pinched his wallet and pocket watch from the pockets and tucked them into his new jeans, and he removed the picture of Vishal he had taken from behind the counter. Before he could slip it into his pocket, Vishal grabbed his hand and turned it so he could see the photo.

"You pilfering my stuff? My culture believes that if you take a person's picture, you take their soul."

"There were so many, I didn't think you'd miss it."

"It's okay. You're welcome to my soul for the time being." Vishal let go of his hand, and Matt Reece pushed the photo into his hip pocket. "Besides, I like the idea of walking around town with my face pressed to your ass." And he laughed that flute sound again.

Matt Reece grabbed the leash and hurried to the front door. He knew if he hesitated even a second, his courage might falter. So with momentum in full stride, he plunged out the doorway and swaggered up the sidewalk until it was too late to turn around.

Vishal drew up beside him.

Just keep walking. He stared straight ahead and bowed his head slightly to hide his face. He couldn't help, however, stealing glances at his reflection in the storefront windows, observing how he moved, how he looked. He also studied Vishal's reflection, his proud smile, his poise. It bolstered Matt Reece's confidence. He could do this; he could pull it off.

Vishal led him down Haight Street and into Golden Gate Park. They wandered along sidewalks, over paths cutting through stands of trees, and passed a Japanese tea garden before stopping in front of the de Young Museum.

A family of five stood before a Michael Jackson impersonator, who stood like a statue with his hat held out for tips. The scene was comical only because this impersonator would easily dress out at four hundred pounds. The youngest family member, a girl no older than six years, placed a bill in the hat. The performer reached down and touched a button on his boom box. "Thriller" beat the air, and the performer began a robotic dance. Matt Reece was spellbound, amazed that such a massive human body could make those intricate moves. And once in motion, it seemed that he would continue on forever, unstoppable, like Jupiter in orbit. The performer was a dead ringer for MJ, had MJ been the size of a Dallas Cowboys linebacker. He danced for two minutes, ending with a moonwalk back to his boom box. He switched off the music and held out his hat again.

As the family clapped and moved away, Vishal said, "Come meet my friend." He led Matt Reece and Groucho to the performer.

Vishal said, waving a hand at MJ, "Ray Ray, meet Kirby."

Matt Reece stuck out his hand to shake, but Ray Ray kept his statue-like pose.

"What kind of a name is Ray Ray?" Matt Reece asked. "Is that a stage name?"

Ray Ray relaxed his pose. "Someone tagged after a fucking vacuum cleaner is dissing my name? Seriously?"

Matt Reece lowered his hand.

"Hey, skinny, be nice," Vishal said.

"Whatever, scarface."

"You didn't give them much of a show," Vishal said. "Bad day at the office?"

"Bitch, I'd slap you, but shit splatters," Ray Ray said. "Besides, those cheapass hicks only popped a buck." He glanced at their retreating backs and yelled, "Get your sorry asses back to Walmart."

Matt Reece couldn't begin to guess Ray Ray's nationality. He had sea-colored eyes, coppery skin, enormous limbs, and intense white teeth.

His smile was tigerish and challenging, but his eyes regarded Matt Reece with a languishing sweetness. He was dressed in a band uniform with epaulettes on the shoulders like the famous pop star.

Ray Ray took in Matt Reece from hoody to sneakers. "Nice dye job, dude. You let this untouchable do that to you? I know he likes dark meat, but this is going too far." He spoke a clipped California dialect with an aggressive emphasis.

"I'm not an untouchable," Vishal said. "My family is Brahman. In India, I'm in the ruling class—"

Ray Ray cut him off with a silvery little stage laugh. "He loves telling strangers tales of being India's elite. But his mother came from a Calcutta gutter, and God only knows who his real father was."

Vishal balled his hands into fists, but Ray Ray only laughed harder. "He thinks he can kick my ass. That's the way he keeps his ego puffed up. But he can't, and that keeps him from growing too proud. Unclench your fist, homie," he said contemptuously, "and next time you brag about being a Brahman, be sure nobody knows you."

Matt Reece cocked his head to one side. "You one of those guys who cuts everyone else off at the knees to make you look taller? He does no harm by being a Brahman."

"It's a lie, like your skin color. If you believe that one, he'll tell another, and another. In a week, he'll try to convince you that his grandfather built the Taj Mahal. He's a tattoo artist, a damn good one. But he's no maharajah."

Matt Reece seized Vishal's hand. "He has aristocratic manners, and there's something else. He seems… gallant. If he says his family built the Taj Mahal or even the Eiffel Tower, I'll believe him. I'm not sure how I know, but I know he is, Brahman I mean."

Vishal's eyes grew proud. "It's true, Kirby, what you said. I come from noble blood." He drew himself up dramatically.

"Christ," Ray Ray said, "I'm going to vomit."

Vishal laughed and took Ray Ray into a long hug. "Sorry your day sucks, but stop stirring my pot of shit too."

The intimacy they shared in that embrace told Matt Reece they had been lovers and possibly still were.

When Ray Ray pulled away, he said, "Okay, I'm guessing you two need my ride?"

Vishal nodded.

"It will cost you. Tonight is Dining Out. There's diving gear in the trunk."

Vishal nodded again.

"You letting that Wookie—" He pointed at Groucho. "—climb his hairy ass into my ride?"

"Unless you keep him here with you? How about it?" Vishal said.

"Only if he can moonwalk."

RAY RAY'S car—a '64 avocado-green Volkswagen Beetle—very handsome, with wine-red upholstery and silver buttons—purred. Matt Reece could tell how much it meant to Ray Ray because Vishal had the jitters about backing out of the parking place.

Groucho curled up in the back seat while Matt Reece rode shotgun. The car had the bouncy, loyal eagerness of a lapdog. It seemed cheerful, and that was a relief after such a shit morning. It seemed the perfect car to escape his life and explore the city.

They zipped through neighborhoods of Victorian homes, with seemingly millions of people on the streets, all dressed in colorful outfits and all scurrying to some important destination. Sidewalk cafés were packed. Traffic clogged the streets. Every one and every thing seemed to scream, "Look at me! For God sakes, look at me!" and Matt Reece did look. He took it all in. They rode an onramp onto the Bay Bridge, rewarding Matt Reece with an elevated view of the city. It was mind-blowing. Nothing in his life prepared him for the grandeur of it. Beautiful and terrifying.

"So what did you think of Ray Ray? He's cool, right?"

"Well, he certainly isn't warm."

"Hey," Vishal said, "can the trash talk. Nobody disses Ray Ray but me."

"Sorry. I just don't understand how two men so different can be best friends."

"You don't know him. He reads e.e. cummings, likes bodysurfing, is studying to be a marine biologist to help save the planet, and went door to door to get out the Obama vote both elections." He paused for effect. "On the other hand, you have to be careful with him because he never forgets an injustice, and by nature he is anything but forgiving."

"Okay, okay, I believe you. But I hope you don't mind if I like you better than him."

Vishal reached over and cuffed the back of Matt Reece's neck.

"So, you two were lovers?" Matt Reece asked.

"What gave you that idea?"

"That hug. It seemed pretty… I don't know."

"Ray Ray's straight and married. And she's not just any frumpy woman, but a high-maintenance, ball-crushing she-devil. He spends most of his time clerking in a clothing store, raising money to keep her happy—which is damned near impossible. It's sad."

"Sad because he'd rather be dancing for tips?"

"I can't help but feel how ignoble marriage usually is for creative people. It drags down and shackles and degrades a man like Ray Ray, who is sweet and bright and full of potential. Trapped in that squalid little shop every day, and the deadly social pattern imposed on him—of dragging his unappreciative woman everywhere he goes for the next forty years. Not to mention the kids. It's a miserable compromise, and after time he'll be apt to punish her for having blackmailed him into it."

"You're down on relationships?"

"With the right man, it's not a prison. Gay men, at least the younger ones, are not into all those material possessions, and kids, and living in the right neighborhoods, and all the keep-up-with-the-Jones's shit that women bring to the plate. Gay men are all about adventure, freedom, advancing the social situation, traveling the world."

"Yeah, well, I think you're shortchanging women. Things are different for everyone these days."

"Wow, who knew you were so PC?"

"PC?"

"Never mind."

Matt Reece asked, "So what did Ray Ray mean by having diving gear in the trunk? If we're going deep-sea fishing, I should tell you I can't swim."

"He's the founder of Food Not Bombs. It's an organization that scrounges up food and twice a week cooks a meal on the streets to feed people in need. That's how I met him. I volunteered to help, and we hit it off."

"You work at a soup kitchen?"

"It's nothing so formal. It's against the law, but the cops let it slide as long as we keep it small—strictly a sidewalk affair. But we feed a few hundred people every week."

"That doesn't explain the diving gear."

"You'll see."

They pulled off the freeway and drove along University Avenue. Berkeley is located across the bay from San Francisco, but Matt Reece could see that they were worlds apart. The buildings were low, two or three stories, and the people all seemed to be in their early twenties.

When they reached the UC Berkeley campus, they abandoned the VW at a parking spot and set out on foot.

Along the sidewalks strolled the most beautiful girls Matt Reece ever saw, ridiculously underdressed, scowling, and accompanied by peacocking men who were equally underdressed in tank tops and shorts or skintight jeans and black T-shirts and sandals, also scowling. They seemed hostile. Something had the campus in an uproar.

Matt Reece kept his hood on and his head lowered in order to hide his face. Groucho went crazy with the different smells along the crowded sidewalks, so Matt Reece held him on a short leash and hurried him along.

He pulled to a halt, however, when he glanced up to see a blond-haired student racing toward him on a skateboard. The guy's skin was dyed lime green, and he wore a red tank top with black letters across the chest that read:

I'm

Matt Reece

Connors!

Matt Reece's jaw dropped as the skateboarder whooshed past them. He and Vishal stared at each other, both speechless. Vishal finally said, "Cowboy, this is Berkeley." As if no further explanation was necessary, he turned and began walking again. Matt Reece followed, tugging Groucho along, still unable to voice his shock.

Matt Reece pulled an address out of his wallet. An hour later, they found Patrick's fraternity house. Matt Reece rang the bell, and a heavyset African-American woman opened the door. He asked to see his brother.

"He owes you money too?"

Matt Reece shook his head. "He's family."

"Humph, some family!" She told the boys that she was the housemaid, and she hadn't seen Patrick in over two months, maybe three.

"Any idea where we can find him?" he asked.

She lowered her voice. "I don't like to gossip, but I heard he dropped out of school, and some girl is supporting his sorry ass. I see him on campus, but he's a moving target."

"Thanks for your help," Vishal said.

"If you find him, you remind him that he still owes Shelly fifty bucks."

"We'll do that," Vishal said, as he took Matt Reece by the arm and led him away.

For lack of a better plan, they wandered the campus, orbiting the student union, hoping they would stumble onto Patrick.

They found protesters at the center of campus, divided into several groups. One crowd held signs supporting the abolishment of weapons, and another protested the religions that were bent on assassinating Kenji. One block of protesters supported the right to bear arms. Religious groups were protesting human efforts to alter God's plan. Each faction had their own take on the issue of longer life vs. gun rights. The protesters were peaceful, but several hundred visor-clad riot police officers and National Guard troops, rifles and shields at the ready, were trying to herd the protesters away from each other. They used the threat of violence to quell the tensions, which of course, only spurred emotions to more perilous levels. There seemed to be two guardsmen for every protester, and three reporters with cameras rolling for every guardsman.

The masters of this situation, as far as Matt Reece could tell, were not the police, nor the students protesting for or against religious issues, and certainly not the men who were demanding to keep their weapons. The real masters were an ensemble of women—young female students, middle-aged mothers, grandmothers—who were being drowned out by angry voices, but they were clearly the best organized and dead set on the idea of ridding the world of firearms. Some held signs with pictures of their sons and daughters in military uniforms, with captions saying Bring My Child Home for Good. Others held signs saying Stop The Bloodshed and Trade Your Guns For The Children. They held up infants smeared with red paint for the cameras as a statement that needed no words. Somebody began to sing "We Shall Overcome," and all the women joined in. Even women who marched with other groups came running to add their voices. And with the media cameras trained on them, the guardsmen slunk past, avoiding anything that might look like a confrontation.

The more Matt Reece saw, the more he grasped that most protesters tended to act with the calm forethought of a beheaded turkey. But these women marchers held themselves with a dignified resolve.

Mothers, God bless them.

But soon the mood turned hostile. Guardsmen brandished their rifles, ordering everyone back. Arrests were made. Some guardsmen became rattled and made as if to shoot. Then a line of armored trucks appeared and trained their machine guns at the different crowds, causing a stampede to the other side of the campus that carried Matt Reece and Vishal with it. There the protesters reorganized into the same groups.

After three hours of walking, all they found was five more green-skinned students, each wearing the same tank top announcing that they were Matt Reece Connors.

Matt Reece and Vishal sat at a sidewalk café where protesters bent their heads over marble tables, speaking in excited voices. Matt Reece couldn't help but wonder how many of them would be arrested—if not this week, then surely the next.

"So," Vishal said, "you a regular coffee drinker, or should we order a low-fat half-caf caramel frappuccino with a twist and who the hell knows what else?"

"Frappuccino? Is that some kind of Italian tropical punch?"

Matt Reece wasn't in the mood for coffee, so they ordered iced teas, burgers, and fries. They sat by the open doorway, close enough for Matt Reece to appreciate the aromas wafting from inside—a mixture of incense, frying bacon, and buns toasting.

Vishal talked about his uncle. Long ago, before G.W. Bush ruined the economy, Vishal's family was comparatively well off. His father and uncle would fly back to Mumbai every year to visit family. Vishal accompanied them and grew up loving those adventures. They had a manager to work the head shop, another person to run the hotel, and a maid to cook and clean for them. Since the Bush recession, Vishal and his uncle ran the businesses themselves, and now it all fell on Vishal's shoulders.

Matt Reece only half listened. The other half of his mind kept an eye out at the passersby, praying Patrick would be among them.

"Now, with Mamaji getting weaker, I've got to take care of him as well," Vishal said. "Some days he never leaves his bed. Not so many years ago I was in school, hung out with friends, traveled, and then it all turned to shit."

Matt Reece was about to share his own experience of caring for Blake when he spotted another green-skinned student sporting the same tank top. Vishal asked, "Do you want me to keep calling you Kirby, or can I call you Matt Reece?"

"Matt Reece doesn't exist anymore. He went MIA when the world turned upside down. But what the hell is going on? Why paint themselves green?"

"You're a cult hero, cowboy. This time next week, thousands of kids across the world will be green. I'll bet there's already YouTube videos of green kids doing all kinds of weird shit. Who knew we didn't have to dye your skin. All we had to do was buy a tank top." He laughed so hard he leaned over gulping for air.

"Cult hero? It makes no sense." The label was not something he could handle just now, being so far afield of his own sense of himself, the narrative he had fashioned that allowed him to function—a confused kid with humble ambitions, former cowboy who now lived moment to moment, searching for a lifeline to save him from this shitstorm.

"Face it, cowboy, you've got what everyone wants."

The waiter deposited two glasses of iced tea and packets of sweetener on the table. As he walked away, Matt Reece noticed a television on the wall inside the café. It showed a panel of "experts," and behind them was a photograph of him—a head shot at age fourteen dressed in a snap-button shirt and Stetson. The panel participants all talked at once, speculating on why an innocuous youth might run off with a deranged killer. One woman said, "Even though Kenji offered the boy immortality, they both have a mark of death on their brows." By then, Matt Reece and Vishal were listening intently. The panel agreed that Matt Reece was with Kenji for immortality, even, perhaps, for sex, and—in the opinion of one "psychologist" who felt able to judge Matt Reece without ever having met him—because certain kinds of teens were turned on by the thrill of danger.

"The world's gone crazy," Matt Reece whispered. He felt a sense of shame, however subdued, yet he knew he was guilty of nothing.

Vishal said, "The media provides a relentless feeding frenzy. Americans are gluttons, and gossip and half-truths are our snack food. Our demand for empty-caloric titillation never diminishes. It arrives in a different wrapping each new day. People don't care who they hurt as long as they can keep their face in the trough.

"Last year, before I was burned," Vishal continued, "I was plowing through Churchill's six volumes on World War II. What I found most interesting was that Churchill called the Versailles Treaty, the product of the combined intelligence of all the top politicians of Europe, 'a sad and complicated idiocy.' From what we've seen today, I think that description can extend to all human politics."

The broadcast made it clear how divided America was on these issues, and the debate that started in the US Senate had spilled onto the universities and onto the streets. The only certainty, Matt Reece thought, was that the country was caught in moral confusion.

Matt Reece looked away, turning his attention back on the crowd swarming by. He moved his eyes from one face to another, noting each set of features. He knew finding his brother was hopeless, but suddenly something vaguely familiar caught his attention. It felt like no more than an itch at the top of his head. That itch, abruptly and without warning, grew. He'd learned to trust his instincts, and right then, they told him that Patrick was nearby. Groucho jumped to his feet, and Matt Reece grabbed the leash to keep him from dashing off. He stood, scanning the faces with more determination.

For an instant there was no sound. The TV stopped broadcasting, and the people stopped burbling. It seemed like just after a conductor taps on his music stand, raises his arms, and holds them poised.

His eyes settled on a man whizzing toward him on a skateboard. For some reason, that man's presence struck him, but there was no recognition. The man's hair was platinum blond and stuck out at rakish angles. The dirt on his clothes seemed old enough to have geological significance. He had a worn, abraded look as if he had lain exposed to the weather for ages. He was Patrick's age but looked to be a vagrant. Spirit-trappings, second sight, ghost stories, etc., never interested Matt Reece, but there was no denying the surety of this supernatural connection. It had to be Patrick. Every feeling pushing up from Matt Reece's gut told him so.

He kept his eyes on the skateboarder. Patrick had always been unclassifiable, as remote and clear as mountain water and as elusive as its color. The skateboarder weaved through the crowd until he smacked into a man wearing a suit and tie and carrying a briefcase. They both tumbled to the ground. The skateboarder helped the man to his feet before taking off again in a hurry. The suit-and-tie man screamed, "My wallet! Hey, you, stop!" and he ran after the skateboarder.

Matt Reece was so shocked he loosened his grip on the leash holding Groucho. The dog leaped away and raced up the street, close on the heels of the skateboarder. Before Matt Reece could react, they had vanished.

On the ranch, Matt Reece and Patrick had been more than brothers. They had been pals forever. They had tied bandannas across their foreheads—Big Warrior and Little Brave. He remembered that more clearly than anything in his young life. Those days riding into the foothills, the two of them, fly-fishing the Promesa Rota, nights at the campfire frying up trout and telling stories under the Nevada sky. He remembered all of it. Swimming races, bareback riding steers, hunting rabbits. A friendship like that makes everything more intense. You share the same food, same blood; you give it together and take it together, no matter what "it" may be. Pals forever. But now Patrick was a petty thief.

"What the fuck?" Vishal said.

In a voice that seemed to arise out of a deep well, Matt Reece said, "I saw Patrick pick that man's pocket and dash away. Groucho recognized him too and ran after him."

"Great, now we know he's here and what he looks like."

"He's a pickpocket. I saw it with my own eyes."

Vishal sat unsmiling. "Are you qualified to throw stones? Don't judge people by what they do. If you judge them at all, it must be by what they are."

At first Matt Reece didn't understand the difference. It seemed pretty evident that one dictated the other. But he nodded vaguely, because that was what he had experienced while listening to that panel discussion on TV. On the evidence, both he and Patrick were outlaws, outcasts, and perilously short on luck—but the evidence didn't tell the whole story. Patrick had qualities that couldn't be expunged.

"Let's run after him," Vishal said. "If he's this close, maybe we'll find him."

Matt Reece stood stunned, his mind enveloped in fog. Was Patrick a petty thief or a man who could help him? Both? Neither? Maybe Patrick needed more help than himself. Pals forever, or an anchor that would drag him further down? He could find no satisfying solution to this puzzle. It had the fascination of an enduring mathematical riddle, like squaring a circle.

By the time Matt Reece wrapped his head around what had happened, it seemed too late to chase down Groucho. He was easily miles away by then, and he held no hope of finding his friend. And by that time, he didn't have the heart to even try. He shook his head. "He's gone." He meant gone forever, and he was not quite sure if he were talking about Patrick or Groucho. "Let's go home."

Chapter Seventeen

It seemed an agonizing drive across the Bay Bridge and into the city. This time the view of crowded skyscrapers did nothing to excite him. The city seemed to contract, to diminish to a dot, scarcely larger than any other speck on the enormous map of the earth. While riding through the streets teeming with people, Matt Reece saw only buildings bunched up against each other, like bones connecting to form a skeleton, a fragile frame sharp with the ache of grinding girders of railway lines and ironwork bridges and discordant clusters of hotels, bars, cinemas, restaurants, and shops. He felt that ache in his own skeleton. And the masses of people, swinging like monkeys from one bone to the next, made it easy to see what America's faithful worshipped; they all knelt at the altar in the Church of the Immaculate Consumption. Now that his only lifeline was severed, the city's sparkling nucleus turned into a sham diamond, glittering in the shabby twilight, giving only the illusion of warmth. It seemed cold and cruel and wounded.

He assumed they would drive to Golden Gate Park to return Ray Ray's VW, but Vishal pulled onto a side street and swung into a dumpster-lined alley between Gerry and Clement Street. He parked the car and climbed out, waving for Matt Reece to join him.

"What gives?" Matt Reece asked as he unfolded from the passenger seat.

Vishal opened the storage trunk and pulled out gloves, surgical masks, and a plastic hamper. He handed a set of gloves and a mask to Matt Reece.

"It's Dining Out night, remember? The buildings on both sides of the alley are the backs of restaurants and grocery stores. We'll gather the good stuff they threw out."

"Do you take all your first dates dumpster diving? Maybe Ray Ray was right."

"Matt Reece!"

He smiled. "Sorry, but you're so fun to tease."

"Laugh it up, cowboy. It's only my feelings you're crushing."

"Why do they trash good stuff?"

Vishal waved an arm. "Follow me and learn, cowboy."

They walked to the nearest dumpster while donning their masks and gloves. Vishal handed Matt Reece the hamper and pulled back the lid. A fly swarm rose up as a stench hit Matt Reece, backing him up a step or two.

Vishal took stock of the contents, sifting through the upper layers. "Bingo," he said. He lifted five bunches of slightly bruised bananas and placed them in the hamper. "This store can't sell these because of the brown spots on the peels, but they're firm, which means the fruit is still good." He dug deeper and found a case of lettuce. "The outer leaves are moldy, but the inner leaves are ripe and crisp, but if the store snips off the outer leaves, the heads look small and shoppers won't buy them. It's a sad fact in this fucked-up country that millions of people are undernourished, yet we trash 40 percent of the food we produce. 40 percent! And most of that is perfectly edible."

They worked down the line of dumpsters, filling the hamper. Luckily, the VW had a second hamper in the trunk, and they filled that too. It was all vegetables. Vishal explained that meats and dairy products were too risky. Next, they swung by a food bank to pick up sacks of flour, sugar, and ground coffee.

They drove to a volunteer center, where Ray Ray helped carry the food into the kitchen. He wore an enormous black T-shirt with lettering across the front spelling out "Fabulous Bitch."

"Did you leave that Wookie in Berkeley?" Ray Ray asked.

"He was so embarrassed about riding in your car, he made a dash for freedom as soon as we opened the door," Vishal said. "He's now hanging with some homeless dude."

Ray Ray nodded. "He's better off. The homeless dude is probably a real Brahmin."

Vishal stood toe to toe with Ray Ray, a hamper between them. "Look, skinny, Matt Reece's feeling bad enough without your sarcasm. So zip it for once in your life."

Ray Ray lifted his hands like Vishal was holding a gun on him. "Hey, just trying to lighten the mood. You started it."

Volunteers dug into the hampers and got down to work. Matt Reece cleaned and chopped vegetables, tossing them into a twenty-gallon pot of stock to make soup. Vishal took charge of baking banana bread. Matt Reece kept his hoody and sunglasses on. Nobody asked why, but they stared. The irony was that one of the other volunteers had dyed his skin green and wore that same tank top stating he was Matt Reece Connors.

Two hours later, he helped set up tables on the sidewalk out front and carried pots and dishes and paper plates and plastic utensils to the tables.

A line of people formed. Matt Reece ladled out paper cups of soup. There was also green salad, boiled potatoes, banana bread, coffee, and peach pudding for dessert.

It didn't seem like much of a feast in Matt Reece's estimation, but the gratitude in the people's eyes was unmistakable. Adults and children seemed at the end of their rope, struggling to stay alive another week. Having lost everything, they were reduced to a pure human spirit, without trappings or pretenses. It made Matt Reece feel embarrassed by his earlier mood of seeing this city as a sham. There were plenty of quality people here. He saw them in every pair of needy eyes.

Vishal stood beside him, dishing out pudding. As they worked, Vishal talked about homelessness, society's safety net, and disillusionment. "Achievement and possessions are only dust," he said. "When gale-force winds blow that away, this is what's left." He nodded to the people coming through the line.

Those haunted eyes had a profound effect on Matt Reece, and so did Vishal. He watched Vishal's profile as he serenely served each person. The man was a giver, donating his time to help him find Patrick, his energy to sift through garbage bins to feed the needy, and freely sharing his wisdom. Matt Reece was seeing a dance of the seven veils dropping one by one from a fragile soul, and what he now beheld was a glimpse of what lies behind that scarred facade, that vitality existing in the vast spirit of nature.

One man came back for seconds. "Young man," he said, "your soup sure hits the spot. Every bite takes me home."

As Matt Reece refilled the man's cup, tears sprung to his eyes. He saw himself standing there holding out a cup, having lost everything—home, family, dignity, hope—and finding something consequential in the taste of something thrown away. Yes, like Vishal, there was nothing separating him from this weather-beaten soul. They were all, he thought, like vegetables in the dumpsters, tossed out because the peel was bruised but still firm and perfectly ripe and beautiful at their cores. It could make anyone weep.

He felt grateful to be here with Vishal, and he began to hope for a lifetime of nights like this, stretching into the future like a beautiful highway through time.

THEY WERE walking through neighborhoods on their way back to Vishal's shop. There were many restaurants and bars still open and full of people. It was a beautiful night with a bright moon illuminating the sidewalks, making the city seem enchanting. Matt Reece felt a light breeze on his face, as light as a feather tip gliding across one's lips, and he also felt a beautiful glow in his chest. Vishal reached out and took his hand. Vishal's hand was firm and strong, their fingers locked and their wrists nailed together where they crossed. All the other sensations of that night faded, and he felt only the touch of their fingers and palms and wrists alone. And that feeling was so intensified, made so urgent, so aching and so strong by the solid pressure of their fingers and pressed palms that it created a current that moved up his arm and spread from crown to soles with a burning sizzle of wanting.

And then Vishal pulled him to a stop, pressed the lengths of their bodies together, bent his head, and kissed him. He felt Vishal trembling as they kissed. He encircled Vishal's waist with his arms. He pulled his head back and dropped his chin, and then kissed the soft part of Vishal's disfigured neck, and that's when he realized he was trembling too. Vishal wrapped his arms around him, lifted him off the ground, and spun him in a circle. Vishal pressed his lips to his throat as his feet found the pavement again.

Matt Reece felt, more than heard, a moan coming up from his chest, and Vishal lifted his head and they kissed again, this time with a bit more roughness, a bit more urgency. Time stood absolutely still, and he felt the earth shudder under him.

Vishal pulled away, and he brought his hand up to caress Matt Reece's cheek. "Thank you for tonight. You were great with those people."

"The night's not over yet. Maybe there's more to come."

Vishal laughed, and Matt Reece saw his teeth sparkling in the moonlight. Vishal locked his hand with his again, and they kept walking in the same direction.

It was nearly midnight when they entered the head shop to find Kenji standing at the counter, still dressed as a priest, shaking hands with Vishal's uncle.

Kenji turned to face them. "Nice dye job. It took me a moment to recognize you."

Matt Reece glared at him, wondering if he should run for it.

Kenji glanced at the uncle. "Seems our boys were playing hard. They look done in."

"The young are the young are the young," said the uncle. "They foolishly play until nothing is left, and then they sleep like the dead. Us older men, thank goodness, are wiser and save our strength for the long haul."

"The passport only took a few hours," Kenji said to Matt Reece. "It's amazing how this new software works. We're moving up our departure time." He handed Matt Reece a blue-bound booklet with golden embossing.

Matt Reece opened it to the picture page and saw Kirby Cain from Saskatchewan staring back at him. He felt the last of his past slip away.

Vishal's uncle held up a set of keys and a stack of hundred-dollar bills. His voice shook with emotion. "Look, Vishal, in exchange for our silence, Mr. Toranaga is giving us his Prius and ten thousand dollars. I have the bill of sale for the car in my pocket."

"I'm not going anywhere," Matt Reece said. "We're done."

"We're a team, son. You can't cut and run anytime you feel threatened."

"You and Consuela were a team, and look what you did to her."

"Son, people want to kill us. There is nowhere you'll be safe, except with me. Where I'm taking you, we'll be sheltered for as long as it takes to de-arm the world."

"And just where is that?"

"I can't risk telling you until we get there. But know this: you can't go home."

Home, the ranch, was the only place Matt Reece truly wanted to go, back to that quiet, lonely life where he was once sheltered from a crazy world. And the thing that became evident was that Kenji made no attempt to deny the allegation of Consuela's murder.

"He's staying with me," Vishal said in a voice that filled the room with a tone of challenge. He draped an arm across Matt Reece's shoulders, pulling him closer.

Vishal's laying claim on him, when he felt most adrift, became intoxicating.

"I see," Kenji said. He bowed his head toward Matt Reece, coldly, like an enemy. The shock of Vishal's claim on him was compounded by Kenji's calm reaction to losing what Kenji considered his property. The subject seemed exhausted, and nobody spoke for over a minute. They stood like mannequins, no one making a move.

"Do I still get to keep the car?" the uncle finally asked.

"I'm prepared to offer you something of greater value," Kenji said, "if you both come with me tomorrow. You can be lovers. Let it never be said that I stood in the way of passionate love, even if it's only a day old. Actually, I'm a sucker for love at first sight. It happened to me once, with Jessup."

"Don't trust him," Matt Reece said.

"I don't need anything you can offer," Vishal said.

"Help me de-arm the world. What could be more important than that?" When neither Vishal nor Matt Reece took the bait, he said, "My treatment doesn't simply make one live for thousands of years. It generates new cells at an astronomical rate, and that includes skin cells. With one wave of my magic wand, I can remove your scars and make you normal again. Skin is the quickest organ to replace."

"He's beautiful the way he is," Matt Reece said.

Vishal only stared, unable to answer. Kenji had found the right button to press.

"Will it turn me green?"

"By the time we get to our destination, you'll look as you did before the fire. Come, both of you. You can be lovers, and I'll be your guardian angel."

"Why?" Vishal murmured. "Why do you need us?"

"Aren't you lucky, you stupid complaining thing?" the uncle said. "He's offering you a *dharma*. But I suppose you would prefer to someday take over this shop, inking pictures on the skin of people who are all show, condemned to die slowly of 'security'?"

"I'll do more than make you beautiful," Kenji said, "I'll cure your uncle's ischemic heart disease and make him young again. Don't take too long to decide. At his late stage, he could die any minute."

Vishal shot his uncle a questioning stare. The old man looked away.

Matt Reece didn't wait for Vishal to answer. Vishal's expression showed Kenji had outmaneuvered him, and this likely was a pattern that would repeat itself for as long as he stayed with Kenji. His choice now was go it alone or stick with Kenji in order to keep Vishal. He took Vishal's hand and led him upstairs to his apartment. As they entered the living room, he made a beeline to the black bag and pulled the tricorder from the side pocket. He steered Vishal into the bedroom and flicked on the lights.

He glanced at the unfortunate furnishings: a waterbed, a low chest of drawers that functioned as a bedside table, lamps with muted lighting, and a chair set by the window.

He led Vishal to the bed, telling him to undress and lie on his back. He knew that wasn't necessary, but he wanted to see him naked, and he hoped they would make love once they completed the treatment.

While Vishal disrobed, Matt Reece moved to the window and peeped through the curtains. Some of the shops below glowed yellow from the streetlights. Matt Reece opened the window. On the sidewalks, young men and middle-aged women walked, whistling at cars. Occasionally, one would wave at a driver and say, "Hey, baby, looking for company?" They seemed desperately lonely. Were they only after money, or did they need companionship to keep the demons away for a few precious hours? Matt Reece could feel that loneliness swelling in his gut, reminding him that he was far from home. But then he turned and saw Vishal lying before him on the bed, naked, waiting.

Matt Reece cried out, "My God!"

Nearly all of Vishal's body held the same nasty scars as his face—horror in its most absolute ugliness, surpassing all understanding. Only that one side of Vishal's face was strangely spared from the devastation. The thought of how much agony he must have endured, and might still endure, caused a deep sadness to wash over Matt Reece. He stared, shocked, while Vishal lay with eyes closed, mouth open, and features calm, as though placidly waiting for the Rapture.

He sat beside Vishal and ran his hand over the top of his head. He had wanted to do that all day, and now he did it. He felt his throat swelling. Vishal moved his head under his hand and smiled up at him. He swept his hand through the silky roughness of Vishal's hair, felt it rippling between his fingers, and then he dropped his hand to caress that disfigured cheek.

Matt Reece turned on the tricorder and waved it over Vishal's body. He felt grateful that he was able to do this for him. If nothing else good came of this nightmare, at least he was able to cure his new love, make him beautiful again. And if he could do this for Vishal, perhaps he could do it for hundreds, or thousands, or millions like him.

He had used the word love, and he knew it was true in its full meaning.

I'll make love to this beautiful soul, we'll go out and find an all-night diner for a bite to eat while Kenji cures the old man, and we'll come back here and spend the night in each other's arms. At sunrise, I'll decide whether to go it alone or stay with Vishal, who will no doubt follow Kenji.

Chapter Eighteen

In Jessup's opinion, the dean of Berkeley's political science department, Professor Terrence Wallace, looked more like the student protesters on campus and less like any university professor he could imagine. With his lean physique, tousled sun-streaked hair, and expensive clothes that were designed to appear grungy, he looked like a living Abercrombie & Fitch ad. Jessup sized him up as a privileged kid, albeit gifted, with far more money than was healthy. His manner was almost boyish, but he possessed the cool carelessness of a man of far greater age and experience.

"Yes," Wallace said, "what happened to Patrick was appalling. Such a gifted intellect."

Jessup and Blake sat across a desk from Wallace in a choky office that had no windows. In that stifling space, he noticed the faint odor of marijuana. He scheduled an appointment with Wallace because Patrick mentioned him often and considered the man a mentor.

"Appalling?" Blake asked.

"He gave me hope. While he attended my classes, he showed up prepared, got involved, and leaned into every lecture. He pushed back when he thought I was being wishy-washy and went for the jugular in every debate. He has an extraordinary mind and also a plethora of internal demons. He was working on a term paper that stemmed from one of my class discussions on why Bush and Cheney goaded our nation into the Iraq war. You see, every one of my students knew the White House lied, and everyone but Patrick was convinced the hidden reason was acquiring cheap oil. Only Patrick, and I believe him wholly, claimed the only reason for that war was so the Republicans could bleed trillions of dollars from the American middle-class taxpayers and funnel that money into the pockets of the defense industry shareholders. Ten years of war and killing and honoring our dead was all done to make the rich richer and the poor flat broke. That's why they strung it out for so long. They didn't want to win. They wanted to keep milking the cash cow for as long as the ignorant voters would allow."

"Ignorant?" Blake echoed.

"Sorry, I should have said 'patriotic.'"

"That's rather appalling, if it's true, but how does that apply to Patrick?" Jessup said.

"Oh it's true. Patrick proved it with his paper. Trouble was, in doing his research, he somehow gained access to some incriminating documents. And the more he dug, the more he realized that it wasn't just the Republicans at blame. They were all in on it, and all getting their piece of the pie, Republicans and Democrats alike. And not just the DC Beltway crowd, many state officials as well."

"That couldn't have been too surprising," Jessup said.

"It was to Patrick, who had his sights set on a political career. He thought he could make a difference until he realized the deck was stacked against him, against anyone with integrity, no matter which way he jumped. He's a passionate soul, and when he uncovered the truth about our political system, that everything is controlled by a handful of corporations, it crushed him. He's that kind of kid. His off hours were spent doing outreach in a clinic to stop child abuse. Patrick harbored Don Quixote-like dreams."

"Crushed?" Blake said.

"He knew then that the only ethical thing to do was revolution, the kind where you hang all the politicians, the lobbyists, and the corporate board members from the nearest trees and start from scratch. I believe that's what he's trying to organize now."

"Impossible. He could never plot to overthrow the government," Blake said.

"Mr. Connors," Wallace said, "the corruption in our government is so blatant now that our politicians don't even pretend to be ethical. So much for peer oversight. How can democracy work when they've all sold out? Or should I say, souled out? Patrick's work proved that. I tell you his paper is Pulitzer Prize–winning material."

"Shit," Jessup muttered.

"It gets worse," Wallace said. "Those incriminating documents I mentioned? They were classified, and he posted them on WikiLeaks to back up his dissertation. Now he's under investigation by Homeland Security."

Jessup stood. "You're not telling me what I came for. I need to find him, Professor."

"How do I know you're not working with the FBI or Homeland Security?"

"As a matter of fact, Professor, the FBI has me under investigation as well. They might even be listening to this conversation."

"To understand where he's hiding," Wallace said, "I'll have to tell you about Patrick's negative side."

"Plotting a revolution is his optimistic side?"

Wallace rose and laid a hand, soft with apology, upon Jessup's shirtsleeve. "Once he dropped out, he became dissolute and undependable. He drinks and takes hard drugs, keeping himself in a romantic haze. He looks so innocent, so needy, that all the girls line up to mother him. From what I've heard, he takes advantage of anyone who helps him."

Jessup clenched his teeth.

"While they comfort him, he seduces them and spends their money on drugs until they wise up and throw him out." Wallace drew a sorrowful breath. "Patrick is a man who brings both happiness and pain to everyone in his orbit. He lies, steals, cheats, and imposes on kindnesses, leaving only a bitter taste in his wake. Everyone loves him, excuses his faults, and protects him. Men admire him; women pity him. Around campus, he's become a bit of a cult hero."

"Where can I find him?"

"It would be unethical for me to reveal his whereabouts."

Blake stood, leaned over the desk, and grabbed Wallace by the shirt collar. "More unethical than me dragging your skinny ass over this desk and putting a serious hurt on you? You gonna whine to the nurse through your wired jaw about what's ethical?"

"You touch me and I'll have you arrested."

"Right, but that'll be after I smash your mouth so that you'll chew with shards of pain for the rest of your miserable life."

Wallace tried to step back, but Blake held him. "There's a girl." He would not say her name aloud, but he wrote it on a slip of scratch paper.

JESSUP AND Blake left Wallace's office with a name—Julie Summers—and an address of an apartment across campus. As they neared the apartment complex, they saw a man in a shabby, gray overcoat beating a stout woman in a Russian blouse and long dark skirt. She was crouched by some garbage bins while the man cuffed her face, arms, and shoulders. She tried to protect her head with her arms, not crying, just covering up like a boxer in trouble. He beat her hard, swinging his fist furiously.

Blake rushed to her aid, grabbing the pale, anorexic man from behind, pulling him away from her, and holding him captive. The man wore faded jeans, a torn tank top under an overcoat, and cowboy boots. The bleached-blond hair on his head and face were as short as a thirty-second fuse. He looked like a stray mongrel on the verge of starvation. As the man turned, behind his pierced eyebrows and a hummingbird tattoo on his neck, Jessup recognized his son, Patrick.

There was no mistaking those gemstone eyes—a tiger's eyes that gave Jessup the impression he should have been more prepared, although prepared for what he couldn't say—eyes identical to his own. Yet those eyes, which had always shined, were now as dull and arid as desert dust.

They glared at each other, both recovering from the shock.

"Dad, what happened to your face? You look like something the cat refused to bury."

The woman leaped up and launched a counterattack. She battered Patrick about the face with her fists until Jessup grabbed her and shoved her away. She stumbled, and from the ground, she turned on him with fire in her eyes, a fire that matched the fury in Patrick.

"Don't touch me," she shrieked.

"What the hell is going on?" Jessup said, noticing for the first time how pretty her face was, this red-cheeked girl of twenty or so.

"She's a murderer," Patrick hissed. "I'll fucking kill her." He tried to break away from Blake but only thrashed in vain.

"Like you even care about me?" she said, her voice noticeably calmer. "What about my life, my career?"

"That's right, you self-centered cunt, it's all about you. You didn't give a shit about the life you carried."

"Like you give a fuck about anything but that needle in your arm." She jumped to her feet, and she came off the ground holding a splintered piece of wood that had been lying beside the trash cans. She charged Patrick, bashing him across the face before Jessup could stop her. Jessup pulled her away and stood between them. She turned and fled.

"I'd have given up the needle," he yelled to her retreating backside. "I could have changed, if only…," he said to himself in a softer tone.

Patrick's forehead was red, and a gash, diagonal to his eyebrow, oozed blood.

"You're bleeding," Jessup said. "It might need stitches."

Patrick swiped a hand over the cut, smearing blood across his forehead. "I ain't seeing no fuckin' doctor." Blake released him. He spun around ready to attack but stopped cold. "Grandpa? Christ, is it really you?"

"Same ol', just a little green around the gills." Blake pulled a handkerchief from his pocket and pressed it over Patrick's eyebrow. "Hold this to stop the bleeding."

Patrick held the handkerchief. "Then it really was Groucho who followed me home?"

Jessup yanked Patrick to within a foot of his face. "You found Groucho?"

"I didn't know it was him, because he's so young, but he wouldn't leave me. He's in my… Julie's apartment now."

Jessup released him. "That means they're here, nearby."

Blake nodded.

ON THE walk to Julie's apartment, Jessup told Patrick all that happened since the morning Kenji and Matt Reece disappeared. Patrick trembled all over. Jessup assumed it was partly from the loss of his child and partly from seeing his grandfather rejuvenated as proof of this wildass tale. As they approached the apartment, Patrick didn't bother with a key. He simply lifted a foot and smashed the door. The rickety thing flew open, taking a chunk of the doorframe with it.

Jessup and Blake exchanged a glance but said nothing.

Groucho raced out the doorway and danced between Jessup and Blake. Jessup bent to one knee and gave the dog a hug. His hopes of finding Matt Reece ballooned. They were close by, within his reach, if only….

They barged into a studio apartment. The décor was of clean, light-colored birch furniture, shelves of books in multiple languages, a seventy-inch flat-screen TV above the bookshelves, and a platform bed along one wall. Opposite the bed lay a kitchen area and a tiny bathroom. Abstract paintings added color—mostly yellows and reds—to the white walls, and more paintings stacked against a wall near the bed convinced Jessup that Julie was an artist.

The largest painting hung over the bed, impressive with its size and blend of colors, bloodred and mustard-yellow blocks framed in charcoal gray. Being abstract, it allowed Jessup to see whatever was pressing on his mind, and right then, while he focused on the lower corner where bloodred blended with charcoal, he saw his son beating a woman who had come from aborting his child. A sour taste rose up his throat, and he swallowed it down. His shame was directed at his son, and a good measure directed at himself, although he couldn't explain why.

Jessup walked to the bathroom and opened the medicine cabinet. He took a bottle of hydrogen peroxide, a box of cotton swabs, a handful of bandages, and carried them back to his son at the desk. He pulled the handkerchief away. It was soaked red, but the bleeding had slowed to a few thick drops. Jessup soaked a cotton ball with peroxide.

"This will sting."

"Do it already."

Jessup cleaned the gash while Patrick remained stoic. Jessup could tell by the set of Patrick's jaw that anger, not pain, drove his son into a deep, sullen quiet. The boy didn't say another word while Jessup dressed his wound.

Jessup and Blake faced each other across the partner's desk with Groucho sitting at Blake's side. Patrick drew a backpack from a closet and stuffed shirts and jeans into it. When he came across any of Julie's clothing, he yanked them from the hangers and tossed them willy-nilly on the floor.

"What happened to you, son?" Jessup said. "You held so much promise."

"That's the paradox of a star, Dad. The more fuel it begins with, the faster it burns out."

"But why? We sunk sixty grand into your education. You were going to make a difference, remember? You planned to change the world."

"Talking about me is a waste of time. Just tell me what you want."

"Waste of time? Hey, I've got all damn day. You squandered sixty grand of my earnings. I think I can afford an hour for an explanation of where that money went."

"Right, it all comes down to the cash. Thanks, Dad. You should be writing Hallmark cards instead of commercials."

"Let's rise above personal attacks and focus on the why?"

"What I learned about political science is it's all about which corporate fucks you ream to get campaign funds, what lies to tell voters to get elected, and the rest is the psychology behind how much shit constituents will swallow before they notice you're butt-fucking them with the rough end of a pineapple."

"Sixty grand to learn that?" Blake scoffed. "I could have told you that for two bits. That story's been around since they built the pyramids."

Patrick walked to the bookshelves and stuffed books into his pack. He held up one. "Since I dropped out, I've been studying the Greek philosophers, Socrates, Plato, Aristotle. They had their shit together. They knew government was for the benefit of the masses, not the 1 percent. But now, there's too much money involved. Trillions upon trillions, and these politicians are drunk on it, stupid drunk. Every damn one of them. The system is rigged so that you can't get any position until the corporate executives have you by the balls."

Jessup said, "Fine, so the question is, what do you plan to do about it?"

"Get a job, pay my taxes, bend over with my ass in the air, and keep my mouth shut as they ram it home. Just like everyone else."

"For sixty grand, I was hoping for more."

"Sorry to disappoint you. Maybe I'll come back to the ranch. I was happy there."

Jessup nodded. "Those were happy times, but that option isn't available to any of us until we find Kenji. I'd rather you become the first honest politician of your generation, even if you don't get too far."

Jessup studied the changes that had altered his son over the last several months. He still had the same facial features, even if some were covered by a five-day-old beard. His movements were quick and precise, as they had always been. And even with the eyebrow rings and bleached hair and tattoo on his neck, he was still inexplicably attractive, perhaps even more so now. It was easy to see why girls mothered him.

"You want me to be the guy lecturing the masses on morality while a page blows me under the table? The guy funneling millions into a Cayman Islands account while cutting Social Security to people on the brink of starvation? Fuck that."

"You can help change the system."

"Are you aware that when Congress refused Reagan the funds to fight his war in Nicaragua, he had the CIA set up an organization that flew billions of dollars of cocaine into American cities to raise the money so the Contras could buy weapons? The whole time he was telling the country that drugs were our number one problem ripping apart society, and that people should just say no. During the Clinton era, the CIA published a four-hundred-page report admitting their guilt, but of course they published it during the Monica Lewinsky scandal, and the country was so outraged that the president got a blow job that they ignored the fact that Reagan's CIA was selling crack cocaine in the nation's ghettos to pump billions into the defense industry boardrooms. But that was peanuts compared to Bush and Cheney, who started the Iraq war to funnel trillions from the middle class to the stockholders of Halliburton, Raytheon, Hewlett-Packard, Pratt & Whitney, General Electric, Northrop Grumman, General Dynamics, Boeing, Lockheed Martin. Lockheed alone bleeds over thirty-five billion from taxpayers each year. The list of corporate fat cats goes on and on, like hogs at a trough. The crimes these politicians have perpetrated on our middle class are even more horrendous than the torture our government inflicted on POWs in Iraq and Guantanamo. And even now, the government is taking military action against its own people. It's not enough that these corporate fucks are richer than God, but now they want to live forever and are willing to kill anybody who stands in their way. Over eight hundred soldiers died this week fighting protesters who demand nothing more than to keep their weapons. They're not even releasing the number of civilian casualties because that would inflame the insurgents into a full-on revolution. And that's just here in the United States. This hysteria is spreading globally."

Jessup wanted to grab Patrick and shake him until his teeth rattled, to force his way into that shell of resentfulness and win his trust, or at least his respect.

Patrick slung the backpack over one shoulder. He marched to the kitchen and ripped open the refrigerator door. A loaf of bread sat on the top shelf beside a brick of Velveeta cheese and a package of Oscar Mayer baloney. On the bottom shelf sat a quarter-full bottle of Jack Daniels. He shook his head. "I don't know why I thought that bitch would make a good mother." He ripped the bottle from the shelf and stuffed it into his backpack. He left the door hanging open, walked to the closet again, and lifted a guitar case. "I'm ready."

"For what?" Jessup asked.

"You're here to find Kenji and my brother, right?"

"We were worried about you. None of us are safe while Kenji remains in hiding."

"Did he kill Consuela?" Patrick asked.

Jessup sensed a softening of his son's anger. He stared at his hands, realizing that Patrick's rage over the abortion was only the surface layer of a much-deeper torment. He said, "I identified the body. Now, everywhere I look I see her face with her throat cut—in my dreams, in people walking by on the street, in the mirror when I'm shaving. Hell, even when I'm taking a leak, her face is staring up at me from the toilet bowl. It's driving me mad, but I know in my bones that Kenji is innocent. He didn't do it, him or your brother. You of all people should know that."

"I'll help you find them on one condition." Jessup lifted his head and raised his eyebrows in question. "I want ten minutes with Kenji, alone."

"Why?"

"Julie aborted our child because of the headlines about Kenji topping the FBI's most wanted list. It terrified her. She wants no part of this fucked-up family."

Who could blame her?

"Kenji killed my child, your grandchild. This is personal."

Yes, guilty or innocent, this train wreck has gone way beyond personal. "Okay, but I have a condition too. For as long as this goes on, no drugs. We need you clearheaded."

"You won't like me much while I detox."

"Could you get any worse than punching a defenseless woman?"

He dropped his head. "Sorry I lost my shit back there. You have no idea what becoming a father meant to me."

"The hell I don't!"

"It won't happen again."

Jessup didn't know if he could trust his son, in the same way he was beginning to question his trust in Kenji. He clearly didn't know either of them as well as he had imagined. Either could be an angel or a devil, and how could he tell which was which? Angels sometimes did terrible deeds in the service of allegedly holy principles, and it was possible to have compassion even for Lucifer, the rebel angel whose punishment rose from challenging the absolutist command of God's will. Isn't that what Patrick had done, and even Kenji? Lucifer's punishment, as Daniel Defoe put it, was to be "confined to a vagabond, wandering, unsettled… without a fixed place." Right now, Patrick stood with a backpack and a guitar case, looking about as unhoused as a person could get, denied the roots that define a sense of having solid ground beneath his feet. Didn't that describe Kenji too? And himself for that matter? They'd all become drifters in search of a home.

"Are you any good with computers?" Jessup asked his son.

"I'm no Steve Jobs, but I know my way around an operating system."

Jessup fished the flash drive from his pocket. "Kenji left this. I need to know what's on it."

As Patrick took the flash drive, his face blossomed with a crooked, ironic smile. "Lucky for us, Julie left her MacBook here. It's her pride and joy. State-of-the-art. I'd love to see her face when she realizes I jacked it." He walked to the desk, opened a drawer, lifted a MacBook Pro and power cord, and stuffed them into his bulging backpack.

"Let's get some chow before I bust this thing open," Patrick said. "I'm starving."

Blake tugged Groucho's leash and led the dog out the open doorway.

Jessup and Patrick followed without another word. Two steps outside the doorway, Patrick stopped and turned back to the apartment. Jessup saw something rising in Patrick's eyes, something like regret, and he assumed his son was having misgivings about the wreckage he was leaving behind. Patrick lifted a set of keys from his jeans pocket, tossed them through the open doorway, and turned and walked away. He left the door hanging open, and Jessup knew it was his son's way of abandoning something for good, not caring what happened to it, leaving it open to the world and welcome to it.

But Jessup couldn't tolerate the thought of punishing this girl for not wanting to be associated with his family. He walked back and closed the door before following his son.

Chapter Nineteen

Once Matt Reece laid the tricorder aside, the room's stillness became overwhelming. He gazed along the length of his lover's body. Vishal's injuries seemed a thing altogether improbable—a presence unfathomable in this place or in any place above hell. Emotion rushed to his throat. He leaned down to kiss Vishal, but Vishal chose that moment to lift up, and their foreheads bumped.

Vishal smiled and caressed Matt Reece's shaved head. "It just occurred to me that we hardly know each other, and you're so young. But this feels right."

"You look so fragile without your clothes," Matt Reece said. He stared into those sad eyes like a man seeking some vision of the increate future of the ages. He'd hardly the breath to speak, but he told him that he was more beautiful this way.

"Will I wake up green?"

"Takes a few days. Will you still be here, with me, in the morning?"

Vishal dismissed that idea with a wave of his hand. He closed his eyes and pulled Matt Reece into a hug. He used the word love for the first time and said he would never abandon Matt Reece. Vishal seemed embarrassed by his confession of love. Matt Reece was embarrassed himself.

"Are you afraid?" Matt Reece asked.

"Maybe a little sad."

The room grew so quiet that he sensed the silence closing in on him. When he spoke, his voice sounded lost. "I saw that in your eyes. Why?"

"Because of everything I'm giving up. Mamaji, Ray Ray, this city, my art…."

Matt Reece sat up. "We can stay here. Fuck Kenji."

Vishal drew Matt Reece's T-shirt over his head and guided him back into his arms.

He felt his lover's rough, mutilated skin along the length of his bare torso. They kissed, but this time with a hunger that made Matt Reece's head spin. When Vishal reached to undo his fly, he instinctively pulled away. Exposing himself was one of the hardest things he'd ever done. Kenji had called him "a runt." His scrawny body had little definition. He had no hips or ass to speak of. How could Vishal, or anybody, find him even remotely appealing?

"What's wrong?"

Vishal waited while he debated what would come next. Finally, he slipped out of his jeans and silk underwear and back into his lover's arms.

Yes, he thought, *I love the feel of his blistered skin, his beautifully marred flesh.* He needed to make love, now, before that skin healed, before Vishal became a different person.

Vishal sat up and whispered, "I don't have any condoms."

"We never have to worry about that. But maybe I should grab my spurs? You look pretty rank and hard to handle."

Vishal grinned. "Yippee ki-yay, cowboy."

Matt Reece pressed him to the bed. "We need to stop talking." His voice was deep and smoky and complex with emotions. He climbed on top of Vishal, and they kissed. His lips were pliant but forceful, and there was determination behind his kiss. Their tongues merged. After a time, Vishal pulled back but kept his arms around Matt Reece's neck. Vishal became starry-eyed. His kisses were as hot and needful as Matt Reece's.

Matt Reece brushed his lips over Vishal's scars. He pressed his cheek against his lover's chest. He noticed everything, the rough warmth, the dark hairs surrounding Vishal's erection, the way Vishal's features changed now that he was excited. Even the sound of traffic rumbling up from the street held a peculiar quality.

Matt Reece teetered on the verge of an epiphany when Vishal took charge, placing his hands on his shoulders, pressing down, guiding Matt Reece between his parted legs. He felt clumsy, inept, as he tasted his lover's sex, but even so Vishal whispered his name again and again. Vishal gave a deep moan followed by a soft gasp.

A moment later, Vishal rolled him onto his back and leisurely demonstrated how to give pleasure. Delicious sensations shot up his spine and enfolded his neck, and then inched up to tingle his scalp. It felt like he'd been switched on for the first time.

Later, lying under Vishal with his legs spread, Vishal also gave pain, yet it seemed a paltry price to pay for the abundance of physical delight of moments ago. The heat of Vishal's erection began to feel sensual, easing in and out cautiously. He moved with the ebb and flow of his lover's body. Then Vishal thrust his hips harder. He could feel the need building in Vishal.

That epiphany that hovered on the edge of his understanding became lost in a sea of confusion. As one minute stretched to the next and the next, he soared in agonizing perfection. He was not Matt Reece or Kirby or even remotely human; he became a ball of molecules bound up with Vishal, adrift, unmade. Over the sound of Vishal's grunts he heard himself gasping, and he caught a brief vision of himself with his legs wrapped around his lover's waist. It seemed as if the walls vanished and the streetlights outside shone in on him, and the streetwalkers, those lonely souls, could see his fulfillment. He was no longer one of them, no longer gripped by loneliness.

Later, Matt Reece nestled his face against Vishal's neck, holding his lover, scarred and naked, against him. "Still love me?" he asked.

Vishal laughed and kissed his forehead.

That laugh made Matt Reece love him even more. He lay for a time staring at the ceiling. "I'm afraid I'll wake up and you'll be gone."

"Tonight I taught you how to make love. And you taught me that home is wherever you are. I'm no longer sad about leaving. You're stuck with me now, cowboy, saddle sores and all."

Vishal caressed his skin as if something precious hung there. "Besides, it's exciting being lovers with the most scandalous man in the world."

"What will happen to us?"

"Either we live forever, or we eventually die. Both are equally terrifying."

A knock on the apartment front door turned both their heads. With the second louder knock, Vishal motioned for Matt Reece to stay put and then wrapped a blanket around his waist and hurried into the living room.

Matt Reece heard a door screech open, muffled voices, and the door shut. He pulled the sheet up to his chin.

Vishal walked back into the bedroom carrying a pizza box in one hand and two bottles of beer in the other. He set the bottles on the nightstand, pulled the blanket from his waist, and flung it over the bed. He sat the box on it and crawled on with the pizza between them. A tangy smell of pepperoni engulfed Matt Reece, and he realized he was ravenous.

"Kenji assumed we'd worked up an appetite." He laughed. "I'm beginning to like him."

Matt Reece lifted a slice. "Just so long as you like me better."

Hours later, he woke from a nightmare. The streetlights bleeding through the windows were all that lit the room. The wind had picked up, and he could hear the soft patter of raindrops on the windowpane. Beside him, Vishal slept. He studied his lover's profile and the steady rise and fall of his chest.

Making love had eased the knot in his stomach, or it could have been the pizza. The nightmare was disturbingly real, yet waking next to Vishal soothed him. This intimacy, this sharing a bed, was something so comforting that it was easy to push his fears aside and experience genuine contentment. He thought about the possibility of extending this intimacy over the next century, of waking next to his lover until the end of time, and he had to smile. *Yes*, he thought, welcoming that unlikely prospect.

He wrapped a blanket around him and moved to stand at the window. On the street, people still strolled by, bunched under umbrellas in twos and threes, keeping the night alive and festive before going back to their bedrooms.

Vishal sat up, rubbing his eyes. "What's wrong?"

"I had a nightmare. I saw you burning."

Vishal crossed the room and wrapped his arms around Matt Reece. "No worries, cowboy. That was last year. Look here." He held out his arm. "I'm fine now."

In the dim light, Matt Reece saw that Vishal's skin had smoothed, hardly any scarring left, only a slight red coloring. He turned so he could see his lover's face, and for a moment, seeing how the yellow light enhanced those now handsome features, he couldn't breathe.

Vishal touched Matt Reece's throat, caressing the arteries that now throbbed.

"You wanna go out?" Vishal said. "Get some fresh air?"

"Only if we don't come back. Let's become invisible instead of invincible."

"We gave our word."

"Don't trust him."

Vishal yawned. "Trust me instead, cowboy. I'll protect you. Come back to bed."

Matt Reece gently pushed him away. "You sleep. I need a few minutes more."

"I love you," Vishal said, and kissed him. He tasted beer on Vishal's lips.

Matt Reece felt like a child with a porcelain heart. His trust in Vishal ran as deep as his sudden joy, and he thought of taking this beautiful man back to bed and devouring him, as a way to consume all the happiness in all the world.

"Is that you talking, or the beer talking?" Matt Reece asked. Vishal had drank both beers, for Matt Reece had no taste for the stuff.

Vishal grinned. "That's me talking to the beer." He chuckled as he strode to the bed.

MATT REECE was still at the window when the sun silvered the sky. The rain muted into a heavy mist; the wind held barely a breath, yet it drifted through a gap in the curtains to caress his face with cool fingers. A vague headache grew into something sharp, brought on by anxiety of what this day would bring. He could not shake that burning dream.

Vishal slept on his back with an arm flung over his face and the sheet covering him to the waist.

On the street, the rat race began as early risers hurried to the MUNI stops to catch buses headed for downtown. Haight Street woke up to itself, more obstinate than ever about not moving into the twenty-first century. But however many anti-Kenji/antigun rallies were planned for today, no matter how many shootings, no upheaval was going to keep the world from turning.

The front door creaked, and the bedroom door burst open, banging against the wall.

Kenji surged into the room, still dressed as a priest. "Rise and shine, lovebirds," he said in a cheerful voice. "Forgive my barging in, but we need to get a move on."

Without waiting for a response, he crossed the room and held up a paper bag and a cardboard tray holding two Starbucks paper cups. "I need you showered, dressed, and fed in thirty minutes. Sorry to cut into your morning nooky time, but we're on a schedule."

Vishal sat up, looking around as if in a daze.

"What's the hurry!" Matt Reece realized he was shouting and checked himself.

Kenji set the food on the empty pizza box that sat on the nightstand. "I brought bagel sandwiches. One roast beef and cheddar, one turkey and swiss, and two vegetarian, not knowing his preference." He nodded toward Vishal.

Never had Matt Reece seen Kenji so animated. This person seemed outrageous, certainly not the composed, introspective man he'd known for most of his life. Kenji filled the room with nervous energy.

Kenji touched Vishal's face, which was now free of all disfigurement. "Christ, it worked so fast. You're beautiful, just like I promised."

"Thank you," Vishal said.

"Okay, boys," Kenji said as he snatched up the tricorder from the nightstand and walked to the door. "Eat, shower, and dress warm. Chop-chop. Our chariot awaits. Don't worry about packing. We'll buy clothes when we get there."

Before Matt Reece could ask about their destination, Kenji raced out the door.

"Christ," Vishal said, "you'd think the building was on fire. Wow, you should see the look on your face. It's priceless."

Matt Reece leaned against the window frame for support. He was more shaken than he would have thought possible. This new, animated Kenji was something unexpected and somewhat frightening.

Vishal was so amused that Matt Reece shot him a crooked smile. Seeing his lover naked from the waist up in this morning light, he admired his smooth skin. Vishal now looked like he'd been fashioned with great skill; his dark head and eyes, bullfighter's physique, and impeccable skin held an exactness, like a butterfly or a hummingbird, something nature refined to perfection.

Vishal lifted the lids off the two cups. "You want turkey, beef, or avocado?"

WHEN HE had eaten his fill, he slipped into the shower. Vishal joined him, and they held each other, luxuriating in the heat and kisses before soaping each other down.

Back in the bedroom, they donned the same clothes they wore yesterday. Those jeans and gray hoody took on new meaning for Matt Reece. Because they were Vishal's, he felt surrounded by his lover, his soft touch and his scent. It felt as if they were somehow still making love.

Before they abandoned the room for good, Matt Reece asked, "Are you frightened?"

"Hell no."

"You won't leave me?"

"Never."

That bolstered Matt Reece's courage. He assumed he could face anything as long as they were together. They tromped downstairs and found Kenji and Vishal's uncle waiting for them in the head shop. The black travel bag sat by the front door, and no doubt the cash, passports, tricorder, and computer were in it.

When the old man saw Vishal's restored skin, his hands flew to cover his gaping mouth. He backed away until the counter stopped him. "Oh my lord," he whispered.

Vishal stepped toward his uncle but stopped. He smiled. "Did Kenji treat you too?"

"I'll take no part in this devilry. Don't come near me."

"This is a good thing, Mamaji. It'll heal your heart."

"No good can come of this." He turned to Kenji. "I curse the day I first saw you."

Kenji held out a set of car keys to Vishal. "Your uncle needs time to adjust. Let's discuss it on the drive south. Just in case the car is under surveillance, I want you and your uncle to drive it out to Ocean Beach and park in the Cliff House parking lot. Matt Reece and I will wait here a few minutes and then grab a taxi and meet you there. Then we'll all drive to San Jose airport where I have an airplane waiting."

"I'm going with Vishal," Matt Reece said.

"You'll do what you're told," Kenji snapped. "It's too dangerous, even in that disguise. You can't go anywhere near that car until we know we're not being followed. Look, I already have the cab waiting, and the meter is ticking."

Matt Reece glanced out the doorway. A yellow car was parked at the curb, waiting.

Vishal snatched the keys.

"It's a cream-colored Prius, four blocks to Ashbury, and a half block to the left, toward the Panhandle. If you think you're being followed, then drive past the Cliff House and come back here. We'll call you and work out a plan B."

Vishal hurried to the tattoo room and came back with a wide-brimmed panama hat that he placed on his uncle's head. He grabbed an umbrella, took the old man by the arm, and led him to the door.

Matt Reece wrapped an arm around Vishal's waist. "I want to come with you."

"It's just for thirty minutes, cowboy," Vishal assured him.

"No!"

"We have to be careful." Vishal pushed Matt Reece away, giving him what seemed an encouraging smile. "You'll be fine."

"What if you're arrested?"

They hugged again before Vishal led his uncle out the door and opened the umbrella. They disappeared in the crowd as they ambled toward Ashbury Street.

As Kenji shut the door, Matt Reece's windpipe began to close. His solar plexus clinched, and his breaths became shallow. "Oh—" He drew in a slight breath. "—shit."

Kenji pushed him into a chair and rushed to his travel bag. He unzipped it and rummaged around until he removed a narrow box. He opened it and removed a syringe and a vial of clear liquid. Holding the vial to the light, he stuck the needle through the rubber stopper, drew a syringeful, thumbed the plunger back to the proper dose, and knelt at Matt Reece's side.

"It's a muscle relaxer, son. You'll be fine." He pushed the sleeve of Matt Reece's hoody up his arm and gave him an injection.

Matt Reece closed his eyes and leaned his head back.

"I'm sorry," Matt Reece said. "Forgive me."

"It's okay, son. I prepared for this. I know how you feel about abandonment."

He opened one eye, studying Kenji's face. He thought about confessing that his apology was to his lover, not Kenji, but by then he could feel his head drifting, and he tried to relax into that sensation.

He was thinking clearly, enough that he knew something was wrong—something to do with Vishal. He couldn't quite put his finger on it, but then…. Passports! Kenji had brought him here to obtain a fake passport. Wherever they were going, he needed one. But there had been no discussion about Vishal needing a passport.

"Why—" he started to ask, but he couldn't make his mouth form the words.

Chapter Twenty

"SADDLE UP," Kenji said.

Matt Reece hardly recognized Kenji's voice. Blood pulsed dully at his temples. Whatever Kenji injected into his arm thwarted his brain, keeping him suspended between bewilderment and lethargy. When he tried to rise off the chair, he stumbled and landed facedown on the floor. His jaw was so lax it was difficult to speak. "Help me."

Kenji muscled him into the chair again and knelt before him, checking his eyes. "You betrayed me, Romeo, but I've set everything right again."

Through his dizziness, Matt Reece realized that everything that mattered to him was in danger. "Vishal," he whispered. He tried to push himself up, but he fell back, helpless.

"I forgive you," Kenji said. "Young love makes everyone crazy—"

He tried to look away, anywhere but into Kenji's predatory eyes. But now he couldn't move his head or close his eyelids, helpless as a mongoose frozen into immobility by the swaying, blinkless eyes of the cobra. He wondered if his heart would stop as well.

So much for living forever.

"—although I admit, you're not so appealing now that you're soiled goods." Kenji's voice sounded detached, clinical. *Perhaps*, Matt Reece thought, *my hearing is affected too*. But a rushing sound blasted his ears, a roar that shook the room and rattled the windows.

A profound terror washed through him.

"Time to skedaddle," Kenji said. He ducked his head under Matt Reece's arm and lifted him. His body sagged and his feet dragged as Kenji carried him to the doorway.

Kenji opened the door and dipped to clutch the black canvas bag of money. Once outside, Matt Reece tried to scream for help but could only manage a weak moan. Kenji stuffed him and the bag into the back of the waiting cab and crawled in after them.

"Hurry it up, Father," the cabbie said. "This place just turned into a war zone. Something wrong with the kid? You want to dash to a hospital?"

"Naw, stupid kid broke into my liquor cabinet when I was asleep," Kenji said as he slammed the door shut.

"There'll be hell to pay if he pukes in my back seat."

"Raising kids isn't as easy as it used to be."

"Never was easy. You want problems? Try raising girls. I got four."

"Marina Green in fifteen minutes gets you a C-note tip."

The cab squealed away from the curb, raced to the corner, and barreled through a red light as it slid into a turn. They turned another corner and sped up the block along the Panhandle. Matt Reece saw traffic snarling the road ahead and a column of smoke rising over the buildings to his right. Slowly, he realized that he was hearing sirens.

The cabbie jumped the curb and raced up the sidewalk of Panhandle park with horn blaring, dodging all the jammed cars. Cursing pedestrians leaped for their lives. As they bypassed the head of the traffic bottleneck, Matt Reece's head rolled to the side and he glanced up the hill to see the cause of the traffic backup—a car parked halfway up the hill with flames leaping above the roof. He caught only a glimpse of it as they sped back onto the road beyond the backup. It was not enough time to make out the type of car, but he held no doubt that it was Consuela's Prius.

A primal scream rushed from someplace deep in his gut, somewhere he never before experienced and against which he had no protection. His vision blurred, and he experienced a spell of vertigo, falling through space with no place to land.

He closed his eyes. A moment later, he detected a different kind of movement in the car. Like a breeze, it seemed as if a window had opened, a change in the air so delicate he could both feel it and not feel it. A trick of his imagination, but he couldn't ignore the pressure and heat of breath on his cheek, his eyelids. The tension on his skin was real. The voice in his ear was also real. "Forgive me." Then came a dreadful silence. The pressure on his skin moved away, a subtle heat that one body exerts upon another cooled, and he felt only emptiness.

Had his stomach been able to move, no doubt there would have been hell to pay with the driver. Vishal was gone. Only a dozen minutes from bliss to utter hell.

He tried to visualize his lover at that moment he sat in the Prius—protected from the storm, surrounded by dull light, raindrops still clinging to his cheeks, his clothes slightly damp and musty, holding his breath the instant before he lit up like a Roman candle for the second time in his short life. What was he thinking before the car ignited: of Matt Reece, of living forever, of the life they would have in hiding while the world disarmed? Or was he thinking of Vishnu and the bargain he'd made to trump the Indian god's will? Was he afraid this bargain made him an abomination in Vishnu's eyes? Or was he simply thrilled to be driving his new Prius?

He felt the blood go thick behind his eyes. A million thoughts flashed through his head—he was too innocent to be wrapped up in this heartbreak. Too smart, too compassionate, too everything. This couldn't be happening; he had always played by the rules, lived an honest life.

He jostled side to side as the cab swerved through traffic. The cabbie used his horn more than his brakes, zooming over hills and down narrow streets. At the Marina Green, Kenji directed the cabbie to a line of boats moored in the harbor. The boats huddled under the mist that was growing into a steady rain.

Kenji slipped the cabbie a C-note and held up five more in a fan of green. "This is a reward for waiting five days before you tell anyone who was in your cab."

The cabbie offered a crooked grin. "Hell, I took the day off. Right now I'm reading poetry at Ocean Beach. I love me some Robert Browning."

Kenji handed him the cash. "I'm a big fan of Browning, myself." He hauled Matt Reece and the bag onto the wharf and hoisted the boy over his shoulder like a sack of rice, lifted the bag, and carried them down a line of sailing vessels. They stopped before a single-mast sailboat, large enough to cross an ocean, small enough for one man to manage. It boasted a teak deck, lots of brass fittings, and a roof covering half of the cockpit to protect the helm. Matt Reece's head was hanging upside down, but he could read the ship's name stenciled on the bow: *Valhalla.*

Valhalla, he knew from reading Norse mythology, was the Hall of the Slain, the final resting place of the gods, where Odin gathered the fallen heroes of battle. That mountain temple became the gods' mausoleum.

A voice from the ship yelled, "Welcome aboard, Father. Right on time."

Kenji tossed the bag aboard and pitched Matt Reece into the water behind the stern.

The fall was short, barely time for Matt Reece to comprehend what was happening. But when a shock of cold hit him, it became all too clear. He plunged, surrounded by bubbles and green water. When the water turned darker, he knew he was sinking, but he couldn't move his limbs to save himself. For a boy brought up in the high desert, and who was supposed to live forever, he couldn't believe his life would end by drowning in a dozen feet of icy seawater.

His body rose into green water again. His head bobbed above the surface, and he filled his lungs with air as his body leisurely rolled onto its back. Kenji knelt on the wharf, only two feet away and making no effort to rescue him. They stared at each other for what seemed hours, with Matt Reece hating, and at the same time imploring, those rapacious eyes.

With an exhale, he sank again. The icy, silent blackness surrounded him. That's when he understood true terror, that point where you're not human anymore. He was pushed into a space where he slipped out of his body, shedding his history and his future, and leaving behind everything he had ever believed in. He knew he was about to die, and he could do nothing but surrender to it. His mind shrieked a silent scream just before he felt an upward rush toward the light. Was this his moment of death? Was he rising to heaven? No, Kenji was dragging his body onto the dock. He gasped for air.

Kenji lowered his face close to his. "I did that to demonstrate how easy it is for me to kill you. My love for you is the only thing keeping you alive, but don't test me again."

Kenji hoisted him onto his shoulder and walked up the gangway and onto *Valhalla's* deck. He dropped him on a bench in the cockpit, next to a hatch that led below.

"Haul in the gangway and cast off the bowline, Father," said a one-legged man who sat at the cockpit controls. Kenji jumped to do what he was told. The rumble of an engine sounded below deck. A minute later they were backing away from the dock.

Matt Reece moved his fingers and then his toes. He realized that his dunking had more purpose than to frighten him. The cold shock helped his system overcome whatever drug paralyzed him. He knew then that soon, he would be normal again.

He managed to lift his head to see a smoky mushroom rising above the city, a black mass that even the clouds' tears could not wash away.

Kenji went below and came back with a blanket. He wrapped it around Matt Reece and sat beside him, holding him steady with one arm over his shoulder. Matt Reece could only continue to stare at that mushroom, feeling an unquenchable loss.

The ship cleared the harbor and entered the bay. The engine throbbed, and the propeller chewed the water as it launched itself toward the Golden Gate. The one-legged man cranked a winch, and the mainsail inched up the mast. Kenji manned another winch, which unfurled a second sail.

The ship scurried under that massive orange bridge. When they cleared the lighthouse, the engine went silent. The world hushed, seemingly holding its breath.

He felt something soulless enter him like another being; he imagined that it smiled malignantly, and he had no reason to believe that it would ever leave. Yes, he was certain some demon was dragging his soul down into the lowest circle of Orwellian hell. He had read that great book, Orwell's *1984*, and he remembered the quote about the thing in Room 101 being worst thing in the world. Of course, that "worst thing" is different for everyone. For Winston Smith, the main character of that novel, Room 101 held rats. For Matt Reece, sitting in the cockpit of the *Valhalla*, it was a burning car on Ashbury Street. But he reconsidered. No, his Room 101 was a murder yet to happen. He knew beyond doubt that at some point in the future, he would wrap his fingers around Kenji's neck and squeeze the life out of him, watching the horror in those eyes as he exhaled his last breath. Kenji turned him into a murderer—like stepfather, like son—it was simply a matter of time and opportunity.

Fighting Kenji may cost me my life. Is killing him worth dying for? He was prepared to die, if necessary, to bring about what he thought of as justice. Yes, not for revenge, for even sweet revenge was not worth imperiling his life over. But justice, he would risk all for justice.

He sat utterly still, quiescent, as he felt that demon's malignant smile widen. His gaze lingered on that smudge of smoke fading from view until the orange bridge and the land disappeared, slowly swallowed beneath the curve of the earth.

CHAPTER TWENTY-ONE

THEY LUNCHED in a Mexican dive on University Avenue in Berkeley. Jessup and Blake sat on one side of a booth. Patrick sat facing them with the stolen laptop before him. Mariachi music played over loudspeakers. There were a handful of students in one corner. Two of them sported green skin and wore shirts saying "I'm Matt Reece Connors," which helped to make Blake's pea-colored skin less conspicuous. A group of women wearing sunhats sat at a center table munching corn chips and sipping margaritas.

Jessup and Blake both ordered huevos rancheros. Patrick ordered three pork burritos. After the waiter walked away, the mood grew pensive but quiet while Patrick typed, trying to bypass the computer's password-protected security system.

Jessup recognized the Apple MacBook Pro because it was the same top-of-the-line model as the one Kenji insisted on. Kenji claimed it was the Rolls-Royce of portable computers, and it came with a sizable price tag.

He sipped his beer while watching his son, who seemed relaxed and confident. Jessup had not eaten a proper meal all day, but he was uninterested in food. Not even the spicy smell of jalapeño salsa could awaken his appetite.

Patrick kept an emotional wall between them, a barricade Jessup would need to chip away at, one swing of the hammer at a time. Ranch life had been hard for Patrick. It was not easy when Gail had left them and filed for divorce. Harder still was all his friends finding out his father was gay. Growing up in that rough schoolyard turned him into a fighter and a loner. *It took years for Patrick to accept a gay father. And despite the love I lavished on him, he is still convinced that the smallest upset will be enough to shatter him.*

The waiter brought a tray of food just as Patrick said, "I'm in," and closed the laptop.

Jessup was about to ask how he had bypassed the security when Patrick gave a dismissive wave of his hand—no time for shoptalk—and dug into a burrito. He ripped away huge mouthfuls at a time, chewing quickly, swallowing with a gulping sound, and wiping his chin with the back of his hand.

Jessup was relieved to find that Patrick didn't have an eating disorder. On the contrary, his son consumed all three burritos and two baskets of corn chips before Jessup had finished his eggs. It was easy to see that his son's emaciation was brought on by lack of money or an abundance of drugs, not anorexia.

Jessup kept eating at a slow pace while Patrick opened Julie's MacBook and slipped the flash drive into a slot. He moved the cursor around, clicked a few times, and looked up at Jessup. "These files are encrypted."

"We're screwed?" Blake asked.

Patrick scoffed. "It takes only a minute to download a program that can crack Word's encryption protection, and this restaurant has Wi-Fi."

"That's how you broke into a government database and stole classified files?"

"I needed inside help with that job, but this I can do with only five active brain cells."

Jessup ordered more beers, Patrick typed away, and Blake shoveled the leftovers onto a to-go plate and carried it out to the curb, where Groucho sat tied to a parking meter.

"Any idea what we're looking for?" Patrick asked.

"I assume it's Kenji's formula documentation, but I'm guessing."

The waiter brought the round of beers. Blake returned to the table.

"Okay," Patrick said, "here's the data, and yes, it looks like scientific research notes, but I'm not feeling it."

"Feeling what?" Blake asked.

"This looks on the up-and-up, but if these notes are for the most important discovery in the history of mankind, why didn't he use better encryption? It's like leaving your car keys on the hood of your Bentley while you walk into a Walmart. It doesn't jive."

"Can you verify its authenticity?" Jessup asked.

"I'm a poli-sci major, not a physicist," Patrick said. "We have to assume this might be genuine. Question is, what to do with it? I mean, there's no one we can trust."

"We use it to find Kenji and your brother." Jessup looked out the window at Groucho. "They're here, close by. Maybe something in these files can tell us where."

That something eluded them. They sat for two hours while Patrick browsed file after file. He finally closed the laptop, removed the flash drive, and handed it back to Jessup. "Nada, zilch, up shit creek with nothing but a gorilla-sized butt plug."

Blake said, "If Kenji can't be found, we need to set a trap and lure him into it."

"That means we come out of hiding," Jessup said. "Too risky."

"Like we have a choice?" Patrick said.

Blake nodded. "And while you two Einsteins are exerting those brain cells, you'd better think of a way to rustle up some cash. After we pay this chow bill and find us a motel for the night, we'll be hard-pressed to buy coffee and doughnuts in the morning."

Jessup fingered the phone in his coat pocket, the one Landau gave him. Perhaps the FBI found something that would help their search. If nothing else, he should let Landau know that Kenji and Matt Reece were somewhere near Berkeley. But the pressing issue of raising money had him stumped.

"I know how to raise some quick cash," Patrick said, "but you won't like it."

Jessup sat up straight, giving his son his full attention.

"We go back to the university," Patrick said, "find a spot with lots of people around, somewhere away from the protesters, and we give them a show."

"A show?" Blake said. "You think we're so damned talented people will throw hundred-dollar bills at us as we pass the hat?"

Patrick shook his head. "Grandpa strums my guitar, and Dad, you pretend like you're drunk as hell while you sing and dance. A drunk always gathers a big audience because sober people like to feel superior. At some point, Dad will stumble into the crowd, knocking people down. I'll help them to their feet and fleece their pockets while they're totally focused on kicking Dad's butt."

Jessup said, "You mean steal?"

"I'm pretty good at it."

"I don't care if you're fucking Harry Houdini. That is not the point." His voice grew in volume until it silenced the entire restaurant.

A stone-faced manager strolled over, looking unflappable. "Gentlemen, you've been here long enough. Kindly pay your bill and take your business elsewhere."

Blake paid at the register while Jessup and Patrick took their argument to the sidewalk.

"Yes, Dad, I applaud your honesty. By the way, how's that working out for you? Is the golden rule shining down on you and making your life all peaches and cream? Is the world rolling out the red carpet so your feet don't get muddy? I mean, maybe I'm missing something, but it looks to me like everyone and his dog is shitting on you."

"I raised you better."

"Yes, you did. And ya know what, when I got into the real world I fell flat on my face while people lined up to kick me in the balls. And ya know why? Because nobody else plays by those rules. Everybody is out to take whatever they can, wherever they can, and whenever they can, no matter who suffers. That's why I gave up politics. That's what those people are. It's all they are."

"You don't have to be like them," Jessup said, his voice rising again.

"You do if you want anything worth having. And by the way, you didn't object to my stealing Julie's laptop when we needed it."

"So now I'm a hypocrite?"

Patrick simply stared at him.

He had failed his son. It lit in him a fiery ring of shame that burned seldom in a lifetime, flickering a cool blue flame, ethereal and insubstantial. *One son wanted for murder and now this.* For the first time, he truly felt lost.

Patrick said, "People only live for vanities. Humans have sunk to the point where they have no kindness, no faith, no charity beyond what serves to increase their pleasure. And you're no better than the rest of us."

Jessup's phone rang. He fished it from his pocket and pressed it to his ear. "Hello."

"Mr. Connors, this is Agent Landau. I'm sorry to inform you that Kenji and Matt Reece are now the victims of a vicious terrorist attack."

Silence.

"I'm in San Francisco," Landau continued, "at Saint Francis Memorial Hospital. Your son is in intensive care, and, I'm sorry to say, Kenji is dead."

Longer silence.

"Mr. Connors, stay put, and I'll have my team pick you up and escort you here."

"You've ID'd the body?" Jessup's voice was shaky.

"Well, no. For a positive ID, we'll need dental records."

"My God!" Jessup cried. "How is Matt Reece? Do the doctors think he'll live?"

"In cases this bad, Mr. Connors, you don't think, you pray. Stay put. My team is only minutes away." Landau disconnected.

Patrick grabbed him by the waist to stop him from collapsing. All his reference points vanished. He knew only that someone would take him to the hospital. All he had to do was stay put and somehow hold on.

HOURS LATER, they crested Nob Hill and Saint Francis Memorial Hospital came into view. Jessup sat beside Agent Longston in the front seat of an unmarked Buick. Patrick, Blake, Groucho, Patrick's backpack, and the guitar jammed into the back seat. Longston, a man with beefy shoulders and no neck, had briefed them while driving across the Bay Bridge. He told how the FBI had Consuela's car staked out in San Francisco, and it exploded when Kenji and Matt Reece returned that morning to make their getaway. Agent Souad was able to pull Matt Reece from the burning car, but there was no way to get Kenji out alive. Souad burned both his hands and arms in the rescue, and was now laid up in a hospital bed for God knew how long. The car bomb was massive enough to have turned the street into a gruesome disaster scene, leaving many pedestrians dead or severely injured. Longston's voice seemed like a sledgehammer pounding nails into his skull, clean and haughty, cognizant of the gravity of its declarations about Matt Reece: massive, deep burns with a slim chance of recovery.

Longston's relentless voice seemed determined to dismantle Jessup, fiber by fiber.

A mass of people clogged the streets surrounding the hospital. Two dozen police wagons, with red lights pirouetting, barricaded the hospital entrances. The Buick, with the help of several police officers flanking each side, inched through the throng.

Inside the car everyone kept still. Longston held a death grip on his steering wheel. Jessup felt like a mouse trying to sneak through a swarm of cobras. He was not a religious man, but the closer they crawled toward the hospital, the more fervent the voice in his head prayed, until it resounded like a subterranean echo. When the car pulled to a halt, they were hustled through a security checkpoint and entered the hospital via the emergency room entrance.

They moved through the ER, where the Saint Francis Memorial Hospital crisis management team was on red alert mode. Occupied gurneys filled every available space. Agent Longston flashed his badge at a doctor and asked about the injury status. The doctor told them the tally of dead stood at five, nineteen others in critical condition, including four children who had been on their way to school. Several people with minor injuries were treated at the scene. The ER seemed to substantiate the worst scenarios. Sirens wailed outside, telling Jessup there were more coming.

Cries from the wounded added to the pandemonium. Many of them were peppered with metal splinters and glass shards, with some suffering severe burns. Jessup noticed a boy, no more than seven years old, nearly naked and hair singed to a bald scalp. The boy's face and arms were bloody and covered with soot. Jessup took hold of the gurney and wheeled it to one side to open up a passageway. Then he saw that the boy's left foot had been severed at the ankle. He kept his nerve, but it took effort. He stayed with the boy, holding his hand, until a staff intern wheeled him away for surgery. No sooner had he gone than Jessup saw a man in a business suit lying on a gurney and demanding to be treated immediately. His coat was ripped open, and his white shirt was stained red across the right shoulder. When no one jumped to treat him, he grabbed a passing nurse by the hair. She shrieked, and Jessup rushed to free her. The man slashed at him with fists. Jessup pinned his arms and held him. The man cursed and struggled to free himself, and as a last resort, spit in Jessup's face. A wad of saliva landed on his cheek and dripped back down onto the struggling man. Two officers rushed over. One held him down while the other strapped his arms and legs to the gurney.

Blake took Groucho to the lobby to wait. Longston led Jessup and Patrick to the burn unit's lounge, where Salman Landau waited for them.

"Have a seat," he said, waving a hand at the sofa. "I assume Agent Longston filled you in on your son's condition. And Kenji Hiroshige, of course. We believe this was the work of terrorists, although at this point we have no idea which religion sponsored them."

Jessup's limited understanding of religious extremists was that it all came down to the same bottom line: money. The clever ones made tons of cash under the table; the simpletons got promised a little corner in Paradise with a hoard of virgins to enjoy. The years of political gay bashing he'd seen over gay marriage by Christian groups made him assume that religious-sponsored hate was the rock bottom of human inanity, but now he knew he had been kidding himself. All he'd experienced before today was no more than circling around stupidity's perimeter.

Jessup nodded, still trying to wrap his head around this.

"There's nothing more I can tell you until the investigation is complete. We assume some group will eventually claim responsibility. Once that happens, we'll take steps toward apprehending them."

"Why would they admit to murdering innocent people?" Jessup asked.

"This case is a worldwide sensation. They'll want to use it to strengthen their base."

"When can I see my son?"

"The doctor is hoping he'll regain consciousness soon, but I can take you to see him now."

"What's happening with all the people outside?" Patrick asked.

Landau shook his head. "Someone on the hospital staff tweeted that Matt Reece was here. People believe if they get a transfusion of his blood, they'll be healed and will live forever. They're all demanding his blood."

"Vampires?" Jessup said.

"More arrive every minute. National Guard troops are being dispatched. If the mob grows violent, we're prepared to airlift Matt Reece to a military hospital at Fort Ord."

"Not to be a buzzkill," Patrick said, "but now that you have us here, is there any way to get us out? Those vampires are jammed into every space for blocks and blocks."

"You'll need to stay here. I'll arrange a room where you can sleep."

Jessup asked Landau when he could take possession of Kenji's remains. He couldn't stand to think of him shut up in some drawer in a morgue with a label attached to his toe. As much as he wanted to stay by Matt Reece's side, he wanted to get Kenji away from this madness.

"You're married, so all we'll need from you is a signature on the release forms. Of course, it could be several days before we can release the body. God knows how long it will take to clear the streets so you can leave."

ALL AFTERNOON the hospital staff kept the boy heavily sedated, unable to talk. Jessup never left the corridor outside the ICU. He found no comfort in the off-white floor tiles or the host of armed officers standing guard.

He wandered up and down the corridor, fixing his eyes on every doctor who went in or out of the ICU door. Finally a surgeon whose name tag read Dr. Falses led him into an office and explained the gravity of the situation, and added that she had never seen anything like this case before. "When he came into my OR, he was a charred shish kebab, critically burned over 90 percent of his body. It isn't just his burns. He has the whole damned menu—scorched lungs, multiple fractures, internal hemorrhaging, lacerations, ruptured spleen, concussion, you name it. By all rights, the patient should have died only minutes after the blast. But he is not only stable, he's generating new muscle and new skin. And this new skin has an olive-green hue."

"Will he live?" Jessup asked.

"Right now I'm giving him a fifty-fifty chance. Be aware, however, that even if his body recovers, his mind has experienced an inconceivable horror. A burn is the most distressing and painful injury, and his is the worst case I've seen in all my thirty years of practice. We'll keep him sedated, but he's already suffered more anguish than anyone in history who lived, and now he still has hell to look forward to. I'd bet my bottom dollar he'll be in what we call a persistent vegetative state. It's a long-term condition where the patient regains consciousness but not awareness. As heartbreaking as it seems, you should prepare yourself for anything. If he keeps mending at the rate he's going, we'll bring him out of sedation in a few days."

A shiver ran up Jessup's spine.

"There's something you should know," she continued. "During surgery, he died twice and fought his way back to life. Please understand, nonscientifically speaking, his flesh had seared until little more than the nerve fibers were left. Kenji Hiroshige's treatment, presumably, saved him, overriding eons of evolution. Even so, he's one hell of a fighter."

"Are you preparing me for the worst scenario?"

She smiled. "I just wanted you to know he's now one up on Jesus."

Chapter Twenty-Two

Declan sat at a dining table on his veranda, overlooking a dense-foliage garden surrounding a pool, spa, tennis courts, and five large stone heads from the Angkor region of Cambodia, each mounted on pedestals surrounding the pool. Along the parameter of the fifteen-foot-tall garden walls stood nine well-armed security personnel and a dozen unobtrusively placed security cameras. Beyond the walls spread a view of Holmy Hills, Bel-Air, and Beverly Hills, which form the "Platinum Triangle," the most exclusive neighborhoods in California. Declan's Holmy Hills Mediterranean-style villa boasted views of the Los Angeles Basin, which now seemed filled with tanks, artillery, and military outposts surrounded by sandbags established at strategic locations. Chopping the sky, army gunship helicopters swarmed in tight formations.

Declan wore his silk pajamas and shoveled down raspberry crepes with as good an appetite as ever. Regardless, it was anger, not hunger, that drove him. He chewed with his elbows on the tabletop as he stared at his laptop showing mob scenes, one after another, from cities across the country. The destruction and looting was mind-boggling. Military and National Guard troops were doing their best to quell the violence, but they were too few and could only enforce martial law in the metropolitan areas, leaving 95 percent of the country to the vigilantes.

Portman, the butler, poured grapefruit juice into cut-glass tumblers.

Declan glanced across the table at Diane McCarthy, who was also wearing pajamas. Even fresh from sleep she was a beautiful woman, one of the few he knew who could give him a run for his money in the boardroom and the bedroom. She was an inch taller than him, with lovely features, and she had that casual athletic grace that so many Californians carry. She often beat him at golf and tennis. She scuba dived, snowboarded, and rode a polo pony with the best of them. Her chief assets were her organizational skills and sharp intellect, which made her a superb CEO of Golden Eagle Industries. He cuffed his mouth with his napkin, leaned across the table, and kissed her.

"What's that for?" she asked.

He shrugged as he sat back down and lifted his coffee cup in Portman's direction. It was promptly refilled.

He turned back to his laptop. On his screen, perhaps five thousand demonstrators, all of them male, waved assault weapons like banners. Occasional shots fired into the air punctuated the mood. Their faces were livid, or, to be precise, their faces were performing rage for the cameras. He could see in their eyes, the exhilaration they felt at the presence of the media. It was the exhilaration of celebrity, of what Saul Bellow had coined "event glamour." They were on history's red carpet, brandishing their weapons and carrying signs reading DEATH BEFORE DISARMAMENT and WE STAND BY THE 2ND AMENDMENT. They gathered for their close-up. The image shook Declan to his core: the happily angry faces, rejoicing in their defiance, believing their identity was born of their insolence. Surrounding them were National Guard troops reinforced by armored vehicles. The look on each guard's face was that of determination.

Declan thought a good deal about what he termed "ultraviolence" over the last few days. About the allure of terrorism, how it made disheartened men feel powerful and consequential. And how the media glorified it so that it became hip—Rambo defending his rights against a corrupt system.

He switched to his CNN app, showing a video of a burning car in San Francisco. It was the same video he'd seen a dozen times. The voiceover described the possible burning death of the scientist Kenji Hiroshige by extremists, and the possibility of his accomplice, Matt Reece Connors, still alive at the Bothin Burn Center at San Francisco's Saint Francis Hospital.

"Still no word on recovering the formula?" Diane asked.

"Nada. And Harrington's created a full-blown civil war," he said. "Bit off more than she can chew is a colossal understatement. Mama Cass choking on a ham hoagie comes to mind."

Diane said, "Polls say 80 percent of voters outside the southern states support her. Even 47 percent in the Bible Belt."

"Sure, but the minority are well-armed, Alt-right wing nuts, fighting for their lives. Literally. Over seven thousand deaths and quadruple that number of injured in just five days since Congress outlawed private ownership of weapons."

"On the positive side, over a hundred thousand assault rifles were turned over to authorities, with the military confiscating another thirty thousand, and twice that many handguns."

"A drop in the ocean."

"Yes, but it's spreading over the globe. I never thought that could happen. I'm stunned. Kenji Hiroshige created something that has the potential to change life on this planet forever. What doesn't make sense is now that he's dead, why continue to de-arm? He was the only one making these demands, so why hasn't the government backed off?"

"I'm guessing it wasn't him in that car. It's the only answer. And as for people turning in guns, they were mostly women, wives turning in their husband's stash. This movement will cause more divorces than any other event in human history."

"That speaks volumes about the differences between the sexes. Not to mention the fact that women are becoming assertive. We're taking charge to bring about a peaceful world."

Declan stabbed a finger at his laptop screen. "You call that peaceful?"

"You see very many women in those mobs?"

"Touché. But assuming Kenji's alive, he's created a clever diversion. Harrington foolishly threw the country into chaos, so everyone is trying to quash the uprising, and no one is left to hunt Kenji. He's free to skip town with my formula."

"Our formula."

Declan raised one eyebrow, and they shared a smile.

The phone at his elbow played the *Captain America* theme song. He reached for it, turned it on, and pressed it to his ear. "Declan."

"It's Jeffery Wolfe," a voice said. "Are you alone? I need to share classified intel."

Declan stared across the table at Diane. "Let me call you back on my laptop so we can talk face-to-face over a secure link."

He clicked on his Skype application. "Portman," he said, "some privacy, if you please." Portman bowed and walked into the house. Diane began to rise, but Declan waved her down. He punched Wolfe's name on his address list, and Wolfe's face appeared on the screen.

Wolfe smiled. "Good morning, or do you say *buenos dias* in La-La Land?"

"Is that a racial slur? Never mind. The only good thing about morning is it ends at noon, which begs the question, how much of your time can you spare? I've got questions about this train wreck of a manhunt."

Wolfe's smile widened. "As much time as you need."

"Unlimited one-on-one time? Wow. You folks in DC must be panicked."

"We like to think we're determined."

"From what I'm seeing, you're determined to rip this country apart before moving on to a global confrontation."

"The enemy has bloodied our nose, but we've begun pounding them into smaller and more impotent groups, cut off from each other because we control the communications satellites. We're now moving to step on their throats, one by one."

"The enemy? You're talking about US citizens? Voters? The people who pay your salary?"

"They've become enemies to the state by forming illegitimate fighting forces bent on defying laws passed by Congress. We're past the tipping point and gaining the upper hand."

"From what I'm seeing, these militants are moving freely through the country, gathering strength and growing more violent."

Wolfe's smile evaporated. "Don't believe everything you hear in the media. Our strategy will put our fighting men in spots where they can subdue the enemy."

"Subdue? You mean kill?"

"Only if need be," Wolfe said.

"May I speak freely, off the record?"

Wolfe nodded.

"Washington implemented a strategy to de-arm Americans regardless of the human and financial cost, so the 1 percent can enjoy longer lives. How can you people justify that?"

"We've given serious thought to the human cost."

"Now I feel better. Seven thousand in five days. What's your estimates for the long haul?"

Wolfe lifted his hands, palms up. "We will de-arm no matter what it takes in terms of time, money, and lives."

"And if this takes five trillion dollars, fifteen years, and twenty million dead?"

Wolfe stared at him.

Declan shook his head, not believing this conversation.

Wolfe continued, "Americans need to understand this strategy to de-arm the world is not only our choice as rational guardians of society, it's our moral obligation."

"I swear if you dare to bring God into this conversation I'll hang up and never speak to you again. I will not be treated like an idiot."

He was about to hang up anyway. He'd had a bellyful of this bullshit already. They both sat silent. He glanced at the armed security guards covering the garden walls, and he wondered how soon the government would strip him of his protection.

Diane scribbled on a notepad and held it up for him to read: *Get on topic! What's his classified intel and what about the manhunt?*

Declan nodded. "Kenji and Matt Reece were not killed by a terrorist car bomb. Do we have a clue where they are now? Any idea about the state of the formula?"

"How did you know?" Wolfe asked.

"Because I have a triple-digit IQ."

"It was not our fugitives who died in that explosion. As of now, we have no idea of the whereabouts of Kenji or the formula, which is why I'm calling."

"The FBI let him slip through their fingers?"

"They're doing everything they can. But now we know the assassins are close. They might even have our fugitives in custody. Because of that, the president intends to escalate plans to protect our interests. President Harrington and everyone in Washington, Moscow, and Beijing feel we must act now or risk losing everything."

Declan knew whatever was coming would not be worth a damn.

"You're alone?" Wolfe asked a second time.

Declan nodded.

"Seven days from now, Moscow will nuke the Vatican—"

"You mean Rome. Moscow will nuke Rome?"

"Let me finish. China will nuke Jerusalem and Tel Aviv. We'll annihilate Tehran."

Politically, Declan knew the choices made sense. There were too many Christians and Jews in America for Washington to attack Israel or the Vatican. And he knew this option of cutting off the monster's head was being discussed with other world powers. Still, it was sheer lunacy, a leap toward World War III.

"Impossible," Declan said, his voice uneven.

"Not impossible, buddy, merely unthinkable."

Across the table, Diane's face lost all color. Her lovely mouth hung open. Declan knew denial was the mind's defense mechanism to counterbalance horrifying realities that produced more stress than the body could handle, and she was caught up in that mechanism now. Hell, he was as caught up as she.

Declan gave her a solemn shrug, wanting to help her through this but not wanting Wolfe to know she was listening in.

"This is madness," Declan said. "I can't support this."

"Let me remind you that the world's current population growth is an exponential progression occurring within a finite space with limited resources. If assassins have kidnapped Kenji, and his formula becomes public knowledge, the end of human civilization will come within our lifetime. It won't be Revelations, fire and brimstone, or even nuclear war... it will be an apocalyptic collapse caused by the sheer number of hungry mouths fighting for dwindling resources. Given that triple-digit IQ you're so proud of, you should know that the mathematics are indisputable."

Declan slammed down the screen hard enough to crack the casing. He grabbed the computer and flung it over the railing, where it splashed into the pool.

Diane held her throat with both hands. "I'm going to throw up."

"We've got to stop this insanity," he said.

She moved to the rail. When she turned to face him again, she had regained her composure. "There's only one way to do that."

He nodded. They had seven days to find Kenji, or at least find the formula. Once these pigs had what they wanted, they would back off these war games.

"We need reliable info," Declan said, "because we can't trust anything coming from Washington."

Diane was moving toward the bedroom to change. "Let's track down this FBI agent everyone's so in awe of, go right to the quarterback in the huddle. I'll make some calls to locate him. Perhaps he'll give us something we can work with. And while you team up with him, I'll fly to Israel to close down our Tel Aviv office and get our people the hell out of there."

Declan grabbed her wrist, stopping her. "No, call them and tell them to wrap up the office and evacuate to Switzerland."

"That'll cause a citywide panic. No, I need to be there to manage this. I'll be in and out days before anything happens. I promise."

She pulled away from his grip, and he knew arguing was pointless.

Declan followed her inside, thinking he would apply all the pressure needed on Salman Landau's two most sensitive body parts to stop this madness.

CHAPTER TWENTY-THREE

JESSUP SAT beside the hospital bed. They were in a private room in the burn unit, and for three days Jessup only abandoned his chair for bathroom breaks and food in the cafeteria. Blake slept in the other bed. Patrick was out walking Groucho.

Two days ago the doctors had lessened the medication to allow the patient to regain full consciousness. The patient, however, showed extreme trauma, so they medicated him back into a coma. He lay with his head and body bandaged, resembling a mummy.

Jessup gazed at the chest inflating and deflating under those dressings. He shook his head while talking to himself. "He just needs to sleep through this. Boys love their sleep. He'll be right as rain once I get him home."

Dr. Falses breezed in, flashing Jessup a wounded smile.

"Well, if it isn't the miracle worker," Jessup said.

"You're mistaking me for your husband. I'm just a run-of-the-mill old sawbones."

She touched the boy's wrist. She peeled back an eyelid and then the other. Donning her stethoscope, she listened to his heart and pressed her fingers here and there on the abdomen. She checked the flow on the plastic drip sack, and moved to the end of the bed and lifted the chart. She checked her wristwatch and scribbled notes on the chart.

She turned to Jessup. "It's time he regained consciousness again."

"You told me sleeping is restorative."

"Yes, but too long in a coma brings on its own set of issues."

Blake stirred, coming awake. He sat up.

"And I want another scan," the doctor said. "I'll schedule it for tomorrow morning."

"Should I be worried?" Jessup asked.

"We're simply covering all the bases to understand as much as possible before taking the next step."

Jessup nodded. "And what exactly is the next step?"

Agent Landau entered the room carrying a paper bag and a briefcase. "How's our patient?" he asked. "How soon can we question him?"

"Perhaps as early as tomorrow afternoon," she said. "On the other hand, we won't know until he regains consciousness."

Landau eyed Jessup. "Mr. Connors, I'd like you to come with me. What I have to tell you will be easier to swallow if we grease the skids." He nodded at the paper bag he held. "You're a rye man, right?"

"I can't leave my son, and Patrick's walking the dog. I should be here—"

"I ran into Patrick in the lobby. He's agreed to be our designated driver for the evening. Trust me. What I have to show you, you'll want some privacy and space to think."

Jessup paused. "Shit."

"Enough to bury us, Mr. Connors."

THEY DIDN'T speak on the ride to Ocean Beach. Patrick drove with Groucho riding shotgun. Jessup and Landau rode the rear seat. Blake stayed behind to watch over the patient. Landau didn't seem to mind that Patrick dodged through traffic like a fleeing deer, speeding through yellow lights and squealing around turns. Jessup, however, had a white-knuckle grip on the door handle.

By the time they reached the beach, Jessup longed for that first snort to calm his nerves. He and Landau perched on the cement seawall overlooking the sand while Patrick raced Groucho out to the water's edge and threw driftwood for the dog to retrieve.

The sky was a radiant twilight. Above them, an anemic streetlamp shed a pallid glow.

Landau passed Jessup a bag of Ruffles potato chips and a bottle of WhistlePig rye. He pulled a pint bottle of single malt scotch from the paper bag and cracked it open. They clicked bottles and both took a healthy swig. Jessup felt a delightful numbing in his head.

Since that first day in the interrogation room, Jessup sensed that he and Landau had come to an understanding. It was founded on a trust that both men were trying their damnedest to bring Matt Reece and Kenji home safely. As far as Jessup was concerned, Landau had proven himself to be tough as an old saddle—seasoned by copious use, weathered and wrought, a repository of valuable experiences. And now that the manhunt was over, even with the terrible result, Jessup felt he had nothing to hide from Landau. They could even become friends. This drinking together certainly carried that possibility.

Jessup opened the chip bag, and they passed it back and forth, munching and sipping. The roar of the surf soothed him, pulling him into its give and take. The moon came from behind some clouds, huge, white, and covered with scars. It poured light down on them, enough milky rays that he could see everything—cresting waves, Patrick and Groucho frolicking. Whatever earth-shaking information Landau had to tell, he was in no hurry to hear. He wanted to enjoy this quiet time for as long as there was more rye in the bottle.

Jessup pointed to the yellow-feathered fishhook Landau had stuck to his lapel. "Why the hell do you always wear that fly?"

Landau's hand came up to stroke it. "I'm a fisherman. I have a cabin up at Big Bear Lake, right on the water. I wear this to remind me of better times. Here's to better times." He lifted his bottle and took another deep swig.

Jessup also took a hot swallow. "When will you release Kenji's body?"

"That's what we're here to talk about. What I'm about to tell you is classified, strictly off the record, something between friends. At least I hope, after all we've been through, we can be friends. This information cannot be repeated. Do I have your word on that?"

Jessup nodded.

Landau set the bag of potato chips between them, procured another swallow of scotch, and removed a laptop from his briefcase. He opened the computer and clicked on an icon. He explained that his team had Consuela's car under stakeout in San Francisco, and that moments before the car blew up, two men who they were dead certain were Kenji and Matt Reece climbed into that car. "But after you came to the hospital, my team showed me this surveillance tape." And he pressed the Play button.

The video showed two men approach the Prius. One opened the passenger door. He paused the video at a point where both faces were visible.

Jessup leaned in for a close look. His eyes widened. "Who the hell are these bozos?"

"That body in the morgue is an eighty-year-old man who came here from Mumbai twenty-four years ago. His name is Mr. Mandial, and he owned a shop on Haight Street."

Jessup held his breath for a silent minute before asking, "The boy at the hospital?"

"His nephew, Vishal Mandial."

"That can't be. That boy's had Kenji's treatment. It's what saved him."

"You can plainly see, these men are no relation to you." He tapped the Play button.

Jessup watched the explosion and the horrific scene that followed, which included Agent Souad rushing in to pull the driver from the flames. The chill in the wet wind surprised Jessup, the shock of feeling any physical sensation at all. Three days and nights of mourning beside a hospital bed left him unraveled, and now this.

When the video ended he said, "You've known all this time, and you left me sitting up there grieving? You bastard!" His voice roared, but he knew it was from relief, not anger.

"I am sorry, but we, the agency I mean, want to keep everyone believing Kenji is dead so the assassins will give up pursuing him."

"They're still alive?"

Landau held up his bottle for a toast and took a long swallow.

Jessup felt the threat of tears, and he turned away to hide his face.

"As I said, this is classified information, which is why we're discussing it here. I can't trust anyone at the hospital, and frankly, not even a few people on my own team."

"Agent Souad?"

"He's a devout Muslim. He's by no means an extremist, but this living forever, this trumping God's will, clashes with his core beliefs. He pulled a lot of strings to get assigned to this case, and I've been wondering why ever since he signed on."

"Are they still nearby?"

Landau explained that once they realized the victims weren't the suspects, they printed their photos from this video and canvassed the Haight-Ashbury area. That's how they found the head shop, and what they found on its security cameras shed more light on the case.

Jessup swallowed more rye while Landau clicked a second icon. They watched Kenji, dressed as a priest, handing keys to Vishal, and Vishal leading his uncle away.

"That's Kenji, but who's the black kid? And where's Matt Reece?"

"Believe it or not," Landau said, "the black kid is Matt Reece, in disguise."

Jessup took a closer look. The facial structure did seem familiar. He watched Kenji give his son an injection, and they waited.

"You can't see it," Landau said, "but we linked up the timing. Right here is when the car bomb exploded four blocks away. As you can see, as soon as Kenji heard the blast, he carried Matt Reece out the front door."

"What are you telling me?" Jessup asked.

"You saw it yourself. Kenji gave Vishal his car keys, sending them to their deaths. He waited until he was sure it happened before he made his escape."

Jessup set his bottle on the seawall.

Landau continued, "We were lucky. The café next door also had security cameras, and one of them was trained on the front sidewalk." Landau clicked a third icon, which showed Kenji stuffing Matt Reece into a taxi and them zooming away.

Jessup said, "This doesn't prove Kenji knew about the car bomb."

"What the hell do you think he's waiting for? Not for the taxi to arrive, because it sat there at the curb the whole time. He waited for one thing only: confirmation that his trap worked before he made his escape. That, I'll grant you, is conjecture, but I'd bet my life on it. What the videos do prove is that Matt Reece is not an accomplice. Kenji sedated him to get him to go along. So in addition to two counts of first-degree murder and one count of attempted murder, we'll charge him with kidnaping, assuming we find him."

"My husband might be a lot of unsavory things, but he could never kill those men. I don't believe it. I can't."

Landau took another deep pull of scotch. "A hotel attached to the head shop was also owned by Mr. Mandial. That led us to find their hideout. Kenji left this in the room. My team fingerprinted it, and I'll need it back for evidence, but you should see it."

Landau removed an envelope from a plastic evidence bag in his briefcase and handed it to Jessup. He used his phone's flashlight app to give Jessup light to read by. Jessup's name was scrawled on the envelope.

Jessup removed a single sheet of paper. He unfolded the letter. It held only six lines, hastily scribbled, but clearly in Kenji's handwriting.

> *Jessup, I wish with all my heart that I could have*
> *taken you with me, but you would never agree to what*
> *must be done. You want to raise our children to be moral*
> *and decent. I want to keep them safe for eternity. We can*
> *both succeed, but for that to happen horrific sacrifices*
> *must be made. Many souls will perish. Please, my love,*
> *don't hate me.*
> *Kenji*

Jessup didn't know where he was. A moment later, with Landau's hand now supporting the back of his neck, he recovered a little lucidity.

Steadier now, and unmoving, he looked up. His vision squared itself, and the night was firmly held by his eyes—solid things like the sand and a smooth moving line where ocean met the land.

The paper fell from his hands. Landau jumped to the sand to retrieve it before the wind could carry it away. He stuffed it into the envelope, placed it and the laptop into his briefcase, and locked it.

Out over the water, an ocean liner twinkled while racing away from the Golden Gate. Waves hurled themselves against the sand. The pounding reverberated in his head.

"How can we be sure that kid is Matt Reece?"

Landau described the agency's pattern-matching software that discounted facial hair, wigs, skin and hair color, since those were the most common methods of disguise, and focused on things that didn't change—shape of the ears and forehead, age, color and shape of eyes. "When we compared these pictures with photos taken from your ranch, both Kenji and Matt Reece were positively matched."

"Christ, I don't know whether to jump for joy or cry my eyes out."

"Take another snort. Let's get toasted."

Jessup found the taste in his mouth disgusting. He lifted his bottle, held it over the sand, and turned it upside down, letting the whiskey pour out.

"That's probably for the best. The bottom of the bottle's no good during this kind of implosion. If you don't bounce back quickly, you'll become a spectator of your own collapse and not realize that the abyss is closing over you. I know, it happened to me, over a woman of all things."

The sea breeze refreshed him. He pulled his knees to his chest, gathered himself around his legs, and rested his chin on his kneecaps. He listened to the waves. His eyes gradually grew blurry, and he held back sobs.

Then he said, "The video of them in the taxi, did it show the cab's license plate?"

"Now you're thinking. We tracked it down. While all the attention was focused on the car explosion, that cab raced across town and dropped them off at the Marina Green wharf, where they boarded a blue-water sailboat. Kenji, being sensitive to the laws of tragedy, achieved the most dramatic escape possible, disappearing into sixty-four million square miles of ocean. You said he was too smart for us. I'm beginning to believe you."

Jessup stared out into the gloom beyond the waves and found the kind of clock-stopping blackness that made his eyeballs ache. "So they're out there?"

"By now, they could be anywhere from Central America to Alaska, or a thousand miles out from shore. The cabbie didn't catch the ship's name, and the harbormaster had no paperwork for it. If it were me, I'd be hightailing it to Peru or Chile."

"He never talked about anywhere outside of Nevada. Tell me, you've dealt with criminals your entire career, did you meet any of them, I mean, really talk to them?"

"More than I'd care to remember."

"How can a seemingly loving, contented person suddenly turn into a psychopath?"

Landau shrugged. "Many of the ones I've talked to had hallucinations that convinced them they were on a divine calling. If we take Kenji's mission at face value, he probably feels that eradicating the world of guns justifies every sacrifice he makes. He sees himself as a hero, rather than a psychopath. And who knows, history might prove him right."

Landau sighed, obviously giving himself time to choose his words. "Even seasoned terrorists don't always know what's happening to them. Something in their subconscious clicks, and they don't see the world in the same light. It's like a tapeworm that wraps around their organs, squeezing everything else out, until it controls them, body and soul. From that point on, they never try to justify their actions. They think the only way they have to return to a normal life is to carry out the mission, assuming that if they live through it, it will be over and they'll be themselves again."

"Is that possible?"

Landau shook his head.

Jessup cleared his throat. "Let me ask you something else."

"You want to know if Matt Reece might be next?"

Jessup nodded.

"Matt Reece is Kenji's Achilles' heel. He's put himself at considerable risk over keeping the boy with him. I assume because he loves the boy, but it's clear Kenji will stop at nothing to accomplish whatever it is he's doing. If Matt Reece opposes Kenji—and Kenji's needing to sedate him indicates he already has—I don't like his chances."

If all this was true, and those videos were pretty convincing proof, Jessup didn't like his chances either. He had to do something to help get Matt Reece back as soon as possible. He hesitated but then dug into his jeans pocket and pulled out the flash drive. "You remember that letter Kenji left at the ranch?"

"Of course, the one where Kenji said he was going to a certain place because lightning never strikes the same place twice."

Jessup held out the flash drive. "This came with that letter, with instructions never to show this to anyone. Patrick broke past the encryption and got an eyeful of scientific documentation. We assume it's the formula notes. Maybe it can help you find Matt Reece before it's too late."

Landau took the flash drive and held it at eye level. "Well, I'll be damned."

CHAPTER TWENTY-FOUR

A WET sea breeze pounded Matt Reece as he leaned against the railing where port and starboard forged a spearhead to cleave the gray plain, and with his back to the ship, he studied the immensity—sea and sky, the sun hovering inches above the vanishing point. It silenced his mind and weighed on his chest with such force that he struggled to take in air. Shouts echoed behind him, angry and belligerent, but they no longer mattered. All he could think of was how to lose himself in that yellow disk as it touched the water.

He stared at it until his eyes burned and he had to look away, anywhere but behind him. To the east he saw a slash of color on the horizon. They had sailed south for three days with wind and current in their favor. According to Vice Admiral Mike, the *Valhalla* crossed two hundred and fifty miles per day in these conditions. That meant the land to the east was Baja, Mexico.

During those first two days aboard, he envisioned red lights and alarm bells going off on consoles in San Francisco, LA, Honolulu, even Washington, DC, hands reaching for phones, orders barked, pilots running for their planes, coast guard ships steaming toward them, even submarines swerving to intercept them. He knew a rescue ship would appear on the horizon. He had only to wait it out. But by the third day, he abandoned hope.

He had always thought of sailing the ocean as something romantic, snorkeling in secluded anchorages, dolphins crossing the bow, the song of the wind swishing through the rigging—

—not.

Those naïve images belonged to novels and travel brochures. This was a sphere of infinite absence—a vacant plain of muted colors, the edges lost in haze. Everywhere the landscape was all one thing, like a boundless curving mirror, infinitely gray and empty, always the same. The solitude felt heavy. The repetition, the hypnotic drone of waves pushing against the boat, became maddening. It felt like the void he dropped into when he pushed himself beyond exhaustion to a strange otherworldly dream.

Since Vishal's death, the days and nights blurred into a single lost cry, and whenever he closed his eyes, he felt that warm body embrace him, smelled the musk of his hair, and felt lips caress him. The next instant he'd see a fiery Prius with smoke mushrooming over the city. After that first night aboard, he stopped closing his eyes. But lack of sleep took its toll. He began to hear voices coming up from the sea; the crest of waves became human faces. Moments later, there was nothing but waves and a lucid slice of moon.

He well understood now the stories of old salts who told of beautiful sirens calling to them and mermaids with flowing, silver hair. These relentless waves, this emptiness, did that to you. Matt Reece was no salt, but the *Valhalla* was, according to Vice Admiral Mike, a blue-water boat, meaning this forty-three-foot, single-mast Shannon Pilot was built to cross oceans. It carried charts and a sextant, GPS unit, refrigerator, water purifier, clothing and books sealed in plastic wrap, fifty pounds of canned meats and vegetables, dried fruit and beans, powdered milk, and enough vodka to stay inebriated through the next century.

But this world seemed only a place of dearth. Nothing but waves coming one after another, making those faces, openmouthed, wide-eyed, incredulous. He became haunted by waves. Those faces mirrored his emotions that were too deep for tears.

He randomly selected a wave and followed its progress—a bulge lifting out of the gray mass with a fringe of white where it crested. It was pure movement, some mysterious containment of energy. It rushed toward him as if bent on some vital undertaking. The size and crispness of the wave held him with an elemental intensity. He felt its solitude, its utter indifference to its fate in that waning light. It came to him that the sea was not some grand pattern or an intricate plan; it was a primal struggle. Nothing mattered against the fact of this. He saw the waves battling each other with no abiding sense of each other's purpose, only to eventually spill themselves against a beach in a final surge and withdraw in shrugging irony. It somehow felt like the last line of a poem by Homer, or the ending chords of Schubert's unfinished symphony.

He smiled. It was a sad smile because he glimpsed something of himself in that wave rushing toward annihilation. He was struck by its meaninglessness and the speed by which it raced to shore. He appreciated, however, that it was a lovely curve on a smooth sweep toward oblivion, and that calmed him.

From his front pocket he removed his watch, still fixed at 8:15, and from his hip pocket he removed the picture of Vishal he took from the tattoo room. Beside the clothes on his back, these were his only possessions, the only link to his past. It was remarkable, he felt, that both survived the dunking in San Francisco Bay before coming aboard the *Valhalla*. So remarkable that it must mean something; it just had to. He stared at both until the sun dipped below the horizon and the sky became ablaze.

Another shout sounded behind him, and he heard the sandpaper scuff of clothing dragging over teak. He glanced over his shoulder to confirm what he already knew and slipped his possessions back into his pockets.

The sails glowed scarlet, reflecting the sky, as Vice Admiral Mike, aka Mike MacDougal, heaved his body along the deck. He was a swarthy man in his midforties, wearing khaki cargo shorts and a blue denim shirt unbuttoned to his belly, so patched and tatty they looked like a flag of perpetual defeat. The hair on his chest was the same red color as his scraggly beard and dreadlocks. His body was stout, and yet he had no legs. That is, army surgeons in Iraq had amputated the left leg at the hip, the right one at the knee. On land he was, no doubt, confined to a wheelchair, but aboard his forty-three-foot-long realm, he was the equal of most men. Few sailors, Matt Reece suspected, could scurry along the rigging as efficiently or handle the sails as well. Vice Admiral Mike said that sailors in San Francisco named him "Vice Admiral Loco" because the landmine in the Middle East had not only taken his legs, but gave him a fondness of vodka (hence the "Vice"), which he consumed in impressive quantities. He said he earned the label "Loco" not so much for being crazy, but for his love of sailing in bad weather. When the raging elements sent other men cowering on shore, Vice Admiral Mike would reef his sails and lash himself to the helm, a fifth of vodka in one hand and the wheel in the other, and ride the *Valhalla* over twenty-foot waves like a bucking bronco.

Matt Reece believed every word, because even though the Vice Admiral's clothes suggested defeat and the blotches on his face spoke of advanced age, his eyes were cheerful and audacious.

Vice Admiral Mike chartered his ship to tourists wanting to run up and down the coast. Most of his time was spent between Seattle and Ensenada. He claimed it was his reputation for skill and boldness in bad weather that brought him enough tourist business to keep his belly full and the *Valhalla* in seaworthy condition. How Kenji found him, Matt Reece had no idea.

Just then, Vice Admiral Mike was panting, sweating, and wild-eyed. He was black Irish, and when his temper was up or he had a snootful, his face boiled a scalded red.

"Hoss, I told you to stay the hell in the cockpit. If you slip and land in the drink, your father will skin me alive." He'd taken to calling Matt Reece Hoss, no doubt something he picked up in a cowboy movie.

Kenji lay below in his bunk. Vice Admiral Mike and Kenji alternated watches: six hours on, six hours off. The ship's clock rang out the hours religiously. Matt Reece kept the same schedule as Vice Admiral Mike as a way to avoid Kenji.

In addition to manning the galley, Matt Reece made entries into the ship's log, noting latitude and longitude, course and speed, wind direction, weather, unusual observations. He was grateful to have that task because it helped focus his thoughts. He also made entries that had nothing to do with sailing, vague poetry that meant nothing, double talk from a restless mind: "No Sir, 'tis not the gulls who fear the sea, 'tis the tiny drops of gray that fear the gulls." And "A wolf never loses sleep over the opinions of sheep."

Matt Reece didn't speak. He hadn't spoken a word since coming aboard. His vocal cords were immobile. Grief had lodged itself in his throat, a lump he couldn't swallow. He staggered back to the cockpit and watched the sky turn lavender as Vice Admiral Mike heaved himself to the helm with the grace of a monkey swinging from branches.

The ship's clock rang the hour.

"Update the log, Hoss, and if that rye bread ain't stale, rustle up some canned corned beef and swiss-cheese sandwiches."

Matt Reece climbed down the companionway. The galley sat on the port side, a desk with charts, log, GPS, and radio lay starboard. Farther forward were the dining lounge, head, and sleeping quarters.

Matt Reece slid behind the desk and eyed the float plan wrapped in plastic wrap. He'd read it a dozen times. It identified stops at Cabo del San Jose, Mexico, to restock supplies, again at Panama City, with their final destination at Lima, Peru. He opened the log, selected a pen, and scribbled:

Stardate 04.26.2017:18:44
Weather unchanged, gray clouds, moderate waves, nothing else. Boat speed: twelve knots. Wind speed: fifteen knots.
Spotted land to the east at sunset.

Vice Admiral Mike spent hours showing Kenji how to calculate our position, to plot a course, and also to operate the sails. Kenji is learning everything about shipboard operation. Why?

Vice Admiral Mike, you've become expendable. If you trust him, then you really are loco.

He moved to the galley and made two sandwiches, and placed them on a tray with a mound of yellow potato salad. He also placed a half-empty bottle of vodka on the tray. He slipped the ship's log under his arm and carried the tray up the companionway. He set it beside Vice Admiral Mike, opened the logbook, and handed it over.

The Vice Admiral read the latest entry by the light over the compass while Matt Reece watched a wispy cloud wrap up the moon.

"I love the sea," Vice Admiral Mike said, his voice low and meaningful. "I love sailing the deep. I love the freedom of it, the sovereignty. I love the fact that there are no people out here. You can sail for months and not see another ship."

Jessup loves his ranch for the same reasons you love your ship. He felt a sudden kinship with this outlandish, legless rogue.

"And yes," Vice Admiral Mike continued, "what you love or value will eventually be used against you. It's the most basic universal law. But you and I can't run from karma. You, my friend, look at the universe through too narrow an opening. Sometimes you have to trust others to be more than they seem, even people you hate, in order to drag your sorry ass further down your own path."

Vice Admiral Mike scooted along the bench until he came to a cabinet beside the wheel. He glanced down the companionway to ensure Kenji was still in his stateroom. Reassured, he opened the cabinet and removed a twelve-gauge, pump-action shotgun from its hidden rack, identical to the Browning Grandpa Blake kept on the ranch. He smiled. "You see, I can't run from karma, but I can stack the odds in my favor. That's what I mean by seeing through a wider opening." He chuckled as he hid the weapon in the cabinet and closed the door.

Matt Reece gazed at the dark horizon. There seemed no way to escape violence, even in the middle of the ocean. The pain in his chest became heavier, more solid, pulling him off balance. He heard not a sound, saw nothing but the monotonous waves coming and coming.

CHAPTER TWENTY-FIVE

LANDAU CALLED Declan Hughes. Jessup heard only half of the conversation, but he gathered Landau was asking for scientific assistance to verify the data on the flash drive.

Landau drove Jessup, Patrick, and Groucho to San Francisco airport, where they were met by a Golden Eagle Industries' corporate jet. They needed a private jet because the federal government had grounded all commercial passenger flights. They first suspended only international flights to keep assassins out of the country, but three days later, they grounded all domestic flights to restrict the movements of the vigilante organizers. Now only military, corporate, and cargo aircraft were flying in US airspace.

Jessup relaxed into a leather-upholstered chair. The sun was lighting up the Oakland hills as they lifted into the sky. Once they leveled at thirty thousand feet, they breakfasted on bagels, Norwegian lox, cream cheese, orange juice, and coffee. Then Landau got down to business. The jet was equipped with desks, laptop computers, printers, and Wi-Fi. Patrick opened the files on the flash drive and printed them. Landau made use of the copier, making five duplicates of everything that rolled off the printer. Forty-five minutes later, they touched down at John Wayne Airport in Anaheim, California.

A driverless, black Escalade waited for them on the tarmac. They piled into the car, with Jessup assuming the driver would soon join them, but to his surprise the doors locked, and a voice from the dashboard instructed them to fasten their seat belts. The engine started and the vehicle moved. Jessup, sitting in the front passenger seat, hurried to clasp his belt. Landau and Patrick did the same. Patrick draped a protective arm around Groucho.

Two armored vehicles manned with high-caliber machine guns joined them, one in front and one following. It was hard to tell from the tinted glass, but Jessup assumed those vehicles were unmanned as well. While he was still thinking about it, two drone helicopters—armed with rocket launchers and heavy-caliber machine guns—roared in the dusty sky overhead.

Once the convoy left the airport, the complexion of everything changed. Jessup saw protesters in Berkeley, but no mob violence; even San Francisco seemed like a rest home compared to what he saw now. The US military controlled the major cities and airports, but in small towns and suburbs, burned-out neighborhoods and battle flags were the order of the day. Bands of vigilantes roamed with impunity, asserting war on the government. Towns in a state of siege; highway checkpoints with long lines of people fleeing into protected areas; roads littered with charred vehicles; the sound of gun battles loud in Jessup's ear. He prayed that the Escalade was equipped with bulletproof glass. His prayers were answered not ten miles from the airport when a spray of bullets peppered the windshield but failed to penetrate. The helicopters open fired on the snipers. The convoy dashed along, swerving this way and that, like passing through a minefield.

"Thank God they're using small-caliber weapons," Landau said. "Lord help us if they get heavy artillery."

As far as Jessup could determine, the vigilantes weren't just fighting the government troops. Beardless boys with assault rifles— some wearing camouflage, some in hoods—lashed out indiscriminately at citizens. Residents were warding off blows of rifle butts with their bare hands. Five more miles down the highway Jessup saw a crowd gathered around six bodies that, he assumed, had just been shot.

Rows of evacuated houses and businesses had broken windows and were covered with war-propaganda graffiti. Bullet-riddled vehicles, some still smoldering, were common. In the distance was the constant wail of ambulances.

It looked like a doomsday Hollywood sci-fi movie. He had been so focused on finding Matt Reece, he had no idea that the state of rebellion had advanced this far.

"This seems like the ending of the world," Jessup said.

Landau grunted. "You think this is bad, wait until the military moves out of the cities and declares full-scale war."

"You think they will?"

"They'll have to. Vigilantes across the nation are holding up shipments of food into the cities. People are hoarding, store shelves are bare, and soon people will begin to starve. The banking system is collapsing because people are amassing cash, anticipating food prices skyrocketing and a black market that deals only in hard currency. The government will have to move their advanced weaponry out of the cities to reestablish the flow of food. Then we'll see Goliath stomp the hell out of David, take my word. It will make what we've seen in the Middle East seem like name-calling in a child's sandbox."

The convoy left the highway on an access road leading into the hills. There were dozens of human bodies at the side of the road, black as pitch and swelled up like balloons. A camera crew and their armed guides were filming the scene—spotlights, shoulder-hefted cameras, fluffy boom mikes, everything seemed to amplify the horror.

"This area is infested with snipers," Landau said. "No wonder they use drone vehicles. Who the hell would drive through this if they didn't need to?"

Jessup said, "We should have left Patrick with Blake and Vishal."

"Piss off," Patrick snapped.

Movement in the sky caught Jessup's eye only a heartbeat before the SUV in front of them erupted in a geyser of flames. A burst of bullets hit the front of their vehicle, flattening the tires and causing a fire to erupt under the hood. Smoke poured from the engine compartment as the SUV jerked to a halt. A rocket took out one of the helicopters escorting them, and as it plunged, it crashed into the third SUV.

Groucho yowled.

"We're sitting ducks," Landau said.

The radio in the dashboard told them to leave the vehicle and find cover nearby. They would dispatch another vehicle, so stay in the vicinity; ETA was thirty minutes.

They were stranded near an abandoned strip mall. On the opposite street corner stood a church. Landau withdrew his pistol and clicked the safety off. He pointed to the church and said, "That's our best bet."

Landau flung the doors open, and they all raced for cover, Landau leading, Patrick keeping a tight grip on Groucho, and Jessup bringing up the rear.

At first, Jessup believed that, because it was a church, it would be spared any assault. But he found that bombs and numerous bullets had already punctured the building. Inside, the pews were splintered and smashed, prayer books scattered, and everything else had been looted or burned. Stained glass crunched under their feet. The room smelled of burned wood, unwashed bodies, decomposing rubbish, and over it all hung a pungent smell of fear.

They found a squad of soldiers crouched behind the altar. They were doing the same thing that GIs the world over do while waiting for the next battle; they were smoking cigarettes, checking their weapons, and drinking coffee from thermoses.

The officer in charge introduced himself as Lieutenant Myer, Task Force Rock—Second Battalion, 503rd Infantry Regiment, 173rd Airborne Brigade. He was obviously a lifelong military man, taller than average with a bullish torso and a square face. He exuded a brisk, forthright confidence, without pretense or misgiving.

"Wait in here," Lieutenant Myer said, "but stay away from the windows."

They crouched with the soldiers. Jessup sat close to the lieutenant and could see the muscles in his cheek twitching and smell the cigarettes on this breath. His tension spread to Jessup. He knew the battle was minutes away.

In one chapel, women and children crouched before a broken marble statue of Mary holding the baby Jesus. In another, four men sat waiting for a pot of coffee to percolate over an open fire. There were more than two dozen civilians in the church, and the place was alive with a mixture of coughing, crying, snoring, laughing, all mingling with the sounds of rifle shots and detonations outside the windows.

A hole had been blown out of one wall, large enough for men to walk through two abreast. The house that sat beside the church had a similar hole, and there were sandbags piled five feet high between the two openings so that soldiers could move about the neighborhood without exposing themselves to sniper fire. They had created rabbit warrens throughout the area, from building to building, house to house.

"Is your squad pinned down, Lieutenant?" Jessup asked.

"We've identified five different houses, all bunched together. We believe they form the local insurgent stronghold. You see, every neighborhood outside the protected areas is now a fiefdom. Most of these people are caught in the middle." He waved a hand at the civilians. "They don't know who to trust, and they've learned it's best for them not to ask questions. Right now we're waiting for a coordinated attack of air support and ground firepower before we take them down."

"What kind of support, Lieutenant?" Landau asked.

"We've established a COP, a combat outpost, three miles west of here. When the helicopters drop their barrel bombs, four Humvees will be dispatched from the COP to give us ground cover. Two of the Humvees are armed with TOWs, tube-launched, optically tracked, wire-guided missiles. The other two vehicles have 50-caliber machine guns. My squad has small arms and a 120-millimeter mortar."

"Barrel bombs, what the hell is that?" Landau asked.

"Fifty-five-gallon barrels filled with shrapnel or chemicals, and explosives. They cost under three hundred dollars and are very effective."

"Leave it to our military to find a cut-rate way to kill its own people," Patrick said.

A civilian walked up and cowered between Jessup and Patrick. He seemed cheerless, a grave man. He held out a mug of coffee. Jessup took it and thanked the man. The man hunkered beside him.

"How did you get trapped in this mess?" Jessup asked him.

"For common people," he said, "war starts with a jolt: one day you're taking your son to soccer practice, the ATMs and your phone and the cable networks work perfectly, and the next day nothing works. Barricades go up. Men with weapons form their own defenses. Local officials are assassinated, and everything falls into chaos. First the police disappear, and then people disappear. Banks close. Money and culture and daily routines are all swept away. The smart ones saw it coming and got the hell away, but I've never been particularly clever."

In the wars Jessup had read about—Chechnya, Bosnia, Afghanistan, Iraq, Kosovo—the time when everything changed from normal to abnormal seemed to share that same quality this man described. He talked about how he went to bed one night smelling the cherry blossoms from the trees in his yard, and next morning he smelled houses burning. He had only a twelve-hour window between peace and war. That morning, his phone no longer worked, and the electricity had been cut off.

"My wife—" The man pointed to a woman resting in a chapel. "—is critically ill—with cancer. But we can't leave this neighborhood for treatment, so she is dying and in tremendous pain. But what can we do? Now we are all sick from the cold, and everyone is hacking from the dust and smoke from the destroyed buildings."

"You need to get her to a protected area," Jessup said.

"All I want is for normal to return, the pleasure of going shopping or enjoying a cigarette at an outdoor café or driving your kids to the park. Is that so much to ask?"

Lieutenant Myer checked his watch and gave the order to his squad to mount up. He moved to a window and scanned the sky. Jessup followed and crouched beside him.

A steely grayness shrouded the sky. The clouds were low but not so low that they couldn't see the army helicopters circling at a high altitude. They were little more than dots, and tinier still were the falling barrels. The whistling sound of the bombs could only be heard seconds before impact.

As soon as the blasts shook the earth, Lieutenant Myer waved an arm, and his men ran single file through the hole in the wall and disappeared into the house next door. The battle became a ferocious, deafening display of bullets fired in many directions at once.

In the heat of the battle, the replacement Escalade pulled to the curb in front of the church, and the doors opened. Landau took the lead. They moved while crouched down. Jessup felt a sense of relief once they were all in the Escalade and the doors closed.

Ten minutes later, they were the only ones on an uninhabited road.

They came to a maximum-security facility with several modern buildings behind two sets of heavily guarded, twelve-foot-high chain-linked fences with razor wire on top. They were waved through, and the Escalade stopped at the entrance of the largest, most impressive steel-and-glass building in the compound.

Four men wearing Kevlar vests and carrying assault rifles descended the steps. They opened the Escalade's doors and stepped aside. Declan Hughes stood behind them.

"Welcome to my research facility, gentlemen. Please, come this way."

Jessup trailed Declan up the steps and into the building. Landau and Patrick followed, leaving Groucho with the guards out front.

"I trust you had a relatively uneventful journey?" Declan asked Jessup.

"I was nervous riding in an SUV with no driver, and I didn't appreciate being shot at, but other than that I found it quite accommodating."

Declan smiled. "Funny that you didn't mind flying in a jet with no pilots in the cockpit but you didn't like riding in a driverless car."

"I'm glad you waited until now to tell us that."

They walked through a lobby to a bank of elevators. The furniture and artwork were ultramodern and appropriately high quality. "This two-thousand-acre campus is dedicated to the discovery of chemical- and biological-warfare weapons. This baby cost a cool two billion dollars, and is the most modern facility of its kind in the world. Only 5 percent of our findings are published in scientific journals. The rest is classified."

Patrick said, "The US outlawed biological warfare after Vietnam."

"Just because we don't use them doesn't mean we can't know about them."

"Golden Eagle spent two billion dollars on researching something you'll never use?" Patrick said. "Why is that so hard to swallow?"

"Not Golden Eagle. No, no. Taxpayers foot the bill."

"My compliments to whoever decorated this place," Jessup said. "Nice to see my tax money is being well spent."

Declan nodded. "Like so much of everything these days, it's all marketing, the endless pursuit of cool. Our geek scientists love it."

"People don't use that word anymore," Patrick said.

"Are you referring to 'cool' or 'geek'?" Declan said with a smile. "The real work, the research, happens in the subterranean levels. This lobby and the upper floors are administration, except for the penthouse, and that's where we're going—our library."

They entered an elevator car and ascended. Declan talked about the person they were about to meet—Sergei Godelinsky. "His wife died a decade ago, his four children still live in Russia, and now he's recovering from a bout of prostate cancer that shriveled him in the course of the last six months."

The elevator car door opened, and they stepped into an open space three stories high. Two levels of balconies surrounded the room on all four walls. Crystal chandeliers gave off a warm, pleasant glow. There was no natural light in the room because there were no windows, only an inset picture of the Grand Tetons set against a cerulean sky. Mahogany tables and chairs were surrounded by floor-to-ceiling shelves that held what looked like a million hardbacks. At one end of the room, an old man sat at a concert grand piano, playing a theme from Tchaikovsky's *Sleeping Beauty*. The music spun through the air like a slow, cool breeze.

Jessup stopped, listened. This peaceful, elegant place lifted his spirits. A commotion above him pulled his gaze to the upper balcony where four armed guards leaned over the banister. Declan waved to them, and they waved back, and then went back to whatever they were doing.

"Don't mind them," Declan said. "We don't get many visitors. We interrupted their game. All these books hold the sum of human knowledge, and they sit up there day after day playing Pokémon. Sometimes I don't think the human race is going to make it."

"I can beat that," Landau said. "I carry a device that can access all the information known to man. Almost everyone has one, even grade-school kids, and yet people use it to look at pictures of cats, post photos of what they're eating, and watch porn."

They moved toward the tables in the center of the room. The music stopped, and the man who had been playing rose from his bench to join the party.

Declan introduced Sergei Godelinsky. He was an elegantly dressed man in his eighties with a ravaged face that must have been aristocratic before his bout with cancer. He gave off a powerful presence, with his closely trimmed gray hair and a gold tooth in the front of his smile.

Landau said, "Dr. Godelinsky, this is an honor. I've read your books."

Dr. Godelinsky waved a hand. "There is no need for formalities here, sir. Please call me Sergei. Even the security guards call me by my Christian name."

"I built this library specifically for Sergei because he hates dealing with computers," Declan said. "Old dogs and all that rot. He lives like a hermit in this cave of books."

Dr. Godelinsky said, "I used to spend my time in the research labs, mapping out DNA strands, designing new treatments, and monitoring our test cases. But I confess, now I spend most of my time here. There is so much I can still learn from my peers and the people who came before me."

Landau turned to Jessup. "Dr. Godelinsky is a Renaissance man who defected from Russia in the nineties."

"You play beautifully, Doctor," Jessup said. He recognized the name. Consuela Rocha y Villareal had mentioned him several times during their many talks. Back when the good doctor defected to the

West, he'd been hailed as one of the top five scientific medical minds in the world, had written two volumes on molecular biology, and spoke six languages fluently. After his defection, he taught at Harvard where he published a series of elegant metabolic papers on HIV antiretroviral therapy that eventually led scientists at the Institut Pasteur in Paris to develop a cocktail that eliminated the virus from the human body, which won them the Nobel Prize in 2012. A few years after publishing those papers, he dropped off the radar.

"I have a number of questions about how the manhunt is going, Mr. Landau," Declan said, waving a hand at the table. "But let's get a peek at the formula first. Please, my curiosity is bursting."

"Yes, the trillion-dollar formula," Dr. Godelinsky said. "I'm curious myself."

Landau said, "Before we begin, you mentioned something that caught my attention, about test cases in labs. In the video that went viral, Kenji Hiroshige made some startling claims that this formula cured dozens of human diseases; cancer, AIDS, and Alzheimer's topped the list. You're aware that we've seen evidence that supports these claims, yet, could he make such bold declarations if he never tested it on humans?"

Dr. Godelinsky said, "To make that assertion he had to perform clinical trials on dozens, if not hundreds of humans."

"If that is true, where are these patients?" Declan said.

Landau stared at Dr. Godelinsky, looking like a stunned calf ready for slaughter.

"I'm surprised you didn't think of this before now, Mr. Landau."

"I'm embarrassed to agree with you, Mr. Hughes," Landau said.

Dr. Godelinsky said, "They must have treated hundreds of people, perhaps thousands over the last decade. People who were old and dying but are now healthy and not getting any older. But how could they stay hidden? Surely someone would notice."

"Unless they're all tucked away in a remote location—an island, a secluded village, or a monastery," Landau said. "The other option is that after he cured them, he murdered them and ditched the bodies. But then he couldn't study the long-term effects."

"You're suggesting," Declan said, "that there is a community of immortals?"

"How else could he complete his research and keep them under wraps?" Dr. Godelinsky said. "He selects someone who's dying and makes a deal with them. I'll grant you life eternal, but you have to live here for the next hundred years, which is a grain of sand in the hourglass. At my age and poor health, I would jump at it."

"So in all probability," Landau said, "our boy isn't fleeing from danger like a deer escaping a forest fire; he's running to something. He plans to join them."

"Find this community, Mr. Landau, and you'll find Kenji," Dr. Godelinsky said.

Landau nodded. "If we're talking several hundred patients, there must be paper trails of people traveling to and from Kenji's lab facility, especially if international flights were involved. Many of them might have been accompanied by medical personnel."

Declan, now pacing back and forth, said, "It's likely a closed-off valley like Shangri-La or Ayn Rand's Atlas Shrugged."

Landau turned to Jessup. "You told me Kenji never traveled outside of Nevada, but did he have connections with a particular monastery or religious group?"

Jessup drew a blank. He shook his head.

"Think. He never mentioned any foreign visitors?"

"None that I recall."

"We have two things to explore," Dr. Godelinsky said. "Shall we look at the data?"

Landau opened his briefcase and distributed paper copies of the flash-drive files. Declan and the doctor began to examine them. Landau phoned his team. Jessup walked to the piano and sat at the keyboard, wishing he had learned to play. It would pass the time. Patrick followed him and browsed the spines of books on the shelves. He pulled a volume from the shelf and sat in a wing chair beside the piano. The book's title: Dante's *The Divine Comedy*. Patrick rested the book in his lap and leaned close to read. Jessup watched him become absorbed.

Patrick read aloud, "And of that second kingdom will I sing wherein the human spirit doth purge itself, and to ascend to heaven becometh worthy." He slapped the book shut, lifted it from his lap, and hit it against his forehead. "Fucking poetry. Why can't they just say what they mean in plain English?"

Jessup said, "That story is about descending into hell and climbing a mountain back out the other side. It describes the seven virtues, the seven deadly sins, and the seven terraces of purgation. It's about the nature of sin and atonement for sins. I found it interesting that Virgil, a poet and philosopher, leads Dante up the mountain out of hell but only leads him partway. In the last four cantos, Beatrice, who Dante loved, takes over as guide and leads him to earthly paradise. For me, it means that the intellect can only take you so far out of hell, but it takes love to lead you all the way into bliss."

Patrick smiled. "I've read the CliffsNotes. They say it outlines the theory that all sin arises from love—either perverted love, deficient love, or the love of objects."

"Funny, I never got that. So to Dante, impure love causes one to fall into hell, yet true love is the only thing that can lead you back out. So hell must be where love is purified?"

"You know Kenji better than anyone. Is he acting out of love?" Patrick asked.

"Damned if I know. One thing's for sure—he's got a lot to atone for."

"But he's not to blame. When people turn over their weapons, when the bloodshed stops, and the guns are destroyed, we'll all live forever. It's these assault-rifle-toting twits who are fucked-up. They selfishly demand to keep their security blankets, only looking out for number one and fuck everyone else."

"Most people in this world don't own guns, except for the military and police. Ninety percent of humanity are compassionate, loving citizens."

"What rock have you been hiding under? At a Berkeley crime prevention course, they teach never cry 'help' if you're attacked, because nobody will bother to get involved. Instead, always scream 'fire,' because people come running. It's something they want to watch. Tell me again how people have love in their hearts."

Jessup sat silent for a minute. Then he said, "I'm not comfortable with you siding with Kenji."

"Dad, try seeing the big picture. This technology will blast our species into the next evolutionary phase, making humans healthier, stronger, with higher-functioning brains, like the leap from Neanderthal to Homo sapiens, only instead of happening incrementally over millennia, we'll have it now. Kenji made a quantum leap."

Jessup said, "But people are dying. How many souls are you willing to sacrifice for this evolutionary leap?"

"As many as it takes."

Those five words hung between them, creating a gulf that seemed insurmountable.

A discussion echoed from the center table. Dr. Godelinsky walked to the far wall, pulled a book from the shelf, and continued searching. When he had an armful, he walked back to the table and deposited them. He took out a cigar and lit up, opened one volume, and scanned the pages. He pulled a notepad from his coat and brought a pen to bear.

An hour later, a steward delivered lunch, navy-bean soup and turkey sandwiches. Landau, Declan, and Dr. Godelinsky continued to work as they ate. Jessup and Patrick sat across from each other at the far end of the center table.

"I wish you could have known your grandmother Audrey," Jessup said to Patrick. "She came from a poor but honest line, who believe that salvation lay in keeping your word, speaking your mind, and living an upright life. She had no ambition beyond the borders of her ranch. She felt that happiness and longevity depended on honoring the land."

Patrick munched his sandwich, showing no interest.

"When she died, I had no wish to inherit her blinders, but once I returned to the ranch after college, I did—hook, line, and sinker. I dreamed of becoming a novelist. Audrey and I had some monumental clashes over that. In her view, most writers were bums. That was the only battle I ever won with her."

Patrick finished his sandwich, cuffed his mouth with his napkin, picked up his spoon, and dug into his soup. Jessup picked at his food like a weary bird.

"Audrey said spells of bad luck were a gift because they made you stronger. God, I wish she were here now. She'd take this bull by the horns and shake it until something gave. She taught me that wars beget wars; reprisals always follow reprisals. She believed in forgiveness."

"You're bringing this up now, because...."

Patrick's tone made Jessup try harder to reach him. "She was the only true Christian I've ever met. She saw her God in every creature; everyone counted equally to her, everyone was deserving of love. She used to say, 'If you start from the principle that your only enemy is the person who tries to sow hatred in your heart, you're halfway to heaven.'"

Patrick finished his soup. "I get it. Dad, you can step off the soapbox."

"What makes your life more special than these people you're so willing to sacrifice?"

Patrick's eyebrows lifted. "Nothing, I guess."
Jessup nodded. That seemed a smallish victory, but a victory nonetheless.

THE AFTERNOON mirrored the morning. Jessup began to think it was a mistake coming here. As evening approached, the stewards brought more food, which was eaten without enthusiasm. Hours later, they had cots brought in. Jessup and Patrick turned in.

Jessup lay in that room, disappointed that his attempts to reach Patrick had failed. Later, his thoughts turned to Kenji: *When did he turn away from me? Or was it always that way? Our relationship lost much of its tenderness lately, and he laughed less and less, but isn't that normal in a relationship? We had loved so passionately. He once said: "If you leave me, I'll never survive without you, not even an hour." It was all a lie, every minute of our relationship, and now Patrick has made him a hero.*

Chapter Twenty-Six

JESSUP AWOKE from a dream just as a steward wheeled in a tray of coffee and doughnuts. The three men were still working, and several others dressed in lab coats had joined them. He pushed away his covers, sat up, and scrutinized the group at the table.

Dr. Godelinsky suppressed a yawn. His eyes were red, his movements slow. He pushed away from the table with a dull and plodding deliberation. Jessup had scrutinized the doctor last night. Whenever the people around him became excited by something, Godelinsky seemed to grow more disinterested. Jessup assumed that was the foundation of this man's success, remaining objective and clearheaded while everyone else chased their tails. He seemed like the kind of man who could fall asleep in a horror movie.

Dr. Godelinsky lifted a cigar from his coat pocket and lit it. He sucked on it for a moment and lit it again. When he removed it from his mouth, he plucked a bit of tobacco from his tongue. "I think we are in agreement. Our presumptive conclusion is that the formulas spelled out by this documentation are compelling. Although, when we compare these theories to the DNA in the blood, bone, and tissue samples taken from Blake Connors after he'd been treated, these formulas, these procedures, don't hold water. Our two Cray computers working in tandem to simulate these theories simply can't produce those results from this set of procedures. If we hadn't had Connors's DNA samples, I would have said this is worth extensive exploration, but now I believe from the bottom of my heart that these formulas are a red herring. We could, and probably will, spend years proving these theories are false. My advice is that we abandon this data, ignore it."

Landau nodded. "I believe you, Dr. Godelinsky, but I'm far from an expert in this field. How can I be sure you're convincing us it's phony so that Golden Eagle Industries will be the only ones holding this formula? I mean, you do work for Declan."

Dr. Godelinsky's back stiffened. Speaking around his cigar while emitting a long curl of smoke, he said, "That's ridiculous to the point of being offensive. I'm a scientist, dedicated to the greater good of mankind, and any claim otherwise is irresponsible."

Landau lifted his arms like a boy caught with his fingers in the cookie jar. "I need to be certain. There is so much riding on this."

Dr. Godelinsky puffed on his cigar and pointed the burning end at Landau. "I'm as certain as I'm capable of, Sal, and so are you."

Declan's eyes clouded over, becoming dim and distant. He seemed disoriented to the point he seemed not to know where he was, and it was only with visible effort that he snapped out of his daze. As he recovered, he said, "I had such high hopes. If this were the real formula, it could stop our nation from stepping over a line that there can be no retreat from, a line that will damn every one of us from now until eternity."

"What line are you talking about, Declan?" Dr. Godelinsky asked.

"I've said too much already," Declan said with a quavering voice. "This new day, like all those that have gone before it, will be incapable of bringing compassion into the hearts of influential men and women. One woman in particular."

The people gathered at the table could only stare at one another.

"I'm sorry. I had no business sharing that. My father used to say, 'Keep your sorrows and disappointments to yourself. They're all you have when you've lost everything else.'"

Jessup joined the group. "Dr. Godelinsky, you must be terribly disappointed."

Dr. Godelinsky took a moment to puff on his cigar and knock the ash into a glass ashtray. "Perhaps it's for the best. We are a species on the brink of an unprecedented environmental crisis. Forests are disappearing, lakes and rivers are poisoned by pollution, our food is contaminated with lethal pesticides, and forty thousand species of plants and animals go extinct every year. That's roughly one species every twelve minutes. And the worst case is the submarine disaster of oxygen-making plankton perishing in fouled seas. With current manufacturing and farming technologies, this planet can comfortably feed roughly four billion humans. We've now surpassed eight billion, and that number will skyrocket to twenty-one billion souls in your son's lifespan."

Jessup glanced at the other scientists. They nodded.

Dr. Godelinsky continued, "Your son will see famine and malnutrition breed plagues to level the entire population. Wars over food and water will be the order of the day. Insects might survive, but not mammals, birds, fish, or amphibians. And certainly not man. Unless man changes his breeding habits, the end is near. If nobody dies, that scenario will play out in your lifetime instead of your son's. I don't know about you, Mr. Connors, but I don't want to witness the extinction of every species on this planet."

Jessup glanced at Patrick, who was sitting up on his cot, listening. His face was still creased with sleep. Jessup turned back to Dr. Godelinsky. "So you feel that to safely introduce Kenji's technology to humans, four billion people would need to be culled and having babies outlawed?"

"My guess is five billion, because you cannot keep people from making babies."

Jessup turned back to Patrick and crossed his arms over his chest. "You said you supported as many deaths as it takes to attain this evolutionary leap. Dr. Godelinsky claims that number is five billion. You still okay with that? If so, then you must be some kind of monster."

Patrick's pallor was gone. His eyes were incandescent. "As usual, you missed the point. Dr. Godelinsky claims that human extinction will happen regardless. What difference does thirty years one way or the other make? Let me ask you a hypothetical question, Dad. If you were certain that humans were headed for extinction within the next, say, fifty years, and you could do something dramatic to save our species, save the planet, would you do it?"

"That's not much of a question. Who wouldn't?"

"Right, but what if that 'something dramatic' meant killing five billion humans, in order to save the other three billion? If that was the only way, would you still do it?"

Jessup simply stared at him.

"And if you saved three billion people from certain death, are you a monster or a saint?"

Jessup knew when he had lost an argument, and there was no point in continuing this one. That university professor, Terrence Wallace, had been spot-on; Patrick had a cunning mind with the ability to see every angle of an argument. A flash of pride flared up in Jessup's chest. He wasn't sure which of them had the right answer, or even if there were a right answer, but the fact that the boy had outwitted them all by turning this problem on its head impressed the hell out of him. He turned to the others. "Dr. Godelinsky, would it help if you had a nonhuman that has been exposed to the formula?" Jessup asked.

"Yes, of course."

"Our dog was exposed. He's here. We left him with the guards at the front door. We can leave him here for you to study."

"Excellent," Dr. Godelinsky said. He turned to Landau. "I'll send you the results of our autopsy. Perhaps it will help your investigation."

"Autopsy?" Jessup's voice rose. "He's our pet. I said study him, not kill him!"

CHAPTER TWENTY-SEVEN

DAYS CRAWLED by. Once every hour Matt Reece walked from stern to bow and back, scrutinizing the condition of the sails and rigging, checking the barometer and compass heading, feeling the strength and direction of the wind. Each day he shimmied up the mast for a look-see at the horizon. The constant rise-and-dip motion of the ship brought about an ache in his lower back and knees, and the damp salt air settled in his throat, which produced a relentless cough. He felt dirty, itchy, but Vice Admiral Mike would not allow him to shower, as fresh water was precious. He was welcome to a saltwater bucket bath but declined. During sleep shifts, while Kenji was up and about, Matt Reece lay in his bunk and dreamed of the claw-foot tub back at the Promesa Rota and clean towels dried in the sun and smelling like a spring meadow.

For days on end he stared out at the swells, hoping to see anything other than water. Nada. At night he saw the twinkly lights of freighters and tankers, but Vice Admiral Mike steered well away from them and ran with no lights.

Without something of interest to look at, it became impossible not to dwell on the events in San Francisco. As painful as it was, he couldn't stop himself from contrasting the most wondrous night of his life with the heartbreak of the next morning. And with each comparison, his abhorrence for Kenji grew, as did his thirst for revenge.

Once just after sunrise, he experienced a distraction. A shark hit the fishing line he trailed behind the stern. Matt Reece grabbed the pole and set the hook. He fought for twenty minutes, watching the dorsal fin cutting the surface. He drew the fish to within fifteen feet of the stern, close enough for a good look. It was a five-footer, seventy pounds of muscle and teeth—no great white, but respectable nonetheless.

"We won't need a bigger boat," Vice Admiral Mike said and barked a hearty laugh.

The pole snapped back. He lost the fish and a ten-inch lure.

Another diversion came when Vice Admiral Mike taught him how to cook meals on the propane stove while the ship was heeled over at a thirty-degree incline and bucking wildly. Preparing meals became the greatest challenge of his day, and he felt pride when the vice admiral would nod his approval after finishing a plate.

He also learned a new vocabulary: *port, starboard, bow, stern, companionway, galley,* and the toilet, for some unfathomable reason, was called the *head.* He slept in a *berth* that was located in a *stateroom,* which sounded grand but turned out to be a three-foot-wide, six-foot-long closet with a two-inch foam mattress and not much overhead space. It seemed more like a coffin than a stateroom.

Matt Reece, accustomed to riding open country, considered this forty-three-foot vessel just another prison cell. He hated the confines of his berth, but whenever Kenji was out of his stateroom, Matt Reece crawled onto his mattress and stayed there until the coast was clear. Most of his time was spent at the chart table while Vice Admiral Mike manned the helm.

As the southward miles ticked away, the gray overcast turned to unbroken blue sky. The sun blistered down. Matt Reece shed everything but a pair of canvas shorts Vice Admiral Mike gave him. Under that intense sun, the henna dye and his green skin faded into a coppery tan, and the bur on his scalp assured him his hair was growing back.

He spent many an hour thinking about pitching the vice admiral and Kenji overboard, taking the helm himself, and letting the winds and currents carry him away—some hidden jewel in the South Pacific where he could ride horses along a pristine stretch of beach. With enough food and water, he could even circle around Asia and end up in the Mediterranean. At the tip of Italy, he could ditch the boat and board a train bound for Paris. The train would work its way north, and he would admire the cities and green farmlands and orderly vineyards of Italy. He would cross the Alps and wind down into France. When he stepped off the train in the City Of Lights, he would find a sidewalk café. He would drink red wine and begin to learn French. He would visit the Louvre, the Musée d'Orsay, Notre-Dame, and the Arc de Triomphe, and sit in the cafés and smile at the handsome men walking by. He would take a flat, and each morning he would go to the open market for his breakfast. He would wander the city, not as a tourist, but as a man who learns and understands what makes the city live. At that point he would be a new person entirely. Then he could look back over his current life and come to fathom all of these hard times and stupid errors since leaving the ranch. He would understand what it all meant. He was not growing crazy or even daydreaming. It was a way to combat the boredom—a way of passing time, which seemed never to pass.

The afternoon of day six, he noticed the odor of land riding beneath the smell of the ocean. An hour later, four black crosses with red breasts circled above the ship—man-o'-war birds. Land was near. He climbed the mast and spotted a slash of brown to the east. He pointed and yelled the first words he'd uttered since coming aboard, "Land ho."

He leaned out toward it, extending an arm and a foot in that direction, limbs spread like angel wings, balancing wind resistance against gravity until it seemed like he was soaring, leaving behind the ship and all his pain. It felt epic, a sensation of freedom he'd never expected. He knew that strip of land held some power over him, a place that could either free or kill him. *Perhaps for me*, he thought, *death is the only freedom.*

He heard the timorous sound of flying fish leaving the water and the whistling that their stiff wings made as they flew. A silver flash soared over the waves a hundred yards from the bow. He was fond of flying fish, as they were a brief distraction from the constant waves. This school seemed like a sign, as if they merged with his sense of soaring to lead the way to shore.

When he returned to the deck, Vice Admiral Mike upended a bottle of vodka he'd nursed all morning. He tossed the empty overboard. "That's Cabo San Lucas, at the tip of Baja, Hoss, but there's too many Americans there for us to anchor." The vice admiral brushed his dreadlocks over his shoulder. "We'll sail another twenty miles along the coast and drop anchor at San Jose del Cabo. You wait, octopus pickled in lime, fish tacos, frosty beers. Man-oh-man. I know a cantina that makes the best mole chicken in all of Mexico."

Four hours later they lowered the sails and motored into a harbor crowded with sailboats, sport fishing boats, and two cruise ships. They dropped anchor in thirty feet of water and lowered the dinghy. Fishermen were in their skiffs, hand-casting nets. Ashore, hugging a cream-colored beach, stood four impressive hotels surrounded by white buildings covered with red tile roofs. It looked like the kind of sleepy resort that anyone could lose himself in.

Kenji went forward to grab some shut-eye. They would wait until dark before going ashore to load up on supplies. As much as Matt Reece wanted to stand on solid ground and wolf down an icy beer and hot tamales, he knew he wouldn't share that dinghy with Kenji.

Vice Admiral Mike cracked open a fresh bottle of vodka. They waited. While dusk overtook the harbor, the sleepy marina came awake. People lounged in their cockpits, eating, drinking, listening to '60s rock music. Darkness fell, and mast lights winked like fireflies.

Matt Reece scuttled down the companionway and opened the logbook. The barometer was dropping.

Stardate 04.31.2017:18:44

There was once, on a swift and magical carpet, the saddest jailbird who ever lived, an inmate so ruinously blue that he had forgotten his name, forgotten how to speak. Day after day he stared out over a sea of unlimited regret. But today he is within reach of civilization. All he needs is to reach out and embrace it.

Matt Reece returned to the cockpit. It was full-on dark now.

Vice Admiral Mike checked the logbook and the barometer and swung himself into the cockpit. He laid a hand on Matt Reece's shoulder. "I read your entry, Hoss. Tell you what. You need to get off the ship, and I need to sober up. Let's swim."

Matt Reece eyed the black water, remembering the shark that he had tried to land only yesterday. A seventy-pounder might not be much of a threat, but what if mama was waiting under the keel? There were a hundred species that could maim or kill him, and they all fed at night. His real fear, he knew, was the terror he'd experienced when Kenji dropped him in San Francisco Bay. He had come face-to-face with death, felt his lungs burn, sensed himself leaving his body.

He shook his head no. He crawled down the companionway and crossed to the galley, thinking he would make the vice admiral a sandwich to sober him.

Vice Admiral Mike's voice echoed from above. "Jesus, Hoss, don't be a pussy."

Matt Reece heard a splash.

He raced back to the cockpit to find nothing more than a shirt and shorts piled on the bench. Vice Admiral Mike surfaced five feet beyond the stern, sweeping his dreadlocks away from his face. "Come on, Hoss."

He slashed the surface with one arm, and a spray of phosphorescent light sailed up. Vice Admiral Mike dived, flashing his bare ass.

Matt Reece's pulse thrummed in his ears. He assumed it was impossible to swim with no legs to kick the water. He tried to muster his courage, dreading the need to save Vice Admiral Mike if he didn't surface soon. Then he heard something scrape the side of the hull, and Vice Admiral Mike pulled himself up over the cap rail and landed on the deck with a wet flop. Every inch of his skin glowed emerald green. Millions of tiny organisms flamed like starlight. It seemed like something out of *Avatar*. Then it faded.

"Trust me, Hoss. You need this more than I do."

Matt Reece realized that there was only one person with a disability aboard, and it wasn't Vice Admiral Mike. His fear was hindering him and had all his life. Fear of violence, of being alone, of Kenji, of something lurking in the darkness—he would always be only half a man until he overcame those anxieties.

Fear is the killer, he realized, not some damned shark, not the blackness, not being alone. His nausea turned to anger, increasing the thrum at his temples. He stripped off his shorts. Vice Admiral Mike had a knotted rope trailing into the water so he could hoist himself back aboard. He stepped to the edge of the stern, uncertain of what he would do.

Voices murmured in his head. Was Vice Admiral Mike urging him on? Was Kenji talking below deck? He thought of the vice admiral leaping into the unknown and trusting himself in any environment. How fortunate he was to work a job without a desire beyond steering his ship through turbulent waters and with no goal greater than reaching port. Matt Reece had failed at life. He was neither brave nor free of desires, had nothing to cling to in desperate times except a broken pocket watch and a dead man's picture.

The voices grew louder. He paused, becoming distracted by the lights of the town spread over the land, trembling under a darkened sky. Almost involuntarily—at least it felt that way—he stepped into the empty space behind the ship.

The frigid bite of seawater shot a chill through him, but it was not unbearable.

He knew true silence for the first time—a divine quiet in every cell of his body. Even the voices hushed. He envisioned Vishal's scarred face, those disfigured dimples accenting his marred smile. He'd heard once that we punish the ones we love the most, and in those seconds of plummeting into blackness, he knew it was an absolute truth. But that was a two-way street; the ones we loved brought the most pain back to us.

He opened his eyes upon a greenish-silvery trail of phosphorescence. He gasped and took in a mouthful of water. He thrashed his way through a vortex of bubbles and light until he broke the surface. The water grew bright with light. The panic of survival became a roar of joy.

The current spun him with muscular force away from the ship, as if a strong man were embracing him. It felt personal, sensual, like being caught in the rush of sex.

As the light began to fade, Vice Admiral Mike plunged into the water not three feet away. Awash in light again, the unexpected wonder of it overwhelmed him.

The vice admiral surfaced with a playful roll. They floated on their backs, letting the current carry them from the ship. They drifted while watching the stars being blotted out by clouds. *As long as I stay fixed on what's above (as opposed to what's below me in the water),* he told himself, *I can do this.*

"In Mexico, they call the sea *La Mar,* which is feminine," Vice Admiral Mike said. "They say that because they love her. Swimming like this, engulfed in her womb, is the closest thing to making love to a beautiful woman. People who don't love her call her *El Mar,* which is masculine. But those people know nothing of love. Let me tell you, she is definitely a woman. I know this because of the way she gives great favors, and she can also withhold them. She can be a loving mistress or a cruel whore. But when she's wicked, it's because she can't help herself. Her moods are determined by the moon and the winds. Take it from me. She is truly a woman."

It did feel close to the joy Matt Reece experienced in Vishal's arms.

"I hate to be a buzzkill," Vice Admiral Mike said, "but a storm's coming. It's better to take it head-on in deep water than here where it can slam us onto the beach. Time to saddle up, haul our asses into town for supplies, and then get the hell out of Dodge."

They swam to the trailing line, but before they heaved themselves up, Matt Reece clung to him. "Do you ever feel fear? Out at sea I mean."

"Yes," the vice admiral said without hesitation. "And no. There are different types of fear."

"Like the fear of being alone?"

Vice Admiral Mike pushed him away. "Jumping into darkness took guts, Hoss. I'm proud of you, but let's not get all milky over it. Up you go."

They shimmied up the stern, and for a minute, they gleamed like galaxies. His eyes roamed over his phosphorescent skin. It was fairylike, the third miracle since his journey began. The first was seeing Groucho turn young again; the second was finding love in Vishal's arms, which forever marked him, flickering in his soul like this third phenomenon flickered on his skin.

He donned his shorts while Vice Admiral Mike yelled below to wake Kenji.

Three minutes later, Matt Reece watched Vice Admiral Mike, Kenji, and the dinghy fade into the darkness between the other ships.

ONCE ALONE, a curious thought crossed his mind. He now had plenty of time to hoist anchor, motor out to sea, and raise the sails. Kenji couldn't call attention to himself by reporting a stolen ship to the authorities. He could make a clean getaway, leaving them stranded. He'd learned to manage the sails, and if he hugged the shoreline, he didn't need to navigate a course. He could sail up the coast and be home in a few weeks.

He grew excited until he realized that he would need to singlehandedly battle a storm. He tried to imagine it, and it seemed too hazardous a gamble. His newfound bravery still lacked that kind of heroics. Still, to rob Kenji of his formula, the laptop, the money, and the tricorder, he felt he could endure almost anything. But what a shame he wouldn't be there to see the look on Kenji's face when he realized he'd been stripped of his power. That regret germinated an even better idea.

He hurried to the bow stateroom, switched on the lights, and stood on the V-berth. An overhead locker seemed the only place to store the canvas bag, and it was locked. He raced back to the galley to retrieve a knife, and he jammed the end into the lock and jiggled it back and forth. Three minutes later, the locker opened. Inside that space crouched a waterproof box, also locked. The knife opened that lock with ease. The box contained the black canvas bag. He pulled the box from the shelf, drew out the bag, and unzipped it. Inside, he found the laptop, tricorder, passports, and, of course, neat stacks of cash. It was all there, looking as overwhelming as it did in Consuela's cabin.

He rushed back to the storage lockers in the main cabin and grabbed an orange duffel storing the ship's medical supplies. He carried it back to Kenji's cabin and emptied the supplies onto the berth, an array of syringes, vials of medicine, bandages, and boxes of pills. He filled the duffel with the money, computer, passports, and tricorder. Then he filled the black bag with the medical supplies, dropped it back into the waterproof box, and placed the box on the shelf precisely as he had found it. He hauled the duffel through the ship and up the companionway. In the cockpit he hesitated only a second before flinging it overboard. It splashed the surface five feet away, erupting in light. It sank, leaving a trail of green sparkles that a moment later went black.

He sat back in the cockpit, anticipating Kenji's return. He would wait until they were out at sea before crushing Kenji's balls with the news. He smiled. For the first time since Vishal's death, he had something to look forward to.

CHAPTER TWENTY-EIGHT

DIANE MCCARTHY marched through the Golden Eagle Industries offices on Eilat Road, not far from the Greek Orthodox compound in Old Jaffa. The whirlwind effort to close down the Israeli offices and evacuate the staff had exhausted her. She had toiled all night. It was a quarter past nine in the morning, and she had a full day of work ahead of her before she could drive to the airport and fly to Madrid, Spain. She arranged for breakfast to be delivered to the offices so they could continue working while eating.

The lion's share of her staff and their families were safely away, and the other eleven executives would be on that 6:00 p.m. flight with her.

It had been difficult to evacuate without giving a reason. She knew, however, that if they suspected the city was in danger, it would have leaked out and caused a panic. Panic was better than a nuclear holocaust, of course, but she held high hopes that the diplomats wouldn't let it come to that. How could they? They were rational people after all.

She poured herself a cup of coffee and walked to her makeshift desk in the records filing room. They'd offered her a corner office with floor-to-ceiling windows overlooking the city, but she chose a room with floor-to-ceiling shelves of books and important documents instead, a room with no windows. She sat at the desk and lifted her phone to inform Declan of her travel times. Through the open doorway, she saw men and women scrambling to scan documents onto portable drives and others shredding documents. It would be tight getting it all done before their departure, but she felt confident in her team.

The staff welcomed the move to Spain. During the last weeks, the mood in Tel Aviv had turned against Americans. Her staff became the butt of ugly slurs. They became jittery and stayed locked in their apartments each night from sunset to sunrise.

Before she could punch Declan's number, the city ripped open in a conflagration of color and sound and felling wind. A flash—more intense than a sea of suns—cut through the offices, momentarily blinding Diane. She only had time to shout for people to move away from the windows before the shock wave slammed into the building, traveling more than a thousand feet per second. It pitched her into the air and hurled her against a wall of files. This time her voice was a whisper. "Oh God, help me to be brave."

A scalding sound followed a blast of severe heat. The shelves lurched forward, and books buried her. The ceiling gave way, debris raining down. A beam fell over her legs, pinning her. Despite the crushing weight, she used one free arm to clear enough space for her to breathe.

Her greatest fear became fire. If all this paper caught ablaze, she was toast. She tried to be brave. She knew bravery was not being fearless, but rather, acting wisely in spite of fear. That was true courage in her book. And she also assumed the apparent corollary: the greater one's fear, the greater your potential courage.

Through the wreckage, she could see into the next office. Walls were missing, knee-deep rubble, cries of agony. She searched for survivors, but without being able to move, she could only hear them. Windows had blown in, spraying shards of glass with deadly force. Blood spattered the debris. She saw bodies twisted into impossible angles, limbs dissected, and blood pooling on the floor.

Being trapped under concrete debris, with her legs possibly broken, waiting for someone to dig her out, for the first time in her life, she felt utterly helpless.

And then she lost consciousness.

She lay under wreckage for forty-eight hours, drifting in and out of consciousness. She was unable to do anything but endure the pain in her pinned legs. The shrieks of the other survivors had stopped. All she heard was the thud of heavy rain, the whine of wind, and the shriek of sirens in the distance. She had lost hope of rescue when she heard the sound of tromping feet and debris being moved about.

She managed a cry, which turned into a cough from breathing the gray ash that covered everything. She cried again and was rewarded with a yell back. She kept shouting, almost hysterically, guiding the rescuers to her. Minutes later men tossed the debris off her and lifted the beam pinning her legs. Two men carried her to the ground floor, wrapped a waterproof tarp around her, and laid her on a flatbed truck with six other survivors. She waited in the rain another thirty minutes while rescuers brought four more survivors from the building—none of them her staff. They were taken to Tel Hashomer Hospital, normally a thirty-minute drive from the center of town. This day, the truck took two hours to traverse the roads cluttered with building debris, fallen telephone poles and wires, and abandoned automobiles. Many fires still blazed from collapsed buildings. The air carried the electric smell given off by the bomb's fission. Ash and rain colored the entire landscape a hellish gray. Block after block they passed rescue teams working to free survivors from buildings and clear the roads.

At Tel Hashomer, ranks of injured awaited treatment. The hair of many was singed off, and loose skin hung from their faces and limbs. She saw several with empty eye sockets. Some were naked; others wore shreds of clothing. She was placed on a stretcher and carried through the crowd spread out in front of the building and then through hallways clogged with more people needing treatment. She was placed in an examining room with eight others.

Diane realized that the ratio of doctors to patients was off the charts, so despite the pain in her legs and weakness of her limbs, she didn't wait for help. She would later learn that of the eight hundred and forty doctors living in Tel Aviv before the blast, seven hundred and sixty-six were already dead or too injured to work. Also, less than three hundred nurses survived. Indeed, the largest medical facilities were at the Ichilov Hospital, off Kikar Hamedina, and that complex had been destroyed.

She examined her legs—cuts, bruising, swelling, but no broken bones. She rummaged through a storage cabinet and found bandages and disinfectant. She cleaned and wrapped her cuts and then began patching up the others in the room. Many of them were so traumatized that they couldn't talk. They had to use hand gestures to communicate.

Her contact lenses had blown off in the blast, so her vision was fuzzy. She pulled the glasses off a man she was treating and tried them on. They helped, so she kept them.

Once she treated those eight patients, she snatched more supplies and moved into the corridor. No doctors or nurses were in sight. Patients crouched on the floor. Disfigured families huddled together, assisting only their relatives, for they couldn't comprehend a wider circle of misery.

People were still in a comatose state of shock. Many were vomiting; others suffered bouts of diarrhea. That sour stink combined with the stench of burned flesh to make her gag. She bent over the nearest person, a girl of six or seven, and began disinfecting her burns. The girl's skin slipped off in glove-like pieces, but Diane continued to wrap her wounds. She worked steadily but without method, doctoring one as best she could and moving to the next person closest to her. People prayed aloud, some trying to bargain with the Almighty, promising to give up drinking or women or gambling if only he allowed his family to live through this hell.

She worked for three hours without seeing any medical staff, yet more wounded poured into the corridors. She was forced to make the hard decision of passing up the lightly wounded to concentrate on keeping the critically wounded from bleeding to death.

She worked through the day, becoming numb to the people weeping and pulling at her sleeve trying to get her to treat them next. She turned into an automaton, a robot wiping, daubing, winding, and moving to the next one. It crossed her mind that she needed to get word to Declan that she had survived, but she assumed all telecommunications were out, and there was no time with so many victims to help.

At midafternoon a doctor approached her. He thanked her for helping, but then he looked at her with the hardened eyes of an abandoned animal. He had been working nonstop for days. His body language spoke of utter defeat, exhaustion. Not simply from the dark half-moons under his eyes, but the way his arms hung at his sides, as if his hands were too heavy to lift.

"A hundred thousand wounded," he said, his voice rising in anger. "Where is the International Red Cross? Who is coming to save us?"

"I don't know. I'm not with the Red Cross. I'm with—"

"I know who you are. I've seen your picture in the news. You're one of the people who profit from war. You did this." He waved his arm at the people begging for help.

She opened her mouth to protest, but she knew anything she had to say was feeble.

He pointed a finger in her face. "Where are they? Where is the international community? Why aren't they helping?"

"We have to save ourselves," she said.

He stared at her for a long time, and he said, "Keep going, but concentrate on the lightly wounded. The seriously wounded will die anyway. We can't help them, so focus only on the ones we can save."

She wanted to slap his face, but she was too exhausted. He turned and walked away, and all the way down the hall he kept shouting, "Where are they? We are alone, just like we've always been."

She continued her work, and the more she thought about his words, the more she knew he was right. She had wasted much effort to only prolong these people's suffering for another handful of hours.

By evening she ran out of disinfectant and bandages and could find no more. She was wondering what to do next when she noticed a child begging her parents for water. She gathered an armful of empty plastic bottles and tried the tap at a sink in the women's restroom. To her great relief, it held water pressure. She filled the bottles and distributed them. She soon realized, however, that there were tens of thousands of casualties and only herself issuing water. Her efforts were too ineffective, but she refused to give up. She noticed a young man, not badly hurt, who was comforting his burned wife and baby. Diane grabbed him by the scruff of the neck and hauled him to his feet. She pressed several empty bottles into his hands, pointed to the sink, and told him to get to work. He glanced down at his family with longing to stay with them but moved off to help. By the end of the hour, she had enlisted eight others. Some carried buckets of water and a cup, going from person to person. Others filled bottles. No one turned down a drink because they were all parched.

Once Diane gathered a sizable water brigade, she thought about food. Her stomach was a clinched fist, so these other casualties must be equally as hungry. *This place must have a cafeteria*, she thought, *which means a storeroom*. She went looking for it.

Tel Aviv was a metropolis of four million people. She assumed that several hundred thousand people had died in the blast, perhaps millions, and many more would perish in the coming days and months. Yet many survived. She wondered why they lived when scores of others died. Each survivor, like herself, unknowingly depended on many small items of chance—a brisk run to catch a bus instead of waiting for the next, a decision to stop at a coffee shop so that they were indoors, parking a car in the underground parking lot instead of on the street—that had spared them. In her case, it was choosing an inner office with no windows. That had not been her intention while selecting that workspace, but she wondered now if it had been a subconscious reason for her lucky choice. And she also realized that in her act of surviving, she was witnessing more death and suffering than any other people in human history. More than she ever imagined possible. There seemed no end to it.

CHAPTER TWENTY-NINE

JESSUP DREAMED about a gun carriage bearing a flag-draped coffin, followed by six clattering gray steeds with blackened hooves, their riders tall with rigid backs and gold aiguillette on their dark jackets. Another horse pranced at their side bearing an empty saddle with stirrups reversed, also with blackened hooves and being led by a military groom. There was something about the orderliness of the procession and the steady swaying motion of the horses that his dream-self found soothing. But then he noticed that twenty yards behind the horses marched a tall shadowy figure dressed in black robes. He had Kenji's face, grim and menacing. At that moment, Jessup's dream-self realized that the riderless horse belonged to Matt Reece.

The shock of it propelled him into consciousness, and he woke to see a young man lying on a bed. He knew at once that he was in Vishal's hospital room, and he saw Blake standing across the bed, staring at the ceiling-mounted television. He smelled antiseptics and heard the beeping of monitoring equipment.

Outside the windows the city lights twinkled below a lavender sky. It was dusk. The flight back from Southern California had been relatively uneventful, and he was happy that he had gotten back before the doctors had brought Vishal out of his coma.

Out of the corner of Jessup's eye, he saw the TV flash "Special News Bulletin" across the screen. He grabbed the remote and increased the volume.

A CNN anchor explained that reports were coming in that four cities across the Mediterranean had been simultaneously struck with what could only be nuclear weapons, Jerusalem, Tel Aviv, Rome, and Tehran. Early reports described the destruction as massive, with millions dead. Jessup jumped to his feet, now wide-awake. Blake stepped closer to the TV. They stood staring at the screen.

As appalling as the bombings were for Jessup, there was more to it, something connected to the case. He felt that familiar tick in the back of his neck, the one he got whenever events were connecting but he couldn't put his finger on it. It was a nagging clue, a tidbit buried deep. Was it something Agent Landau said? A clue having to do with the formula? He couldn't remember any discussion of bombs, nuclear or conventional, but he knew he read or discussed something about the case that triggered an association with this bombing.

He pressed his hands to his head, squeezing against his temples, trying to force the link to the forefront of his brain, but he failed.

He considered himself an intelligent man, yet he often thought his brain let him down at inopportune times, as if his will and his memory were regularly at odds. There were even times when he doubted the utility of thought, and all intelligence. Right then he thought dolphins swimming in the sea or bears roaming the woods were somehow superior to humans because their brains were not as developed. At least those seemingly happy creatures did not have the intelligence to poison the earth or destroy themselves with weapons of mass destruction.

Indeed, human intelligence was creative, yet equally destructive; charitable, yet more often spiteful and avaricious; precise and calculating, yet often muddled with conflicting emotions. The human brain, the most complex structure in the known universe, could theorize the beginnings of time and space, the creation of the universe, and the workings of subatomic particles, yet Jessup now assumed that it would also cause the end of all life on earth. Much like climate change drove the dinosaurs into extinction, Jessup felt that unbridled intelligence would be the downfall of man.

And right now, his cleverness was failing him. He knew that some puzzle piece had dropped into place, linking others together for a clearer picture, but the more he grasped for it, the more it slipped through his fingers. He gave up trying, and a moment later, there it was, staring him in the eye.

He grabbed the phone Agent Landau had given him, punched in Landau's name, and pushed the Call button. Landau answered his call.

"Are you seeing the news, about the bombings?" Jessup almost screamed, he was so excited.

"Yes, I just saw it—"

Jessup cut him off. "I know where Kenji is going," Jessup said in a breathless voice. "Remember the note he left me. It said, 'I'm taking Matt Reece to the one place that is perfectly safe, because lightning never strikes the same spot twice.'"

"Yes! That's it," Landau shouted. "It's the one industrialized country that already outlawed gun ownership back in 1971, the only superpower that has no weapons, no army or navy to speak of, so no country would bother to attack them. They are no threat. It makes perfect sense. But if you're right, it means Kenji knew his actions would lead to nuclear war. He planned this horror from the very beginning."

Blake shot Jessup a stupefied look.

There was a long silence before Jessup said, "How soon can we leave?"

An hour later, Dr. Falses, wearing a white coat over scrubs, breezed into the room and took a clipboard from the foot of the bed. She removed a stethoscope from her pocket and leaned over Vishal. "You're awake! My goodness. I'm Dr. Falses. Remember me?"

Vishal nodded.

"You've been burned much worse than the first time you were here." Her demanding voice was tinged with tartness, yet it was a protective voice.

"My uncle?" Vishal said, his voice weak and raspy.

The doctor took his hand. "I'm terribly sorry. His remains are in the morgue."

Vishal closed his eyes. "Matt Reece? Where's Matt Reece?"

Jessup nearly jumped out of his chair and moved to the bed. "You know him?"

Vishal nodded. "We plan to marry."

Surprise hit Jessup like a mule kick to the gut.

"Breathe deeply," Dr. Falses said as she pressed her stethoscope to the left side of Vishal's chest. She moved it to his right side and pulled away to jot notes on the clipboard.

Jessup said, "We assume he's still with Kenji. God only knows where they are, but we might know where they're going."

Vishal tried to raise off the bed. "I.... Oh God."

Dr. Falses pressed a hand on his shoulder and guided him back to the pillow. "Are you in pain?" she asked. "Do you need stronger medication?"

An insane question, Jessup thought, after learning his uncle was dead and his betrothed was kidnapped.

"No more meds. My head is so woozy."

Jessup asked, "Does Matt Reece feel the same… about getting married, I mean?"

"It was his idea."

"In that case, I'm proud to call you son. I'm Jessup Connors."

Vishal reached up and took Jessup's callused hand in his.

"Any idea of what they're planning?"

Vishal shook his head. "Stop saying they. Matt Reece is against Kenji."

"I knew it."

"The car?" Vishal asked.

Jessup's face grew stony. "The FBI believes Kenji rigged that bomb."

"What do you think?" Vishal asked.

Jessup hesitated. "I think we need to find Matt Reece, quick as hell."

"You said you know where they're going?"

"Agent Landau from the FBI is flying up from LA, and I'll meet him at the airport. We're chasing a hunch, but it's all we've got to go on."

"I'm going with you."

Dr. Falses replaced the clipboard at the foot of the bed. "Out of the question. It'll be weeks before you can leave that bed." She walked to the doorway and glanced over her shoulder. "I'll have the kitchen send up some soup."

"Don't bother. I'll be gone by then," Vishal muttered under his breath, but loud enough for Jessup to hear.

"You're not fit to travel, son," Jessup said. He pointed to Blake. "This is Matt Reece's grandfather. He'll stay with you. If you'd like, he can take you to our ranch as soon as Dr. Falses releases you."

"I've had Kenji's treatment."

Jessup nodded. "They tell me that's the only reason you're alive."

"Then you know I'll recover fast."

"I only know what Dr. Falses tells me," Jessup said.

Vishal turned his eyes to the ceiling. "He was an ordinary boy, except that from the moment I saw him, I was struck. I don't know how he did it, but even before we could get to know each other, he'd become the center of my universe. Whenever he smiled, it was like being smacked by lightning. When he was down, the world turned black. When we made love, well… words can't describe. Lemaitre once said, 'Either one stays at the beach, playing as a child does with all sorts of colored stones and shells, or one follows the path of truth.' My only truth is Matt Reece."

Patrick ambled into the room. "They're serving beef ribs and mashed potatoes. I'll spell you two while you go eat."

"You must be Patrick," Vishal said. "Matt Reece and I went to Berkeley looking for you." He turned back to Jessup. "Let me put it another way, Dad. Where I come from, we don't abandon family, and you're not leaving without me. Now, find my clothes and help me out of bed."

"Dad?" Patrick said. "Why the hell is he calling you Dad?"

CHAPTER THIRTY

THE FLIGHT from Cabo del San Jose took place with such speed that it seemed like a teleportation—one minute they piloted out of the harbor, the next they bounded over ten-foot swells under heavy rains. The sea became hills with deep troughs carved by strong winds. To a landlubber like Matt Reece, it was hostile and beautiful, but also terrifying.

From San Francisco to the tip of Baja, the ship's rolls and plunges were moderate, and Matt Reece kept his sea legs, a fact that gave him much satisfaction. But after two days of enduring gut-heaving dips and vaults, he realized his pride had been premature.

The *Valhalla* creaked over each wave, structural groans that sounded like rusty hinges slowly opening. He was not too worried. The ship was, no doubt, a marvel of modern engineering. The wind screeched at a pitch that hurt his ears, and it was punctuated with frequent detonations of thunder. They sailed with three reefs in the mainsail, no jib, and the engine running at low speed. He, like everyone else, had not slept for days because the ship rode the waves with a paroxysm of twists, lunges, and plunges, the whole enchilada. He had to concentrate on keeping his stomach calm and his feet on the deck.

He stood at the stove grilling a Spam sandwich, which he held down on the grill with a spatula to keep it from hopping around like a jumping bean. It was a slow process because he could cook only one patty at a time.

Vice Admiral Mike sat at the dining table, clutching an overhead handhold and swaying with the ship as he wolfed down his second sandwich. His face glowed reddish-purple from the vodka he consumed, making it appear locked into a permanent sunburn. Yet each time he emptied a bottle, Kenji hurried to the lockers and fetched him another.

Matt Reece yelled, "Two days of this—how long will it last?"

"How long will what last?" he said, grinning. Vice Admiral Mike was in his element.

Between the midnight swim at Cabo del San Jose and riding out the storm together, they had formed a definite, albeit fragile, camaraderie.

"Forget that last sandwich, Hoss," Vice Admiral Mike said, zipping up his foul-weather jacket. "I better get topside and spell your father."

"He's not my father. He's not my anything."

Vice Admiral Mike swung himself to the gangway ladder and climbed with his hands. When he opened the hatch cover, the roar of the rain grew louder. At that moment a wave crested over the ship, and water plunged into the cabin from the open hatchway—a waterfall that kept coming and coming. Mike held on.

The bilge flooded. The engine sputtered and died. Matt Reece was washed off his feet. As more water rushed in, one by one, the floorboards popped up, floating a few inches higher than the floor.

"Keep the bow into the wind," Vice Admiral Mike yelled to Kenji, who was harnessed to the helm. The vice admiral fought through the cascade, pulled himself into the cockpit, and slammed the hatchway shut, leaving four inches of achingly cold water covering the cabin floor.

As the ship pitched forward, an interior wave surged to the bow, soaking everything in the V-berth. A moment later, it rushed aft, carrying everything not tied down.

Matt Reece crawled out of the water and onto the dining table bench just in time, for next came a roar that he could never have imagined, loud enough to shatter eardrums. Then an explosion of hot air hit him. Outside the windows, the sky flashed white. Inside, blue filaments of electricity sizzled through the interior of the ship. The hair on his arms and legs singed away. The lights went out; the cabin vanished into darkness.

Lightning had struck the mast, he realized. He was thunderstruck in the truest sense of the word. Fear bound up in his chest. Had it struck a moment before when he was kneeling in water, he would have been a charred shish kebab now.

He had been manipulated by fear all his life, enough to know it had no decency, showed no mercy. It always found his weakest spot with unerring ease. His heart galloped, his limbs trembled, and he couldn't breathe. This was tangible fear, the kind that shakes you down to the foundation, seeping into your brain like ischemia.

He wondered if Kenji and Vice Admiral Mike were fried. He was more afraid of being alone than the risk to his own life. In order to find out, he would need to cross that flooded deck to the ladder. He sat there for several minutes, clinging to the table while trying to beat down his anxiety. Without lights, however, the interior felt like a crypt tumbling toward hell. His fear morphed into panic, squeezing his lungs to the point he couldn't breathe. He had to get the hell out of there.

The question was how to make his will overpower his fear. He had to somehow shimmy into that stealthy chamber of his heart, where lay the circuitry for all he was capable of, the full range of what he might be. He needed to crawl in there and set off a spark, something that would ignite a blaze of valor.

He swallowed hard, wriggled free from the table, and waded across the flooded salon, feeling his way over the holes left by the floorboards. He gripped the ladder and hauled himself above the waterline, grabbed the emergency flashlight attached to the bulkhead, and switched it on. A beam of light illuminated the hatch. When he opened it, another waterfall rained down. He held on to that ladder and the flashlight with a death grip. It felt like the weight of the world pressing against him. It finally let up enough for him to hotfoot it into the cockpit.

He focused the flashlight beam on Kenji, who was still harnessed to the helm and fighting the wheel to keep the boat into the wind. His eyes were bright with astonishment. The irony hit Matt Reece that the one person he had come to fear the most was now the very person who brought him calm, who allowed his clinched lungs to open and accept air again, simply by being there, alive.

Matt Reece gulped oxygen as he swung the light beam over the ship. The dinghy was gone, along with the propane tanks. The sail was still intact, and the rigging looked fine, but there was no trace of Vice Admiral Mike. He swept the beam over the ship again.

"Where's Mike?" he yelled.

"When lightning struck the mast, the boom swung free and knocked him overboard," Kenji shouted. "There was nothing I could do."

An emptiness opened inside him, and it filled with dread. "No," he screamed. He flashed the beam over the water, knowing it was hopeless. Even in daylight, once you lost sight of something in the water, you never found it again. They couldn't have saved him without divine intervention, and he had no doubt that God had forsaken them.

"Why—" Matt Reece whispered. He threw the flashlight at Kenji, and it sailed overboard. "He was no threat to you, you fucking animal," he said, and even to himself, he sounded pitiful and lost.

"We'll be okay. The winds are already half what they were an hour ago."

Matt Reece might have felt lost, but he was not yet defeated. He staggered back to the companionway hatch. "I'm going to send out a distress signal. I'll radio the coast guard and tell them who we are and where we are."

Kenji laughed.

Of course, Matt Reece thought, the lightning strike not only fried the ship's lights, it would have also charred the VHF, GPS, radar, autohelm, inverter, and batteries—everything electronic, including the water purifier. How much fresh water was in the tanks, and was it still good? Also, the propane tanks went overboard, so no more cooking. With no electronics and the engine submerged, they were in serious distress. Even if they survived the storm, there was no way to navigate without GPS. They would be blind, groping through an area seven thousand miles wide.

He crumpled to the deck and hugged his knees. More water sloshed into the cockpit and poured down into the cabin, but he couldn't make himself care enough to close the hatch, even when Kenji yelled for him to do just that. What was the point? Whether the *Valhalla* was half-full of water or overflowing made no difference now.

It was not just another abandonment. After all, he hardly knew the man. But he was now trapped on this ship—a few dozen square feet of space—with the man who murdered the one person who illuminated his heart.

THE WAVES dwindled, and the winds calmed into lethargic gusts. The stormed moved on. Exhaustion pulled him into a fitful sleep where he crouched in the cockpit.

He woke in time to watch the sun rise thinly from the sea, the water turning from lead to liquid light. His shorts were nearly dry. The sun grew brighter as it cleared the horizon, and its rays tumbled over the sea and into his eyes, making them burn. There was only enough wind to push the *Valhalla* a few miles an hour through a moderately calm sea.

He lifted himself on one elbow and scanned the water. All about them was flatness, an unbroken panorama of blue. He assumed they were light-years from the nearest land.

Kenji sat at the helm. While Matt Reece slept, he had closed the companionway hatch, taken the reefs out of the mainsail, and hoisted the jib. Still, with little wind and carrying tons of seawater below deck, the ship made almost no headway.

Then he realized the sun was behind the stern. They were traveling west? Insane…. With no GPS, the only rational course was east, toward the American continent, so they could follow the shoreline south to Lima like the float plan indicated. Kenji, obviously, had another destination in mind, which was why he had rid himself of Vice Admiral Mike. But the only land due west from the tip of Baja was Hawaii, and that was three thousand miles away. Did Kenji think they could make Hawaii in a crippled ship without means of navigation?

"Welcome to the living, Sleeping Beauty," Kenji said. "Go below, and see what you can scrounge up to eat."

Matt Reece opened the hatch. Three feet of water sloshed below deck, and the force of the internal waves had smashed open the supply lockers. Pineapples and papayas and bananas and potatoes and blocks of cheddar cheese floated along in a soup of clothing, books, maps, cushions, and floorboards. Boxes of pasta and sacks of rice, flour, and black beans were ruined, as was the fresh bread they had brought aboard at Cabo del San Jose. A film of gas coated the water. The air was heavy with petroleum fumes. The slightest spark could burn the ship to the waterline.

Climbing into that sloshing mess, he hoped that the holding tank from the toilet had not overflowed into the flood.

He found a dozen eggs still wedged in the refrigerator, but they would have to be eaten raw. He pumped water from the galley sink into his cupped palm. It tasted clean, thank God. He had no idea how much water was in the tank because he couldn't remember the last time Vice Admiral Mike had run the water purifier. To make more, they needed the engine, and that was kaput.

With his bare feet, he felt cans slopping around the floor. He reached down and retrieved a can of SpaghettiOs. Yes, they had canned food aboard, and somewhere in all this mess was an opener. The blocks of cheese were shrink-wrapped, so they were edible. The vegetables and fruits were still good, and there were dozens of unopened bottles of vodka. They would not starve, not this week anyway.

He opened the forward hatch to circulate air through the cabin. Then he made his way to his stateroom. The mattress was waterlogged, but the shelf above where he stored his clothes was dry. He pulled his grandfather's watch and the picture of Vishal from his jeans pocket. They were unharmed. He opened the watch to ensure it was still stuck at 8:15, and he stared at Vishal's smiling face for a time, long enough for a wave of comfort to wash through him. He crossed to the galley and found a Ziploc bag. He sealed the watch and photograph in the bag and stuffed it into the pocket of his shorts.

Fortunately the chart table was high enough that the master chart and the logbook were relatively undamaged. In the cabinets above, a real find—a sextant in a box that included instructions on its use. They might not be able to sail this half-sunk tub, but they could pinpoint where in the hell they were. Beside the sextant was another box holding a red Orion flare gun and six casings that looked like shotgun cartridges. The shells reminded him that in a cabinet under the helm was Vice Admiral Mike's shotgun, and he hoped it was still operable. Now he had two secrets, one the hidden shotgun and the other, Kenji's loot that was on the bottom of Cabo del San Jose's bay.

He carried the two boxes and the master chart to the cockpit, and then he went below again to gather the food. It was slow work sifting through the swilling mess, most of the time on his hands and knees feeling the bottom for canned goods. Three hours later he found the can opener and decided to call it quits. He had a monstrous headache from breathing petroleum fumes.

Back in the cockpit, Kenji had organized the supplies.

"You want the good news?" Kenji asked.

He refused to answer. He had no wish to talk, not to this man.

"We have enough food to last three weeks, and I found a solar still in the emergency kit. It can purify four pints of seawater a day."

Kenji explained that although they were surrounded by trillions of gallons of seawater, it was deadly. The salt content in seawater was so high that when a person drank it, the kidneys must generate urine to flush away the salt, but to do that took even more water than was drunk, so the body pulled water from its cells, until the cells began to fail, causing fatal dehydration.

A solar still, however, created unsalted water through evaporation. It was an inflatable, round, life buoy–like chamber with a transparent plastic cone over it. It floated on the ocean, and water heated by the sun on the inside of the chamber vaporized, gathering on the inside surface of the cone. The salt-free, condensed water dribbled down the cone and gathered in a catch in a cavity on the cone's perimeter. "That'll work as long as we're caught in this calm with the sun beating down and no waves. But it won't work once we're underway again."

Did he say, "caught in a calm"? He glanced out at a strange stillness. The sails luffed, and the rise and fall of the *Valhalla* ceased. They made no forward progress. The ocean stretched out in every direction in polished smoothness, reflecting the sky in glassy perfection. The water looked so solid it seemed like he could step out of the boat and walk home.

Kenji said, "The storm sucked everything into its wake, leaving nothing behind. We're caught in a high-pressure area. Not a breath of wind, and no telling how long this will last. On the positive side, it gives us a calm sea while we pump out the water below."

Kenji's offhanded tone annoyed him all the more.

He had read accounts of slave ships, in the days before steam engines, becalmed for several weeks at a time in areas of the Atlantic called dead zones. When stranded ships ran low on supplies, the crew would drive their human cargo on deck and whip them over the side. The livestock cargo—horses, cattle, sheep—they slaughtered on deck and ate them down to the hooves.

As for the solar still, one person could survive on four pints each day, he knew. But could two?

It didn't take an Einstein to figure out that three weeks of food for two people meant six weeks of food for one. Killing him would double his stepfather's chances of survival. He assumed that if the food and water rationing got tight, Kenji would have no qualms about killing him.

Karma. Murdering Vice Admiral Mike has flung us into some dead zone where we'll die of starvation. So be it. At least here there is only one more person he can kill. Will he simply push me over the side? Or eat me to keep himself alive?

At that moment he felt more like a lamb than a slave.

Chapter Thirty-One

Days passed, a week, and then another in a dead calm. The sea held not a wrinkle, no movement, no wind. Nothing to read, nothing to see, nothing to do. Hours lasted years. At night the sky held masses of stars all crowded together in a soup of gems. During the day the sun hammered them from a cloudless sky. The sea was a molten circle, and they became a pinpoint surrounded by a radius of blue that was shattering to the senses. The air glimmered with heat, as if each molecule were a tiny mirror reflecting the sun's blaze.

The first week they took turns below, sitting up to their necks in seawater and cranking the bilge pump handle back and forth. Each day the water level inside the hull lowered by four or five inches. Now, below deck was shipshape with the exception of green mold growing wherever it could get a foothold. So much mold that they slept in the cockpit to escape the smell below.

The engine was a total loss, but the sails and rigging were functional. Thirty gallons of untainted water sat in the tank, and the solar still purified four pints a day. The fruits and vegetables were finished, and they were down to one block of cheese, six cans of Spam, and ten cans of beans. Matt Reece kept a fishing line off the stern with a hunk of Spam on the hook. It yielded nothing.

He and Kenji had not exchanged words since the night the vice admiral died. He stayed to his side of the cockpit, Kenji to the other side. Conversation would have passed the time and kept their spirits up, but he refused to give his stepfather the satisfaction.

After several days of semistarvation, his stomach contracted, his gastric spasms subsided, and he found himself drifting into a curiously peaceful condition, which turned into an ideal space for meditation on things past, passing, and to come, in just that order.

He wore nothing but a pair of shorts and a turban he made from his shirt. He slept twenty hours per day. It wasn't proper, restful sleep, but rather a state of semiconsciousness where dreams and reality were indistinguishable. Whenever he wasn't sleeping, he prayed for wind. The sun beat down without mercy. When he felt his brains boiling, he dipped a plastic bucket into the sea and poured seawater over himself. It was warm and hardly refreshing, but evaporation helped cool him. He often thought about diving overboard, swimming down a few yards where the colder water lay, but he felt so weak he had no confidence he could pull himself back into the boat.

He lay prostrate in the cockpit hour after hour, parched, sweating, and utterly vacant. Boredom dripped in his gut like acid, with each droplet eating away at his vital organs.

On the other hand, he grew to appreciate the utter quiet and the scent of sun-warmed teak decking. He avoided thinking about Vice Admiral Mike, and it was hard not to feel anything but relief to be alive in a place where Kenji couldn't harm anyone else.

He stared at the horizon, careful not to squint, trying to detect any movement. The edge of the sea blended seamlessly into the sky. His hunger pains weren't bad, but he had begun to see green spots hovering twenty to thirty feet in front of him.

Every hour, Kenji slung binoculars around his neck and scurried up the mast. Once every few days, he also removed the sextant from its box and took bearings to see how the currents were moving the boat. They were drifting southwest, roughly forty miles per day from the original setting of one hundred seventy miles west from Baja.

Matt Reece decided that fish simply had no appetite for Spam, and who could blame them? He reeled in his line, replaced the bait with a sizable hunk of cheddar cheese, and cast out behind the stern. He let twenty fathoms of line go down before clamping the pole to the fishing socket. To pass the time, he took the plastic bag from his shorts pocket. It still held his watch and the snapshot of Vishal. He pocketed the watch and stared at the picture. "Gone," it seemed to whisper. "I'm sorry but I'm gone, so deal with it." He struggled to remember details of his lover, which he could not. Jessup, Patrick, Grandpa Blake were all vivid to him still, but the more he looked at that photograph, the less he remembered of Vishal. His lover was passing from his mind, and he realized loving the dead increased their unreality, and the more he tried to envision this beautiful man, the further Vishal receded into the depths of his cloudy memory.

And so, half-awake and half-dreaming, he ripped the photo in half, and again, and again. He scattered the pieces over the water like rose petals. It was a stupid gesture. Sentimental too, he thought, but mostly just stupid.

At that moment he hated Vishal. Yes, hated him. Loved him too, but it was an unforgiving love. *The poor bastard just flat-fuck refused to heed my warnings. Boom. Dead. Nothing else.* And it was Matt Reece who'd lured him into that web of demise. "You can't fix mistakes," he mumbled. "Once people are dead, that's it. The end. Move on."

But he couldn't shake the blame; he would carry this like a stone in his gut for the rest of his life. And even without the picture, he still visualized him vaguely, dishing out food to the needy while smiling tender encouragements.

He was realistic about it, knowing this memory was somehow self-loathing. Regardless, there grew a hardness in his stomach. His eyes burned. He wasn't crying, but he was up against it. And Lord knew he had no water to spare for tears.

He slipped into sleep, and he was carried home, purely borne into the land of his memories. Now, whenever he slept, he lived at the base of those snowcapped mountains, with peaks so white they hurt his eyes. He heard the song the wind made moving through the trees, the heavy breaths Comet made after a hard gallop, and the three-note melody of blue jays. He smelled the resin from pine trees and the fresh scent of snow drifting down into the canyons. He felt the sun on the back of his neck and sweat trickling down the V between his shoulders. It warmed and comforted him after a cold morning sunrise.

Normally, when the sun's warmth grew strong, he woke up. But now he kept dreaming, wanting to ride all the way back to the ranch house to see Jessup, to see the place he grew into manhood.

He no longer dreamed of traveling the world, nor of finding love, and he definitely stopped himself from dreaming of Vishal, which had proved too painful. He only dreamed of the ranch now and riding Comet through the canyon lands. But this time he woke to a strange new sound. He opened his eyes and saw the fishing pole bent toward the water and line spinning out, making a clicking sound from the drag.

"I need to set the hook," he said aloud. Two hundred yards to port, a school of flying fish broke the surface, flashing silver in the bright sunlight.

He rushed to slide the pole from the socket, tightened the drag, and pulled back sharply to set the hook. He knew from the weight that this was no flying fish; it had to be a predator stalking the fleeing school.

His excitement rose as he held the pole firmly and commenced to haul it in. He reeled it up slow and steady until he saw the fish's blue back and the gold of its sides just under the surface. With no net, he prayed his thirty-pound test line would hold as he pulled sharply to swing the fish over the stern and into the cockpit. The tuna was bullet-shaped, pure defiant muscle thrashing out its life. Large, fleshy, and sleek, it was a magnificent fish.

Kenji came up the companionway carrying a curved knife. "Albacore," he said. "Good eating. We'll use the guts for bait to catch others. He'll weigh fifteen pounds."

"Twenty," Matt Reece whispered.

He couldn't pinpoint when he'd started talking to himself. Sometime during the storm while being thrashed about the ship's interior, he began to pray out loud, an appeal to see Jessup and his brother again. The words helped take his mind off the motion of the ship, but the exact moment when that happened was a mystery. He began by talking at night, while Kenji slept, but now he couldn't control himself. On the ranch, it was considered a virtue not to talk unnecessarily, and Matt Reece respected that. But now, whichever words knocked about his head came out his mouth any time of the day or night.

"Sashimi feeds the blood," Kenji said, handing the knife to Matt Reece.

Matt Reece knelt over the fish, held the knife by the blade, and hit the tuna over the head with the wooden handle three times for kindness. It stopped thrashing. As it died, its shimmering color turned dull and lifeless. He removed the hook, scraped off the scales, and cut thick wedge-shaped strips of red meat from the backbone down to the belly. He laid the strips in a row along the bench. Hunger took over, and they both chewed the flesh until they barely had to swallow, releasing all the juices and spitting out the skin. It was not unpleasant, but he wished they had limes to add flavor.

The strength of the fish surged through his veins. So much nutrition after weeks of near starvation made him drunk on protein. After they each consumed three strips, Matt Reece gutted the tuna. He ate the heart and gave the liver to Kenji, and then used the intestine bits to rebait the fishhook. He cast off the stern, set the pole in the socket, and cut more wedges.

They forced themselves to eat leisurely, knowing that too much too fast would make them vomit. There was no hurry. A twenty-pound fish yielded over ten pounds of firm edible flesh. That gave them each five pounds of meat to consume before it went bad.

"Let's eat it all before it spoils," Kenji said. "No telling when we'll catch another."

I'll dry strips that will keep for days, Matt Reece thought. *This full-blooded fish will restore us. We'll be good for a week.*

Two hours later, Matt Reece turned the fish over and sliced wedges from the remaining side. By late afternoon they ate all of the flesh, leaving nothing to dry. Even after eating so many pounds of flesh, Matt Reece's stomach didn't feel full. His body absorbed the meat as fast as he chewed it, leaving his stomach demanding more.

He cut the head from the backbone to keep as bait and wiped his blade on his shorts. He lifted the carcass by the tail and dropped it overboard.

They both stretched out on the benches. A half hour later, Kenji grabbed the binoculars and climbed up the mast. After only a minute, he bounded into the cockpit. Excitement sparkled his eyes as he grabbed the flare gun and rack of cartridges.

Matt Reece lifted the binoculars. He scanned the port side and starboard. A speck of white flashed on the horizon. It had to be a sail. Kenji shot a flare in the new ship's direction. It made a beautiful arc, so high that Matt Reece had to tip his head back to watch it rippling against the sky with a trail of gray smoke, followed by a burst of red.

He raised the binoculars again to see the sail disappear. He knew, as Kenji shot another flare, that the new ship had turned toward them. Gradually, a sleek double-mast vessel motored closer, growing larger as it drew near.

Kenji dropped the pistol and hurried down the companionway. He came back lugging the waterproof container that held his black canvas bag. He set it on the cockpit bench, ripped off his white T-shirt, and waved it over his head. Matt Reece realized that Kenji was not planning to beg for food and water; he was abandoning the *Valhalla*.

"Are you surrendering?" Matt Reece asked.

"We're saved," Kenji said.

"But they're doomed," he mumbled to himself.

He followed their progress with binoculars until he read the name on their bow: *Nirvana*. She was a trimaran, ten feet longer than the *Valhalla*, with two solar panels gleaming on her stern and a maple-leaf flag at the top of her mast.

Her motor grew loud. After weeks of silence, those mechanical noises stunned him into a peculiar silence. Two people stood at her helm. Salvation was a bare-chested man wearing a straw hat and a heavyset woman dressed in a yellow blouse, with her hair pulled into a ponytail. Matt Reece liked her instantly. He liked them both. They seemed the kind of people who dropped everything to assist those in need. It would, no doubt, be their last act of kindness before their deaths.

"Come to Papa," Kenji said. When they were twenty feet off the starboard beam, he yelled, "You're a sight for sore eyes if there ever was one."

Matt Reece dropped to his knees and opened the cabinet under the helm. There it lay, the pump-action shotgun. He knew what he must do— but it would be the hardest thing he had ever attempted. He snatched it from its rack. It felt impossibly heavy. He pumped a shell into the firing chamber, lifted the barrel skyward, and let go with a blast at *Nirvana's* mainsail. By the time he pumped another shell into the chamber and blasted a second hole in that canvas, *Nirvana* spun clear of *Valhalla* and raced away with the engine droning furiously.

He pumped a third round into the chamber and leveled the barrel at Kenji, who now held the knife Matt Reece used to gut the tuna. It had happened so fast that he felt as stunned as Kenji looked. They glared at each other, and Kenji dropped the knife.

"You'd have murdered them," Matt Reece said.

"This is survival, where there are no second chances. You killed us instead of them."

"Whatever it takes to keep you from butchering more people."

Kenji laughed. "Oh how wrong you are. Everyone has something they're good at, painting or music or business or gardening. Look at you. You handle a horse like nobody else because you took that skill and perfected it, and in the process you became an artist. Death is my art, and right now I'm painting my masterpiece." Kenji pointed to the waterproof box. "In there is everything the human race ever wanted— immortality—and people will rip this world to shreds trying to own it. That YouTube video set the ball in motion, and sitting here, where nobody can touch us, won't stop it. The only way to prevent total carnage is to give them what they want. The longer we sit here, the more innocent people will die."

Matt Reece longed to pull the trigger, but he said, "Everything you put in that box is on the bottom of the sea." He didn't feel the rush of triumph he expected.

The smile melted from Kenji's face. He ripped open the lid, unzipped the canvas bag, and stared at the contents. He lowered the lid and laughed again, his tone even more condescending. "Put that down. You aren't capable of shooting anyone. You're a spineless little shit, although I admit you surprised me just now. That took guts."

He knew Kenji was right. He hurled the shotgun overboard and felt an immediate sense of relief.

Kenji reached for his pocket and pulled out a flash-drive cartridge sheathed in a protective casing. "The tricorder documentation is stored on this. I can recreate it. All you did was make us poor." Then came that condescending laugh again.

A sense of failure ignited his frustration into pure fury. He leaped at Kenji, tackling him. They burst through the companionway hatch and fell into the ship's salon. They fought, rolling on the floor, fists flying, fingers gouging. Kenji attacked with surprising might and speed, his jabs wickedly efficient. What was more impressive than the speed of his fists was his pure animal confidence, his total absorption in the moment. His level of calm concentration would be the envy of the highest yogis.

Matt Reece received cuts over his face and torso. Blood oozed down his cheeks. Each blow felt like an arrow piercing his flesh. He thrust himself past the pain, and fury pushed him to a level of savagery he never imagined possible.

He focused on wrenching the flash drive from Kenji's fist. Holding that arm with both hands, he gripped those fingers with his teeth and bit down with every ounce of rage in him. The hand opened. The flash drive bounced on the floorboards. He snatched it up and tried to tear away, but Kenji held him down.

With the flash drive held in his right fist, he gathered his pain and what was left of his pride, and he rolled over and smashed Kenji's gut with that fist—once, twice, and a third time in rapid succession. He put everything into those blows, real lung-busters, and he felt ribs break. It knocked the wind out of his stepfather, enough so that Matt Reece wrenched himself away and scurried up the ladder to the cockpit. He was thinking clearly. He stuffed the flash drive in his shorts pocket and snatched up his grandfather's pocket watch. The timepiece showed the winged boy engraved on the cover. He raced to the stern, and as soon as Kenji's head appeared at the top of the companionway, Matt Reece flung the watch into the water. It made a plopping sound and sank.

Matt Reece, now panting, turned to face his stepfather. He had a strange taste in his mouth, coppery and sweet. He was afraid of it, of what internal injuries he had suffered.

Kenji looked stunned. "Billions of people will die," he said, with no arrogance in his voice now, "and because of what you just did, it will all be for nothing."

His ruse had worked. Now Matt Reece was in possession of what the world craved, and that scared him. He believed Kenji about the mass killing. And Kenji had said the only way to stop the bloodshed was to give them what they wanted. But how could he do that sitting on this damned boat?

Four hours later, with Matt Reece settled on his side of the cockpit waiting for sleep, he felt a pressure building around him. The ship's lolling motion shifted.

They both turned in unison, listening, feeling the air.

The paddles of the wind generator turned ever so slightly: once, twice around, and then it accelerated into a sluggish spin. A sweet, lovely breeze freshened the sky. A wave lifted the bow, and another. Waves meant wind. Everything was moving now. After nineteen days of stillness, those waves felt larger than they actually were.

The sails leaned to port and began to draw.

"We'll be underway soon," Kenji said. "Let's hope we make Hawaii before our water runs out."

Hawaii? Matt Reece's excitement imploded. He knew then that something specific waited for them there. Why else would Kenji risk a journey with little food and less water? But what was the point now that Kenji thought the formula was lost?

The route to Hawaii would take weeks longer than to Mexico, and every day longer meant more people dead. He thought about fighting Kenji again, so that he could turn the ship east, but his strength was spent. He wiped some dried blood from above his eyebrow. "Rest against the wood deck, and save your energy for the next battle. Hopefully that won't come until Hawaii."

Exhaustion washed over him, and all he could think about was sleep, so that he could dream of being back on the ranch. He had destroyed his picture of Vishal and now lost his grandfather's watch. He was no longer a keeper of time, no longer had a lover. He had nothing left but riding the scrublands in his dreams.

He hovered in a dreamless state until the *Valhalla* pushed through the waves, carried along by the strengthening breeze.

CHAPTER THIRTY-TWO

AIR FORCE One sat on the tarmac at Edwards Air Force Base in Southern California. On the upper deck, Declan Hughes placed a folder on President Harrington's desk. She wore her customary dark blue suit, which like her hair, was immaculate. *She must travel with a hairdresser*, he thought, *or perhaps it's a wig?* Regardless of grooming, there were deeper wrinkles on her puffy face; her lips were more severe. She'd aged five years since he last met with her only seven weeks ago. He'd been picked up by helicopter at the research facility with no notice, and he didn't know he was having a briefing with the president until the copter landed beside Air Force One.

Distant gunfire lifted his attention to the windows lining the fuselage. He saw a brigade of armored vehicles supported by a battalion of ground troops. It seemed a bit ironic that inside the plane felt like a family huddled around the fireplace with wolves howling in the distance. His next thought was one of relief that the 747-200 was equipped with armored glass windows and armor plating to withstand nuclear blasts on the ground.

The reason she was here rather than flying him back to Washington, he knew, was that after the nuclear assaults in the Mediterranean, suicide squads had attacked the White House and Senate, leaving thirteen senators dead and virtually shutting down the federal government. She and her advisors now spent most of their time at thirty-five thousand feet, flying from one military base to the next, a moving target.

Harrington stared with distaste at the folder: a manila cover marked Possible Immortality Formula. She glanced at Jeffery Wolfe, who sat leaning back in his chair with his hands clasped behind his head. His face sagged, giving him a basset-hound look.

"You've read this data, Jeffery. Do you agree it's a ruse?" Harrington asked, her words slightly slurred. She nursed a glass of vodka over ice, even though it was 9:00 a.m. It occurred to Declan that she might be one of those people who could imbibe impressive amounts of alcohol without becoming sloppy drunk. He began to see her in a new light, as an alcoholic, drinking to repent, to bury her shame and her sins.

"We can't say for sure," Wolfe said in his normal creamy voice, which Declan was beginning to loathe. "Dr. Godelinsky is the foremost authority in DNA science, so I lean toward his findings until we can test the theories mapped out in those files."

The president slammed a fist on the folder. "Seven weeks after Kenji Hiroshige's YouTube announcement, and what do we have?"

"Thanks to you," Declan said, "a shitload of death!" He had not planned to confront her, but now that it slipped out, he was glad. He felt tightness in his chest and needed to sit. But he stood there, wanting the advantage of height if this turned into a bitch fight.

Harrington's mouth drew into a tight line. "I beg your pardon?"

"You turned the Mediterranean into radioactive ruin, destroying the adherents of three major religions, and turned every nation in the world against us. You singlehandedly started a civil war, waging a bloody conflict against the middle class, while the rich wrap their wealth around them and run for cover—Iceland, Canary Islands, Tahiti, Seychelles, anywhere isolated so they can lay low until the killing stops. Six million dead and wounded, with a hundred thousand of those being the people who voted you into office, all in just seven weeks. Hell, it took Hitler seven years to match that tally. Pretty soon you'll rival Mao Tse-tung, who I believe notched up a hundred million."

Her eyes flashed. "Jeffery tells me you lost someone in Israel?"

"Ms. Diane McCarthy was in Tel Aviv, closing down our Middle East operations, but it seems you jumped the gun." Even to him his voice sounded strained, rather than defiant. "I'm flying there to search for her as soon as my jet returns to California." He wanted to add that for the president's sake, he'd better find her alive. It was on the tip of his tongue, but he knew this was no place to make threats.

She swiveled her chair and stared out at the perimeter of military vehicles. "The Muslims, Christians, and Jews forced us to take measures. We had to protect this asset until we can acquire the formula. I don't think you appreciate how important it is that America controls this technology, and thus controls the fate of the human race. There is no prize for second place in this competition, Mr. Hughes, only total success or unmitigated failure."

A general on the Joint Chiefs once explained to Declan: "Wielding power requires a measure of inhumanity. Compassion is baggage nobody in our business can afford to carry. If you think about people as individuals with souls, then you'll never make the tough decisions, and you'll never be able to live with yourself after." At the time, Declan thought those were wise words. Now he wished he'd have punched that sorry son of a bitch in the nose.

Declan said, "I don't know how you sleep at night."

"I rarely do." She straightened her shoulders and turned back to Declan, fixing him with a resolute glare. "And for the record, the United States bombed only Tehran, a government guilty of sponsoring half the terrorist activities of the last two decades."

"Which did nothing more than massacre a million innocent women and children, strangle our supply of Middle East oil, and start a new jihad," Declan snapped. Actually it did a lot more, he silently corrected himself. It preyed on some of the kindest, most worthy people on the planet, wiping family lines away in a flash, and obliterated a beautiful landscape. Yes, their holy leaders sent assassins, and a crude justice may have been won, but inhuman cruelty had also won.

"It's true we've lost allies," Wolfe said. "Europe and Latin America and Israel, everywhere that Catholicism and Judaism is a factor. But now that we've established a Vatican in Boston, and the new pope has given his first address over Vatican Television's broadcasting network, absolving everybody of sins, we're hoping to win back the faithful. All of the surviving cardinals support us. As for the Jews and Muslims, once we have the formula, they'll come begging. Let me remind you, owning that formula presents us with an opportunity to settle the Communist question once and for all."

President Harrington's lips seemed poised on the edge of a smile.

Declan grated his teeth. He should have known they'd drag out that tired, fear-mongering cliché. It was the old standard carrot they dangled in front of the ignorant masses. It angered him more that they used it on him. But he knew this was the essence of politics—creating plausible explanations out of bald-faced lies, and using the media to spread propaganda. It was nothing short of putting an acceptable spin on mass murder.

"I'll bet you could polish a turd to a gleaming finish so people would hang it on their walls. Go shovel your bullshit to the evangelicals. We're up to our ears in it here."

Wolfe steepled his fingers and pressed them against his lips. "Canada, New Zealand, South Africa, and Australia have begun to disarm, and China is disarming all of Southeast Asia and North Korea. The UN sent inspectors to verify they get every last peashooter. It's a good start, although the Aussies can be goddamned infuriating. As for the civil war in America, who knew that hysteria among the lower classes was infectious? Thankfully it won't last much longer. We've halted production of all weapons and ammunition and confiscated arms and ammo in every store across the land. The vigilantes will soon run out of bullets, and that will be the end of them."

Declan said, "After Kenji's video went viral, ammo sales skyrocketed. They buried arsenals in backyards and basements. You'll be at this for the next decade." The tightness in his chest grew sharp. He knew his blood pressure must be off the charts, but he carried medication in his pocket. He was not worried.

Wolfe waved a dismissive hand.

"Mr. Hughes," said Wolfe, "whichever country acquires this formula will rule the world, and everyone else will be enslaved. Which camp do you want to be in? I suggest you decide, and in a big fucking hurry."

So it's Mr. Hughes now, not Declan? "We're on the brink of war with Europe, India, and the Middle East. The banking system is near collapse. The price of gas is seventy dollars a gallon, a chicken costs a hundred bucks, an assault rifle is now twenty grand. Globally, people are starving in vast numbers, and here in the States the suicide rate for people who've lost their guns is astronomical. World commerce is at a standstill, so no food is moving into the cities. And grounding all nonmilitary flights has only exacerbated that problem and bankrupted the airlines. You're butt-fucking the planet so a bunch of rich, white, geriatric fucks can be young again."

Harrington paled. She clearly did not enjoy being lectured. She did, however, maintain her appearance of confidence and purpose.

"I would like you to know," she said, "that our government has a two-year stockpile of oil, grain, and canned goods stored in strategic locations. The Air Force is distributing those supplies where they are needed. And be assured that America is not the only country steeped in civil war. With the exception of Japan, every industrialized country in the world is in the same boat."

"And what of the excessive number of suicides? How can you explain them away?"

She shook her head. "I confess, it's beyond comprehension why these deplorables would die rather than live without their assault rifles."

"It's not difficult to understand." Declan's voice softened. His chest twinged, and he made a mental note to visit his doctor as soon as he returned to LA. "We have a profound mistrust of governments, other religions, other races, and other tribes. This distrust has gone on for so long it's become embedded in our psyche, become instinct to want to defend against anyone who doesn't share our views. And what you've done in the last seven weeks has intensified their distrust. At the same time you've emasculated them by taking away their only means of self-defense."

"There are other ways to defend yourself."

"For 'deplorables,' I think you called them, the world is pretty black-and-white."

"You're still slow on the uptake," Harrington said. "Regrettable as this situation is, do you remember our conversation about the need to administer this treatment only to the country's elite, the 1 percent who contribute the most to our society?"

Declan remembered only too well.

She continued, "Imagine what will happen to those chosen few if the rest of the population, those well-armed deplorables, are deprived of the treatment. The only way to protect the influential is to emasculate the masses first."

Declan's hand twitched from the need to slap the smirk off her face. But of course, she was right. When your loved ones lay dying, people would do anything to save them. The have-nots would rise up and take from the haves, given a chance. It became clear. She wasn't fulfilling Kenji's demands. De-arming was purely for self-preservation.

"Let's get back on point," Wolfe said. "Can your team duplicate the formula?"

"We've discovered an enzyme in the blood that we've never seen before. It may be responsible for changing the host's DNA, but we can't say for certain yet. We don't even know if this is a new enzyme or a known enzyme that has been radically altered."

"I assume you've injected Blake Connors's blood into other humans?"

"Out of desperation, we experimented with transfusions on three different critically ill patients. All died within hours of receiving the treated blood. Their body's natural immune system warred against these cells with the altered DNA. But these cells are indestructible and multiply at an alarming rate by consuming all other cells. Thus, the war intensifies until the host systems collapsed, one by one—liver, kidneys, brain, lungs, heart. We believe that for the host to live, the treatment has to be administered to the entire body all at once, or at least within a matter of minutes. Simply injecting the new cells into the body is fatal."

"So it needs to be administered with a fast-acting nerve gas or an ion spray? Something with high saturation across the lungs to inundate the bloodstream instantly?"

"Possibly. My leading hematologist suspects it might be some type of bacteria saturation through the lungs that quickly spreads throughout the bloodstream, altering the red and white blood cells. There are a variety of bacteria that rapidly affect the blood. Staphylococcus, for example, produces two enzymes that alter blood cells."

Wolfe nodded. "Our Johns Hopkins team experienced the same results with blood transfusions. We want to try a bone marrow transplant in combination with transfusions."

"Too risky until we know more," Declan said.

Wolfe said, "My team is adamant, and we want your full cooperation."

"Over my dead body."

"You leave us no choice. In the interest of national security, the federal government is annexing Golden Eagle Industries, and I'm taking control of your research facility."

Declan laughed a sad, cruel bark. He had met with members of the National Security Council on the main deck below them, and they seemed nervous. This takeover had been planned in advance. "That won't help with your transplant because we no longer have donors. I suggest you retract your fangs if you wish any support from my team."

Harrington scribbled a note on the cover of the report. "No donors? We have Mr. Connors and this new man, Vishal Mandial."

"You people need to stay up to date on the details. Agent Landau, who's heading the FBI investigation, found a reasonably solid clue as to the whereabouts of our fugitive. Since you've grounded commercial flights, I allowed him to use my corporate jet to investigate his lead. He's taken the Connors family and Vishal Mandial with him."

A long drawn silence.

"Why wasn't I informed of this lead?" Harrington said.

"I suggest you ask the FBI."

Wolfe gripped the arms of his chair. His voice failed to hide his fury. "As welcome as that news is, why did he take our test subjects?"

Declan ignored the question.

Harrington pressed both her hands on her desk and rose to her feet. "You seem determined to become my enemy."

He became her nemesis the moment the bomb dropped on Tel Aviv. He was about to tell her so, but he held his tongue. His top priority was flying to Israel to search for Diane, and he didn't want this bitch stopping him.

When Declan refused to respond, she said, "Where is Kenji Hiroshige hiding? Don't be coy. If you don't tell us, the FBI will."

Declan spoke a silent "fuck you" with his eyes. He and Landau had discussed the possible scenario that Harrington might nuke any location she thought Kenji was hiding, to keep Russia or China from acquiring the formula. This operation was top secret; not even the pilots knew their destination until they were well away. The jet had flown out of San Francisco, thirty feet over the water to escape radar until it was two hundred miles west from American shores.

"Jeffery, alert the Pentagon," she said. "Force that plane to land at a base we control."

Declan glanced at his watch. "They touched down five hours ago, and they'll have the full cooperation of my staff in—" He stopped himself from naming which city. "And as for stealing my company, I'm about to show you what real power is." He knew who held authority in this country, and it wasn't this bitch. Real power was reserved for the exclusive club of money people, billionaires who pulled the strings to make her dance. He was not only a platinum-card member, he had cozy relations with the others. Bureaucrats like her came into office and went out again at this club's whim. The money people would be in authority long after the next electorate replaced these transient officeholders. "A few well-placed calls and you'll be choking on my shit."

Since the bombings in Israel, his most demanding question came from a gut level: *Whom can I trust?* And he found only one answer: *People who have nothing to gain.*

A band of pain encircled his chest. The pressure became severe. The room wavered like a mirage in the desert, whirling around him. He felt a sensation of falling, and he saw the spiked, Jimmy Choo heels under the president's desk rushing to him.

Wolfe's voice said, "I'll alert the medical team."

"Wait," Harrington said, as she bent over Declan and cradled his head so he was looking up into her eyes. "Declan, listen carefully. You're having a heart attack. We have medical staff aboard. If you tell me where Kenji is hiding, I'll send for the doctors."

Declan tried to shoot her another "fuck you" with his stare, but he was in too much pain. Then the blessed rise of unconsciousness eased his agony.

PART TWO
KINDRED SPIRITS

Your most precious desire is on the far side of your deepest fear.

Chapter Thirty-three

Sailing a westerly wind, Matt Reece and Kenji lay motionless. They shared no words, for they had no thoughts. They paid no attention to the horizon unless it held clouds that promised rain, for their drinking water was used up. Most of the time, however, the sky was blue and shimmering with infernal heat.

For the last two weeks, they ate only what they caught and drank whatever fell from the sky. They had bagged three sharks, the largest being six feet long, colored a grayish brown with white-tipped fins. Each one they drew alongside and clubbed its head to kill it before dragging it into the boat by the tail. Even with a sharp knife, sharkskin was as easy to cut as a coat of mail. The flesh was tough and smelled faintly like ammonia. The livers were the easiest to eat.

Each fish had been caught at sunset. So they feasted through those nights, drying whatever was left the next morning.

Matt Reece had withered down to little more than burned skin stretched over bones. His lips became hard and cracked. His shrunken muscles ached.

Thirst had a curious effect on him. He withdrew into a dead-like state, drifting in a febrile fog. He felt no fear, no enthusiasm, no joy, no sadness, no concerns about death, and no hopes of rescue. Time became irrelevant. The life within his flesh retreated further into his core, leaving the extremities, until he no longer felt the heat or the wind on his skin, heard nothing but the pulsing deep in his chest.

From what seemed far away, he heard a measured tap, tap, tap. *Death knocking on the door?* He ignored it. *Let him wait.* But it grew in tempo and volume. It became annoying, like someone flicking the end of a towel in his face. It ripened into a hissing noise, a swarm of furious snakes. He grew angry, so much so that he opened his eyes.

Rain, pure and cool. The scent of it reached into his chest and pulled him all the way to full consciousness. The *Valhalla* became engulfed in a squall. Fat, glistening drops drummed on the ship and the sea around them. Kenji was unfolding the tarpaulin sail they used as a rain catcher. If Matt Reece could help him, they were saved, or at least they could prolong the agony for another week or two. His resolve grew strong, and he dragged himself to his feet. He clutched a corner of canvas and stretched it out, he on one side of the cockpit, Kenji on the other, channeling rainwater into a five-gallon plastic bucket.

They both leaned out over the sea, stretching the tarpaulin wide to gather the most water possible. All he had to do was lean back inside and release his grip, and Kenji would tumble overboard. The ship was moving fast enough that he would be left behind. Matt Reece had suffered so much. You can go only so long without food and water and still maintain your sanity. Revenge lay in his grasp, but as sweet as that idea seemed, he would be left alone to suffer his own death in the weeks to come. Once again, being alone seemed more fearful than the satisfaction of retribution. Of course, he could let go and fall backward himself so they both toppled into the sea. A quick end for them both, and they could cling to each other as death pulled them under.

And so this moment blossomed until he was more intent on revenge than survival. They held each other's eyes, and he knew Kenji realized his intentions. Kenji's superior strength now seemed like weakness because Matt Reece became fearless. They faced off, wide-eyed and defiant, both equal for the first time.

"*Hasta la vista, padre.*" His words were raspy. Yet, using his voice for the first time in weeks flipped a switch in his head, and he held fast. That moment of insanity lapsed.

Rain raged against him. He tilted his head back, gathering a mouthful of water. The *beat beat beat* of raindrops smacked his face as he swallowed and opened wide for more. Freshness lifted his heart, and he swallowed again.

They leaned in long enough for Kenji to replace the full bucket with an empty, and they filled that one too. By the time they topped a third bucket, the storm had swept by.

He fell beside a bucket and submerged his face. He drank, slowly, pulling his face out only long enough to breathe. He knew that even though the weeks ahead might prove agonizing, life was precious, to be savored even while crawling through hell.

When he staggered to his feet again, he knew he needed to help Kenji pour the rainwater into the freshwater tank and help fold up the tarpaulin. But something caught his eye, near the horizon. He assumed it was another storm, but he saw a line of green against a storm-blown Pacific. The *Valhalla* was driving right for it.

As they sailed closer, he saw a low-lying peninsula backed by tremendous cliffs rising from the sea, and a mountain behind rising thousands of feet. After weeks of nothing but flat blue, this sight was shocking.

He lifted an arm and pointed, making a grunting sound.

Kenji spoke his first words since the calm, "Molokai."

It took Matt Reece time to process the word. Once he did, he didn't know how to feel about it. Could they have escaped death? He peeked into the future and found he had a life with hope once again. It seemed strange, yet it lifted him up, and he felt himself floating.

The island grew large with many shades of green interspersed with black cliffs that looked like ancient battlements and a mountain rising up several thousand feet. It looked primitive and sinister, but the organic scent of vegetation became a perfume to get drunk on.

He didn't know much about the island. He'd read about the leper colony at Kalaupapa on the northern peninsula, and the mountain was a national preserve. There had once been a massive pineapple farm that had turned into a cattle ranch, and then Monsanto bought up the island to produce seeds for GMO plants. Few tourists traveled there, and the locals liked it that way. He assumed Monsanto wanted that exclusivity because they were afraid to let the public know what the hell they were doing.

When he no longer needed binoculars, he saw four boats speeding toward them, each carrying armed men and had a heavy-caliber machine gun mounted near the bow.

He raised the binoculars again. The men in the gunboats all wore the same brown uniform with an insignia at their shoulders.

The boats formed a barricade across *Valhalla's* path. Kenji lowered the sails, and they became dead in the water. A boat approached with all guns trained on them.

"You've entered a restricted area," a man said using a handheld hailer. Officer bars were pinned on his collar. The amplifier carried his voice with harsh mechanical tones. "Turn back or we will open fire."

Kenji waved his arms. "My name is Yukio Toranaga. I'm a guest of Mr. Ogden Moloch. He's expecting me."

That name jarred Matt Reece's memory. Moloch was a mega billionaire who owned several leading corporations across the globe, a man who had his fingers in everything from GMO foods to hydraulic fracking to military weapons manufacturing. He was public enemy number one with organizations like Sierra Club, National Wildlife Federation, Greenpeace, and Earth First.

The officer said, "Nice try, Mr. Toranaga, but we have instructions to repel all vessels. Orders is orders. You have two minutes to raise your sails and turn about."

Kenji stood still. "We have no engine, no electronics, no food, little water, and an engraved invitation from Ogden Moloch. I'm not leaving until you radio Moloch and tell him I've arrived. If you don't, he will personally roast your balls when he finds he's missed the opportunity of a lifetime." He winked at Matt Reece. "That should give them pause," he said under his breath.

The officer barked an order to one of his men and was handed a phone.

With no forward drive, the *Valhalla* rocked precariously in the choppy sea. Matt Reece stared at that heavy-caliber machine gun, ready to bolt overboard if it opened fire. At the rear of the boat stood a staff with an unfamiliar flag snapping in the wind. It showed seven islands against a field of blue, and the words, "United Islands of Hawaii" embroidered along the bottom.

The officer lifted the hailer once more. "What was your point of departure?"

"San Francisco," Kenji said.

"I'm authorized to escort you to the island. Gather your belongings. We will board you, and you will come with us."

"Affirmative," Kenji said. "What did I tell you," he said under his breath. "Now these peons know who the hell they're dealing with."

Matt Reece was unconvinced, so as a precaution, he fished Kenji's flash drive from his shorts pocket and slipped it into his mouth, wedging it between teeth and left cheek.

The boat came alongside. Six soldiers leaped into the cockpit. Two men grabbed Matt Reece and forced him down, mashing his face onto the deck and holding him. He didn't struggle as his arms were forced behind his back and his hands cuffed. The other four men did the same to Kenji, but he fought them, cursing and spitting. He took a hell of a beating before they dumped them both into the gunboat.

They waited while two men combed the ship, above and below. The searchers returned to the gunboat, telling the officer they couldn't find passports or any kind of identification. The officer grabbed Kenji by the jaw and raised his face so they stared eye to eye. "If you aren't Toranaga, I'll be the one roasting your balls, wise guy."

The helmsman gunned the engine, and they raced away. As soon as they were free of the *Valhalla*, the other gunboats opened fired with their mounted machine guns.

The shots were directed at the waterline. Despite its small size, the boat stayed afloat as shot after shot ripped into the hull. An arc of flame leaped up from the stern as a bullet found the gas tank. With a roar, the ship tilted back, and the stern slipped beneath the water. In seconds, the cockpit was awash, the mast fell to one side, and then there was nothing left but pieces of flotsam bobbing on the waves.

Whoever these men were, they had no sympathy for seafarers. That ancient camaraderie of sailors, and the historical high regard for wind sailors, held no weight with them. This was beginning to feel like the worst sea rescue of all time.

As much as Matt Reece was glad to be heading for solid ground, there was something sad in the *Valhalla's* passing. It had been a hellish prison, yet it carried him thousands of miles and allowed him to meet the vice admiral. He had learned much about himself, and even more about Kenji. It was an undertaking, and not a totally unsatisfactory one.

THE RIDE into port took over an hour. Kenji was clearly upset, but he kept his mouth shut, no doubt fearing more blows from the crew.

Despite the hot sun, Matt Reece shivered as the knot that was his empty belly tightened even more. He wedged himself into a corner of the boat and tried to appear as insignificant as possible. He wondered what kind of reception they would receive ashore. Clearly, hospitality was not a priority here.

To the south, a fleet of cargo ships was anchored in neat rows. The boat slowed as they cruised into the narrow bay. Ahead, a wharf town had two piers jutting into the bay. There were three cargo ships unloading crates and cages. The wharf was busy with activity and crowded with crates.

The helmsman swung the boat around when it reached the pier. With the bow pointed toward the bay, the officer barked orders, and two crewmen jumped to make fast lines. The other boats were behind them, preparing to dock as well.

The officer glanced over his shoulder at them. "Welcome to paradise."

Two men grabbed Matt Reece's arms and hoisted him onto the dock like tossing a sack of rice. He stared down the barrel of an automatic weapon. The man holding the rifle was a foot taller but was just as lean as Matt Reece. He wore a ragged, brown camouflage uniform with the same arm patch as the other men and a wide-brimmed hat with the left side of the brim turned up Aussie-style. His face was narrow, with a predominant nose and excessive overbite that pointed his features like a ferret. Matt Reece could smell him, a stink that matched the man's soiled uniform.

The dock was crawling with militia, all of whom were exhibiting wickedly high levels of testosterone. There were a dozen older men, looking faintly harassed, their dignity threatened by the ferocious younger men who carried that swagger of superiority. Many of the younger soldiers were beautiful and virile, with a sort of ruthless sex drive propelling their own sense of power. Within this community, he detected a constant struggle for status and position, and underpinning it all lay a bedrock of violence where every man was judged by a single standard, and that was his readiness to kill or be killed.

A man with a shaved head standing behind the ferret wore an immaculate uniform and captain's bars on his collar. "Uncuff 'em," he barked. "They're not going anywhere."

A soldier swung a set of keys from his belt as he stepped forward. He unlocked Matt Reece's handcuffs and stepped back while putting the keys and cuffs back in his belt. Matt Reece stood rubbing his wrists. Before he could think, the same soldier ripped his shorts down. He was left naked. He hugged himself while looking at Kenji, who had also been stripped. They were both as thin as whippets.

The captain pointed at Kenji and Matt Reece. "Deliver them to the big house."

"I'm not going with him," Matt Reece said. "Anywhere but with him."

"You're coming with me," Kenji demanded.

The captain nodded at the ferret, who stepped toward Kenji and rammed his rifle butt into his gut. The smooth motion told Matt Reece the ferret was proficient in combat. Kenji dropped to his knees, gasping.

The captain smiled. "I don't care whose dick you sucked to get on this island, you give me any more lip and I'm going to rip your head off and fuck your bloody neck with my ten-inch cock." Two soldiers dragged Kenji to a nearby pickup truck. They tossed him in the bed and climbed in after him. The truck spewed red dust as it sped away.

The captain leveled a stare at Matt Reece. "Like the man said, welcome to paradise."

CHAPTER THIRTY-FOUR

Jessup followed Landau, Patrick, Vishal, and their Japan contact Randall Aubrey, into a bar at the Shinjuku rail station in the heart of Tokyo, where after a ten-hour flight and a two-hour limo drive from Narita Airport, they planned to enjoy a drink before plunging south on a bullet train. He sat beside Vishal, who looked better every hour. For the first time since sneaking him out of the hospital dressed in Blake's clothing, Jessup was glad to have him on this expedition. His skin was mending so rapidly that by sunup he could pass unnoticed in a crowd.

Jessup checked his watch and calculated the time difference in California. Blake should have arrived at the Promesa Rota ranch by now, and he prayed there was enough left of the place for Blake to rebuild the barn, the house, and even the livestock if need be. He had little hope that much remained, but he refused to imagine a life with nothing to return to.

It was a quarter after midnight, Tokyo time. The flight over had seemed endless, even in the luxurious Golden Eagle corporate jet, a Boeing 787-800 Dreamliner. Everyone else slept in vertical-reclining seats while he stared out a window, seeing nothing until they descended into a land of ceaseless lights.

While waiting for the waiter, he stared out the floor-to-ceiling windows, noting that a hard rain began to fall. He gave a sigh of thanks for being on the ground again, safe and dry in a comfortable chair in a saloon of burnished wood and chased mirrors. Outside, lighted boulevards crisscrossed the rain-drenched landscape.

A waiter came to take their order. Randall Aubrey spoke a sentence in Japanese, and the waiter walked away. Randall's voice was a sexy whiskey-and-cigarettes baritone.

Elegant businessmen sat at the bar, but Jessup assumed that anytime Randall Aubrey occupied this bar—or any saloon—it became his private lair. An African-American fortysomething with a sexy swagger, he gave the impression he believed that little was out of his reach once he put his mind to it. Here they sat in one of the premier cities of the world, the metropolis capital of Japan, waiting for God knew what drinks, and it didn't matter because Randall defined the glamour of the urban night. Randall personified the nocturnal creatures of an all-night city that believe that the most intense living begins at midnight.

He wore a dark, slim-cut suit, knotted gold tie, and a pale blue shirt with silver cuff links. A whisper of gray touched the dreads at his temples, but he had an athletic build, and although he didn't fall into any conventional idea of masculine beauty, Jessup thought he had an unfairly handsome face.

To a rancher like Jessup, Randall was his exact opposite. People of the night, Jessup had always assumed, were bartenders and sporting women; gamblers, con artists, and gangsters; artists and newspapermen; people who had no one to go home to. Randall was an expat high-ranking executive at Golden Eagle Industries.

The waiter brought a bottle of Glenfiddich and five tumblers. He arranged the glasses, poured a generous amount in each, set the bottle on the table, and walked away.

Landau lifted his spectacles and stared at the bottle. "You've done your homework, Mr. Aubrey. I appreciate a man who makes an effort to acquire the essential details."

Randall smiled. And even though they were opposites, Jessup admired his panache.

Randall said, "You're an easy target to research, Salman. Declan Hughes sent me a file on you as thick as my…. Well, pretty thick. And please call me Randall."

"Thick as your what?" Jessup asked as he picked up a tumbler.

Randall hesitated. "I was about to say thick as my arm, but that seemed like too drastic an exaggeration."

"Yes," Jessup said, "from what I see, only President Harrington has a file that ample."

"For fuck sakes," Patrick said, "you two have been totally eye-fucking each other since we sat down. Why do you people always make any situation so awkward?"

"You people?" Vishal asked. "Which people would that be?"

Patrick bristled. "This is family business, Vishal, so butt the fuck out."

"My relationship with Matt Reece makes me your—"

"You are so not my brother. Matt Reece is eighteen, which makes you a pedophile, and I hate pedophiles."

"Matt Reece watched you pickpocket a man. You stole his wallet and raced off. After that, downhearted and desperate, he became suicidal. I was the only one he could turn to. I gave him the comfort he needed."

Jessup shot his son a hard stare.

"That doesn't make you any less guilty," Patrick snapped.

Vishal said, "Which proves you're not only a petty thief, you're also a moron."

"He's no moron," Jessup said. "He's a moroff. You know, more off than on." Jessup turned to Randall. "I'm so sorry, Randall. My son's homophobic comment was directed solely at me, as you've done nothing inappropriate." He turned to Vishal. "And I welcome you to this family, even if he doesn't. I'm so grateful to you for having my son's back when the rest of us failed him."

Jessup glanced at Patrick, and his face grew hard. "I've tried to instill the best manners, ideas, and morals into both my children, but at least one of them ignored me. It's my fault, I grant you, although what I could have done different is a mystery to me."

Patrick's eyes blazed, but he kept his mouth closed, for the moment.

"No offense taken, Jessup," Randall said with a wink, a slow stroke of his eyelash that told Jessup everything he wanted to know.

"Tell you what," Landau said, "no more bickering until I've enjoyed at least one scotch. My back is killing me, and I'm in no mood to hear any of this." He lifted a plastic bottle from his jacket pocket, opened the tab, and shook out two pills. He popped them in his mouth and swallowed an impressive amount of scotch. He drank like a connoisseur, lingering on the taste. "How about some food? These pills will eat my gut raw if I take them on an empty stomach, which I just did."

Randall waved a hand at the waiter and spoke rapid-fire Japanese. The others lifted their glasses and drank without another word.

As the scotch evened out everyone's mood, Randall asked Landau why he assumed Kenji was returning to Japan.

Landau described Kenji's note, specifically, the comment about lightning never striking the same place twice. "You see, after the atomic bombs were dropped, I became convinced of what he meant in that note."

Randall lost his smile. "All this carnage, he planned it?"

Landau nodded. "In the study of psychological trauma, one often discovers both human vulnerability and the capacity for evil in human nature. I've always found it strange how those two things go hand in hand."

The waiter appeared with a tray of plates, each one containing a turkey sandwich and french fries. Jessup expected bento boxes or noodle soup, and realized that his edgy mood was brought on partly due to hunger. He couldn't wait to dig in.

"He's not a monster!" Patrick said as he picked up his sandwich. "He's purging the world of weapons. It's not his fault people are too stupid to see his vision." He lifted the sandwich, ripped off a hunk, and chewed with force.

Vishal said, "Tell that to the women and children in Tel Aviv."

"He didn't order those nuclear strikes," Patrick said through a mouth full of turkey.

"Right, and Hitler never shoved people into the ovens," Vishal said. "Kenji's a hero!"

"He's a cold-blooded mass murderer," Vishal said with equal force.

"This squabbling is less than constructive," Landau said, lifting his glass.

"You're betting a lot on a hunch," Randall told Landau. "You have to admit, that's pretty thin evidence."

Landau nibbled a french fry. "Firearms are illegal here, so only the police have them. And after World War II, Japan relies on the US for protection. Their own military is almost nonexistent. If we end up in global war, Japan won't be attacked because it's not a military threat. When all the other industrial nations have decimated each other, Japan will arise as the world's industrial leader, dominating all nations for the next thousand years."

"That was in Kenji's note," Jessup said. "He wrote, 'the meek are about to inherit the earth.'"

"I grant you the numbers add up," Randall said, "but there is still a hidden X in this equation, and that is motive. From what you tell me, he must be reasonably sane. So what would prompt him to engineer a world war?"

"Keep in mind he grew up with the horror of the postatomic blast. He saw his loved ones, the ones who survived, being routed by radiation sickness. Imagine being raised in a place of nothing but death and sorrow. Based on the profile that we compiled, I think something evil has been growing within his psyche over the last seventy years, something rising out of primal despair. It grew out of Japan's bloody past, and then its domination by Western powers. Perhaps he sees himself as a nemesis to Western nations, galvanized to address all of the accumulated wrongs suffered by his people."

"A madman obsessed with vengeance? You're grasping at straws," Randall said.

Landau poured himself three fingers and lifted his glass. "Kenji has suffered great spiritual anguish, an utter wrenching of his soul. I believe, once he stumbled onto this breakthrough, he realized a way to make others share his anguish."

Randall looked unconvinced.

"He's brought great torment to the West. If we can agree that he planned this, then the only logical motive, the one playing out, is revenge." Landau downed his drink and placed the glass on the table. "Sure, it's a long shot, but it's all we have to go on."

Randall held up his hands in a motion of surrender. "Okay. I'm not convinced, but I'll help in any way I can." He glanced at Jessup. "Just let me know what you need."

There was no denying Randall held an internal power. His way of facing the world was upright and open. Although he was only slightly older than Jessup, he listened and spoke with an intense directness of a man twice his age. It was unnerving and uplifting.

"We assume he'll arrive by sailboat," Landau said. "We need to initiate a search around Hiroshima, and we need to keep it to ourselves. We don't want any governments knowing what we're doing. If they think he's here, lightning could strike twice."

"Our own government too?" Randall said. "Don't answer that. Stupid question."

Landau said, "Kenji will be armed. We're confident he's already murdered at least two people. We'll need a way to defend ourselves. I couldn't bring my handgun through customs. Is it possible to acquire weapons here?"

"There's a black market for everything," Randall said, "but it's hush-hush and very expensive. And we draw firearms only in a life-threatening situation."

"What will the law do to us if they catch us with guns?" Jessup asked.

Randall smiled. "It's better to know the judge than to trust the law. I have contacts at the highest levels to get us out of anything short of murdering Emperor Akihito."

After a leisurely meal and a third round of drinks, they hurried to catch the 1:30 a.m. train. The doors closed, and the train moved as they found their seats. As they came out of the station, Jessup saw the glow of that vast city. He felt engulfed by it. He was a stranger in a country where everyone spoke only Japanese. He couldn't even read the signs in the train station. How the hell was he supposed to find Matt Reece in this alien land?

Chapter Thirty-Five

"This haole's too scrawny to work," the ferret told the captain. "Feed him to the cats and be done with him." Matt Reece followed the ferret's gaze to a line of cages holding big game cats—three Bengal tigers, a half-dozen lions, and a pair of cheetahs.

He assumed the ferret was pulling his chain, but he wasn't sure. The other sensation he felt was astonishment at all these exotic animals. Not only cats, but elephants, zebras, giraffes, buffalos (African, Asian, and North American varieties), and cages crammed with monkeys, baboons, and mountain gorillas. Someone was creating an impressive zoo. Were they hoping to expand tourism? If so, they had a strange way of going about it.

The ferret drove his rifle butt into his back, and it caused a different pain than the rough ride into port or the humiliation of standing exposed. This pain awakened that stronger person—that part of himself brave enough to fight Kenji, to shotgun blast *Nirvana's* sails. It was a core of strength buried deep, obscured and hidden all these years. This rifle in his back, this naked humiliation, caused an inner warfare to flare, and a new, almost lunatic-sounding inner voice clamored for retribution. It wanted to hurt these people, and most of all it wanted to punish Kenji for bringing him here. This new lunatic voice was something separate—a new persona. He thought of it as Kirby, the creature Kenji invented in him. Kirby felt like a beam of coherent, homochromatic light lasering from within his head. No warmth in it, only cold rage.

This new identity didn't feel like a rite of passage into manhood, but rather, like being freshly born into this new world. He tried to quell this force, but he sensed Kirby's embryonic power, and it terrified him. The ferret shoved the rifle in his back with more vigor, and before Matt Reece could stop himself, he turned and heaved the man away from him. It happened so fast and the man was so surprised, he couldn't move his feet back fast enough, and he toppled over.

Matt Reece's mouth went dry as the soldiers around him lapsed into silence. There was a sense of rage from everyone, held poorly in check and ready to be unleashed.

As the ferret rose, the sound of pounding hooves caught Matt Reece's attention. He glanced over his shoulder. A column of riders appeared at the margin of the jungle. Five horses thundered toward the docks. A woman—she seemed more like an ethereal shadow—with dark hair flying behind her rode the lead horse, a chestnut-colored Holsteiner. She wore military pants, combat boots, black tank top, Cochise headband, and something more—an inflexible, aggressive challenge that was underscored by the automatic weapon slung across her back and the ice-blue-mirrored shades hiding her eyes. The horses pulled up to a stop, and the riders slid off their mounts.

In the late-morning glare, the riders floated across the earth like spirits, vaporous and unreal. Indeed, they seemed to glide without moving their limbs. The others held back, but the woman with mirrored eyes came close enough for Matt Reece to see her features.

She was near Patrick's age, carried an AR-15, a Glock sidearm holstered to her waist, and wore bandoleers that held ammo clips crossing her chest. She was dark-skinned with lean arm muscles hard as green fruit. She ripped off her glasses to give him a once-over. Her face looked boyish—protruding nose, full lips, and emotional eyes that were blue and slightly crossed, giving her a sweet, ever-questioning air—yet her ensemble made her look lethal. She swung her rifle into her arms, cradling it loosely.

He saw his reflection in her naked eyes. It was utterly strange, with all that was happening, that he should notice his image imprinted on each pupil. He stood twinned in those orbs of blue, and for a moment he could think of nothing else. He sensed her desire to touch him and her powerlessness to do so in front of the soldiers. He wore nothing but skin over emaciated muscles, which now that he was in the midst of these troops, seemed pitifully inadequate, even laughable. He felt himself blush under her gaze.

"So you thought you'd be safe here?" The words seemed harmless, but her tone made him think she had stainless steel balls. "Thousands of miles of water in every direction makes us an outpost to hide in while the world self-destructs. Well, you assumed wrong, you haole shit. We don't take kindly to white trash coming to take what's ours."

Right then he didn't much care about the world or this island, and he didn't give a fig about this woman with mirrored eyes and steel balls. He glanced beyond her. The four men she rode with were all dark-skinned, in their twenties, shirtless, and had middleweight-boxer's builds. They wore military fatigue pants with the same Cochise wrap across their foreheads, and they were as heavily armed as the woman. They seemed a different breed from the other soldiers. He assumed they were native Hawaiian and members of an elite forces unit.

He was grateful that over the weeks he spent aboard the *Valhalla*, the henna dye had faded, and so did his green tint. His skin was now bronzed, and his hair had grown to a comfortable length. Another week of sun and he would be as dark as this woman. He tried to make himself be understood while talking with the flash drive still pressed between his teeth and cheek. "All I want," he said with a raspy voice, "is a spot of shade to sit and rest."

"When's the last time you had a meal?" the captain asked. His tone and manner seemed to soften, yet the ferret's rifle was once again jabbing his spine.

Matt Reece shrugged. "Weeks. I can only guess how many. I don't know what day it is." He looked into the captain's eyes, hoping for a bit of sympathy.

Nothing.

"You have to work if you want to eat. What can you do to earn your keep?"

"Horse wrangler. I ride as well as any man." He glanced at the woman. "Or lady."

"Oooo weee," she said with a snicker. "Damn, boys, we got ourselves a genuine John Wayne who wants to halter break an island filly."

She held Matt Reece's stare. He found it strange they had yet to ask his name or where he came from, and he decided they already knew. News reports about him and Kenji must have reached the island.

The captain smiled. "Don't get your hopes up, cowboy. She's the Boss Man's bastard, and nobody's cinched a saddle on her rump yet."

The men standing around guffawed, but there was no humor in the sound. That's when he knew there were old alliances here, a pecking order well established. This woman was royalty; the elite soldiers with her were knights. The captain seemed priestly.

The rest—including the ferret—were court squires fighting for the princess's favor.

"That's because she's more stallion than any of you," he said.

A shove from behind sent him sprawling onto rough wood planks. Reflexes took over and he rolled onto his back as the ferret stepped over him. He cocked a leg and sent a foot flying into the ferret's crotch. The man doubled over, groaning a sound that was more outrage than pain. When he straightened up, he dropped his rifle and pulled a bowie knife from the scabbard strapped to his belt.

The ferret leaped on him, straddling his chest. He swayed a foot above Matt Reece, his knife pointed at the heart. Matt Reece gripped the ferret's wrist with both hands, trying to push the blade away, but the knife inched downward. "No," Matt Reece said in a thin voice. Matt Reece's head spun, and he felt himself blacking out. He gasped for breath.

"Freeze!" The woman stepped forward, clicking off the safety on her weapon. She pressed the barrel to the ferret's temple.

The knife raised an inch.

The ferret swiveled his head until he looked at her with his ratlike eyes. "Back off, girly. This haole *mahu* attacked me. I have a right to gut this bitch like a tuna."

She didn't flinch. "That'd be problematic with a 9-millimeter bullet in your brain."

"Captain wouldn't like that," he croaked, nodding to the captain.

The captain seemed to enjoy this little drama and made no move to intrude.

"You're betting your life on whether I give two shits what this buffoon likes?"

The captain's smile faded.

The ferret glanced at his rifle lying a few feet from him.

"I'm not that slow," she said, "and you're not that lucky."

The ferret scrambled to his feet and slipped his knife back into its scabbard.

Matt Reece regained his feet. His head spun from relief and exhaustion. He was rather surprised to still be alive. Everyone but the woman visibly wanted the fight to continue, which made him queasy. He would not fight. He knew this with calm certainty, in the same way one knows the depth of one's own soul.

"*Haole* and *mahu,* what does that mean?" Matt Reece asked.

"Haole is a non-Hawaiian," the captain said. "Mahu means faggot."

Something happened, something astonishing. He wasn't quite in his body anymore. His mind was shoved aside to some inner place where the events on the dock were still being assimilated. It felt as if many different fragments buried deep within him, like shattered statuary, were now flying together to assemble something hard and big enough to thrust him out. That inner part of him he thought of as "Kirby" was strengthening recklessly, and then Kirby rushed out like an eruption. "You man enough to make it a fair fight?"

The ferret's eyes sparkled.

Kirby egged him on. "Once I kick the shit out of you, there won't be nothing left but a belt, boots, and that faggoty-ass hat."

"No," the woman said. She raised her rifle. "I need him alive."

The captain stepped between her and the others. He touched the barrel of her rifle and forced it down. "He made a challenge. This is how we roll."

She stepped back, a surprising submission. The captain pulled his combat knife from its sheath and held it out. Kirby grasped the handle. It felt solid and lethal.

The captain lifted a pack of cigarettes from his shirt pocket, shook one free, and lit up. He offered it to Kirby, who refused, so he passed it to the ferret, who took a drag and blew streams of smoke from his nose as he reached for his knife.

The air seemed dead; the wind hushed. The wharf now seemed infested with soldiers appearing out of nowhere. Beyond the ring of men and farther beyond the dock, others came running to watch. Kirby heard one of the horses whinny and a hoof scrape the earth. He also heard the big cats panting in their cages. He would not have heard these things unless every human sound on the dock had ceased.

"One walks away," the captain said, "the other is cat chow."

"What if I don't accept those terms?" Kirby said.

"Two shots to the chest and one to the head. That's another possible ending."

Matt Reece's mouth tasted like ash. Still, with Kirby in control, he was not afraid, perhaps for the first time in his life. He'd cheated death to this point, and if his luck petered out, so be it. The sea had driven him to the brink of insanity, and now he must fight for his life. There was no escape, no savior to help him. He would meet this challenge alone, perhaps his only remaining burden as a human being, despite his weakened state from malnutrition and dehydration. The cosmos had given him a last challenge, a death dance to perform. He intended to make it count.

By accepting the terms of his situation, he learned a secret about fear. It's an absolutist, all or nothing. It rules your life with blinding omnipotence or else you vanquish it, and its power evaporates. And another secret followed: conquering fear is not about "courage." It's propelled by something much more common: the simple need to move on with your life. He stopped being afraid because his life was limited to minutes. He had no future to fret over, and he didn't have even a second to spare for anxiety.

It was nearing the middle of the day, and the heat was intense. He knew the sun's glare could be an obstacle, especially in his weakened condition.

An idea took root—or had it been there for years? At the center of his being, he believed he existed to perform some unknown calling, something more momentous than fighting this ferret—an undertaking both sacred and noble and yet still unknown to him. Surely those years of loneliness and the last several weeks of loss were leading up to an act ordained by a higher power. Didn't that mean he would survive this combat? Would that higher power abandon him before fulfilling his purpose? At that moment an image flashed in his mind: his grandfather's silver pocket watch with the winged boy engraved on the cover, sinking into the sea.

"This is not a fair fight. He's so weak he can scarcely stand," the woman said. "You're a bunch of spineless swine."

The ferret dropped his cigarette and stubbed it out with the toe of his boot. He raised his knife and stepped toward Kirby. He reached out with his free hand and pushed the woman back into the circle of men that formed around them. "Knowin' I'm pissing you off, girly, makes it that much sweeter."

Kirby took the flash drive from his mouth and tossed it to the woman. As she caught it, he said, "Don't let that fall into the wrong hands."

She scrutinized the drive and nodded. "Wearing clothes is an unfair advantage," she said. "If you were a real man, you'd strip."

The ferret shrugged, then stepped out of his boots and peeled off his clothes. When he was naked except for his knife, he stood with his arms spread to give her full-frontal satisfaction. He turned back to Kirby and bent his knees, lowering his center of gravity. He gripped his knife in his right hand and raised both arms in front of him.

They circled each other.

Matt Reece understood now. The ferret was the hunter waiting at the water hole, gaze unwavering, every sense concentrated on the kill. The ferret smiled, forming it with exquisite slowness, his lips turning up, mouth slightly parted. He lunged, his knife slicing the air. Kirby sidestepped it and jabbed with his own knife. Kirby heard a click coming from behind him. Then the woman jumped close to the ferret, and two shots rang out. The ferret dropped to the ground, holding his left ankle and screaming his head off. "You fucking skank!" Blood poured from the wound.

"Now it's a fair fight," she said, her eyes smoldering. She removed her headband and tossed it to him, and he used it to wrap the wound.

The soldiers, now angry, surged toward her, but her four companions clicked off their safeties and raised their weapons. The regular troops backed away.

A silent standoff ensued.

Kirby withered as he assumed the fight was over. Matt Reece wrenched control of the mind they now shared.

The captain helped the ferret regain his feet, and the ferret pushed the captain away. Pogoing on his good leg, he raised his knife. Pain etched across his face, but he swallowed it down. His greasy hair flung across his eyes. "Give me my hat," he said.

The captain lifted the hat from a pile of discarded clothes and handed it over. The ferret held it out in front of him in his free hand, waving it about as a distraction. "Because of this bitch, I'm going to cut you bad but not kill you. I want you alive when those cats bite your fucking head off."

Matt Reece was unsure of how to fight. How could he know? Other than wrestling with Kenji on the *Valhalla*, he had never thrown a punch in his life. He would have to exploit his superior movement, he realized. His mobility raised his chances only the width of an eyelash, but that might be enough.

Hope flourished like a great weight in his chest. Yes, for the second time today he realized that life was precious, and he wanted to hold on to his. This faint chance had him feeling both hot and cold with fear. He needed Kirby to rush back to quiet that fear, but he didn't know how to make it happen.

CHAPTER THIRTY-SIX

DECLAN HUGHES sat in a wheelchair before a table facing the only window of his hospital room at Andrews Air Force Base. He wore the blue pajamas he'd received from Diane McCarthy on their second anniversary of living together. The table was set with a plate piled with bacon, four eggs, rare beefsteak, fried potatoes, rye toast, and marmalade.

Isn't steak and eggs the traditional Marine meal before going into battle? Besides, what the hell kind of meal is this for a man surviving triple-bypass surgery? Why don't they just shoot me?

Outside, the uniformed color guard that raised and lowered the flag every day could be seen marching toward the hospital. It was cloudy, a sky to match the gray F-15 aircraft lined up on the tarmac a few blocks away. On the other side of the runways sat the ruins of a fuel storage station, destroyed in a commando-style attack two nights ago.

Overlaid on the glass was his reflection, looking much frailer than a week before.

The door opened behind him, and Liam Cullen, his chief legal counsel at Golden Eagle Industries, entered the room and said, "Hello. How are you feeling?"

Declan didn't turn around. "Any word on Diane?"

Liam, who still looked like a graduate student at age thirty-five, his eyes sharply aware, hair falling over his forehead, lips always ready to flash a smile, voice that held the tones of Eton, was one of the brightest legal minds in the business, and one of the few men Declan now trusted. He was Diane McCarthy's first cousin. She'd groomed him for an executive position at the company. Now they shared the same sense of loss and betrayal.

It was painful to have him so close, because his looks and mannerisms so faithfully resembled her. Two days ago, he sent a team into Tel Aviv to search for Diane.

"No word yet," Liam said. "Our offices were demolished. If she was in that building, her chances are remote at best."

The door opened again, and Liam introduced himself to a woman who said she was Rachael Laughton of the FBI.

Declan had met Rachael once before, when Landau and Souad had given him an update on the case. She seemed pleasant enough, using softly accented responses to Liam's questions, but Declan was in no cordial mood. He'd never before been this tired, and the news about the search for Diane only disheartened him more. He wondered if he even had the energy to lift his fork, but he knew if he simply went back to bed, as he wished, once he put head to pillow, necessities would crowd his mind. He would not sleep. He was consumed by the heart-draining need for action. And for action, he needed strength. He lifted his fork and swallowed some egg.

"Who sent you, Mrs. Laughton?" he said without turning around.

"The FBI agents working on the Kenji Hiroshige case report to me."

"Yes, I remember our prior meeting. I know who you are and what you are, Mrs. Laughton. That was not my question."

"My senior agent, Salman Landau, has gone rogue. You know his whereabouts."

"I asked: Who sent you?"

"I'm here on my own initiative."

"If I refused to tell the president that information, what makes you think I'll give you the time of day?" He lifted his knife, spread marmalade on a slice of toast, and ate a mouthful. He detested hospital food but had resigned himself to it.

"The president and I have different agendas. I only want to protect my agent."

Interesting, he thought. *Her tone altered on that last word, as if there is more than professional interest in Landau.* The bacon was undercooked. Declan liked it crispy. He ate it anyway, knowing he needed protein. Besides, there was no telling if there would be another meal before dinnertime, and God only knew what they'd serve then.

"I keep asking questions and you insist on dancing around them. I have no patience for this kind of conversation. Goodbye, Mrs. Laughton."

"I'm here to bargain. A life for a life."

Declan dawdled over his second slice of toast. He was in no hurry, as he had no appetite for this food anyway, and he had no intention of seeming eager. When he didn't answer, she said, "You're being held for treason. I can get the charges dropped. Your freedom for Landau's location."

It was tempting. His only goal now was finding Diane, and he couldn't do that sitting in this hospital. "Surely you understand why I can't divulge his whereabouts. Four cities incinerated, the planet at the brink of World War III, and people in Washington willing to do anything to acquire, or destroy, that formula, which I'd like to remind you legally belongs to Golden Eagle Industries. Landau understood that perfectly, which is why he's now undercover. It's for his own survival." He paused a half minute. "Even if I trusted you to keep this information to yourself, I have to assume everything I say is being recorded."

"The administration has much to answer for," Rachael said. "There are bad seeds in high places who've been pushed to the wall, and people with their backs to the wall make dangerous decisions."

Declan ate his last bit of egg with a bite of toast, drained his coffee cup, and pushed away from the table. "What I wouldn't give for real French croissants and savory butter."

"I can arrange that too," she said with a smile.

"It's gone beyond a few bad seeds. We are now in the realm of madness, and this lunacy has become a plague upon the world. We have succumbed to what Frederick Douglass called 'the fatal poison of irresponsible power.'"

Rachael crossed the room. She put both hands on the table. "Mr. Hughes, I agree his location must be kept secret. I plan to join him, not place him in danger."

Declan smiled.

"Will you at least tell me if he's okay?"

Declan stared into his empty plate, oddly subdued by the sudden tears in her voice.

"Mr. Hughes, ten, hell even five years ago, I wouldn't have worried. But—"

"But what?"

"He's old and feeble. More than he's willing to admit."

Declan read true distress in her eyes. "What I can tell you, Mrs. Laughton, is he is now in one of the safest places on earth. He is not alone. I have people helping him. And based on what he told me, I believe he has a chance of snaring his prey."

She took his right hand in both of hers. "I wish we had met under different circumstances. I will do everything I can to dismiss these charges and garner your release. My voice echoes pretty high in the justice department." She slipped one hand inside her purse, removed a business card, and placed it on the table. "If there is any way I can be of service to help Salman or you, please don't hesitate." She turned to leave.

He bowed his head. "*Arigatou gozaimashita,*" he said. "*Sayonara.*"

She stared at him with her mouth open, and tears sprung to her eyes. She bowed her head in a gesture of thanks and left the room. As the door closed, he cursed his stupidity. He felt he could trust her, and he hoped more than anything she wouldn't let him down. It would be a steep price to pay if his instincts were wrong, again.

He turned to Liam, whom he could tell had something hot to divulge, but they both knew the room was bugged and nothing of importance should be mentioned. Still, they had worked out a subtle code.

"Sergei has been exercising in the fresh air," Liam said, "to the point his color is bright again. But the health trainers have put a curfew on his workouts, and they're making him wear a hat to avoid what happened to you." That was code for: "Sergei Godelinsky's team had a breakthrough. Problem is, the new government overseers. We don't want to tip our hat until we know what will happen to you."

"My, my. Must be that fresh air. What I wouldn't give for a stroll in the garden."

"Perhaps I can persuade those Marines outside the door."

THE BEEFSTEAK and eggs lay heavy in Declan's gut. The wheelchair felt like a torture device, making his back ache despite its modern design. Being pushed through the garden reminded him of the walk he made with the president at Camp David. When they were a dozen feet in front of their Marine escort, Liam leaned close, and Declan said, "What the devil did they find?"

"Is this safe?"

"Tell me, dammit." They might be listening with advanced spy equipment, but he had to at least get the gist of what they discovered.

"You were right about altering enzymes. We believe Kenji altered the genes that control the rate at which new cells are produced."

Declan felt his own hairs tickling his neck. "Go on."

"Expression of genetic information contained in a body's genes is controlled in part by specialized proteins called transcription factors, which bind to DNA."

Declan slapped his leg with a fist. "I don't need a goddamned biology lesson."

"Okay, let me start over. Actions of a gene is concerned with formation of a particular enzyme, which is a protein. Genes control the amino acid makeup of specific proteins. By rendering certain DNA combinations incapable of producing certain amino acids, we think we can inhibit the body's ability to control the rate that cells divide."

"They found a way to control the rate the body creates cells by altering the DNA, and you can do it throughout the body all at once?"

"No, that's the missing key: how to make it happen all at once. And what we change is the RNA."

"Go on," Declan said, feeling happy.

"It's about RNA found in nucleic acids. RNA and DNA relate to each other like a template and the finished product, much like a mold and the casting that comes from it. The treated host manufactures protein dictated by the RNA. When new DNA is formed within the nucleus of cells, it resembles the sequence of the nucleotides of the modified RNA and not that of the host DNA. Miniscule alterations within miniscule structures change the body's RNA, and the RNA changes the new cell's DNA. Then the newly sequenced DNA cells begin to divide and multiply at astronomical levels."

Declan did not like to contemplate a genetic information system running rampant, and that's what he was hearing—disabling or modifying one or more components in the DNA/RNA string in the nucleus of each cell in the body. Kenji had thrown a spanner into the genetic makeup of human beings. Being a true man of science, he could only hope to somehow restore order at the subcellular level yet still achieve the same results.

"Okay, don't breathe a word of it to the government overseers until I give the green light. Now give me a rundown on the political front."

Liam nodded. "The military is still concentrating its efforts on the cities and suburbs. The rebels control the other 95 percent, which means they control food production and ground transportation routes. Across the country, railroad lines are torn up, airport landing strips are strewn with wreckage to block military landings, roads are blockaded by vigilantes, and troops are slowly losing those urban areas since the Jews and Catholics joined the rebel forces."

"What made them do that?"

"When they nuked Rome and Israel, all hell broke loose here. Israel was debilitated, and the other Middle East nations pounced on them. It's been a bloodbath for both sides."

"Good God…. Diane."

"I pulled our team out of Tel Aviv for the time being. It's simply too dangerous."

"Of course," Declan said. "I understand." He did understand, but he felt something in his chest fall, and he knew it was what little hope he still carried.

"Here in the States, people in cities have begun to starve. They've been getting by on canned goods and grains stockpiled against atomic attack, but belts are tightening, so many are joining the rebellion," Liam said. "To keep the military from using Air Force gunships, the vigilantes are sending suicide squads onto military bases to blow up the aviation fuel supplies and also the refineries that make fuel."

"We've got to put an end to this madness," Declan said.

Liam went on to explain that the government had lost New Mexico, Arizona, Oklahoma, and Texas except for Dallas and Fort Worth. Alaska and the Hawaiian Islands were gone, and also the Northwest, everything above Sacramento. The same thing was happening in Russia and Eastern Europe. And with the plunge in the world economy, fighting had spread over the globe. The one bright spot was, most nations were so busy trying to quell their internal fighting, looting, and financial collapse, that they didn't have the troops or the money to wage war against each other, yet. The one exception was China. There was no word coming out of it, but satellite observations released by the Pentagon suggested mass killings during protests over what the Chinese military was doing to disarm Southeast Asia, India, Pakistan, and North Korea. In Burma and North Korea, the resistance was so effective the Chinese had begun carpet-bombing.

Liam stopped pushing the wheelchair to stare out at the jet fighters lined up on the tarmac. "Did this madman really believe he was bringing an end of violence?"

Declan folded his hands in his lap. He knew now that peace was never Kenji's goal. An estimated hundred million people died fighting during World War II, making it the most costly war in history, yet what was occurring now had the potential of dwarfing those numbers by a factor of fifty. Did Kenji care? Did he have any remorse?

Declan had to assume the worst, that Kenji set this cataclysm into play knowing full well what would happen. There was only one way to stop the lunacy, and Declan's team was now poised to do that. But before they revealed their findings, he had one dirty little chore that needed a resolution.

He waved Liam closer and whispered, "The root of this government's catastrophic policy is driven by one woman and her staff, who I've come to believe are the real madmen. For this country to survive, we need to eradicate that menace."

Liam pulled back, but Declan grabbed him by the collar and pulled him closer again. "She now spends all her time at thirty thousand feet in Air Force One. Golden Eagle manufactures the most lethal attack drones on the planet, and the warheads to arm them."

Liam sighed. "Politicians and their puppeteers can bury or forgive their blunders only so long as the blunders are small. This act you desire is colossal. You can't know what events it will set in motion. The string of consequences of a single act are often quite different from what one would guess. You must be sure that the intention in your heart is large enough to hold all possible negative outcomes. Not every act is worth its aftermath."

Declan absorbed his words in a silence that lasted long after Liam finished speaking. Finally he said, "This is not about revenge. I believe this will save a hundred million lives in this country alone."

Declan saw comprehension settling into Liam's eyes. He added, "Relay this conversation to Bob Howth at our headquarters. He'll know how to proceed."

Declan had never dreamed he could suggest such a thing. It was a momentous decision, but he felt it was the only option open to a genuine patriot. He knew it was a hard thing for Liam to swallow, so he tried to appear confident and full of purpose. What happened next would hinge on his ability to ply his will on his subordinates.

Now that hope of Diane's survival had dimmed, he had only one path, and that was a path for the country's survival.

Chapter Thirty-Seven

Matt Reece raised his knife as he bent his knees. The ferret sprang toward him, waving his hat at eye level. Matt Reece fell back, fending him off. He saw the blade pass under the hat, straight for his throat. He leaped to the side at the same time he slashed at his foe, catching the ferret in the forehead. A lock of hair fell away, and a line of red opened above the ferret's eyebrows. Blood flowed freely, and the ferret seemed surprised.

The anxiety in the silent crowd grew palpable.

The ferret feinted with his hat and passed his knife across Matt Reece's chest. It stung like a bitch, which awakened Kirby. He wanted to look down to see how bad he was bleeding, but he kept zeroed in on those black eyes. Blood from the ferret's forehead wound ran into those orbs, and Kirby waited for his foe to wipe away the blood.

Kirby could smell him, a stench of grit.

The ferret dropped his hat, but he didn't wipe his eyes. He blinked rapidly. His movements were fluid and emotionless, as intent as a man could be. He stabbed again, his blade missing Kirby by an inch.

They circled each other. Kirby wanted to draw this fight out, thinking the ferret's loss of blood from his ankle wound would drain his strength.

The next few minutes became a blur. The ferret's knife flashed. They locked together. Grappled. A razor slashed across Kirby's chest again, and a fist pummeled his jaw. His mouth went warm with blood, and he felt its thickness in his throat. He slashed out with his own knife in a high arc, the blade piercing his foe's shoulder, scraping bone.

Kirby panted through bloody lips. He focused more intently on those eyes, and there seemed a whole malign history burning cold and remote in the depths of blackness. He sliced back and was cut again on the forearm. This time the wound was deep, crippling his hand. He switched the knife to his left hand.

They traded slashes again, and the ferret's blade passed across Kirby's ribs on his right side. For a one-legged man, the ferret moved with surprising speed and balance. He stood facing Kirby, crouching on his good leg, silent, faintly weaving, scrutinizing Kirby's eyes. Kirby knew his foe was hoping to see terror in his eyes, that more than anything this man wanted to be feared. Kirby, on the other hand, watched for an opening, for that moment he could turn this situation to his advantage. But he realized now that his foe was an adept fighter and would not lose his focus until the fight was over. Only when he beat Kirby would he relax his intensity. Kirby knew then he was outmatched. He fought with all his limited skill, but it was not enough. The ferret, stronger and more keenly focused, held the advantage, and two more slashes across Kirby's chest brought that message home.

He covered his ribs with his free hand and felt bare bones and blood oozing through his fingers. Kirby backed away and lowered himself to the dock. His legs sprawled under him. His shoulders fell; his posture deflated in a show of defeat. He held his knife loosely at his side, and he lowered his gaze to the wood planking.

The ferret pogoed to him, grabbed him by the hair, and pulled his head back to expose his throat. Their eyes met for a last time. The ferret smiled, a mere cold baring of teeth. "Before you die, bitch, I'll cut off your ears for a souvenir, like bullfighters."

An apt analogy, Kirby thought. He knew that bullfighting was not merely brutal baiting of a wounded, maddened animal for sport, but a tragedy of death and grace under pressure, since the matador could get gored or even killed. It was rare, but it happened. All it took was a momentary lapse in focus.

The ferret raised his knife arm with a Jaggerish flair, and he glanced at the crowd to ensure the woman still watched.

There was a somber pause as a silent communication passed between the woman and the ferret. Kirby didn't know what message was being conveyed, but he did know that pause was his opportunity. He swung his knife up with all his remaining strength and buried the blade in the ferret's chest. His enemy stood paralyzed with shock as Kirby ripped the knife back and drove it home again.

The ferret's smile faded. He let go of Kirby's hair, his knife fell to the dock, and a moment later he toppled into Kirby's arms.

Kirby was confident he had not punctured the heart, but he must have severed an artery because spurts of bright arterial blood fanned out from the wounds.

Matt Reece rushed to wrestle control back from Kirby. Much as he deplored violence, he felt he would never regret goring his tormentor, never forget the ferret's astounded expression as the knife slashed deep, never forget that fading smile. And he was not sorry he'd unleashed Kirby, even though each time it happened, Kirby became much stronger.

The men standing in the circle turned to leave, like theater patrons anxious to avoid the crush. The woman sprinted to Matt Reece's side and helped him to stand. He was covered with blood, and he hoped not all of it was his own.

The captain drew his knife from the man's chest, wiped the blade on the ferret's arm, and returned it to its scabbard. He grabbed the ferret's shoulders and began dragging him toward the cages. "Come with me," he said to Matt Reece. "You earned this."

"What's your name?" Matt Reece asked the woman as they followed.

"Lilikoi Kamamalu," she said with what sounded like a defensive pride. "Lilikoi is Hawaiian. It means passion fruit." Matt Reece waited for the same question, but it didn't come.

They reached two rectangle cages the size of shipping containers, fastened together. One was empty, and the other held three Bengal tigers, the largest of which was a lanky, glossy male that must have dressed out at six hundred pounds. Bars and a trapdoor separated the two cages. The sweltering air was humid and smelled of cat urine.

Their almond-shaped eyes gleamed in the morning light. He felt the presence of their knowing what was coming, and it electrified the air. They bunched at the trapdoor with their ears cocked.

Lilikoi gripped him from behind, helping him to stand close to the bars of the empty cage. The captain unlocked, opened, and entered the empty cage, dragging the ferret with him. The tigers were now up against the dividing bars, their ears flat against their skulls and each one letting go with deep-throated roars that shook the cages and made Matt Reece tremble. The captain hauled the dying man to the middle of the cage. The ferret's lungs heaved violently, but he remained silent. His tongue hung from one corner of his mouth. The captain left him there without so much as a goodbye.

As the captain shut and locked the cage door, the ferret writhed to his knees. He made an odd belching sound as he struggled to rise, but the effort proved too much for him, and he fell back.

The cats paced back and forth, fluid, effortless motion, their eyes fixed on the ferret. Matt Reece knew what was coming, and it sickened him, but he couldn't turn away. He would have stopped it if he could, but he knew that was hopeless. He could only stare as he panted through his bloody lips. The pain from his cuts kept Kirby strong in his head, and Kirby began to overpower him. The struggle to control his mind made it hard to concentrate on what was happening in the cage.

The captain stepped to the rope attached to the trapdoor between the cages and paused to steady himself. The three cats went silent in anticipation. "Take a good look," the captain said. "That should be you in there."

Lilikoi's hand pressed against his heart. He well knew his luck in the fight had been a fluke—or perhaps divine intervention?—and he accepted his good fortune without enthusiasm. *If this is what the world is sinking to, then who the hell wants to live forever?* But then he wondered if the world had always been like this, and he didn't know because he'd been protected living on the ranch.

The captain heaved the rope. The trapdoor flew up.

The ferret was back on his knees, facing the cats. Blood no longer fanned out of his wounds. He closed his eyes as a flash of orange streaked from one cage to the next.

It happened so fast that Matt Reece was unsure of exactly what occurred, but it looked like the first tiger to reach him reared up and hit his head with a massive paw, crushing his cranium. It made a whoosh sound, like a watermelon splitting open. Then there was nothing to see but a squirming mound of orange and black stripes.

Matt Reece jerked back.

"Let's get the hell out of here, you little shit," Lilikoi said, "before you get someone else killed."

He couldn't respond. What he saw in the cage shocked the living daylights out of him, sent Kirby into hiding, and made him a vegetarian for the rest of his days.

Chapter Thirty-Eight

On the covered veranda of a ranch house snuggled into the lower slopes of Mt. Kamakou, Matt Reece lay in a hammock strung between two posts supporting the roof. The night grew pitch-black. Cool winds and relentless rain pounded the house. He could reach out to the waterfall flowing off the roof in an unbroken stream, but every time he stirred, pain stretched out a fist to smack him down. Every breath was razors across his chest.

The odor of wet vegetation blended with the pure scent of rain. The drumming on the roof became a welcome melody after so many weeks floating on a silent sea.

He lay with his torso trussed in bandages and his lower body covered in rough cotton pajamas and a wool blanket that wrapped around him cocoon-like. Only half-awake, he hovered somnambulantly as though still drifting on an endless ocean. A crack of lightning lit up the sky. Thunder rumbled, sounding like the deep-throated roar of tigers, and his memory of that morning came back to him in vivid highlights, pulling him fully awake. As he remembered that mauling, part of him clung to his last moments of half-conscious ignorance.

Lilikoi came out of the house carrying a bowl and a lantern, still dressed in her combat kit, minus the rifle and mirrored sunglasses. She sat the lantern on the railing, rested on a stool beside him, and spooned chowder into his mouth. The heat was as marvelous as the fact that something was filling his belly. This was his third feeding since coming here. The chowder was the same as the first two meals, chunks of fish floating in a thick broth.

"That's brilliant," he said in a weak voice. "Spicy enough to grow hair on my balls."

"Keep your balls to yourself. I've already seen them, and they're nothing to crow about." Her face was pretty and took on warmth in the lantern light, yet her tone remained frosty.

He took another spoonful. "I haven't thanked you for saving my life. If you hadn't—"

"Can it. Your big mouth got Ted killed, which puts you numero uno on my shit list."

"I got the impression you two weren't planning to elope anytime soon."

"And your point is? Sure, Ted had a mean streak that ran bone-deep, a genuine *moke*, a native thug. But that made him dependable in a fight, or so everyone thought. He hated mainlanders, which you can say about everyone on the island. And he was a first-class rhino-chaser."

"Rhino-chaser?" With the exotic animals being unloaded at the docks, he envisioned someone literally chasing a rhino through the brush.

"Rhinos are giant waves. Chasers are the surfers with enough cojones to ride them."

He smiled and was equally impressed. "He tried to kill me. What else could I do?"

"Why does every man on this island think he's friggin' Rambo? Men...."

Blackened pots and kettles jumped to mind, but he thought better of voicing his opinion. She continued to feed him. He wanted to ask why she bothered to save him, considering her attitude, but he thought it could wait until she was in a better mood, if that was possible.

But then a thought occurred to him. She was the one who shot the ferret in the foot, leveling the playing field. If she hadn't, Matt Reece wouldn't have stood a chance. So she shared in the responsibility of killing the ferret, and that troubled her.

"I can't get the roar of tigers out of my head."

She set the bowl aside and pulled a pipe from her pants pocket. She lit the bowl, took a puff, and pressed the stem to his lips.

"What is it?"

"Maui Wowie buds laced with opium."

He shook his head.

"Don't be a dick. It'll help the pain," she said. "Also, to forget what happened today."

Two puffs brought on a fit of coughing. He felt himself lifting, hovering like a wisp of smoke. He heard her voice from a distance. "You'll forget today, and totally forget about tomorrow." Even before the voice receded, he immersed himself in a world of luxurious images. He saw mountains reaching halfway to the sun, a carpet of wildflowers running yellow and purple to the horizon, sunshine on clouds that approached the perfection of his childhood. He stood in the Promesa Rota River, fly-fishing, waving his pole to an inner rhythm, watching the fly defy gravity as it whizzed back and forth. The water chilled his legs, but not unbearably so. On the other side of the water, buttery light spilled over untamed grass that waved like the sea in a fresh breeze. In the meadow, a pair of colts raced the wind, one an untainted white, another a rich chestnut color. They kicked up a haze of pollen that hung in a long trailing spume, made powdery gold by the sun. A pair of red dragonflies darted about his head. No pain lived here, only the resounding beat of horses' hooves and the breeze pounding his face with velvet fists.

He felt himself running with the colts, and he realized that he was not only fishing, he was also the horses, and also the fly defying gravity. They moved, all of them, to a melody that could not be heard, only celebrated.

But it started to rain and the stream swelled, its waters growing turbulent. The current bit deep under him, and a moment later he was borne along, soaring, arms and legs spread, hair streaming. He fought for a handhold, but there was nothing to grab hold of. He twisted and tumbled in a broken-backed fashion, pressed down by the current until he came to rest in a sluggish cloud of muck. Somewhere above him, beyond the surface, was a sky filled with life-giving air, but he couldn't reach it. It seemed so close, if only…. He realized he was dreaming and tried to reverse the events, to go back to watching the horses. It was hopeless; the muck sucked him deeper, and no amount of concentration could buoy him up. His life from childhood to landing on this island seemed detached and apart from him, and all he could do was struggle in this miry grave.

He woke. His body was cold and drenched in sweat.

He wondered if he would ever be free of the muck, and he assumed that from now on life would be dark, full of suffering with only brief passing moments of joy. He recalled Vishal, and as happens when a memory is too intense, the past became the future, and he pictured his lover standing over him. Before he could voice feelings, the vision faded. Crushed. He knew he would continue to live on the knife-edge between his dream world and reality, and he only had himself to blame. He'd stepped onto this path by his own volition the moment he picked up Kenji's tricorder. He felt a burning behind his eyes, the precursor to tears, and he stopped it cold. *Screw that*, he thought. He inhaled a lungful of air and continued living the hand that was dealt him, breath by breath, without remorse.

Sometime in the narrowing hours, the rains diminished into a drizzle.

Hours later, the sky to the east turned orange. Color throbbed and mounted behind a pattern of royal palms, straining against the blackness still dominating the sky. But at that supreme moment when the sun should have appeared, killing the night, nothing happened. He peered into that timeless dawn, and it felt like virtue had failed to overcome evil. A profound disappointment washed over him. Later, the sun rose without splendor. The sky, still heavy from a night of rain, awakened with a lazy stretch. Distant sounds of surf rose in a steady pulse, like the beating of a heart.

A high-pitched giggle turned his head toward the house. Children hunkered down in a line against the wall. The youngest, a boy wearing red shorts, said, "I can't see you breathing."

"I must be dead," Matt Reece said.

The boy nodded.

"Don't be stupid," another said. "Dead men don't talk."

It was time to climb out of that hammock, and he took a long time getting ready. First he moved his right arm to sweep the blanket off him. That shot fire into his side. After deep breaths, he pushed to a sitting position and was astounded by the pain.

The urchins jumped away screaming and ran into the garden.

He took his time, trying to beat down the inferno in his chest. His feet touched the floorboards. The planks felt cool. He stood, and the detonation in his rib cage overwhelmed him. He dropped to his knees, gasping. He raised his head and looked around.

The house was a simple structure. Its walls were fashioned from whitewashed stone. The foundation was chiseled into an ancient bed of lava, and the roof was made of corrugated tin and covered with palm thatch. A wide covered porch overlooked a bay. To one side of the house stood a barn, also made of stone, and a corral that held two horses. *This*, he thought, *is my kind of spread*. Weathered and sturdy, yet it was still one more version of what he thought of as Not Home. A nonplace he existed in but didn't belong to.

On the far side of the porch sat two Adirondack chairs, but made from thick bamboo. The seats and backrests were made of woven bamboo fibers.

The screen door creaked open, and a monkey-brown dog walked onto the porch. Gray about the muzzle, the poor thing suffered from arthritis so bad he walked slightly sideways, crab-like, and had milky, half-blind eyes. He kept his head down, sniffing the floor. The dog caught Matt Reece's scent and growled.

A voice came from inside the house. "Coolie! Can it."

The dog crabbed over to Matt Reece and began to lick his face. Matt Reece inched his hand to Coolie's head and ruffled his hair and then scratched behind one ear. The dog's face nuzzled his as he began a friendly pant.

"Be careful, you little shit," Lilikoi said. She stood in the doorway holding a white mug. "Coolie doesn't take to haoles."

He almost didn't recognize her, because now she wore only a white T-shirt that hung below her hips and a pink orchid behind her ear, which softened her intense face. Hair cascaded down her back, making her alluring and exotic. The T-shirt had a picture of a can of Spam across the chest with the words "Hawaii's Prime Sirloin" under it.

She walked toward him. Her movements were light-footed and proud, as if walking barefoot was all she had ever known. He felt the kind of numbing sensation, half awe and half alarm, that one feels when encountering a wild creature in the forest.

"Coolie? That's a peculiar name for a dog."

"Right, like Matt Reece is going to win you any awards."

Her words confirmed she knew who he was and what he was running from. Her eyes looked fatigued, and he wondered if she had gotten any sleep last night.

"Look, I don't know why you're all in my face with these personal attacks. I didn't want to come here. I'm just a guy trying to stay alive. I'm no threat to you, so please cut me some slack."

Her body stiffened, but then her face softened. "You're a threat to everyone."

When he didn't respond, she asked, "Do you feel faint?"

"These days I seldom feel anything else."

She cupped a hand under his armpit, and he pushed to his feet with her support. The pain was not as bad as moments ago. He tested his balance.

"Drink this," she said, handing him the mug. He sipped tepid, delightfully sweet coconut milk. When he finished it, she took the mug and helped him to the doorway.

"I'll change your dressings while you eat."

His mind drifted into a backspin. The memory of yesterday came to him, at the point of riding behind her on her horse. He had kept his eyes closed to help tolerate the pain, and he had an awareness of the horse moving up dirt paths through a low-shrub landscape. He heard the occasional sound of helicopters thumping the air, and her curses over the horse's plodding hooves. He didn't know if she was cursing him, the copters, or the speed of the horse. At the house, she hauled him off the horse and onto a chair on the porch. She brought out a medical bag, cleaned and sutured his wounds, bandaged him, helped him into pajamas, and lifted him into the hammock. When he asked if she was a doctor, she said, "Veterinarian, which is no more than you deserve."

He stepped into a living room that smelled of frying grease. Lime-green geckos scurried across the walls. The room seemed stuffy, but everything was neat and clean. One electric fan hung from the ceiling, revolving like a wounded bird. On the mantle above a stone fireplace sat a statue of a Ganesha—the pot-bellied, elephant-headed beast with six arms, each hand holding various objects except one that was held out in a blessing. It was the same mythical creature he had seen in Vishal's shop. He pointed to it. "That's Hindu, right?"

"He's the lord of dumb luck, wisdom, and the overcoming of obstacles. If it weren't for the wisdom thing, he'd be your patron saint."

He nodded to the framed painting above it, a man with four arms held out in choreographic gestures, poised atop a fierce-looking creature, one foot on the demon's back, the other foot lifted in the air. "And that?"

"That's Shiva as Nataraja, the cosmic lord of dance. He rules the movement of the universe and the flow of time. He dances on the back of ignorance, and when his raised foot finally touches the earth, time will stop."

"Kenji," he whispered. The thought caused a wave of hatred to wash over him, and he shook his head to clear it from his mind.

The furniture was as worn and solid as the house itself. He was struck by the room's banality and humbled by its sparseness. The house had personality: strong, substantial, with a Zen-like elegance. No church or temple ever felt so sacred to him. It seemed dense with piety.

At the edge of hearing, a female voice was humming in another room. No, not humming; the voice was chanting in a native dialect, and he felt the mystical pull of the words and heard how the native color and exactness in her tone claimed her song as something spiritual.

A stillness pervaded him, diminishing the throbbing in his chest. His shoulders dropped, and a feeling of relief infiltrated his being. He stood listening. Behind the chanting, he heard distant pounding waves. There was something else in the air he couldn't quite grasp, but it made him feel as if he'd come to the end of his journey.

The only other artwork hanging on the walls was a framed oil painting of a Polynesian scene hanging next to the entrance of the kitchen. It depicted several native women gathering fruit from trees; behind them hung a yellow sky. The women seemed frozen, distant, and silent, with eyes cast down and solemn faces. He was no art expert, but he knew this was a Gauguin. He studied the picture and gave a soft whistle.

"I know," she said. "It's called *Nave Nave Mahana*, which means 'The Careless Days.' Sadly, nobody paints like him anymore."

At the doorway to the kitchen, she pulled him to a stop and whispered in his ear. "Listen up, shithead. You're about to meet my grandmother. If you take the Lord's name in vain in front of her, I will personally lasso your scrawny ass and drag you back to the tigers at feeding time. No 'Oh my God!' or even 'Good Lord.' Got that?"

"I'm guessing 'Jesus fucking Christ' is out of the question?"

"You're looking more like Purina Cat Chow by the minute, smartass."

He knew how to present himself to his elders, a combination of manners, respect, and sincerity. It came easy to him because he generally liked seniors.

He shuffled into the kitchen, which was every bit as humble as the rest of the house—oak table and four chairs, rattling refrigerator, blue-tile counters, doorless cupboards showing bowls stacked within bowls. A sixtyish woman stood at a gas stove, frying something in a wok. On the wall behind her hung a picture of the Virgin Mary of Guadalupe with flowers cascading from her open mantle.

Lilikoi rushed to take over the frying and begged her grandmother to sit and conserve her energy. Then she introduced the old woman as Gran Kamamalu.

The old woman gave him an unabashed look, revealing a childlike curiosity. She wore a richly patterned pink muumuu, which hung loose on her gaunt frame. Folds of slack skin drooped from her jowls, cheeks, arms and legs, telling him that she had once been an enormous woman but had lost much of her bulk. Her silver hair parted at her crown and flowed down both cheeks to her boney shoulders. Her legs and arms were elegantly tattooed, looking like a melting canvas.

"Aloha," she said. "You gotta name?" she added with accented English. She sat down at the table before a colander holding a few dozen shrimp. She grabbed one and began to devein it. Her fingers seemed to work apart from her, as if they had performed this task a million times, elevating it to an art form.

"Yes, ma'am. Matt Reece."

"Reece your last name?"

"No, ma'am, Matt Reece Connors."

"Two first names was your daddy's idea?"

"My mother named me."

"Have mercy."

"You can call me Matt."

"I ain't seen you before. Is your home here on the island?"

"I don't have a home, ma'am. I guess you could say I'm a drifter."

Her face grew troubled. She told him everyone had a place of rest and comfort on God's green earth, and she would pray for him. Then she asked where he was raised.

"On a ranch in Nevada, ma'am."

"A cowboy." She scrutinized him with a raised eyebrow, as if giving him an opportunity to deny the accusation.

"I like to ride, ma'am. I'm also a fair cook. Can I help you with those shrimp?"

She held up a staying hand. "I ain't dead yet." The snap in her voice loosened. "Welcome to my *ohana,* Matt Reece. *Ohana* means family."

"Don't roll out the red carpet just yet, Gran. You don't know anything about him."

Gran Kamamalu pursed her lips. "Neither do you, apparently. There is much to see in this boy's eyes, yet you make little of it." The old woman reached up and touched Lilikoi under the chin, moving her head until they gazed eye to eye. "You forget your Christian duty? You presume to know the heart of our Lord, of Kane, of Pele? Curb your arrogance, young one." Her voice was a whisper, but it held the assertion of a shout.

"I'm so pleased to meet you, ma'am," he said and held out his arm. He shook her fishy hand, and when he tried to pull back his hand, she held it firmly.

"You liked my soup? There's nothing better for the body. The white bits are dorado, and the purple ones are octopus. I simmer the stock for a day with fish heads, roasted red peppers, dried seaweed, and fresh ginger." She released his hand and pointed to a chair beside her. He sat at the table before a steaming, green-glazed coffee mug, and next to that lay the flash drive he had given to Lilikoi before the knife fight. He snatched the drive, feeling the weight of it in his hand.

Gran Kamamalu dropped a cleaned shrimp in a bowl of water and picked up another.

"What's on it that's so important?" Lilikoi asked.

He paused before answering. "Something that can either save or destroy mankind."

Her eyebrows lifted. "The one ring to rule them all? Maybe I was too hasty in returning it," she said.

"Welcome to the fellowship," he said. "How are you at fighting orcs?"

Lilikoi placed a plate in front of him. Breakfast was two beautiful poached eggs over vegetable fried rice, hot from the wok and accompanied by homemade sourdough toast, sliced pineapple, melon, and passion fruit. Coarse ground pepper and sea salt sat in separate bowls to sprinkle over the eggs.

He dug in. Lilikoi opened a cupboard, removed a bottle of vodka, and poured herself a sizable glassful. She took a hard swallow and set the glass on the counter. "Should I pour you one?"

"I don't drink alcohol."

"Well, normally I'd say let me know when you grow a pair, but I've seen you fight. Come to think of it, I've also seen you naked."

Gran Kamamalu shook her head. She asked, "Have you found Jesus today?"

"No, ma'am. Have you lost him again?"

Lilikoi slapped the back of his head with her spatula.

"No, sir. I ain't never lost him since the day he saved me. I see you ain't a believer because you didn't bow your head to give thanks before eating. That's okay with me. The Lord led you here, and we'll help lead you to him."

"I'll be much obliged if you do, ma'am."

"Do you attend church?" Gran Kamamalu asked.

"No, ma'am. I've always found grace by riding the open range."

She nodded sagely. "Our Lord is everywhere. All we need to do is open our eyes and let his glory flood in." She glanced at Lilikoi with an air of satisfaction. "Lilikoi once basked in the light of God, but she flew off to college and came back six years later with a closed heart." She shook her head. "I pray every day she finds Jesus, and I pray she finds a man to marry and have children with. But the men on this island, every last one, has a hole in his heart. What can you do with a man with a hole in his heart?"

He flinched with trepidation, afraid of where she was headed.

"All the violence and hate created that hole, and it keeps growing bigger and blacker. The only way to fill it is to throw those guns away and accept the Lord Jesus. It's what I pray for. Ten times a day I beseech our Lord for that."

"If you don't mind my asking," he said, "what's your success rate?" Which got him another slap on the back of his head.

Gran chuckled and gave him an affectionate pat of her hand.

Lilikoi brought her medical bag to the table. While Matt Reece ate, he noticed that above both her wrists were neat parallel scars, three inches long. They were healed over, but the scars still held some pink in them; they were not that old.

She opened the bag and removed a pair of surgical scissors that were cold against his skin as she slid them under the bloodstained bandages and cut them away. She pulled the dressings from his torso and examined the stitches. Her eyes grew large, and her mouth formed a zero. She pressed her fingers to the sutures that were almost healed.

"Christ Almighty," she said.

He laughed and pointed a finger at her, but she was still too amazed to catch his meaning. He said, "Yesterday you said the world was tearing itself apart?"

"You been hiding under a rock for the last seven weeks?"

"Adrift at sea with no radio."

She soaked cotton balls with her vodka and dabbed his wounds. "The world is at war, with four cities nuked already. The new axis of evil is the US, China, and Russia. People are taking up arms to defend themselves, others have their heads stuck in the ground, and still others, like my father, are making a financial killing." She patted his chest with a towel while she lectured him on assassinations, cities on fire, universities under siege, people starving, and then she took another long pull of vodka. "The politicians say it's all to bring peace, but it looks like the end of civilization to me."

Gran sang out, "You can put truth in the river five days after a lie, and truth is gonna catch up, sure as Jesus is my savior."

Lilikoi's tone was too sincere not to believe her. More food sat untouched on his plate, yet he had lost his appetite. "Four cities nuked? But why?"

"To show they mean business, that there is no going back."

"Can I use your phone? I need to let my father know I'm alive."

"Are you stuck on stupid? Nobody can know you're here. They would kill us all to get you."

She didn't bother to redress the wounds. She rose, dropped the scissors into the bag, and closed it up. "The Hawaiian Islands have broken away from the United States, and the US military is too busy stateside to do anything about it." She looked down at her patient with her eyes still unbelieving. "A hot bath, clean clothes, and you're good to go."

He picked up his coffee mug and sipped, letting what he saw yesterday fit together with her words now. From over the rim of the mug he said, "Those animals at the docks—you're a modern-day Noah?"

"I chair an organization that is amassing more than just living species—literary treasures, religious documents, priceless artwork, scientific formulas, designs for computers and machinery, medical procedures, movies and documentaries, the full wealth of human knowledge that must be preserved for the survivors of the next holocaust. We buy the originals from wherever we can find them. And it's not just this island. Thanks to my father's fortune and a few visionaries who see what's coming, islands all over the Pacific are being used as storehouses. We're buying up zoos and museums and literary collections and shipping it all as fast as we can to any place that's too insignificant to blast to smithereens. On Hawaii's big island, we're building a seed bank, huge storage vaults to stockpile seeds of all kinds, food, trees, grasses, flowers. We have a fleet of container ships chock full of priceless art, floating in the South Pacific. Day by day, that fleet keeps growing."

"I would think nations would preserve their own treasures."

"They have their hands full dealing with the violence. So as long as my father keeps funding my organization, we'll keep at it."

Gran Kamamalu said, "The new Jerusalem will radiate with the majesty of our Lord, and we alone will be left to worship his splendor. Amen."

"You gather animals," he said, "but turn humans away. Aren't we an endangered species now?"

"Right now, tycoons are desperate to find a safe hiding place to wait out the carnage. They show up in their glittering yachts, trying to buy their way ashore. What these nitwits don't get is that, day by day, their money is becoming worthless. They cling to a crumbled dream, like dinosaurs after the meteorite struck the earth, who went on eating and eating, not realizing they had been rendered extinct."

She explained how armed mobs took over pockets of territories, strongholds ruled by lawless brutes—French, Spanish, German, Canadian, American, Mexican, and Australian mobs…. Even in China, Russia, and India. These mobs turned on the upper class. Suicides, murders, and lynchings had become a dominant pattern. On top of that, cobalt radioactivity was spreading over Europe and the Middle East.

At her mention of suicide, he glanced at her wrists again. He felt her mood of imminent blame for these scars and for this global catastrophe. It seemed she wanted to pin it all on him, personally, but couldn't make it stick in her mind, and that made her more annoyed.

"This horror could be avoided if all sides could just understand each other," he said.

"Don't kid yourself, cowboy. It started because they understand each other only too well."

"It's wrong to turn away refugees looking for a safe haven."

"I'm delighted you mentioned that." Although she didn't sound at all delighted. "They're gluttonous swine who supported this war in the first place thinking they would get their magic immortality pill, and now they're shitting themselves because it blew out of control and they're being hunted like dogs. This island already has one voracious pig, perhaps the fattest, most gluttonous pig of all. There's no room for more. Besides, you're in no position to pass judgment, you little shit. If we open the floodgates, we'd jeopardize everything we're trying to protect."

"I feel sick," he said. How could the end to gun violence have gone so appallingly wrong? He swept this gaze around the kitchen, seeking someone not there—the one person who could put a stop to it all. He felt Kirby rising from within, with visions of him taking Kenji by the throat.

"What's happened to Kenji? Where is he?"

"He's a guest of that voracious pig I mentioned. He's being treated well. You don't have to worry."

"I'm only worried he'll escape before I can kill him." The look she shot him made him want to explain. "He'll butcher the whole world if someone doesn't stop him."

"Right, and you're the ring bearer. I thought you had enough of that yesterday."

He shrugged. His sole task now was killing Kenji and stopping the violence. How he could do that was a mystery, but he knew he had to find a way.

"Looks like you'll get a chance at him because he's not going anywhere. And like I said, you're good to—"

"Go. Yeah, you told me, but go where?"

Lilikoi guzzled her vodka. "Finish your eggs, and we'll talk about that."

He picked up his fork and shoveled more food into his mouth, despite his lack of appetite. He didn't ask further questions because he didn't want answers. Gran heaped more rice onto his plate. Her kindness lifted his mood. After weeks trapped in the throes of starvation, he gorged himself. It amazed him how a full belly went, measure for measure, with contentment.

CHAPTER THIRTY-NINE

UPON ARRIVING in Hiroshima, Randall rented a van and drove to the airport. Jessup, Landau, Patrick, Vishal, and Randall boarded a sixteen-passenger helicopter that was every bit as plush as the corporate jet that flew them to Japan. The twin engines idled, and the blades turned. Jessup steadied Landau's arm as he stepped in and found a comfortable leather seat beside a large window.

Randall carried a cooler loaded with soft drinks, beers, and bento boxes full of steamed rice, fish and meats, and pickled vegetables. He stored the cooler between Patrick and Vishal, who were making a point of not talking to each other.

Jessup felt a rising freshness in his chest. Not quite optimism, but a healthy clarity that had been missing for years, because he was fully engaged in reuniting his family.

While Randall bent over a chart book with the two pilots, Landau seemed not nearly as optimistic as Jessup. "There's a thousand miles of ocean to cover. What we're doing," he told Jessup, "is nothing short of a crapshoot."

"It beats the hell out of sitting in a hotel room," Jessup said, glancing out the window. The skies were dull and opaque with good visibility. They'd calculated a reasonable sailing time from San Francisco and were confident the ship couldn't have arrived already. But to be certain, they had checked with the harbormaster to ensure no new ships sailed into port in the last week. Randall had his staff checking other ports along the eastern shore as well. With luck, Kenji's sailboat would be within a few days of reaching them. All they had to do was spot it before it reached land.

Randall walked back from the cockpit. "Buckle up, everyone," he said. By the time he plopped into a seat, they were airborne. From a thousand feet up, the city was shaped like a fan. The main areas covered six islands formed by the estuarial rivers that branched out from the Ota River. It was a vast, modern, vibrant metropolis, as beautiful as any large city could be, in Jessup's opinion. Amazing to think that this place had been leveled only seventy years ago. As they turned east, Jessup got his first glimpse of the island-studded Inland Sea.

For thirty minutes they held a course straight east. They passed over several uninhabited islands, and then the copter banked right and slowed, flying southeast. The bareness was startling—a flat plane of waves and nothing else. They cruised on that course for thirty minutes without spotting anything more than fishing boats. Jessup felt himself sliding into reverie. He scanned the waters for a sail, a boat of any kind, anything that would break up the solitude of gray. He began to think of the food in the bento boxes, not because he was hungry but because he needed something else to do.

They had divided the sea in quadrants from the helicopter, with each person inspecting only one quadrant. Vishal began humming a tune while he searched, a tune that went spinning through Jessup's head. He couldn't ignore it, and all at once, as the tune dipped and curled, he recognized it and the words popped into his head—*Take me home, country roads*.... He remembered riding his horse alongside Matt Reece and Kenji, the smell of wet sagebrush, the three of them riding through a fresh morning shower. The image morphed into other scenes, odd flashes of his past—he and Kenji in bed on a Saturday morning, making love in the chill of December; Patrick and Matt Reece on horseback, racing each other across a spring meadow heavy with blooms; sitting with his family for Sunday dinner of roasted chicken; snuggling with Kenji on the couch and listening to gentle breathing after he fell asleep.

"Jessup, you still with us?" Landau asked.

Jessup glanced up. "Sorry, in all this monotony I drifted off." Landau reached into the cooler, drew out a bottle of water, and held it out. Jessup shook his head.

"Pass that water to Patrick. He seems green in the gills," Vishal said.

"Bite me," Patrick snapped.

Jessup glanced at his son. "Looks like you'll lose your breakfast any minute. Maybe we should head back and get you on solid ground?"

"Not a chance."

"You do look kinda—" Randall started to say.

Patrick made a hard cutting motion with his hand. "Can it, all of you. You want to worry about something, worry about your own fucking selves."

Jessup knew Patrick was hurting from drug withdrawal. He wished to God he could do something to ease his boy's suffering, but Patrick had dug that hole himself, and he needed to crawl out himself.

"Enough bickering," Landau said. "Let's all shoot for a little politeness. If you can't manage that, then keep your mouths shut and your eyes open. Focus on the job at hand."

Vishal said, "I was only trying to—"

"Enough," Landau said, his voice sharp.

Being told to keep silent made Jessup want to give his own oration. He wanted to explain that however he had failed Patrick, he was sorry, and the same for Kenji and Matt Reece. He fought down the urge, because he knew Landau was right. Shut mouths and open eyes were best.

Four times they spotted sailing craft in the distance. As they approached each one, the copter banked low and hovered alongside to scrutinize the crew as they came on deck to wave. All four were Japanese ships with Japanese crews.

They flew at a moderate speed for another two hours, but all they saw were cargo ships and tankers, and not many of those. At noon they ate what was in the bento boxes while the copter zigzagged its way back to shore. Jessup occasionally glanced at Patrick, who was sweating and in obvious discomfort. His hands shook, and his skin turned yellowish. He looked like a pressure cooker ready to blow. Jessup told himself that all he could do was give it time, wait it out, and hope that Patrick was stronger than the drug. He'd have given almost anything to go back in time with Patrick to a point where he could hug the boy, and the boy would hug him back. Patrick needed human touch, and so did he. But he knew that couldn't happen now. The wall separating them was too high and too thick to breach.

IT WAS late afternoon when they landed at the airport. They had covered five hundred nautical miles with no luck. Their mood turned somber.

They walked across the tarmac to a bar where the airport employees gathered after their shifts ended. Jessup tried to lighten things up by saying, "Damn, I had such high hopes this morning."

"No shit, Sherlock. We all did," Patrick said.

Jessup took hold of Patrick's arm and led him away from the group. When they were out of hearing distance, they stopped. The others entered the bar and chose a table at the front window. Jessup could see them ordering a round of beers.

He didn't have a clue what to say. He started hesitantly, "I know you're hurting, but I've had a bellyful of your lip. Stop making this all about you, dammit." Patrick set his jaw and knotted his brow. They glared eye to eye, both defiant. Anger drove Jessup to blurt out his own secrets. For once in his life he held back nothing. He described how he was feeling his way in the dark and couldn't find even a glimmer of light. Which was true. He didn't know where he was, how he'd gotten there, or where the hell to go next. Being a failure didn't begin to describe him, but at least he kept it to himself, not letting it drag down the others.

Patrick, who stood silent during Jessup's tirade, dropped his head. Jessup walked away, joining the group. He watched his son struggling with himself for another few minutes before the boy turned and walked toward them.

Patrick sat beside Jessup as the waitress dispersed frosty glasses of Sapporo beer.

"Sorry I lost my shit, everyone," Patrick said. "It's just that I'm feeling so damned helpless. And I keep being bothered by what Vishal told me, how Matt Reece needed me. If I hadn't let him down, we wouldn't be here now. I'm so fucking mortified."

"He loves you deeply," Vishal said. "That's why he was so hurt."

Jessup clamped a hand on Patrick's shoulder, squeezing, while his other hand pushed a beer at his son. Then the impossible happened; Patrick leaned into Jessup and wrapped his arms around Jessup's waist. They hugged.

"Tomorrow we'll have better luck," Jessup said, even though right then he felt pretty damned lucky. He stared at Randall over Patrick's shoulder, and Randall winked at him. "And if not, then the day after. Nobody quits. That's the only thing I can promise you."

Patrick squeezed harder, and then he pulled back and grabbed his beer. He took a deep swallow and visibly tried to brace himself. "Thank you," he said.

Randall said, "To lift everyone's morale, I'm taking us to a *ryokan*. It's a traditional inn that will give you a real taste of Japan you won't forget anytime soon."

"We won't have to sleep on the floor, will we?" Jessup asked.

"Trust me, you'll sleep like a baby. It wasn't easy finding a place that allows Caucasians. Most ryokans don't, because Westerners offend their Japanese clientele."

Jessup was suspicious that was code for, yes, they would be sleeping on the floor.

AS THEY drove into the city, they passed empty lots where men worked hoes and women pulled weeds away from lines of vegetables. Children played soccer. It was a clean city with tidy gardens and temple roofs of golden tiles. They bore south until they came to a road that dropped down beside one of the numerous canals and cut west, skirting the bustling town center. They seemed to wander through neighborhoods dotted with houses that had rooftops made with gray tiles overlapping like fish scales. The houses stretched from the downtown skyscrapers to the base of the mountains, behind which the sun had begun to set.

They came to an alley, parked the van, and walked up the pavement to a two-storied, wooden building weather stained to a blackish gray. At the front door, a man offered them each a cup of green tea and knelt to remove their shoes. He hurried behind the desk to check them in. A dozen antique lacquered lamps lit the lobby, giving the room a warm glow and veiling the corners and alcoves in shadows. The clerk showed them to their rooms.

Jessup and Landau shared one room, Vishal and Patrick another, and Randall had a room to himself. Randall followed Jessup into a room to ensure everything was to their liking. Jessup studied the furnishings. A low table sat in the center, a smaller table beside it, and a hibachi of hot coals beside that. Along one wall sat lacquered chests. The rest of the room was bare wood polished a golden brown. In one corner stood a screen that displayed a mountain scene painted in the Zen style, muted colors of a bridge suspended in the moonlight over a rocky gorge. In the alcove hung a scroll with Japanese calligraphy on it. Landau asked Randall to translate.

"No gambling, No prostitution, No mahjong, No parties, No credit!"

The wood and paper sliding door was thrust aside, and a woman knelt in the doorway. Her lavender kimono covered three undergarments that showed at her neck, framing her ivory-colored face, which had a light eczema of some kind that she had covered with powder. Her hair fell about her shoulders and flowed down her back in a ponytail. She bowed and rattled off a cascade of Japanese.

Randall bowed. "This is Myeko, and she will treat us to the *furo*, the traditional Japanese bath and hot tub, and then prepare dinner."

She carried a bamboo tray laden with steaming hand towels, a pot of green tea, and three cups into the room. She set the tray on the dining table, adjusted the temperature setting on the iron stove, and bowed.

Jessup bowed and said, "*Domo arigatou gozaimasu*, Myeko-san."

She seemed pleased that he spoke even that trivial bit of her language, and she bowed again and said, "*Do itashi mashite, dozo*," before leaving.

There were no other doors leading to bedrooms. "Where are the beds?" Jessup asked.

Randall pointed to a cabinet. "Myeko will make up the beds later."

Jessup contemplated sleeping on the floor. "Oh hell no. Look, I can eat raw fish and even eel, but I need a comfortable bed."

"Then you should have stayed home," Landau said. "Man up, for Christ's sake." He lifted a bottle from his pocket and shook out pills, which he downed with a cup of tea.

Jessup felt the heat of a blush on his cheeks. He had been ready to demand they move to a regular hotel, but Landau's tone cut that idea off at the knees.

"I'll see you men at the hot tub," Randall said on his way out of the room.

Jessup and Landau shucked their clothes and pulled on the blue-and-white-checkered kimonos that they found hanging in the closet.

Jessup sat beside the window overlooking the garden. A line of cryptomeria trees and thick clumps of bamboo bordered an exquisite rock garden. The night-blooming jasmine was a bit early this year, he thought, but it was an undeniable scent on the air. The place seemed a refuge of coolness and order, and his frustration bled away. He grew pleased at the prospect of occupying this serene landscape that was far from the bustle of downtown.

Landau poured more cups of tea and brought one to Jessup. "The garden is lovely," Landau said. He pulled a book from his bag and sat on the floor near a lamp. He read as he sipped his tea. Jessup was content to stare out over the waving bamboo and the stone-lined paths.

Fifteen minutes crawled by before the sliding doors opened, and Myeko was on her knees, bowing. Landau glanced up. "Time for my bath." He laid his book aside and crawled to his feet. He seemed unsteady as he staggered out of the room.

Jessup returned his attention to the garden and admired a bonsai tree that could have been as old as three hundred years. It was breathtaking.

Myeko returned and led him down a narrow stairway and into an outdoor bathroom in a corner of the garden. He stripped off his kimono and sat on a stool beside a cypress-wood tub where Landau and Randall were submersed up to their necks. Myeko dipped a wooden bucket into the hot water and poured it over Jessup's head. With a bar of soap and a washrag, she scrubbed him head to soles. Lather clung to his body like white frosting. She washed him as gently as a mother with her newborn, and it was a delightful return to a state of infancy.

A thorough rinse, and Jessup eased into the tub.

He closed his eyes and drifted in the lovely heat. Over the past eleven years, he and Kenji bathed together many times, and they shared the same bed. He missed that intimacy, and being naked with Landau and Randall gave him a deep-seated comfort.

Randall's coarse dreads were slicked down like an otter's pelt. Naked and up to his neck in water made him look like a different person.

"At the airport," Landau said, "what did you say to Patrick that turned him around?"

Jessup smiled. "I told him what I was feeling. I guess he feels similarly, because we connected." He paused and asked, "Do you think we'll find them?"

Randall said, "Confucius said: 'If you sit by the river long enough, the body of your enemy will float by.' Although I agree we should have a more proactive approach."

"It's vital to keep searching for their ship via helicopter," Landau said, "but we should find those people Kenji already treated. Assuming they're living together, I'm certain he'll try to join them. Find them, and we can set a trap."

"Jessup, Patrick, and Vishal can continue the sea search," Randall said. "You and I can investigate possible hiding spots. We can start with monasteries in remote areas."

"It's the most logical," Landau said, "because no one would pay attention to what happens behind those walls. Someplace remote."

"I'll have my staff compile a list of monasteries in a fifty-mile radius."

Jessup said, "Patrick brought a laptop. If this hotel has Wi-Fi, he can google it." He splashed hot water on his face, loving this relaxing heat. "Have either of you given any thought to the kind of world our children will inherit if we don't find them?"

A deep silence hovered over their heads.

Landau finally said, "The State Department has given this subject exhaustive thought. The pattern is evident. Fear will propagate. Suspicion of strangers will prevail. The world will reorganize into small governments with closed borders and very little movement between states. They're calling it the Switzerland syndrome. And as for disarming the world, as fast as governments destroy guns, people will produce more underground."

"Perhaps smaller, more manageable governments could be a good thing," Jessup said. "Looks to me like our government has grown too massive to be effective. Big money and greedy politicians have sure as hell screwed the rest of us."

Landau nodded. "No argument there. I haven't respected a politician since Kennedy."

Jessup continued, "I've always thought the federal government's role was maintaining a military for national defense and insuring a judicial system that upholds the constitution. If they disband the armies, why do we need a federal government?"

Landau chuckled. "Do you want to take civilization back to feudal times? Stop trade? Let local governments decide on a judicial system or an education standard?"

Jessup shook his head. "If we achieve a single worldwide currency, an electronic currency, then trade could continue."

"You're dreaming, Jessup," Landau said. "All we'll have is chaos. Dog-eat-dog."

"The real power," Randall said, "will be in the hands of the one government or corporation or person who holds the golden egg—Kenji's formula. They decide who lives and who dies. They will be worshipped as the new god. And frankly, that scares the crap out of me."

Landau eased himself out of the tub and grabbed a towel from a stack by the door. As he dried himself he said, "You asked what kind of world we'll leave our children? I'm not sure there will be a world for them to inherit. That's why we must succeed." He dropped his towel in the hamper and slipped on his robe. He opened the door and walked inside, shutting the door behind him.

A vague regret filled Jessup's throat: he wished….

Randall tilted his head to one side. "Jessup, you look sad."

"Bathing like this is hard for me because Kenji and I had so much pleasure in the tub. I can't help missing him."

Randall's sigh almost qualified as a laugh. He drew Jessup into his arms.

Jessup didn't resist. He felt hard muscles under silky skin enfolding him. He closed his eyes and laid his head on Randall's shoulder.

The sunset bled from the sky. The night was clear, with a half-cut moon low over the mountain. Jessup could see the ocean through an opening in the trees.

They stayed nailed together until the skin on Jessup's fingers pruned. Then Jessup pulled away. With a start he realized that Randall's eyes were big and soulful and more expressive than eyes had a right to be. "This is getting too real."

"Real?"

"What we've got here is a handful of stolen moments. If we keep going, when this thing ends, whatever this is, we'll both spend the next decade finding a flattering way to call it a mistake."

"You're not giving either of us much credit," Randall said.

Jessup lifted himself from the tub. "No doubt you'd think that. But then, you're the guilty party here."

They toweled and dressed and returned to their separate rooms. In Jessup's room, Myeko knelt beside the low table with two place settings. On the floor, the charcoal hibachi sat next to the smaller table that held a tray of raw fish, eggplant, and mountain vegetables. Another tray held bowls of soup, noodles, and tofu.

"Where's Landau?" Jessup asked. She didn't understand so he pantomimed sign language. Her eyes brightened as comprehension blossomed. She pointed across the hallway to Randall's room, indicating Landau had switched rooms.

He sat at the low table across from her. She prepared a cup of tea and placed it before him.

Randall knocked and said through the door, "I'm across the hall, Jessup, if you need anything." There was something in his voice. Jessup could sense his hand on the handle with his forehead pressing the door.

"Nothing now," he said.

Frogs croaked outside.

"Can I join you for dinner? Nothing more than food and a spot of sake."

Jessup was hesitant, and he stayed silent for a heartbeat. Before he could say no, Randall opened the door and stepped into the room. "I'll take that as a yes."

Randall spoke a sentence in Japanese to Myeko. She poured two cups full of sake and held up the tray to serve them. Randall settled cross-legged at the table and took both cups. He handed one to Jessup.

Randall held up his sake in a toast. They clicked cups.

"I was about to say no thanks, but now that you're here, I realize how much I hate to eat alone." He drank his sake and felt his head expand with delightful heat. He checked the size of the ceramic bottle Myeko poured the drinks from and knew he was going to need a lot more than that before bedtime, because he hated to sleep alone as well.

He closed his eyes, and a moment later he felt Randall's breath on his face. He opened his eyelids to find Randall's lips were only inches away from his. He stared into those soulful eyes, and his stomach tightened in anticipation. The cage holding back his desire opened, and Jessup sailed into those lips.

He heard the off-key wail of sirens going off in the distance, its direction distorted by the growing wind.

When he leaned away from that unfairly handsome face, he said, "Tell her to heat up more bottles," and he felt himself blush.

"Indeed. Are you still disappointed we'll be sleeping on the floor?"

For the first time in recent memory, Jessup threw back his head and laughed. Really laughed.

Chapter Forty

Lᴉʟɪᴋᴏɪ ꜰɪʟʟᴇᴅ the bathtub with hot water laced with Epsom salts. Matt Reece settled in for a long soak. His muscles loosened. He tilted his head back, enjoying the heat and a full belly. His pores opened, and blood sluiced through his arteries. He felt something—Life? Hope? Courage?—stirring.

The door opened, and Gran Kamamalu eased into the bathroom, carrying an armload of clothes and a well-used pair of cowboy boots. She wore a hat with the left side of the brim turned up Aussie-style. It perched on her head like a bird's nest. He moved his hands to cover his private parts. *Good God*, he thought, *first it's kids watching me sleep, now this woman barges in on my bath.* "Can't a man get some privacy?"

She dropped the boots beside the toilet and stacked the clothes on top of the lid. She straightened back up, hands on her hips. "Lordy, no need for modesty. You got nothing I ain't seen before. I've buried two husbands." She crossed herself. "You let me know if those boots pinch your toes." She laughed as she left the room, closing the door.

He was pleased to see the brown camouflage uniform like the men on the dock wore, snowy-white underwear and T-shirt, and wool socks. The only thing missing was a hat.

The door opened again, and Gran poked her head in. "I almost forgot." She pulled the hat from her head and dropped it onto the stack of clothes.

Later, toweling off before the mirror, he stared at the bags under his eyes, the stubble on his cheeks and chin. He looked older, and tired. He was no longer the boy who started this odyssey. But who the hell was he now? Yet, somewhere deep in those eyes, he vaguely saw the boy who once dreamed of escaping the ranch to find love, who crusaded to save mankind from guns. The thought made him weary.

Ten minutes later, he walked onto the porch wearing his borrowed uniform and carrying his boots and hat. Once outside, he stepped into his boots and set his hat, but he folded the brim down so it looked American.

The shirt and jeans were a size too large, and he had to roll up both sleeves and pant legs, but the boots fit. Now he felt taller, stronger, ready for the day.

Lilikoi waited for him. She was dressed in jeans, work shirt, cowboy hat, and boots, and she wore her blue-mirrored sunglasses. She handed him a tortilla wrapped around grilled fish and a cup of coffee. He was still full from breakfast, but after so many days of starvation, he couldn't refuse. He followed her toward the corral, eating his food and sipping his coffee.

"You wasted half the morning in the bathroom," she said. "I was about to send in a search-and-rescue party."

He let it roll off his back. She'd saved his life, so she could say anything she wanted.

"Who do I have to thank for these clothes?"

"Those belonged to Ted."

"You mean dead Ted? Mr. Cat Chow?"

"How many Teds do you know on this island?"

The coffee suddenly turned bitter, and Kirby leaped to the forefront of his brain. "I won't wear a dead man's hand-me-downs."

"Then don't. Tie a fig leaf to your crank and we'll call you Adam."

They stopped at the corral fence. He downed his coffee and set his cup on a rail. They stood looking at two horses while he ate the rest of his tortilla. He focused on beating Kirby back into submission, rather than on his clothes, but his skin began to itch.

"Let me introduce you to Top Hat, the horse I rode yesterday. She's a purebred Holsteiner, and a fine workin' horse. But she can be naughty."

Top Hat was a large, spirited horse, too much horse for most riders. It told him Lilikoi was a skilled horsewoman. Top Hat's neck arched, as if she knew they were talking about her. She minced around the corral with a proud, borderline defiant gait.

"The stallion is Kantaka. He's an Arabian, part royalty and part desert whirlwind. Sword Bearer, out of Cairo, sired him, so noble blood flows through his arrogant veins. He's named after the steed of Gautama Shakyamuni, the Buddha. After Gautama rode Kantaka out of the palace and into the forest to renounce the world, the mount returned to the palace riderless and died of sorrow."

Studying the stallion made Kirby disappear. He felt a lump form in his throat, which happened whenever he admired the contours of a fine but elusive horse. An exquisite stallion was always an emotional experience for him. All his life he talked about horses—hell, most of the time he talked of nothing else—but he had never been able to unravel his love of them using commonplace adjectives. To him they were an ethereal dream, to be admired but not talked about, because he could never voice the right words.

"What a waste of good horse flesh."

"How did I know you'd be such a romantic?"

He was awed by Kantaka's self-possession. He had the slow and dignified steps of Bonaparte in exile, with his head held high, his nostrils flaring, and his black-rimmed ears pricked in their direction. Like Matt Reece, he was slender in the chest, but unlike him, the stallion had strong legs as clean as limestone. He was a sorrel, and his reddish coat gave off a golden sheen in the morning sunlight. His hooves kicked at the earth, his body shivered, and his lungs let out a rush of air, letting Matt Reece know he craved the freedom of open space after being cramped up in that corral. This horse needed a good, hard run, and Matt Reece found that he needed the same thing. The sheer idea of it whisked him into a space of pure silence, broken only by the pulse beating at his temples.

"He's got the fury of hell in his heart," Lilikoi said. "Nobody can break him."

Matt Reece gazed into those large moist eyes. The horse knew men and feared and hated them. He sensed that Kantaka understood that men were there to serve him, that they were his servants, not the other way around.

He walked to the barn.

Coolie had followed them down to the corral, and now he whined and seemed torn between following Matt Reece or staying with Lilikoi. Matt Reece told the dog to hush, and the dog crouched near a fence post and waited.

"Well?" she said to his back.

"Well what?"

"You claim you're a hotshot horse whisperer. Can you break him?"

The world was going up in smoke and she was worried about breaking a horse? Had everyone gone mad? But what else did he have to do at that moment? "I need you to do two things. First, lose those sunglasses. Second, lead both horses back to their stables. And I'm going to need more coffee."

"Answer my question, you little shit."

"And another tortilla would sure hit the spot."

He found the tack room and gathered what he needed—rawhide gloves, a gunnysack, two catch ropes, saddle blanket, hackamore, and a saddle. He carried it all back to the empty corral, undid the wire holding the gate, and slipped inside.

A group of kids gathered. He waved them back a few yards so they wouldn't make the horse nervous. He also found a fresh mug of coffee and a tortilla perched on the rail.

He dropped his gear and stuffed his mouth with food while he squatted to sort it all out. When he had everything the way he wanted it, he took a handful of dirt and rubbed it over his pants, shirtsleeves, and chest because he assumed that Kantaka didn't trust anyone who did not smell of the earth. The dirt held the tang of freshly plowed fields.

He slid the gunnysack under his belt, took one of the ropes, and began building his noose. He moved to the center of the corral and asked Lilikoi to bring back Kantaka.

When Kantaka raced into the corral, Matt Reece and the stallion stared each other down. A tremor ran through the stallion, and he shook his head with nostrils flaring and blowing snot. He trotted in short nervous circles.

Matt Reece twirled his lariat over his head. He glanced over his shoulder at Lilikoi, who for once, was speechless. He was not altogether sure of what she saw differently in him, but it was obvious she now looked at him with new eyes. And how could she not? With rawhide gloves covering his fingers, a rope in his hand, and a stallion to break, he was in his element, a man with ability and purpose.

He rolled his loop as smooth as butter and forefooted the animal on the first try. Kantaka hit the ground and kicked out with his hind legs. Before the surprised stallion could regain his feet, Matt Reece crouched on his neck and heaved its head up, pinning the muzzle to his chest. Hot breath shot up from those nostrils. Matt Reece smelled fear in those frantic breaths. He ripped the gunnysack from under his belt and pressed it over the horse's eyes, and then he blew softly into each nostril while gently rubbing Kantaka's neck between the jawbones. As he stroked that long muzzle, he talked in a low, soothing voice, telling the horse in Spanish everything that would happen next.

Following Matt Reece's instructions, Lilikoi retrieved the hackamore and fitted it over Kantaka's muzzle and ears. She ran back to the gate, took two of the ropes, and made a slip noose, one in each. She hitched one around the pastern of Kantaka's right hind leg and passed the rope to Matt Reece, who half hitched it to the hackamore. They did the same thing to the left hind leg.

"What makes you think Kantaka understands Spanish?" she asked.

"It's the language of love. I'm forging an intimate relationship here."

She smiled. "Yeah, well, I hope you two play safe. Although I've seen him excited, and I don't know where you'll find a condom to fit him."

"I'll bet Gran is real proud she raised such a vulgar smartass."

She laughed. "Okay. What's next?"

"Food."

"What?"

He waved her back, and he stepped away from Kantaka. The horse leaped up, shot out a hind leg to run away, but being tied to the hackamore, it jerked his head back, and the horse lurched in a half-circle before falling on its side. He raised up, kicked on the other side, and promptly fell again. His eyeball rolled back to stare at Matt Reece, who stood above him, still speaking Spanish in a low, calm voice. The children laughed and began playing a game to see who could fall to the ground with the most flair.

Kantaka struggled to his feet a third time, but stood still, trying to fathom this new situation. He minced around with small steps, which tugged at the hackamore binding his head, but as soon as he kicked out his hind leg, his head jerked around and he hit the dirt.

"Let's eat while Mr. High-and-mighty gets used to this turn of events," Matt Reece said.

"Hobbling him will only piss him off, and I don't blame him."

"Some animals you can throw a saddle on their back, climb on, and ride them until they surrender. But with a hellion like this, I like to show them who rules the roost before I climb on. Saves wear and tear on my butt, and I don't have much padding down there."

"But this is batshit crazy. I—"

"Being trussed up like a Thanksgiving turkey for an hour or two will have a powerful effect on his ego."

He turned and walked back to the house, and she followed. They found Gran Kamamalu sitting on the veranda with an open bible on her lap. She wore a pair of half-moon reading glasses, and her lips moved as she read.

They carried the kitchen table onto the porch so they could eat while keeping an eye on Kantaka. Later, Lilikoi carried out platters of meaty conch soup with crusty bread and a shrimp salad. Once Gran sat, they took their time eating, the three of them. He finished his soup, and Gran filled his bowl again. He protested, but she ignored him.

Later, he sat sipping coffee while Lilikoi polished off another glass of vodka. He could feel frustration building in her until she said, "Why did you have me take Kantaka to the stable and then lead him back in? And what's so wrong with my sunglasses?"

"Horses need to see your eyes to know you're an animal, not some creature from outer space with glowing eyes. As for the rest, social rank is central to any herd. Rank determines everything. By leading him out, that let me own the center of the corral, so that when he came back, he was invading my territory, not the other way around. That ownership made me the alpha. He became hostile and aggressive, which is an expression of insecurity. Right then, I'd already won. Everything I'm doing, including trussing him up, is to demonstrate that I'm superior. My posture, demeanor, steady gaze, speaking a language he's never heard, and owning the corral are a psychological ploy."

"So, Mister Expert, what's the verdict? Can he become a good riding horse?"

He sipped his coffee and set his mug on the table. "Once he's a finished horse, he'll be the finest animal I've ever seen."

"People say he'll never be any damned good."

"He's just arrogant. You can add up an animal's qualities and faults side by side on a sheet of paper to show you a bottom line, but it won't tell you what's in his heart."

"You talked in Spanish, but God knows he didn't understand a word."

He looked out and saw two parrots gliding over the canopy, flashes of inflamed red against a cool green background. "He heard my respect for him, my promise to care for him. No, he understands I'll give him exactly what he demands."

She poured more vodka and swallowed a mouthful. "You can tell what a horse is thinking?"

"Maybe I'm as arrogant as he is, but yeah, I generally can. A horse knows true from false. If you have a true heart and mean to let the animal keep his dignity, a good horse will figure that out. That way you form a partnership, and the horse stays whole and respects you back. If you're false, he'll see that and fight you. Animals have justice in their hearts."

"You have a mighty high opinion of animals," she said.

"Yeah, well, they're more transparent than humans. When it comes to people, I'm dumb as a fence post and getting dumber by the day."

Gran smiled. "You don't need brains if you got the Lord looking over your shoulder."

He felt reluctant to finish breaking Kantaka, knowing once that was done, Lilikoi would have no further use for him. What would he do then? Where would he go? He lingered on the porch until the sun began its descent.

"What's with that slaughtered-sheep look?" Lilikoi asked.

"What the hell," he said to the birds gliding over the treetops. He pushed back his chair and shuffled to his feet. He drained his cup, set dead Ted's hat on his head, and moseyed back to the corral. By the time he got there, Kantaka had been trussed up for two hours and was relatively calm. Coolie lay by the corral gate, waiting for him.

The crowd of children had doubled in size, and there were a dozen men standing around as well. Most of them looked like ranch hands, but there were also the four men in military drag that had accompanied Lilikoi at the dock.

"There a rodeo coming up I don't know about?" Matt Reece asked as he entered the corral and refastened the gate. He slipped on his gloves, picked up the saddle blanket and hobble rope from beside the saddle, and walked to the horse, speaking Spanish in a calm voice the whole way. The animal shivered but didn't try to rear, which was a good sign. It showed the horse had figured out his situation and was more intelligent than emotional.

He stood there for fifteen minutes, telling the big brute everything that would happen. He talked as he crouched and hobbled the front legs together. Then, for the next half hour he talked about whatever popped into his head while he floated the saddle blanket over the animal's back, under his belly, over his face, and down his neck. When he felt the animal's fear drain away, he slid the blanket into place on his back and gave Kantaka's neck a pat. He talked as if he and the horse were lovers. He leaned into the horse until they were head to head, rubbing their faces together. He murmured in Kantaka's ear, telling him how much fun they would have running in open country. Now the horse had no fear.

He sat the saddle on the animal's back and gently rocked it into place. Kantaka took a few panicky side steps with his hind legs. Matt Reece stroked his neck and kept talking.

Someone in the crowd said, "You planning to ride him or talk him to sleep?" Everyone laughed. Kantaka's ears laid back, but Matt Reece kept speaking in that same manner, a voice of authority mixed with compassion.

He reached under the horse and pulled up the strap and cinched it. He kept talking while he waited for the animal to exhale. When he did, he cinched it tighter. He waited for one more exhale before he heaved up the cinch strap and buckled it. Kantaka stayed relatively calm, which surprised him. He asked Lilikoi to bring him the bridle.

As she crossed the corral, he untied the side ropes from the horse's hind legs and hackamore. He slipped the hackamore from the animal's head and then fitted the bridle into place, setting the bit in the horse's mouth. Kantaka protested, tossing his head up and down, becoming afraid of the bridle bit clink, but Matt Reece held him firm.

"Undo the hobbles while I hold him. Once I'm on his back, go saddle up Top Hat. We'll take them for a run."

"A run? Were you born batshit crazy, or is this some new development?"

"I'm not sure. I've never put it to the test before now."

"This demon is going to launch you over the moon."

"If he does, notify NASA in Houston. They'll want to track my trajectory."

She freed Kantaka's legs, and all the spectators moved to the corral rails. Men sat children on their shoulders for a better look. The excitement grew.

When she backed away, he gathered the reins, put a foot in the stirrup, and pressed against Kantaka's shoulder. "Okay, brother," he whispered, "don't make a fool of me."

He swung into the saddle, ready for anything, his heart slamming inside his chest.

Kantaka stamped his hooves with Matt Reece still talking low and smooth. The horse shot out a hind leg, and when he realized he was no longer a prisoner, he spun in a circle and danced sideways. He came to a standstill, breathing hard, taking in this new turn of events, with Matt Reece still talking steady and stroking his neck.

Matt Reece touched his ribs with his boot heel, and Kantaka jerked into a trot. He pulled up on the reins, and Kantaka stopped, waited. He touched the ribs again, and Kantaka moved around the corral. He reined him left, and the horse turned and cut across the center of the corral. He reined him right, and the horse trotted the opposite way.

"Show's over folks," Matt Reece said.

Lilikoi and the others were clearly disappointed but respectful. "Is Top Hat saddled yet?" he said as he passed her. "We feel the need for speed."

Minutes later, as he trotted Kantaka around the corral, Lilikoi led Top Hat out of the stables, saddled and bridled. He dismounted, opened the gate, and walked the stallion out.

When the horses stood side by side, she leaped onto the filly's saddle, and he slid carefully onto Kantaka's back. He waited for a sign of anger from between his legs, but none came. Once again, he became an unwelcome yet acceptable passenger.

They turned the horses toward a dirt path and nudged them into a trot. Kantaka pranced, seeming as happy as Matt Reece to be free of the corral.

The path cut through dense algarroba, sandalwood, and coconut palms that canopied in lush sweeps of green, towering over leafy banana plants dangling hard fruit. They rode leisurely, heading north. Bees crisscrossed the path like golden bullets, and finches dipped out of the sky. He kept waiting for a burst of wild anger from his mount, but Kantaka was getting comfortable with his touch. The horse was a quivering furnace of heat and muscle between his legs, and he moved to Kantaka's rhythm, as if they were dancing a tango, and he let the horse lead.

They came to a sandy beach on the Kalaupapa Peninsula, west of the old leper settlement. They booted their mounts into a gallop at the water's edge and set off side by side. The stallion leaped into a run, and it felt like Kantaka became airborne. He stretched out his neck and reveled in effortless speed. Matt Reece crouched down until his cheek almost pressed to the horse's neck. Lilikoi and the filly fell far behind. The horse between his legs with the sun on his back felt almost religious.

The stallion wanted to prove something, and Matt Reece felt his own need to work out the frustrations of this new life that he had not wanted. For the first time, he seized firm control of the stallion, booting him faster, harder. Kantaka responded, racing the wind like a magic carpet. Matt Reece's frustrations fell away, and he clung to the moment in the same way he clung to the saddle. Nothing existed except the joy of movement. He lost that part of himself that had a name, becoming only the stallion racing the cosmos. This was what he lived for. He wanted that beach to stretch out into timeless infinity, and he was pretty damned sure Kantaka felt the same.

When they came to a wall of rock, he reined the stallion to a halt, turned him, and raced back. If infinity had boundaries, then they would run in circles, anything to keep the rush going. They ran until they were both spent.

Later, while resting in the shade of a rocky outcrop, he caressed the stallion's jaw while pressing his forehead to the place below his ears and above his eyes. Kantaka snorted and raised his head to ruffle Matt Reece's hair with his muzzle. While he and the horse were locked in this budding affection, he saw a new glimmer in Lilikoi's eyes. She lost that edge she wore like a shield. Her eyes, her face, were more feminine.

They rested a long time and then mounted and rode back up the mountain. The earth was still damp, spongy with crushed ferns and primeval smells. The heat came in layers. It was a draining heat, the sort that sucked moisture out of every living thing.

When they came to a clearing, Kantaka lifted his head high and stood staring at the mountain peaks, aloof and proud, with a heritage of arrogance that he seemed to cherish, as Matt Reece was learning to do.

WHEN THEY reached the corral, Matt Reece walked the horses into the stable and locked them in separate stalls. He unsaddled and unbridled both and stored the equipment in the tack room. He brushed the horses down and dropped a leaf of hay into each stall. Coolie stayed with him. When he walked back to the house, Coolie followed.

When they reached the veranda, a smiling boy no older than five held out a mug. Matt Reece took the mug and drank the tea with Coolie leaning against his leg. He heard women's voices coming from inside the house. He stood in the sun sipping the brew and watching two hummingbirds dart here and there. Lilikoi came onto the porch, took his empty mug, and led him into the house and to a bedroom.

He stood in the doorway of a room with high ceilings and blue walls, and furnished with a double bed, a dark wood armoire, and a humble chest of drawers.

"Take a nap," she said. "I'll wake you in a couple of hours."

He was tired, and that mattress with clean sheets looked inviting, but he said, "The hammock on the porch will do."

"Don't be silly. It's in the sun. You'll be more comfortable here." She pulled him toward the bed and slipped around him and closed the door on her way out.

He shed his clothes and crawled between the sheets. He listened to the sounds of the household, trying to piece together this island-family life. He felt something resembling happiness, or perhaps only a profound contentment that came from being so tired.

Thirty minutes later, he hovered at the edge of unconsciousness when the door opened and Lilikoi walked in and closed the door. He jerked back to full awareness, realizing she had taken a bath and changed her clothes. She now wore a low-cut calico dress with printed flowers on it. Her hair fell over one bare shoulder. She looked and smelled more feminine than he would have thought possible. Without a word, she reached behind her back and unzipped her dress, letting it fall to the floor, revealing her white slip. She held his stare, looking like a virginal bride. Then she let the slip fall to the floor in a perfectly forthright manner—no awkwardness or lewdness. Naked, she smiled. She seemed like an endearing child, tenderly raised, but lost.

He was perplexed by the heart jump he experienced when her slip hit the floor.

He admired the rich color of her unblemished skin. Almost as tall as himself, she had a strong, slim frame, conical breasts with nipples the same darkness as the rest of her, and a wedge of black pubic hair. She was the first woman he'd ever seen exposed, and she was stunning. He was particularly struck by her strong legs—a ballerina's strapping thighs and calves. She pulled the sheet back and slid in beside him.

"Make love to me," she said.

"You can have any man on this island."

"They're all out to prove something. I'm not anyone's trophy."

"I'm not what you want either."

She pulled back. That sparkle in her eyes extinguished. She managed a crooked grin.

"You little shit. I should have known. Actually, I suppose I did know, but I had to make sure. I live on hope."

"I'm sorry."

"You're not at all like Patrick."

He held his breath, trying to fathom this new development. "You know my brother?"

"Every girl at Berkeley knew Patrick, or at least, knew about him. He's infamous, which is a polite way of saying he's scandalous, notorious, and villainous. Most of us fell in love with him because he seemed lost and fragile. We wanted to protect him."

"You sound like he broke your heart."

She dropped her eyes and stared at those three-inch scars above her wrists, which told him his barb had hit the bull's-eye. Finally she said, "There are one or two men on the island I can introduce you to. I mean, the kind who'd love to get to know you."

"Thanks, but I don't need a pimp."

She laughed, and the embarrassment and sadness of the moment fled. They leaned toward each other and hugged.

CHAPTER FORTY-ONE

JESSUP, PATRICK, and Vishal flew over the ocean the next morning, and every morning for the next two weeks. Each day the sea was massive and empty. The weather held—crisp clear days, cold nights. There were a few days of drizzle, but then the skies cleared and a warming wind came up from the south, bringing bright and steady sunlight.

Each sunrise, the copter would be ready. Randall and the pilots would study the chart book. Then Jessup, Patrick, and Vishal would fly off to continue the search.

They flew in massive sweeps, searching a panorama where sameness was the rule. Horizons folded into sky, and solitude bent back on itself. Everything was nothing. Perfect unity, oneness, mirroring the country's religious beliefs in Zen.

One night, Jessup suggested they bring in the Japanese government to help search.

"No," Landau said.

"It's been weeks, and we're getting nowhere."

"No means no," Landau said. "This must be kept secret."

Over dinner on a veranda overlooking the garden, Jessup brought it up again. Paper lanterns hung overhead, the moon overpowering their soft glow. Landau wouldn't budge.

Jessup cursed, crumpled up the napkin, and threw it onto his plate. "I'm sick of flying over an empty ocean, waiting for him to kill again. If this was his destination, he should be here. I mean shit! Talk about a slow boat to China."

"This is the job," Landau said. "Months of preparation and it all comes down to a good hunch, a lucky break, and a few minutes of excitement if all goes well."

"Dad's right," Patrick said. "This sea search is a bust."

Randall lifted a cup of sake. "Same luck searching the monasteries. We've found a big fat nothing. They're right, Sal. Maybe it's time to rethink our strategy. This lunatic is probably right under our noses, but we're too busy looking in the wrong places."

"Don't call him a lunatic," Landau said. "There's a fine line between insane and inspired. Even if he is insane, it doesn't mean he's stupid. He's been a jump ahead of us since the beginning. He knew each move we'd make before we did."

Randall downed his sake and refilled his cup. "Okay, Freud, you're the expert. But that's not the issue. What we're discussing is how to attack this from a different angle?"

"Right, the million-dollar question," Jessup said.

Landau nodded. "This man is no lunatic, unless all men are. He represents the strength, the resistance, the stumbling thinking of all men, and all the joy and suffering, too, canceling each other out, and yet remaining. He is a repository for a little piece of each person's soul. What he's discovered is monumental. I'd hate to think what I would have done in his shoes. I'm not sure any of us would have handled it any better."

Vishal said, "Just because he outsmarted the FBI doesn't make him an Einstein."

Randall said, "Making ninety-year-old invalids young and healthy does make him smarter than the average bear. But we don't have to be smarter than him to catch him."

Landau held up his hand for silence. He stared off into space. Jessup could almost see the wheels turning in his head. Everyone waited.

Finally, Jessup said, "What?"

"What you just said gave me an idea," Landau said. "We're assuming that all the patients he used over the past twenty years were eighty and ninety-year-olds on their death beds. That way, if they died, nobody would raise an eyebrow. And if they became young again, they had to go into hiding. That's our theory, right?"

"Okay," Jessup said, "but how does that help our search?"

"Randall, you have government contacts at high-security levels. Can you get access to government assistance records?"

Randall snapped his fingers and pointed at Landau. "Jesus fucking Christ, of course. You earned your pay today, Sal. I know just who to approach, but it will cost. Bribery doesn't come cheap in this country."

Jessup slammed his fist on the table. "Dammit. Would someone tell me what the hell's going on?"

Chapter Forty-Two

Matt Reece grew stronger. He thrived on the fish-vegetable-fruit diet. At the rate Lilikoi forced food on him, he felt like a goose being fattened for Christmas.

He never knew which day it was, and he didn't care enough to ask. Each day looked identical to the previous one, because there was no change in the weather. Colors seldom varied. Life became the monotonous heat with an occasional downpour, and of course, another plate of food to consume.

He took on Lilikoi's mission to safeguard the animals arriving daily by cargo ships. Most of them were set free to fend for themselves. The mountain and rainforest were a magnificent zoo, the treetops a menagerie. Only the predators—cats, bears, hyenas, wolves, alligators, crocodiles—were kept in enclosures. A sizable goat herd was maintained to feed the predators. Matt Reece discovered that uninvited guests coming to the island supplemented the predators' diet.

Roaring lions woke him each morning as the sky aged toward sunrise. No Swiss clock was as regular. As Lilikoi made breakfast, he fed, watered, and saddled the horses. They would enjoy breakfast with Gran on the veranda. That first meal of the day was punctuated by chattering black mynahs, Moluccan cockatoos, macaws, toucans, and the cries of howler monkeys. They rode out while the morning light was still as soft and friendly as an embrace.

He adapted to his new life like falling into a dream. The hell in San Francisco and the weeks at sea were replaced by verdant mountains, sunsets over the purple sea, and the pristine clarity of the air after a rain shower.

He loved the simplicity of his life: the humble house, Gran, and riding Kantaka. It seemed the closest thing possible to being back on the Promesa Rota. Also, he came to respect Lilikoi's belief in the Quaker-like principle of emphasizing spiritual over material. She had no interest in marriage, which she perceived as a ball and chain that foreclosed any future ambitions. She called it a "golden-threaded straitjacket."

On the morning of his sixth day on the island, while lingering over coffee and noting a squeaking colony of fruit bats, Lilikoi told him Gran was dying. He was not surprised. The old woman looked sickly and seldom left her place in the kitchen.

"I'm so sorry," he said to Gran. "Is there a clinic here?"

"Stage four," Gran said. "But it's fine by me. Not a sparrow falls that God don't know. He's calling, and I'm ready."

He reached up and held her hand. "I wish there were something I could do."

Gran said, "Child, flesh is but a memento, yet it speaks truth. Every man's path is every other's, for we all end up at the same destination. There are no separate journeys, for there are no separate men to make them. We are one. That's the only story to tell."

"There is something you can do," Lilikoi said.

Slowly, but with accelerating alarm, his comprehension illuminated. "That's why you saved my life? You think I can help her?"

She returned a cheerless pinch of a smile. "A life for a life, you little shit."

"Right, so I'm back to being a little shit unless I help you?" He held her gaze, hearing the squeaking bats, smelling the coffee. He nodded. What else could he do?

"The procedure is called parabiosis, a technique that unites the vasculature of two living animals, so that they share the same blood supply, like conjoined twins. By joining the circulatory system of an old mouse to a younger one, scientists have produced remarkable results. The heart, brain, muscles, and every other tissue of the old mouse became stronger, smarter, and healthier."

"What happened to the younger mouse?"

"The article I read didn't say," she said.

"What changed me was a tricorder that surrounded me with radiation."

"That doesn't matter. A stem-cell researcher at Harvard used this method to pass immunology from one host to another. I've confirmed that you're both type-O blood."

He stared out at the sunrise, feeling uncomfortable. "We're dealing with something only Kenji understands."

"My father, gigantic asshole that he is, did the research. That's why he invited your father to come here. He plans to use parabiosis to make himself immortal and to eventually treat everyone on the island, all Hawaiians. As the rest of the world goes up in flames, he sees us rising from those ashes. His flock of indestructible phoenixes."

"I'm afraid of what her blood will do to me."

"I'll inject ten vials of your blood into her and monitor her for five days. If she does well, then I'll inject ten vials of her blood into you. If all's well at the end of next week, then I'll connect your systems so you share each other's blood for twenty-four hours."

He sighed. "I'll do it under protest, but don't blame me if she mutates and an alien creature rips out of her chest."

She laughed as she stood. "If that happens, I'll know who to blame, and it won't be you." She breezed into the house and came back with her medical bag.

She laid out a towel, ten empty vials, and a syringe. He rolled up his left sleeve, and she drew blood from his arm. After injecting that blood into Gran's veins, they walked to the stables and mounted up. It all seemed so simple, too simple to work.

Sunrise and sunset were his favorite times because that's when all the animals scampered out of hiding to water, to eat, to parade their apparel, to croon mating songs. The forests crawled with gibbons, gorillas, chimpanzees, orangutans, baboons, tapirs, elephants, and deer. On the flats roamed herds of buffalo, zebra, wildebeest, camels, rhinos, and stately giraffes. At the shores of the lake, hippos lounged beside a stand of flamingos. Becoming a steward to this cornucopia of life electrified his senses.

They rode toward Kaunakakai, the largest of Molokai's towns. Lilikoi's posse—Mako, PJ, Duke, and Songoree—who were also riding horses, soon joined them. The men's reek of carrion told Matt Reece they had come from feeding the caged animals.

Since joining the group, he had not yet fed the carnivores. He proved to be a barely competent game warden helper, but he managed to hang tough without embarrassing himself. He carried no weapons, kept his head down, his mouth shut, and by and large seemed well liked among the four men.

He had come to understand that the posse was more than soldiers. They, along with Lilikoi, shared a bond of trust that transformed them into one thing—indefinable, a rare unit in tune with itself, the animals, and the island.

As happened each of the last six days, Songoree, handsome Songoree, rode up beside him on his pinto horse named Boozer and flashed him a smile. Matt Reece knew by now that Songoree smiled whenever he was happy or nervous or tipsy with drink, and he could never tell which. Today, however, his smile seemed to hint at a secret they shared—something about youth and lust and their claim to both. Or perhaps youth and lust had laid a claim on them? Trying to sort out these claims grew into a notion of losing one beautiful man with the promise of finding another, which morphed into the idea that hidden in a man's marrow, beauty and loss and lust walked hand in hand, were one.

His new friend proved sociable, freewheeling, and handy with a joke, but Lilikoi had warned him that Songoree could unexpectedly turn somber—never bitter or hostile, but guarded, because he kept part of himself hidden, a place he didn't let anyone touch.

They fell into their usual pattern: talking trivialities while letting the others ride ahead. Occasionally Lilikoi turned in her saddle and glanced back with a mirthless grin. Her obvious matchmaking embarrassed him, but on the other hand, Songoree was a fetching twentysomething man with a strong jaw, high cheekbones, and tough-guy scars that he wore with pride. It was flattering that Matt Reece could so easily form a relationship with a man six or seven years his senior. And besides, Songoree had a reputation for being a first-rate rhino-chaser, and Matt Reece wanted to try surfing.

"Hola, Songoree. Don't tell me what you fed the cats today. I'm feeling queasy."

Songoree tugged on his ponytail. "Roger that, cowboy, but only if you start calling me Song-boy."

"Song-boy," he said, trying it out. Only Lilikoi and her posse called him that.

"God, what a kickass day," Songoree said. "The only thing better than riding horses on a day like this is riding waves on a day like this."

"I wouldn't know," Matt Reece said.

"High time you did. We'll drive to Halawa Beach, and I'll give you your first lesson."

"You're fucking with me, right?"

Songoree smiled. "Hell no. Not yet, anyways."

At Kaunakakai, they rode down the middle of Ala Malama Avenue with not a car or truck in sight. The town was only three blocks long, with a few mom-and-pop eateries and stores selling groceries, staples, and other supplies. He noticed that the restaurants outnumbered the churches by a multiple of four. Apparently eating was more important than religion on this island. Many of the buildings were the original volcanic-stone construction. An abandoned movie house still held a faded poster of a Bruce Lee movie on the marquee. The place had a population of less than five thousand, and it was the kind of town where neighbors came together for an impromptu Saturday night dance or a Sunday afternoon fish fry. Old men sat outside the barbershop watching the world wag on.

They continued to Lono Harbor, where the regular militia was unloading cages from a cargo ship. The docks were teeming with men and animals and cranes and trucks. The militia all wore their military uniforms and kept their weapons close at hand. Armored vehicles were parked up the rise as if they were expecting Marines to charge ashore at any moment.

They dismounted. Matt Reece led the horses to a makeshift corral. He unsaddled, watered, and brushed them down while Lilikoi oversaw the unloading operations. He finished settling the horses and sauntered back to help Songoree load cages of impalas onto a beat-up, one-ton Dodge flatbed with no plates and sporting bald tires. They tied down the cages and jumped into the cab.

Songoree said, "Once we drop these puppies by the lake, let's grab some boards and a six-pack and drive out to Halawa."

"What about helping the others?"

"Hey, cowboy, you never played hooky? We're sitting on a full tank of gas and a high tide coming this afternoon. Lilikoi enjoys her authority too much. It's good to take her down a peg now and then. Let me handle her."

The last thing he wanted was to get back on Lilikoi's bad side, but he couldn't help feeling thrilled. "Roger that, Song-boy."

They drove northwest toward the flatlands that had once been a thriving cattle ranch. An automatic weapon perched on the seat between them. They drove past a field of low brush, and a cloud of rooks lifted into the sky. The birds whirled in a black spiral that laced out into a line winging eastward.

"Can I ask what might be a touchy question?" Matt Reece said, and Songoree nodded. "Lilikoi and her posse are all about gathering and protecting these birds and animals."

"That's not a question," Songoree said.

"Why are you so heavily armed?"

"We help with the animals because the boss man likes to keep her happy," Songoree said, "but our primary objective is to keep her safe. We're bodyguards."

"Protect her against what?"

"We Hawaiians declared independence. We have a fledgling government on Oahu, but the power is with the militia, and that means the gun rules us all. Men who have assault rifles have power, and those who don't have nothing. At any moment, as you know all too well, some nutcase having a bad hair day can threaten your life."

"Anarchy? You've regressed to feudal times. Or should I say futile?"

Songoree shook his head. "It's always been the rule of the gun. It's just that the government had the biggest guns. Nothing changed, except we're the government now."

"So the posse protects Lilikoi from the militia?"

"Affirmative, but that's not all. At some point, Washington will defeat the vigilantes on the mainland, and when they do, they'll be back. That's when the real fight begins. We can only hope that by that time, they'll be so sick of killing that they'll lose heart and let us be."

"And if they don't?"

"Thanks to Lilikoi's father, we have the weapons, ground-to-air missiles, and plastic explosives to defend ourselves. We may not win, but we'll make them pay dearly."

"With bombs?"

"I'm the go-to guy when it comes to making explosives. I'm more of a tinkerer than a warrior. I love electronic gadgetry and mechanical shit, and yes, I've designed explosive devices."

Matt Reece absorbed what he already figured out subconsciously. "And this new government in Oahu, is it any better than what Washington dished out?"

Songoree turned a sly grin toward him. "Same old bickering and everyone out for themselves, but at least it's Hawaiians on all sides of the argument. It's happening the world over. The days of big governments may be done." Songoree's hands were clinching and unclinching on the steering wheel. "This is as good a spot as any." He stopped the Dodge at the side of the road.

They hauled their asses onto the flatbed, opened the cage doors, and stood back as the impalas scampered away. When the last one disappeared, they climbed back into the cab.

They stopped at a house on the outskirts of Kaunakakai only long enough to pick up two surfboards and throw a six-pack of Kona Pacific Golden Ale in an ice chest, and then took Highway 460 past the airport and continued along the shoreline heading east. With the windows down, the sea breeze hit their faces with full force.

Matt Reece marveled at the sheer rock cliffs rising from the shore. They seemed impressive from the ship a mile out at sea, but now, looking straight up made them seem otherworldly. Songoree pointed at the dark stains that colored the rock near the top of the cliffs and explained that those markings were the stains of blood left by island defenders who were beheaded and thrown from the cliffs during the war that united all the islands a few centuries ago. "The iron in their noble blood had blackened the rock forever. We still have that same pride, the same spirit as those warriors, and when the US government comes back to take what's ours, those cliffs will turn solid black. Dover has its white cliffs; we'll have black, like a veil of sorrow."

He was almost shoulder to shoulder with Songoree, with only the assault weapon between them. They pressed shoulders whenever the truck swayed around a curve. After a time, Songoree swung his arm around Matt Reece's shoulder, drawing him closer.

Several miles farther east, Songoree turned the Dodge inland where the road narrowed to one lane. The truck slowed while climbing a steep ravine carved between the inland mountain and another hill on the eastern tip of the island.

They descended into a wilderness. The road followed a stream that snaked through a valley. Except for a few huts that bordered some taro patches and fishponds, the valley was laced with waterfalls and an array of fruit trees nestled within a forest of bamboo. The place seemed lost in time, untouched by modern man.

The valley opened onto a wide expanse of beach. Songoree drove to the end of the road and parked before a four-foot seawall separating the vegetation from the sand.

They surveyed the surroundings. The beach looked cool and inviting. The waves came in like unfolding mountains, one draped behind the next, spreading themselves out with a repetitive energy, given and returned. Beyond the white-headed combers, he saw a half-dozen boards and bodies lolling in a tight group.

He focused on two men paddling in front of a swell that rose from the sea. A heartbeat later they jumped to their feet and rode the comber's crest. Their arms spread like wings as they flew landward, two fleeting darts on an ephemeral curl of spume.

The wave jockeys performed trick maneuvers, competing to see which one could do the flashiest ride. Matt Reece held his breath watching the ballet of speed and balance and athletic grace. As the wave died, they whirled their boards up over the wave. Then, belly to board, they paddled back out to sea. Matt Reece felt the urge to immerse himself in water, yet a cold tickle crept over his scalp. His body didn't want to do this.

"Will you save me if I start to drown?"

With a bark that could have been a bout of laughter, they crawled from the Dodge and retrieved their gear. They trooped to a campsite of blankets, a boom box, and a fire pit with driftwood piled high. Now that they were away from the truck, Matt Reece felt their relationship evolving into something new.

They dropped their gear. Songoree kicked off his boots and pulled his shirt over his head. Matt Reece watched him strip, admiring the dark skin that was lighter from waist to knees, and how something about that body seemed to smile at him. Once he removed his own clothing, an overpowering tenderness seized him, and he wanted to be hugged. He stepped in front of Songoree, and arms enfolded him. They stood locked together, the sun and wind playing on their skin. It was not what he had felt with Vishal, but it was an agreeable substitute.

Songoree gave him a nudge. "Let's go, cowboy, before the tide changes."

He pulled back to look into Songoree's eyes, which were gleaming with triumph.

They each grabbed a board and attached the ankle straps that roped them to the board. They walked to the surf, and a minute later he found himself in knee-deep water. Before him, rollers crashed, immense, almost suffocating. But he examined them with a new strength. Energy forced its way from deep in his chest to the surface.

Songoree charged a wave and leaped on his board—fearless and bursting with confidence. Matt Reece waded straight in, determined to show this stallion he had vivacity as well. He moved farther out and was about to leap on his board when another surfer came out of nowhere, riding a wave. He shot past Matt Reece, a dolphin absorbed in his acrobatics.

That same wave bowled Matt Reece over. He slammed against the sand and tumbled under the foam with a nose full of water. Gaining his footing again, he choked out a laugh while drunk on the lightness, bright and fast and buoyant, of a helium buzz in his brain.

He retrieved his board and glanced out to sea, only then appreciating how large the waves were. That close, they towered over him, dark movement unrolling out of sheer mass. It was thrilling and terrifying, but he was too intoxicated to be afraid.

Another wall caught him in a thundering wallop. It pulled at him with a powerful undertow, but he managed to grab hold of his board and pull himself on. He faltered until he saw Songoree sailing down a toppling precipice, intent upon his own rite of passage. Matt Reece lay in awe, his mind microscopically close to the meaning of life, but then he received another baptism of wild surf. His thoughts, desires, and whole sections of his history flowed from him as the undercurrent pulled him farther out. He didn't care. In the same freedom he experienced while running with Kantaka, he felt happy, clean, and yet less than he had ever been, as if something more than just his clothing had been stripped away.

Total freedom was not to be, however. Something gripped his neck, roughly, and he realized Songoree was muscling him toward shore. His joy doubled with the thought that they were sharing this mind-blowing freedom—the amazing light, the surf, the power of the undercurrent were all being played out for their pleasure. Again, he felt close to understanding that thing that had eluded him all his life. He could feel it, but he couldn't put it into thoughts. All he could do was put himself in Songoree's hands and enjoy the ride.

An apocalyptic tower grew out of the sea, tumbling in on itself with a roar that sounded like the ending of the world. They were still too far out, besieged by the receding flow. They rocketed toward heaven, up the face of that monster, and were hammered down to hell. He had the breath knocked out of him as he pounded the sand. He held on to Songoree, and he had no fear.

The next thing he knew, Songoree hauled him up the beach while he vomited seawater. He took gasping lungfuls of air before Songoree said, "Enough for today, cowboy," sounding like an overprotective nanny.

"No. I'm fine," he rasped. "Let's do more." He hated that he had yet to ride a wave. He hated more that they had fallen into a nanny/child relationship. Moments ago they were stallions racing through a universe of liquid omnipotence. He refused to abandon that sensation.

Songoree laughed, and the sound made him laugh too. Within that howl, he seemed to shrink while everything about Songoree grew larger: the white of Songoree's smile, beads of water clinging to his hair, narrow hips, heavy sex, and his shoulders that shivered.

Songoree leaned into him, his face hovered close, and they kissed. It was not an act of passion, but one of searching, and done with such tenderness that Matt Reece was stunned. He tasted salt, like a two-hundred-proof margarita. Suddenly, they were stallions again, equals.

Songoree pulled away, not so far as to lose the scent of his breath. His gaze felt like moments ago when they tumbled at the whim of the undertow. He reached into the cooler, drew out two beers, and opened them. He passed one to Matt Reece. They drank deeply, letting the brew wash away the salt taste. When they finished, they dropped their empty cans back into the cooler.

"Come on, cowboy. Time to take you back to my place and throw a saddle on you." He slapped Matt Reece's ass.

"It's going to be like that, is it?"

Songoree shot him a half smile and nodded.

THEY PULLED on their clothes, stored their gear in the back of the Dodge, and hopped in. Songoree draped an arm over his shoulder and pulled him close. They kissed—a sensual, leisurely press of lips. "I've waited a long time to find someone like you," Songoree said. "Now you're here and you turn out to be FBI's most wanted criminal. This is mind-blowing."

Matt Reece laid his head against Songoree's shoulder. "I'm sorry."

"Hell, I wouldn't want it any other way."

They drove back along the same highway. By the time they crossed to the southern side of the island, the sky was darkened by a storm front blowing up from the south. Raindrops splattered the windshield. Gloom consumed the sky; colors surrendered. Even the reddish-purple sunset to the west became grays and blacks. Songoree slowed the truck as the rain grew heavy.

He craned his neck to stare up the face of the cliffs. Wind carried the rain up the bluff, not down, and he could not see the top of the ridge now. The sky lit up with lightning, and thunder echoed off the cliff.

They saw impala in the headlights, and Songoree had to brake hard. They were the herd that they set loose earlier that day. They turned their eyes into the lights, and those eyes glowed red. By twos and threes, they leaped to the ditch at the inland side of the road, scrambling for cover.

Matt Reece said, "Where the hell do they think they're headed?"

"They're probably wondering the same about us."

Flinty gusts came off the ocean, almost blowing the truck into the cliffs.

"We shouldn't have played hooky," Matt Reece said. "They'll need our help at the docks with the animals and the horses. You think Lilikoi will give us hell?"

"Christ, as crazy as she gets," Songoree said, "there's no telling what she'll be like."

"Crazy? She seems fine to me."

The color drained from Songoree's face. "Can I speak in confidence?"

"I assumed everything we tell each other is just between us."

Songoree turned his head and kissed him on the temple. "She's had some hard lessons. We all have, and with what's going on in the world, there'll be plenty more."

"What's your hardest lesson?"

Songoree thought for a moment. "Lord knows I'm no scholar, but I'd have to say that when things are gone, they're gone forever. Ain't no goin' back."

"Amen to that."

"She ain't been the same since her mother died. They were close."

"Yeah. I noticed those scars on her wrists."

"She blamed her father. He's damn smart when it comes to business, but dumb as dirt about how to treat people. Lilikoi's mother was his maid. He knocked her up and tossed her out. According to Lilikoi, she carried that pain for years and then died of a broken heart."

Matt Reece stared into the oncoming darkness.

"That's why he gives Lilikoi anything she wants," Songoree said. "She's his only child, and he's trying to make it up to her."

He turned the words over in his head. "I guess that includes luring Kenji and me here so we could cure her grandmother?"

"Funny thing," Songoree said, "about the time she cut her wrists, I was set to quit this job and move back to Honolulu, where there's some gay action. But seeing how unhappy she was, I just couldn't leave."

"You think she's over it? Suicide, I mean?"

"I think rounding up all these animals gave her a grand purpose. But I don't think she'll ever be 'over it.' She's fragile, on the inside anyway. She always will be."

"Can I trust her?" Matt Reece asked.

Songoree was silent for a long time. Finally he said, "She's the best of us. She's capable of amazing things, and it's all wasted here. Her passion is too immense for this island. She's like those tigers we keep penned up in a cage. It's a shame. Her life was meant to be different."

Matt Reece snuggled into his new boyfriend, staring into the black storm, considering Songoree's words as if they were a contract with the world to come.

CHAPTER FORTY-THREE

THUNDER ROARED, and the wind bent the palms. Songoree slowed the Dodge as the worst of the violence passed over them. Then they saw a strange sight on a narrow beach a stone's throw from the highway. Men bearing torches were carrying a litter on their shoulders.

Songoree parked the truck, and they rose up to see better. Matt Reece could see little more than their heads and shoulders jostling in the torchlight, but all the men wore an assortment of native adornments, primitive headpieces decorated with feathers and animal fur. By the torchlight, he saw the litter they carried held a human body, and between the rumble of thunder, he heard the thumping of drums.

Songoree grabbed his weapon, and they leaped from the cab. "Oh fuck," he said, and sprinted toward the procession. Matt Reece followed. They ran to a figure in the forefront, and the procession halted before them. The leader wore a carved gourd helmet adorned with feathers and shark's teeth, and except for two gaping eyeholes, it covered her head. A beak was carved between the eyeholes, and set below that were two rows of teeth, upper and lower, making her appear like a cross between a bird of prey and a shark. The mask was simple yet forceful, projecting an image of wild savagery.

Behind him, from somewhere near the shoreline, drums gave a resonating beat.

"While you were off lollygagging," the masked leader said in a voice he recognized, "your blood killed Gran. She died in pure agony."

Matt Reece felt the need to defend himself. He had wanted no part of this blood-swapping business. But he said, "Lilikoi, I'm so sorry."

"Sorry? That's the best you can do? Sorry? You fucking asshole."

He sighed. "No need for brutality. I put that down to the intensity of your grief."

"You can put it wherever the fuck you want, shithead." She charged by him, and the men carrying the litter trailed her.

The procession stopped at a network of logs woven into a funeral pyre that stood five feet high, and crouched only a yard from the water's edge. A strong scent of gasoline fouled the air. The pallbearers placed the litter atop the logs and jammed their torches into the pyre.

Flames shot fifteen feet high. The drums and chanting grew in volume. Songoree joined in. Only Matt Reece didn't sing. He was struck dumb as the heat drove him back, watching orange fire belching chuffs of smoke.

Lilikoi set her helmet on the sand. Dressed in only a wrap that hung halfway to her knees, she held up a knife in her right hand, and she began to dance.

Songoree told Matt Reece, "She's performing the Dance of Great Sorrow. We use this as a way to honor the passing of a loved one."

Lilikoi began to chant. Her body swayed as her feet moved in slow circles. Her arms wove patterns on the air. They seemed to sculpt the words she was singing out of the sky. Her voice rose and fell in a melancholic scale.

Matt Reece knew with a heaviness that weighed him down that Kenji caused this death, and millions more. There was only one way to stop the killing, and he had it on that flash drive at the house. He had let this tranquil island life distract him from sharing that information with the world, and this death was a wake-up call.

She moved from one foot to the other, her supple body showing unusual strength, a cat stalking its prey. The dance built in momentum, and her movements became powerful.

Songoree whispered, "She's mimicking the fight she'll have with her father."

Behind her, the fire blushed crimson, sending sparks high in the night. She seized a handful of her hair and the knife slashed, cutting off a hunk close to the scalp. It was carried off on the wind. The knife slashed again and again until she was nearly bald. She slit three shallow cuts across the meaty part of her left shoulder. Fine lines of blood trickled down her arm. She did the same on her right arm.

Songoree said, "Our custom is to cut the hair and mark the body to show our anguish. In the old days, some people knocked out their teeth or put out their eyes."

The dance slowed and became graceful again. Songoree told him that this part of the dance mimicked a gentle wind blowing through the trees and the waves lapping the beach, showing that Gran Kamamalu's *mana*, her spiritual power, had merged into the fabric of life and was now in everything that they could see.

She came to a standstill. One by one, they hugged her. Matt Reece folded his arms around her and held her. Her warmth seemed to ease the sorrow in his heart.

The fire raged another thirty minutes, and the pyre fell in on itself, growing hotter, until the rising tide consumed what was left. The drums grew silent, and the singers stood watching the waves draw Gran Kamamalu's ashes into the sea's bosom.

Matt Reece suggested he drive Lilikoi back to her house. She nodded. Songoree surrendered the keys to the Dodge, and Matt Reece led her to the cab and they crawled in. It was a long, slow drive up the mountainside.

MATT REECE ushered her into the house and turned on the lights in the living room.

Lilikoi stood gasping—not fighting for air, but rather, repressing a scream. She rushed into the kitchen, splashed her face with cold water, picked up a dish towel, and patted her cheeks dry. "They brought this to the island, and now they'll pay. Once I kill him, he'll finally understand."

"Your father?"

"And that frostbitten bitch. I loved him once, even after he turned out my mother and married that ice queen. His motto is: 'Destroy or die.' He will never understand what life is about, and only one thing can penetrate that wall of gluttony—a bullet."

No doubt she had the ability to kill another human, even her patriarch. Nevertheless, he felt the awkward urge to laugh. Much as he tried to stifle it, he did snicker. Not a genuine laugh, but rather a sympathetic shrug turned into sound. "How can I help?"

"You could never kill anyone," she said dismissively.

He grew angry, because he knew it was true.

"I was like you," she said. "All that time he tortured my mother, I wanted to kill him, but I couldn't because I loved him. So I tried to kill myself instead. Now he means nothing to me."

That was something he could identify with, and he kissed her on the cheek.

"Tell me about your other father," she said.

"He was never abusive, yet he was often not there for me, for anybody. When he was at his desk writing, he had this wonderful magnetism—this glow—that made you feel like you were sitting under a sunlamp or something. But then he went back to the booze and the sunlamp burned itself out. He's tortured, and I never could figure out why."

She hugged him.

LATER, THEY lay on her bed with him holding her. They talked of their days to come, how they would comfort each other. They might at some point even have sex. It was not something he was interested in, but he felt she needed a rosy future to believe in, something to focus on besides this terrible loss. They thought up names for the children they would make to repopulate the world, children that would live forever—funny names, sometimes, so they could laugh—and they talked about the house they would build far from this island, filled with wood furnishings and Persian rugs and brass lamps. They talked of traveling the world to see what was left after the war. "Lima, and Cusco, and Machu Picchu," she said. "Surely no one will bomb Peru."

They talked through the night, while rain washed away everything outside. They were swallowed by the thrum of falling water, knowing that nothing of humanity would survive the storm, not a footprint, not anything. It felt as if they were the last people on earth. And then she kissed him, parting his lips with her tongue and drawing the breath from his lungs.

When he pulled away she said, "Let's not wait."

"I don't love you like that." But even he heard doubt in his tone. *Either you do or you don't. Love's the one thing that is unequivocal.*

"Screw romance. Love is a sucker bet. I loved Patrick, and it crushed me. I'm talking sex. Sex is like ice cream. You don't worry about calories; you dive in and gorge."

She moved her hand across her forehead, as if brushing something away. He knew it was the thought of Patrick. He held no interest in screwing her, especially if it was simply meaningless sex, but he also felt her desperate need to be intimate. Could he do it for her? And if he did, what would that mean for his budding relationship with Songoree? He smiled. "Well, my favorite ice cream is passion fruit."

A glint crept into her eyes, and the muscles in her throat moved, but she didn't speak. Earlier she had displayed a deep and abiding grief. Now he saw only regret, and again, he was left with the impression it was remorse for pushing his brother away.

The rain grew louder, yet the air inside was still and carried a slight sweetness.

They kissed as he took her in his arms. She pulled back and hesitated long enough for him to know that she, like he, was contemplating this betrayal to Patrick. She pressed her face against his shoulder, and he could feel the wetness of her tearstained face. Yes, she had begun to cry. He asked her if she was sure about this, and she didn't answer. They came together again and kissed with animallike force. All that before had been shielded became unshielded, all vulnerabilities exposed.

He felt her smoothness and firm rounded flesh pressing to him, a long warm coolness, cool outside and warm within. Their mouths were tightly pressed together, hands probing. The feeling became a scalding coolness. He felt that chest-aching, tight-held loneliness that was Matt Reece giving way, and he was cut adrift within new sensations.

They made love, or to be more precise, he fucked her. She needed comfort, and he gave himself freely. And in his giving he became happy, unthinking, and he felt a great delight pushing him on. He became a tender counterpoint to her ferocity until they both cried out. Her passion collapsed, and they fell into slumber with her in his arms.

Later, the rain fell hard enough to wake him. The curtains swayed into the room, and a wet breeze washed over him. He stretched and realized that she was there, curled beside him, breathing lightly and regularly. He kissed her smooth shoulder, which did not wake her. He lay awake feeling the long, seeping luxury of his fatigue, and the tactile happiness of their bodies touching. He felt this new development in their relationship should lead to something. That destination remained a mystery, but he knew it couldn't just stop here. Making love was not an endpoint; it was a beginning. It had to be.

She opened her eyes and snuggled closer. He held her, feeling her heart beating in gushes. He asked her to marry him and said they could have a fine life here on the island nurturing the animals. He'd do his best to make her happy.

She buried her face into the soft of his neck and laughed. There was kindness in that sound, but it was also tinged with mockery. "Darling, you're not yet a man."

"There are countless ways of being a man. Mine is to voice my soul."

"Oh dear, how can I respond to that?" She closed her eyes, and he held her until they fell back to sleep.

THE SOUND of an engine cranking to life awakened them. Lilikoi draped a robe around her and walked to the porch. He stumbled into his pants and followed.

They found Songoree behind the wheel of the Dodge, gunning the engine. Lilikoi slipped an arm around Matt Reece's bare waist, drawing him near to make their new situation clear. Songoree leaned his head out of the cab and spat, giving Matt Reece the impression he was pissed.

Matt Reece felt a chill and wished he had grabbed his shirt. He was about to invite Songoree into the house for coffee, but Lilikoi said, "What do you need the truck for?"

"To load up the jet. Boss man's sending his prize off-island. I brought your horses back. They're in the stable. Saddles and bridles are in the tack room."

"I don't suppose they filed a flight plan?" she asked.

"Naw. We only know he's leaving tonight with a full load of fuel and a little going-away present I hooked up in the landing gear. Something to give him a warm reception when he reaches his destination." He spat again, and said, "The boss man sent me to fetch you. He wants you to bring your lover boy to the Moloch house."

Matt Reece realized they were talking about a plot to murder Kenji. He felt strangely apathetic about it, as if they were talking about a horse with a broken leg.

She said, "If that's the plan, then I've got a little present of my own, one that will fix that fat bastard and his ice princess once and for all."

"They ain't worth it, girl," Songoree said.

"I know."

"Then don't do anything dumb."

"Too late."

"Let it go, girl. Just chock it up to rotten luck and let it go."

"The nature of this war is changing the rules. For the first time, rich white pigs will suffer the same fate as the rest of us. He brought death to this island, and it's time he explained why to his maker. I intend to arrange that meeting."

Songoree gunned the engine. He waved as the Dodge swung around and headed toward the highway.

Matt Reece assumed his fledgling romance with Songoree was now over. What had hardly spread its wings would never fly. He stood shivering until the truck was out of sight.

Chapter Forty-Four

THE CALIFORNIA deserts never looked lovelier, Declan thought as he peered out the window of his hospital room. He had suffered a second heart attack and survived another surgery. After two attacks, he couldn't accept the idea he would leave this bed alive. When businessmen and politicians betrayed him, he always found a way to best them, and in some cases, crush them as a warning to others. But now the betrayal came from within. The only thing that could save him was the formula. He might have survived had President Harrington chosen a different path, but there was no going back now.

She ended his lofty ambitions, and he couldn't console himself with the knowledge that she might live forever, but he had only days left, perhaps hours. He was barely fifty years old. There was so much more he could accomplish.

Air Force One sat on the tarmac. The ground crew had refueled it, and it would soon take to the air, leaving him behind; there was symbolism in that. That's how he knew he was done for, because even if his heart was strong enough to recover, as Dr. Wong said, he was Harrington's prisoner. She controlled his fate, and she had no reason to keep him alive.

It was somehow fitting that he would die at a military base, far from the parks and restaurants and theaters and malls where civilization gathered to enjoy life. He spent his life making weapons, which left no time for social activities. How much had he missed in his quest for power? Art and culture he wielded only as a tool to grease the skids of the high echelon. He became a stranger to his wife and two children after a messy divorce, and lost those he once considered close friends. Love, friendship, the arts were sacrificed on the altar of ambition. And now, was there anyone left to weep at his funeral?

Yes, and he stood only a few feet away. He reached out an arm to Liam, who took his hand. As soon as Liam touched him, the desolation locking his chest relaxed.

The engines of Air Force One throttled up.

Liam nodded at the window. "There she goes."

For the first time in his life, he didn't give it a second glance. It now belonged to another life, one that no longer concerned him. He gazed into Liam's eyes, and he saw that same ambition that drove him and Diane McCarthy.

"My children," he said. "Can you bring them here? Christ, I'm having trouble remembering what ages they would be now."

"I've contacted them, and Deloris. They'll all be here by midafternoon."

"Just like Diane, always a step ahead of me. Christ, what would I do without you?"

"Hopefully in a few days you'll be out of that bed and we'll find out."

"You talked to Deloris?"

"She was charming and concerned about you."

"Don't bullshit me."

"I got the impression she never stopped loving you. And so you know, Mark is twenty-three and Grace celebrated her twenty-first birthday last week. You sent her a red Mercedes convertible for a present. She couldn't stop bragging on Facebook."

His eyes misted, and Liam squeezed his hand.

"If I ever get out of here—"

"When, not if. It's time you start believing the doctors."

"Okay, when I get out of here," he said, apologetically, "I want to take my kids someplace safe, away from all this killing."

"I hear Tasmania is lovely."

"What the hell's in Tasmania?"

"A shitload of virgin forests that nobody would ever drop a bomb on. And let's face it, there's nothing like nature for restoring the soul or putting problems into perspective."

Yes, he thought, there were so many truths he'd forgotten, like the fact that he was only one of the trillions of creatures that shared this planet. And that he and the human race, with its triumphs and follies, might soon become nothing more than a blip in history, an ugly blemish on this planet. He could feel the winds of eternity blowing through his soul. Christ, he'd squandered so many years thinking he could make a difference and be appreciated for it. What a joke.

He had a sudden inspiration. "Look into a ship, something for long-distance sailing. That way I won't be tied down to one location. I want to see it all, or what's left of it." That idea came from a memory of the time before he married, when he'd sailed from Peru, through the South Pacific to Singapore. He reached back to see the glistening deck and the peaceful swish of water passing the prow. That was over thirty years ago and had been a time of contentment.

With a bit of a start, he realized he was planning a future, and that his soul still yearned. He promised himself each day, each hour, would be a universe of experience. He would, for the first time in three decades, really live. If only....

HE STILL held responsibility to the people at Golden Eagle. Liam canceled his appointments and left his staff to pick up the pieces. Declan owed it to the senior associates to break the news as soon as possible and leave them some kind of structure to keep going. There were issues to settle, in the boardroom and in his own mind, before he began the task of unwinding his affairs.

The roar of Air Force One grew louder as the jet climbed into the sky. As much as he tried to ignore the sound, it galled him that Harrington was getting away scot-free. He knew it was a remnant of his stubborn pride, but that pride was too much a part of his personality to be put aside. He thought about the antiaircraft missiles that Golden Eagle manufactured, with their heat- and motion-seeking guidance systems. It would be so easy.

"Liam, did you ever contact Bob Howth, like I asked?"

A splash of white light, ten times the intensity of the sun, arrived a few seconds before a double booming shockwave slammed into the building, almost pitching him from his bed. Outside, a vast roiling cloud, glowing bluish gray, spread out over the desert. Below it, the land boiled. The double boom meant AF1 was hit with two drones carrying small nuclear warheads to ensure the plane was vaporized. He assumed they had caught the jet at a position over a barren landscape, so there would be no significant injuries to humans on the ground.

This would be the last, and finest, act of revenge in his career. *Now for the follow-up*, he thought. While he was stuck in this bed, he could dispatch letters to people who held real power, written in his own hand, to see what options were available to force Washington to end this war. There were plenty in the labyrinths of the capital who would jump at some kind of peace. She had powerful enemies, and now she couldn't retaliate.

"Liam, I'll need writing paper and a pen. Let's get to work on getting me the hell out of here. And before you look into sailing to Tasmania, we have unfinished business in Tel Aviv." He held up his hand to cut off Liam's protest. "It's something I've got to do."

Chapter Forty-Five

THEY LOUNGED around the house well into the afternoon. After a late lunch, Matt Reece saddled the horses. Lilikoi strolled to the corral armed to the teeth, looking every bit the ninja that she did on that first day at the docks. It confirmed what he had only suspected thus far, that they were riding into a showdown.

She handed him the flash drive. "In a tight spot, it's our bargaining chip. Use it wisely." He tucked it into his pocket. They mounted and rode west. Before leaving the yard, he glanced back at the house. It looked warm and inviting, yet he somehow knew that he was done with it. He turned to face the trail and did not look back again.

An hour later, the terrain turned flat and grassy. While passing the airport, Lilikoi pointed to a red-and-silver Gulfstream G650 parked on the tarmac with a flight crew standing by. She talked about her father, claiming he was worth a hundred billion dollars. The lion's share of his fortune he'd made by shorting subprime mortgages back in 2007 when the bottom dropped out of the housing market. In addition to the ranch on Moloki, he owned a palace in the Hamptons that boasted twenty-three marble bathrooms, a disco/ballroom and revolving dance floor, a forty-seat theater with dressing rooms for live stage performances, and a ten-thousand-bottle wine cellar. He was honored to have Dick Cheney as best man at his five-million-dollar wedding extravaganza. And because he predicted the current state of world affairs, he was poised to triple his fortune.

He asked, "Then he had to know what Kenji was planning."

"I'm not sure how, but he knew, and he knew Kenji would come here once the shit hit the fan. He talked about this nuclear war over two years ago. That's why I've had time to buy land on islands and gather animals and irreplaceable works."

He went silent, absorbing this new information.

"If I know my father," she said, "he's the one who gave Kenji the idea."

They trotted up a gravel road running to a thick wall of stone enclosing a sizable compound perched at the western tip of the island. Two Jeeps parked at the front gate; both had soldiers manning high-caliber machine guns mounted behind the driver seat. As they rode between the Jeeps, an officer said, "Mr. Moloch is expecting you."

Manicured gardens encircled a mammoth, five-story, steel-and-glass, circular building with a clear dome covering the top floor. A number of bungalows nestled along the north and south walls—no doubt housing for the hired help, he thought. The western side was open to the shoreline, with vistas of the sea.

They dismounted, and a military officer ushered them into an entry hall. His name was Lieutenant Kien, and he said he would escort them through a decontamination process and to the rooftop garden where they would be served dinner. Besides Lieutenant Kien, two uniformed men sat at a security counter that had several LED displays monitoring different parts of the compound. Both had assault rifles within easy reach. Beside each man sat a German shepherd. Their eyes were burning a hole in the intruders.

"Army-trained sentry dogs," Lilikoi said. "Bred for savagery."

Kien had Matt Reece place his hand on a glass-top screen and looked into an infrared camera. He felt a slight tingling on his fingers while a light passed over his right eye. A mechanical voice said, "State your name—last name first, first name last."

"Connors, Matt Reece."

Lilikoi performed the same drill, and Kien said, "You're cleared. Follow me."

A door behind the security counter slid open, and Kien led the way into an adjoining room holding a wall of lockers and three benches. "We'll leave our clothing, weapons, and any jewelry here. Select any empty locker."

Matt Reece glanced at Lilikoi, and the surprise on her face told him she had not expected this level of security. Without weapons, they were helpless.

When they stored their clothing and weapons, another door opened. Kien led the way into a windowless room with a dozen glass booths, each with a chair inside. As soon as Matt Reece stepped into the room, an alarm sounded, and a red light flashed on the wall.

Kien turned to him. "You didn't remove everything. Rings, a watch?"

He opened his palm, showing the flash drive. "I'm supposed to deliver this," he lied.

Kien took the flash drive and inspected it. "What's on it?"

Lilikoi said, "That information, Lieutenant, is beyond your pay grade." She threw her head back and laughed. "I know that's a cliché, but I've always wanted to use that line."

Kien, with no trace of humor on his face, returned it to Matt Reece.

"Please take a seat inside the nearest booth," Kien said. "While you relax, scanners will monitor your health, checking for abnormal heat variations, sensing blood flow, heartbeat rate, and so forth. Once you're deemed healthy, it'll start the decontamination process. Ultraviolet lights will kill pollen, fungus, germs, and contaminates on your skin."

Lilikoi said to Matt Reece, "My father takes mysophobia to a pathological level. Now that the world is using atomic weapons, his OCD is ramped up on steroids."

As soon as they were seated in their separate booths, Matt Reece wet the flash drive with saliva and slipped it inside his rectum—partly to protect it from X-ray light waves, but mostly because, now that he was naked, that was the best place to hide it.

Lights shimmered and moved up and down the booth. The air held an antiseptic odor, convincing him that he was breathing some kind of sanitizer. The tube filled with steam, hot enough for Matt Reece to break out in a dripping sweat. The lieutenant had explained this process; the steam opened pores to discharge contaminates held in the skin.

The longer the process dragged on, the more it felt like the inside of a glass coffin. He needed fresh air. He longed to be back riding the grasslands. His solar plexus heaved, imploring him to escape. A nervy rush drove him to his feet, and he pounded on the glass.

"Oh—" He drew in a shallow breath. "—not now." His heart raced; his lungs were closing. He had to get out of there, but the door was locked. Anxiety wrapped itself around his chest and squeezed with such force that he fell back on the chair.

His panic awakened that energy he called Kirby. He slapped at the glass wall. With Kirby taking control, his air passages inched open, and then more. He wasn't sure which he feared most, Kirby or suffocation, but a breath later, he surrendered to Kirby.

The lights stopped, and the platform in each booth rose until they came to a halt on the floor above. The door opened, and he tumbled into a room that was floor-to-ceiling tile. It looked like a Turkish hammam with racks of clothes hanging on poles on one side, a line of showers on the other.

A moment later, Lilikoi was cradling his head, her face inches from his. "I'm here," she said, kissing his forehead. "Breathe with me."

He closed his eyes and felt her empathy flowing into him. He knew that without Kirby, he couldn't have survived that glass coffin. His lungs unclenched, but Kirby refused to retreat.

They stayed like that, her supporting his head and Kirby remaining dominant, until Kien said, "Grab a shower, and get dressed," waving a hand at the hanging clothing. "The uniforms are grouped by size."

She helped him to stand. In the shower stall, a sign printed on the tile read "Do not swallow shower solution. Avoid undue exposure to eyes and mucous membranes."

He stood with feet a foot apart, arms raised and eyes closed. When the flow turned off, blowers clicked on, and he stood in a rush of hot air until the blower clicked off.

The uniforms were gray underwear and T-shirt, a snowy-white dress shirt, and coal-gray tweed slacks with matching Nehru jacket that had a yellow emblem on the left breast. No socks, but there were leather slippers with rubber soles. He'd never before worn such rich-looking clothing. The material felt as luxurious as it looked.

As they dressed, Lieutenant Kien said, "All floors above the ground level are sealed, sterilized environments. The air is a pure, oxygen-enriched atmosphere. Everything coming into this ecosystem is sanitized—people, clothing, equipment, air, food, and water. You have entered the cleanest self-sustaining environment on earth. There are five levels aboveground, five below. Subground levels are workers' apartments and storage, with enough food and water to last six years and spare building and computer components. Level One houses security, sanitization equipment, computers, worldwide communications equipment, and maintenance gear. Levels Two and Three are office space for the sixty-five workers who manage Mr. Moloch's financial empire. Level Four is Mr. Moloch's personal living quarters. Level Five is the rooftop gardens, which is used only by Mr. Moloch, his family, and his guests."

"They all go through sterilization every day?" Matt Reece asked.

Kien said, "Nobody likes it, but it comes with the job, and nobody wants to lose their job here. Losing one's position means being shipped back to the mainland." He led them through a door, which said in black letters: Level Two.

The door slid shut behind them and sealed with a hissing sound. The air in the room had a densely packed texture, with a faint woodsy odor that he guessed was disinfectant. He turned to study the door, which had more words on this side: "Return to Level One is not possible through this access."

They marched down a corridor, passing men and women who were wearing the same gray tweed uniform. A few people wore light blue insignias over their breast, which Matt Reece assumed designated their particular job or rank. They stopped at an elevator, Kien looked into an eye scanner, and a red beam of light passed over his right eye. The elevator car door swished open, and they rode up two levels.

They exited the elevator car into a room that looked like the lobby of a futuristic hotel—polished terrazzo floors, cream-colored walls, chrome edging, abstract paintings on the inner walls, and outer walls of floor-to-ceiling glass with views to the horizon. The furnishings were modern sofas with countless pillows suspended over Prussian carpets. There was also a scattering of antiques and paintings from old masters. On their way to a spiral staircase, Kien pointed out two-hundred-year-old woodcuts by Kusaka Kenji. Beside them, a fifteen-foot standing Burmese Buddha carved in teak looked lost in a foreign land. Matt Reece stopped to admire a landscape by Cezanne, which seemed to vibrate with subtle geometries. Beside it hung a voluptuous Renoir nude.

Matt Reece knew this place was the embodiment of refined taste. To him, however, it was sterile, more a museum than a home. It seemed vulgar. Of all these priceless objects, he thought Ogden Moloch's most beautiful possession—perhaps his only beautiful possession—was his daughter, Lilikoi.

Beside the spiral staircase sat a musician in a tuxedo and white bow tie, playing a concert grand Steinway. Matt Reece recognized the chords of a Schubert Impromptu. His father had it on a CD and had played it often at the Promesa Rota. Hearing it now, he felt a stab of longing to sit and listen with Jessup.

Kien led them up the staircase. At the top, Matt Reece held on to that last bit of chrome railing for balance, not believing his eyes.

What stood before him was a rainforest enclosed under a clear dome, complete with newly drenched orchids hanging from the trunks of palm trees, massive ferns dotted with flowering vines, a waterfall tumbling into a sizable pond, and all of it untouched by wind. Tropical birds flew within the confines of the bubble. A layer of mist hung three feet off a ground dense with foliage. In the center of this jungle hunkered a pavilion with sofas, hammocks, a table dressed with a white tablecloth, and china and silver settings for five. Speakers within the undergrowth amplified sounds from the piano below.

He stood entranced by the timeless feel of the place, and although they seemed to be the only ones in the rainforest, he had the impression that people were scrutinizing him.

Movement caught his eye, and he turned to see Kenji standing under the twenty-foot waterfall, naked, enjoying the torrent of water. Like himself, Kenji had regained all his body mass lost during their starvation at sea. He stepped from under the falls and snatched a towel from atop a boulder. The toned muscles in his shoulders and arms and chest shook with delight. His pale stomach made the dark patch of pubic hair look like a wedge of velvet, capping his unblemished legs.

Matt Reece became a voyeur hypnotized by perfection. No carnal modification could improve him. He was as faultless as this remarkable rainforest.

Kenji set about dressing, easing into the same style outfit that Matt Reece now wore. Kenji seemed to carry himself with a boldness that Matt Reece found difficult to stomach. Kenji visibly embraced this environment with the carefree approach of a monarch, indifferent to his past, leaving all injustices behind without regret.

Kenji slipped into his jacket, and he looked more impressive fully clothed—chic, unassailable, and indestructible. He appeared ready to rule the world for eternity, a god. He stepped into his shoes and turned toward them, and his eyes narrowed.

Kien bowed his head at Matt Reece and Lilikoi and said, "I'll leave you to it." He spun around and walked back to the spiral staircase, but he stopped before descending. "I should mention, sir," he said to Kenji, "the boy brought a flash drive through the decontamination process. He said you and Mr. Moloch were expecting it."

Kenji smiled, and Lieutenant Kien hurried down the stairs.

Matt Reece swallowed something hard at the back of his throat. Lilikoi reached over and took his hand in hers, entwining their fingers.

Kenji said, "I'm grateful you had the wisdom not to destroy it. You saved me many years of recreating those formulas." He held out his hand, palm up. "Let's have it?"

"It's inside of me."

Kenji chuckled. It was not an amused sound. "They've taken good care of you." He waved an arm that took in all the rainforest. "I've been living in luxury myself. But alas, today we say goodbye to this island. I've arranged transport to our final destination."

"I'm not going anywhere."

Kenji shrugged, a gesture that seemed to say *We'll see about that*.

Chapter Forty-six

A DOOR slid open in what Matt Reece thought was a solid rock wall beside the waterfall, and a man and woman emerged from an elevator car. He rode on a motorized scooter and puffed on a Sherlock Holmes–style pipe. The reek of tobacco preceded them.

As a human specimen, Ogden Moloch was a bit of an oddity. His body easily topped the scales at over seven hundred pounds, but his vast face was as symmetrical as swelling fruit, unwrinkled, yellowish, and with tawny eyes. His head had short gray hair bordering a cue-ball dome. He wore a black tux, white tie, and diamond cuff links. The outfit, it seemed, could have once belonged to Pavarotti.

His breath came in shallow gusts as he rearranged his weight on the industrial-strength scooter. He called out, "Ah, Matt Reece…," like an old acquaintance. The scooter glided forward until he could shake Matt Reece's hand.

"Allow me to present my wife, Adela, who's been longing to meet you."

Matt Reece gave her an exaggerated bow.

"Ah! The boy we've heard so much about," Adela said in a cordial tone. She assumed a posture of… coquetry… command… ancient wisdom…? It was impossible to tell what effect she was striving for.

Tall and thin, she was as handsome as an old-fashioned film star. Her fingernails were painted platinum, the same color as the straight hair that hung to the middle of her back. Her cocktail dress shimmered with thousands of embroidered sequins, giving it a scaly texture; it hugged her chest and draped to the floor. Her neck was decorated with an impressive diamond choker, and an ermine stole adorned her shoulders.

The feature that struck him was her long lashes, which must have altered her view of the world to something shadowed and filtered. She shot him the smile of someone about to make a sequence of witty remarks. She, however, said nothing more. Indeed, her superior demeanor gave him the certainty that they would never speak again.

Ogden waved a hand at Lilikoi. "Kenji, have you met my daughter, Lilikoi?"

Kenji raised his hand to shake.

She glared at him. "The thought of touching you makes my skin crawl."

"Lilikoi!" Ogden rumbled. "Have you no appreciation for a man who, out of the goodness of his heart, has exiled himself in order to rid the world of deadly weapons?"

"He has no heart."

"Ungrateful child. Let's have drinks while we discuss our situation like adults," Ogden said, waving a hand at the pavilion. "Darling, should we open the champagne now, or would you prefer a cocktail before dinner?"

"Nelson," Adela said to a uniformed waiter standing beside a drink tray a few yards from the table, "Ogden and I are both drinking Bloody Marys."

"Sparkling water for me," Kenji said.

Ogden whizzed his scooter to the pavilion. There was something unnerving about the waddle of fat quivering under his chin and the tobacco reek that did little to hide the stench emanating from this tuxedoed Jabba the Hutt. Still, he was a guest in this man's house, and he knew better than to let his feelings show.

Ogden asked Matt Reece what he would like to drink.

"Nothing for me," he said.

"Perhaps you'd like coffee, tea?"

"My stomach is still out of sorts from that decontamination process."

"My apologies. As if industrialization hadn't dumped enough toxins into the atmosphere, the nuclear contamination from those bombed cities is now spreading across the globe. We must take precautions even on this remote isle."

"When was the last time you were outside?" Matt Reece asked.

"We're outside now." He waved an arm at the pristine rainforest. "But of course you mean outside the bubble. Let me think. That was sixteen months ago."

Sixteen months!

"We have everything we need right here, young man. Why should we go out? I'm sure in time you'll come to love this garden as much as we do."

This building was no sanctuary, just another prison. His every fiber recoiled from the sight, smell, and feel of this habitation. These people took whatever glittered in their eyes, regardless of consequences, and hid in their lair drooling over their treasures. He squeezed Lilikoi's hand and then kissed her on the cheek—a gesture that proclaimed *You are not your father's child after all. Let's get the hell out of here.*

Lilikoi gripped back with astonishing strength. "I'll have a double Stoli martini, straight up." She marched to the bar, dragging him with her.

Ogden sighed with amusement. "Yes, of course, my pet."

Ogden motored to the head of the table. As the women took chairs on one side, Kenji sat with Matt Reece on the other side. Kenji said, "I knew you wouldn't destroy our chance to save mankind. You're not so heartless. A parent knows."

He was talking about the flash drive, Matt Reece knew. How ironic that he fell into the cliché nonsense that a father understood him best. But no, he opened himself to Vishal, who in so short a time, had known him to his core. He had to stop himself from thinking of Vishal, of what could have been.

"You've always had remarkable perception," he said and smiled to himself.

Nelson set tall red drinks with leafy celery towering above the rims before Ogden and Adela. He set a glass of sparkling ice water before Kenji. He poured a double martini and placed it before Lilikoi and set the half-full shaker on the table.

Lilikoi downed half her drink in the first swallow, took a gasping breath, and finished it. As she set the glass on the table, Nelson refilled it from the shaker and retired to the bar.

"Surely you realize, Mr. Moloch, you can stop the violence," Matt Reece said. "You have what everyone is fighting for. Why not hand him over to the authorities."

Ogden drew on the stem of his pipe and exhaled. He studied the rising smoke as if in its uncoiling lay the contours of history. "Which authorities would you suggest? Who should rule the planet for the next thousand years?"

Matt Reece didn't have an answer, but he still held faith in the United States.

Ogden tapped his temple with the stem of his pipe. "The sign of an immature mind is that it reaches for the quickest, easiest solutions. A mature mind first looks deep into a person's soul for motives and understanding, and looks well into the future to anticipate consequences. Do you understand what I'm saying?"

"I think so."

"Excellent," Ogden said. "I can typically tell how clever a man is by how stupid he thinks I am."

"It's not your intelligence I question, it's your motives, and I don't like you," he said.

"I like a man who expresses himself honestly."

Matt Reece crossed his arms over his chest. "So you plan to do nothing?"

"My goodness," Ogden said, "you think I'm responsible for people choosing death over immortality? They were given a choice. All they had to do was surrender their weapons. You understand, a choice, like picking the proper tie in a clothing store? I have no intention of stopping anything, because like Kenji, I see the need for culling. The earth cannot sustain the current population, and if this formula were available to all, then the results would be catastrophic. This bloodbath would have happened on its own, once the population doubles again and resources fall to inadequate levels. Consuela and I recognized that several years ago."

"You knew Consuela?" Matt Reece asked.

"She and I have had an ongoing professional relationship for decades, during which time I funded much of her research." Ogden glared at Kenji. "I'd hate to think you had anything to do with her death," he said, cradling his Bloody Mary, his face strangely offset by the narrowing of his eyes.

Kenji gazed out of that part of the bubble that overlooked the sea. "Circumstances changed. It's never personal. You should know that as well as any man alive."

"Culling?" Lilikoi said, the edge in her voice sounding toxic. "Being your daughter is my deeply felt shame. Yet I've come to embrace it, to own it. It's all that keeps me from becoming the animals I protect." She had the look of someone who no longer existed, and her eyes held the shadows of a crypt, a martyr waiting for the moment when she would press the button on her vest. She gulped more of her martini.

"If you're going to drink like that," Ogden said, "we should eat now to get some food in your stomach." He waved a hand at Nelson.

"Before we eat," Kenji said, "I believe we have business to transact." He reached into his jacket pocket and pulled out a packet holding twelve vials of dark red fluid.

Ogden's tongue darted out and licked his lower lip. He held a look of pure lust. "By all means. The Gulf Stream is fueled and ready, the crew is aboard, and Lieutenant Kien is waiting on Sublevel One to shuttle you to it. An underground tunnel connects this building with the airport. You are free to leave as soon as you hand over that blood."

The situation became clear: Kenji was exchanging his lethal blood for a flight off the island, which was rigged to explode before reaching his destination. For Matt Reece, it felt like being caught in a Tarantino film where everyone had a gun pointed at each other. He waited, assuming Lilikoi would spill the beans. She sat silent. Would she let it play out? Would he?

Lilikoi held him with a stare, and he realized she had no intention of stopping this. Kirby grew excited, looking on this scene with a twisted smile, preparing to murder three people by not lifting a finger to stop it. Such effortless revenge, he had to stifle a chuckle.

"The pilot will fly me to any endpoint I require?" Kenji asked.

Ogden said, "My Gulfstream has a range of eight thousand miles. If your destination is within that radius, there's no problem. I only asked that you take care with my plane. It cost me sixty-five million. Please don't fly it into a war zone."

"Have no fear. I'm going to the safest place on earth."

"Where is that?"

Kenji said, "Let's not spoil the surprise."

"It makes me imagine some remote yet exotic landscape. I admire the kind of men who have the uncanny ability to travel over thousands of miles of wilderness, pitch a tent on some godforsaken mountainside, and call it home, and, of course, it would be home because that's the way that kind of man's mind works. It's that pioneer spirit that built America. I, on the other hand, need to put down roots, develop a sense of place and history, have indoor plumbing and cupboards to store the family china. If it had been up to the likes of me, we would have never made it as far as Plymouth Rock."

Kenji held out the vials. "I need to alter our agreement. I'm taking my son with me."

"Impossible." Ogden shook his head, and the fat under his chin jiggled irritably.

"It has come to my attention," Kenji said, "that the boy has something inside him that belongs to me. I'm leaving with it one way or another."

Kenji was a killer, but Matt Reece had assumed family connection was protection enough.

Apparently not.

He grabbed Lilikoi's glass and gulped the rest of her martini, because even Kirby needed to buck up his courage now. The alcohol hit him with a rush, numbing his head.

Ogden set his pipe on a crystal ashtray, reached into his jacket, brought out a pistol, and placed it on the table. "Our agreement states you leave the boy in case I have need of more immortal blood. He is my incubator, my insurance, and I will not lose him no matter what he carries inside his gut. You'll find I have no patience with people who don't honor their contracts."

Kenji gazed at the pistol, but whatever was rattling around his head, he lowered his eyes and dropped the subject, for now anyway.

Nelson walked up and presented a bottle. Ogden checked the label, and his eyebrows lifted. "A '72 Dom Pérignon Brut! Perfect for this celebration."

Nelson uncorked the bottle and poured. They toasted their health. The flavor opened Matt Reece's head—but he was too anxious to appreciate it.

Ogden said, "Superlative. Nelson, put another bottle on ice for after dinner."

"Brilliant idea!" Adela said and laughed gaily while swiping a tear from her cheek.

The rock-wall elevator door swung open and a middle-aged Hawaiian woman entered the garden. She was dressed in a nurse's uniform.

Ogden said, "Here is the balance of our agreement." He handed a check to Kenji, who noted the amount, folded it once, and slipped it into his pocket.

The nurse crossed the pavilion and stood beside Ogden. She placed a purselike bag on the table and opened it like a set of butterfly wings to display a hypodermic, an ampoule of liquid, and cotton swabs. She took Kenji's vials and drew blood into the hypodermic.

The precarious mood seemed to soften. Matt Reece grappled back into control as Kirby shrank back, content to watch. He rose to his feet. "Wait, you can't—"

"Chill," Lilikoi barked. "We're witnessing history in the making."

"History indeed." Ogden's eyes were fixed on the hypodermic. The nurse took his arm and rubbed a spot with cotton. "Sit down. Enjoy your champagne."

He sat. "Father—"

"Son, Mr. Moloch planned to get my blood with or without my consent."

Ogden didn't respond to this accusation. He seemed to see only the needle as it pressed into his arm. They all sipped their champagne while the nurse injected six vials of blood into his veins, and six into Adela.

Matt Reece knew then that the last traces of the woman who saved him that first day he came to this island had vanished. She, like he, was party to murder. And with her disappearance, so went the last of his animosity for her father and stepmother. Now his only abhorrence focused on Kenji.

The nurse packed up her paraphernalia and descended the staircase.

Nelson served a platter of roasted hares with currant jelly, asparagus, and potatoes. Ogden lifted a carving knife, sliced the meat, and dished out generous portions to everyone. His own plate became what was left on the serving platter, piled high with four times the normal serving. Nelson poured a robust red wine into each crystal goblet. Downstairs, the pianist began playing Beethoven's "Farewell" sonata.

Matt Reece lost his appetite, and hearing the Beethoven made him more depressed.

When Ogden noticed him just sitting there, he said through a mouthful of hare, "Eating at my table is not the same as breaking bread. You'll not place yourself under any obligation to me. I only asked that you continue to be a friend to Lilikoi."

Matt Reece picked up a fork but merely pushed food around his plate. "The thing I don't understand," he said to Kenji, "is that if you planned this culling, what made you certain people would fight rather than give up their weapons?"

"Relevance," Kenji said, and Ogden gave him an approving nod. "People will do anything to believe that their life holds significance. They'll kill for it, and they'll die for it. I've identified three dominant notions people have to convince themselves that they are relevant in an irrelevant universe. The first, of course, is religion, the idea that some omnipotent being created them for a higher purpose. That provides value to their existence no matter how ordinary and sterile their life. The myth of God and a hereafter gives them a false sense of importance.

"The second is greed, the idea that we are what we own. The insidious thing about greed is that gluttonous pigs not only want the best of everything they can get, but they don't want others to have what they've got. They want it only for themselves. That way they're the envy of the have-nots. They think that having the masses envy them affords them relevancy, so they propagate the idea that we are what we have and then keep the masses from getting anything worthwhile. They breed a society where people are judged by what they own, rather than what they accomplish.

"The third side of this argument is people willing to defend themselves and their cause at all costs. Their sense of heroism gives them relevance. I call it the Rambo Effect. They have a deep mistrust of governments, other religions, and other tribes. This distrust has gone on for so long that it has become embedded in their psyche, become instinct to distrust others and want to defend against anything different from what they are. They own assault weapons, and they fear change more than violence. Many, in fact, have a lust for violence because it's the only way they can feel empowered. They are people who try to be relevant by how well they can defend their ideals rather than what they have or what they can accomplish. They can't compete with intelligence or financial success, so they reduce society to a dog-eat-dog world where they are one of the pit bulls."

"Okay, but I still don't—"

Kenji held up a hand to silence him. "The most precious thing in the world is time—to squeeze more exquisite seconds or months or years out of life. When you wave that red flag in front of the greedy pigs with the stipulation that they must rob the 99 percent of their relevance—religion and weapons—war becomes inevitable and will continue until the pain of death becomes greater than the pain of being irrelevant."

"I think you are overlooking another aspect of human nature," Ogden said. "Much as men proclaim peace and unity from pulpits across the land, the hard truth is, men love war. And whatever men love, they will wallow in."

"What you've done is pure evil," Lilikoi said.

Ogden shook his head. "Good and evil are merely value judgments. He's playing one facet of human nature against another. Tell me, in a battle between greed and lust for relevance, which do you think will win?"

"There is good and evil in the world. Good will eventually win," Matt Reece said.

"Yours are the wrong conclusions of a godless people," Ogden said. "Time is the only truly precious thing. And now I have all the time there is." His words unfolded slowly and were punctuated by a wheezing cough, which forced him to stop.

"You think Christians, Muslims, and Jews are godless?" Matt Reece asked.

"People claim to believe in a god, a final judgment, and heaven and hell. But they merely mouth the words, not live the deeds. If they truly believed the teachings of Abraham, Christ, and Mohammed, the world would be a different place. Every man would be a Gandhi, every woman a Mother Teresa. There would be no killing, no homelessness, no hunger. Don't judge people by their words. Judge them by their deeds. The actions of mankind show they worship only themselves. It's a sickness that flourished in Western culture and spread the world over through the power of media."

It took no great analytical skill to conclude he was talking about himself, a man consumed by ego and gluttony, who judged everyone else by his own inadequacies.

"You and my stepfather," Matt Reece said, "are setting yourselves up as gods. And I think you're enjoying that role."

"Your father and I value having an intellect that gives us control over life and death."

Matt Reece was tempted to point out the irony in that statement—considering the fact that they were plotting to kill each other—but Kirby did not allow him to speak.

Lilikoi asked Kenji, "I'm pregnant with Matt Reece's child. Am I or the baby in danger because his sperm has different DNA?"

By this time Matt Reece thought he was immune to any deeper shocks, but she proved him wrong. He stammered, "How can you say that. We only made love last night?"

"It's my time of the month. I'm sure of it."

Kenji said, "We never experimented on reproduction with a normal-cell person."

"It's your time of the month, and you fucked me anyway? How could you?"

"Why do men always blame women?" she asked.

Ogden held up his hands as a way to silence everyone. "We have capable medical staff here in the building. An abortion can be minutes away."

She shook her head. "I'm having this child. Matt Reece offered to marry me."

Ogden was clearly not amused. "Young people, they refuse to consider the gravest questions of their lives. No—" He held out a hand for silence, again. "He is not, and never will be suitable. Our kind does not marry trash, even white trash." He turned to Matt Reece. "I'm sorry if I've insulted you, but the facts are you are uneducated and vulgar. You're the kind who eats chicken with his hands and then licks his fingers. The kind who coughs without covering his mouth." He turned back to his daughter. "The only reason this boy is not shoveling shit on some godforsaken ranch is because Kenji dragged him out of there. And now he thinks he can become one of us by using his dick."

Matt Reece took no offense, because everything the man said was true, except wanting to become one of them. He was common, and perhaps even vulgar.

Lilikoi said, "Whether I marry him or not does not alter the fact that I'm having his child, and I want assurance the baby is safe."

Ogden said, "If you refuse an abortion, we'll make you immortal by injecting you with his blood. I had planned to do that anyway."

Lilikoi shook her head. "We tried that with Gran. It killed her within an hour."

A long silence became uncomfortable. Ogden pointed a finger at Matt Reece. "Your grandmother died because you introduced his blood into her system?"

"Say a prayer for Gran Kamamalu, you gluttonous bastard. She's dead," Lilikoi said.

"That can't be," Ogden said. He glared at Kenji. "You said the enzyme in your blood would multiply and change my DNA so I would live forever."

Kenji said, "You asked me if the enzyme would multiply and spread, changing your DNA," Kenji said, "and I told you yes, it certainly would, faster than you can imagine."

"But…. What killed Gran?" Ogden said.

Kenji made to rise, but Ogden laid his hand on the pistol. "Consuela could have given you a more scientific explanation, but think of this enzyme as the creatures in those *Alien* movies—it's indestructible and has a voracious appetite. It feeds in order to replicate and spread. It's much like a broad-spectrum antiviral agent. It destroys and consumes all organisms built on a unicellular structure, or less. Virus, proteins, amino acids, bacteria, fungi, germs, even parasites. It consumes nearly everything except cells and organs, which have a more complex structure.

"Over time, the enzyme modifies the RNA structure, and that modifies the DNA structure of the blood cells, and they in turn modify the DNA structure of the organs. The problem is lag time between killing protective bacteria and converting the organ DNA."

Now Kenji did stand and paced back and forth as he continued, as if giving a university lecture. "Over centuries of exposure to a harmful environment, mankind has developed a carefully regulated immunity to most organisms. On the skin, in the air, in the lungs, the gut, and bloodstream are hundreds of different viruses and bacteria and proteins and amino acids that keep the body in balance with all the harmful influences bombarding us from outside. This enzyme quickly kills all those good agents, upsetting the balance created by evolution. The protective agents are killed off before the organs have a chance to convert to the new DNA structure. During that time, they fall prey to superinfection from airborne and food-borne organisms bearing diseases."

Ogden waved a hand. "The air in this room is pure as a NASA clean room."

Kenji pointed to the platter of half-eaten food still sitting in front of Ogden.

"You're telling me the meal I ate will kill me?" His words held the unmistakable entropy of a near stupor, that thickening whistle of death in each wobble of his voice.

"Judging from the look of you now, I'd say you'll suffocate from pulmonary edema first, but yes. The food that was nourishing for me was poison for you."

"But why doesn't this alien enzyme destroy the harmful bacteria and viruses coming into my body as well?"

"It does, but not quickly enough. Consuela could explain it better. She was the expert on subcellular sciences, while I'm just a glorified veterinarian. But I do know that to convert to this new DNA structure, it has to happen all at once, through the blood, muscles, organs, brain, bones. The only way to safely accomplish that is saturating the body with a specific radiation frequency. It first happened to me while I was still in my mother's womb, from radiation created by the bomb dropped on Hiroshima. With my son here, he used a device that Consuela invented that saturated his body with a safe form of radiation that modifies the structure of five of the twenty-three pairs of chromosomes."

Ogden brought the pistol onto his lap, caressing it as if it were a pet Siamese. Beads of sweat emerged on his forehead. "I gambled on the chance to live forever, and I lost. I'm not afraid to die. Men who take great risks often suffer dire consequences."

"A good attitude," Kenji said, his voice a whisper. "It will help you to die. It will not, however, help you to live."

Ogden's eyes blazed. It was easy to imagine that early in his life he discovered the violence and power and voracity in an arrogant creed, and he wrapped that brashness around him like a suit of armor. But Kenji used Ogden's own creed to penetrate that casing. Now, behind those eyes, arrogance gave way to anger. He pointed the pistol at Matt Reece and said, "The hell with attitude. If I can't live forever, nobody will."

Matt Reece's mouth went dry.

Ogden's finger tightened on the trigger, but before he could fire, Lilikoi leaped at him like a tigress. He smashed the pistol on the side of her head. It was a heavy blow, which coldcocked her. She dropped to the floor as the pistol discharged. Unfortunately, Adela had staggered to her feet, which placed her in his line of fire. She jerked back as a bullet caught her in the center of her forehead.

Nelson ran for the staircase and descended.

Matt Reece leaped to Lilikoi. He bent over her, lifted her head, and saw she was unconscious but still alive.

Ogden sat staring at Adela's lifeless body. "Oh God, what have I done?" His breathing became audible gasps. The pistol fell from his hand and rattled on the floor. He looked like a gigantic inflatable doll that was losing air, slowly collapsing on itself. He leaned to his left until he fell from his scooter. He lay wheezing, yet no one moved to help him.

Kenji lifted the pistol off the floor and slipped it into his pocket. "Let's get out of here. They'll kill us if we're caught."

On the level below, the piano music was replaced by shouting.

"How?" Matt Reece said. "There are guards below us, and the elevators only work with an authorized eye scan."

"Drag Lilikoi to the elevator," Kenji said, snatching up the carving knife beside Ogden's plate. He bent over Ogden and began hacking through the man's neck.

Matt Reece pulled Lilikoi to a sitting position, lifted her onto his back in a fireman's carry, and staggered to the stone wall that was an elevator door. By the time he got there, Kenji joined him, holding Ogden's severed head. He held the head up to the scanner and pressed the button in the wall.

The elevator car door opened, and Kenji tossed the head aside.

Matt Reece swung around for a last look at Ogden, who was now a headless mountain of flesh beside a lake of blood. He had never dreamed anybody could hold so much fluid.

Kenji pulled him into the elevator car. The doors closed, and they dropped swiftly. When the door opened on Sublevel One, there stood Lieutenant Kien beside a golf-cart-like shuttle that stood before a huge door.

"Quick," Kenji shouted. "There's no time to lose."

Matt Reece hurried to the shuttle. He laid Lilikoi onto the back seat and climbed in. Kien leaped behind the steering wheel, and Kenji sat beside him. Kien pressed a button on the dashboard, and the doors opened, revealing a tunnel. Ten minutes later, the shuttle surfaced aboveground at the airport runway and stopped beside an executive aircraft. The forward stairs deployed. The engines fired up, and a pilot waved from the cockpit window.

Kenji leaped from the shuttle with Ogden's pistol in his hand. He ordered Kien to carry Lilikoi aboard and lifted the pistol until Matt Reece stared into the barrel. He tried to explain about the booby-trapped landing gear, but as soon as his lips parted to speak, Kenji jammed the gun barrel into Matt Reece's mouth. His throat muscles moved, but no sound came from him.

Kenji said, "One word out of you and I'll blow your head off and gut you."

He swallowed down his panic. But the steel in his stepfather's eyes convinced him that Kenji didn't care how he got that flash drive, so he raised his hands above his head. He and Lilikoi were dead one way or the other.

While the lieutenant carried Lilikoi up the steps, Kenji grabbed Matt Reece and pulled him to his feet, all the while keeping the gun firmly rooted in his mouth.

Inside the fuselage, the door fused with the wall. It clicked and sealed, and something locked within his heart with that same automatic sound. The walls merged with the ceiling, a single curve leaving no place for his eyes to rest, no corner to huddle in. Round and round the off-white surface swirled until his heart grew sick and his head wheeled.

The engines surged, and the plane moved to the end of the runway. A voice came over the speakers, "Ladies and gentlemen, please take your seats for takeoff."

The cabin shook as they raced down the runway. Matt Reece felt that first moment of weightlessness, and they climbed through a layer of gray clouds. Kenji didn't take the gun from his mouth until Molokai tilted away and the wheels retracted.

CHAPTER FORTY-SEVEN

KENJI POCKETED the pistol and stared at Matt Reece with a self-satisfied leer. The jet lifted into the sky, the wheels retracted, and the wheel wells closed with a thump, followed by a rapid climb out over the sea. In the few minutes between Kenji removing the pistol from his mouth and the wheels retracting, he could have warned Kenji about the booby trap in the landing gear, but he sat mute. He didn't know why, but it seemed the only answer to a question he wasn't quite sure of. Or it could have simply been payback against Kenji's leer.

The inside of the jet was a declaration of restrained luxury, contoured walls with lustrous ash paneling. Gray leather seats were arranged in pairs. The air held an affluent hush.

He ensured that Lilikoi was resting comfortably and sat back to gaze out a window at an unbroken carpet of ocean. This was his first-ever ride in a jet, the first time his feet had been higher than a few dozen yards off the ground. He became fascinated by how much of the globe he could see from thirty thousand feet.

He envisioned the bomb exploding and wondered what would happen if he survived the blast. He would no doubt plunge to the sea, but would the fall kill him? Or would he drown? He couldn't decide which was worse, and he saw no third alternative.

He didn't feel overly concerned about his oncoming fate. In fact, he felt no concern at all. He read somewhere that prisoners slotted for the death penalty have no trouble sleeping on their last night in prison, because nothing settles a man's mind more than the knowledge that he will die in a matter of hours. He suspected that the converse was true as well—nothing unsettled the mind more than a slim chance of a reprieve.

The pilot's voice came over the intercom. "Relax and enjoy the flight, ladies and gentlemen. I'll level off when we reach thirty-two thousand feet, and at that time you can move about the cabin. Until then, please stay seated with your seat belts buckled. Our flight time is just over ten hours. We'll arrive at our destination just after sunrise."

"Before we land," Kenji said, "you will remove that flash drive and hand it to me."

Matt Reece knew it made no difference now. They would all be dead before gliding back to earth, and the flash drive would be lost forever. The irony somehow seemed fitting that this immortality formula would kill everyone who came in contact with it. He unbuckled his seat belt. "I'll just step into the restroom for a little privacy."

Kenji pulled the pistol from his pocket and pointed it at Lilikoi. "If you flush it down the toilet, she'll get a 9-millimeter hole in her brain."

They had only been in the air ten minutes, but the flight already felt endless. He lifted himself from the seat, walked into the bathroom, and turned on the water in the tiny metal basin. He rinsed his face and looked at himself in the mirror, staring at death. *This is karma at work*, he thought. He said nothing at the dinner on Molokai. He wanted them all to die, and his silence was tantamount to murder. Now he and the woman he had developed a fragile love for would pay with their lives. No one ever got the better of karma.

He dropped his pants, and in a very awkward process, recovered the flash drive. Minutes later, walking into the main cabin, he tossed the drive into Kenji's lap.

Back in his chair, he asked, "Why did you kill Ogden? I mean, what was the point?"

Kenji said, "I didn't kill Ogden, you did. He was convinced a blood transfusion would make him immortal, and I was in no position to disagree since you destroyed my tricorder. Had I told him the truth, we would have never left the island alive."

"And why leave? We could have had a sweet life there."

With his fingers lightly grasping the pistol, he gazed out the window beside his seat and told the story of his birth, how his pregnant mother was living in Hiroshima when the United States dropped the bomb. That day took his mother's life. His father ripped him from his mother's womb, and in the years afterward, his family and his people continued dying as he grew stronger. He described how radiation sickness caused many different birth defects, but there were a handful like him who had not only survived, but flourished without exhibiting the normal aging process. These men and women eventually found each other and became comrades, living apart from the rest of society so as not to draw attention to themselves. Thirty years ago, Kenji left the others and followed a quest to find out why they didn't age. Now he knew, and he had the means to duplicate it. It was time to return.

Matt Reece listened, his gaze fixed on his stepfather's eyes. Some of it was a repeat of what Kenji had told him around the campfire that first night on the trail. Some of it was new. It was somewhat less frightening to know there were others like them living in Japan.

Although they lived together for most of Matt Reece's life, Kenji became a stranger—a man who kept secrets, had survived tragedy, a man who suffered in inconceivable ways over the last seventy years. He imagined his stepfather in his teens, like himself now, growing up in a war-torn city with nothing but sickness and death around him. He struggled to picture the horror of Hiroshima after the blast, the surrounding countryside burned and littered with mangled bodies, tens of thousands dead. He tried to imagine a boy growing up in that environment, with no family and little hope for any future. Against his instinct, he tried to visualize life without his own family, without the protection of the Promesa Rota ranch, a world with only suffering.

"You could have told me," Matt Reece said. His voice was reproachful, yet tears stung his eyes.

"There was no need to burden you with all that," Kenji said.

Matt Reece felt oddly ashamed. "I'm sorry."

Lilikoi stirred. She opened her eyes, trying to orient herself. Her eyes grew larger, and she jumped to her feet. She glared at Matt Reece. "Did the landing gear retract?"

He nodded.

"You little shit! How could you let this happen?"

"He held a gun in my mouth."

Kenji stood. "Relax, you're safe as long as you do what I say."

Lilikoi pointed a finger at him like a gun. "Thought you were slick by killing Ogden? He had a plan too, asshole. When the landing gear retracted, it armed a charge of Cemtex powerful enough to blow us into atom-sized matter."

Kenji asked, "It won't detonate until we lower the landing gear?" His tone was even and held no trace of concern. When she nodded he said, "Lucky I brought you two along." He turned to Matt Reece. "You knew about the explosives and said nothing at dinner? You're full of surprises. But you'll soon find I punish disloyalty."

Matt Reece became annoyed by Kenji's calmness—Kenji was not acting like he had prepared himself for. His confusion grew into anger because he couldn't decide if his stepfather was uncommonly brave in the face of death or so mentally weak he emotionally caved into acceptance. That Kenji might be both never occurred to him.

CHAPTER FORTY-EIGHT

RANDALL LED Landau, Jessup, Vishal, and Patrick through an out-of-the-way neighborhood, strolling along streets lined with shops. Patrick carried his ex-girlfriend's laptop in a backpack. It was past breakfast time, but the smells of grilled fish and miso soup still clung to the air. They passed a teahouse, a vegetable stand, a noodle shop, all opening their doors to a new day. The gabble of women gossiping echoed on the street as they swept away the night's debris from their doorsteps. Temple bells called for midmorning prayers.

When they came upon a shrine, Vishal walked under a *torii* and into a stone-floored courtyard. Jessup and Patrick followed, and they stood before a Shinto shrine that was a single room built like a pillbox with stone walls and a tiled roof. The place smelled of silicates and old incense. Vishal grasped a rope that was attached to a bell hanging from the roof. He clanged the bell to wake the temple spirits. He then took three sticks of incense from a stone box and lit them before placing them in a bowl of sand, which sat in front of a statue of a cross-legged local deity. He told the others to make a wish and bow three times. They closed their eyes and bowed.

Back on the street, Vishal asked Jessup what he had wished for.

"What do you think? I want my son back so we can go home."

"At least you still have a home waiting for you."

Jessup slid his arm over Vishal's shoulders and drew him nearer. "We! We have a home waiting for us. Never doubt that."

Patrick gave an unconvincing nod.

Two doors beyond the shrine stood a sushi shop. There were no customers that early in the day, but that was their meeting place. They ducked through the entryway where a middle-aged lady wearing a kimono sang out, "*Oideyasu!*" She bowed and waved a hand at a table by the window. Landau bowed and asked for a table with more privacy, and then he hung his overcoat on a hook by the door. They moved to a large round table in the back that couldn't be seen from the street.

The woman shuffled over. Everyone but Landau ordered beers. Landau asked for tea. "*Hai!*" the woman said, and Randall spoke a sentence in Japanese.

They sat gazing at the drawings of samurai warriors on the walls until the woman returned carrying a tray with four frosty glasses, a steaming cup, and a platter of raw fish slices artfully arranged. She organized everything on the table and shuffled away.

Jessup picked up a set of chopsticks and reached for a slice of fish.

"That's pufferfish," Randall said. "Their liver and skin contains a lethal toxin called tetrodotoxin. It takes a ten-year apprenticeship before chefs are qualified to prepare it. It's a delicacy if it's cut right. But one wrong slice, and you're toast."

Jessup studied the restaurant, trying to judge how professional the staff might be. He threw down his chopsticks. "So why didn't you order a fucking California roll?"

A stocky man in a trench coat over a black suit entered the shop. He was an Asian man in his forties with dark sloe eyes and slicked-back hair, and he carried a brown leather attaché case. In Jessup's opinion, the man looked like some hired muscle for an underworld gangster. He fell into the chair beside Jessup and barked a sentence in Japanese.

Jessup waited for an introduction, but when one didn't come, he realized that no names would be used during this deal, which was better for everyone involved.

Randall said, "He wasn't expecting anybody but me. Too many people make him nervous." He spoke to him in Japanese, and the man waved an arm and slurred again.

Randall said, "Show him the bag."

Landau lifted a paper bag from his inner jacket pocket and set it before the man. It held neat stacks of US denomination bills bound by white paper strips. The man snatched the bag and took a long time inspecting the contents. Without even a smile, he lifted his attaché case onto the table, turned it so everyone could view its contents, and opened it.

Three Glock 9 mm handguns, three holsters that clipped to a man's belt, and two boxes of cartridges were nestled in urethane-foam compartments. Patrick gave a slow whistle.

Randall checked to make sure nobody was in the restaurant and then lifted a weapon from the case and handed it to Landau. He felt the balance, checked the action. "Yes, this will do. Now I don't feel so naked."

"And our other item of business?" Landau said.

Randall rattled off another stream of Japanese.

The man pinched a plugin USB disk drive from his pocket and handed it to Patrick.

Patrick fished his laptop from his backpack, turned it on, and slipped the drive into a side slot. He opened the only file on the drive and said, "That was money well spent. It's all in Japanese."

The man picked up Jessup's chopsticks and chowed down on the plate of fish.

"Let me see," Randall said. Patrick passed him the laptop, and he scanned the data. He smiled at the man and nodded. The man stood as he pocketed the money. He had polished off the fish, and he lifted Jessup's beer and gulped half of it before setting the glass down. Then he beat a speedy retreat through the front door.

Jessup stared at his remaining beer. "Tell me that data is what we're looking for, 'cause I'm about to punch you in the face."

"It's spot-on, all sorted by length of time these people have been on public assistance. And you're not going to believe this, but Miyajima Island is home to almost two hundred men who have been receiving social security and medical aid for over forty years. Twenty of them have records going back more than fifty years. Miyajima Island is only a few miles from this harbor."

Patrick said, "So, Japanese people live longer, right? From eating this god-awful diet."

Landau said, "We assume Kenji experimented on people who were in their eighties and nineties." Jessup nodded. "Wouldn't these old, infirm people be collecting government assistance? And wouldn't they go on collecting money even after they turned young? I mean, the government would keep issuing them checks, right?"

"Okay," Jessup said, "so what we've found is a high concentration of people who have been receiving government stipends for an inordinately long time?"

"Bingo," Landau said. "Assuming these people started collecting in their midsixties, that would make them all senterarians, and at least twenty would be supercenterarians."

"Supercentenarian?" Patrick asked.

"Someone over the age of one hundred and ten," Randall said.

Landau continued, "Only thirty-nine people in recorded history lived to age one hundred fifteen, and here we have twenty people living on the same island who are that old. What are the odds?"

Patrick nodded, seemingly unimpressed. "Great. What say we take this data to a pizza parlor and grab a real meal? I'm so tired of rice and fish I could shit gluten-free bricks."

"I think it's time to get the local authorities involved," Randall said.

Landau nodded. "Okay, but we'll need to handle them judiciously."

THEY RETURNED to their hotel around 10:00 p.m., and they were all stunned to find Rachael Laughton and Ahmed Souad waiting in the lobby. Dressed in a black pantsuit, she looked ninja-like. Souad was dressed in his working suit with a tan overcoat, and he had bad scars on this face and hands from being burned while pulling Vishal from the fiery Prius.

"Close your mouth," Rachael said to Landau. "You left a mile-wide trail of bread crumbs."

Landau took Rachael in his arms, and to Jessup, it looked like a lot more going on there than professional gallantry.

Souad laughed. "That's your problem, partner. You think you're the only one with a triple-digit IQ."

Rachael slipped out of his grip and turned to the others. "I need to borrow Sal on official business." She clutched his arm. "Let's walk. The cherry blossoms are abundant."

"In the middle of the night?" Landau said.

"There's a full moon out."

"Look," Landau said, "if this is some kind of scheme to get me back to the States, forget it. Tonight we found where his patients are hiding, so we know where he's going."

"Which means you haven't found him yet," Souad said.

Okay, Jessup thought, *that means the FBI still don't have a clue where he's hiding.* That gave him confidence that he and Landau were on the right track.

Rachael said, "Excellent. So we can turn this over to the local authorities, and you'll all come back with me." When he shook his head, her voice hardened. "Things have changed. The president and her cabinet are dead. The Joint Chiefs of Staff has detained the vice president and taken control of the government. They are taking a more cautious approach, one we hope will stop the civil war. Also, the nature of this case has changed. Now that the hunt has gone international, we've turned it over to the CIA."

She stunned Jessup when he first saw her in the lobby. Now he was shell-shocked. "Harrington dead? How? Who?"

"Who?" Rachael said. "A badass dude named karma."

"Who else knows we're here?" Landau asked.

"No one," Souad said. "We chartered a flight to Bangkok that had a stopover at Narita. Nobody knows we didn't take off on the second leg of the flight. The plane is on the tarmac in Thailand, waiting for our call to come get us."

"I'm ordering you to come back," Rachael said.

"Positively, unequivocally, Shermanesquely, no. I'm a Jew. They vaporized my people's homeland. You of all people should know I can't walk away now."

"Shermanesquely?" She sighed. "What I know is that you're addicted to the chase. You always were, and you can't change your spots. But this is too dangerous even for someone half your age. If they'll go so far as to blow Air Force One out of the air, what chance do you have?"

"You just said nobody knows we're here."

"Another news flash hit the wires two hours ago." She took a deep breath, seemingly gathering her courage. "Ogden Moloch, the multibillionaire, was murdered on Molokai. Kenji had been his guest and stole his jet minutes after Moloch's death."

"He's flying here. I knew it." Landau's hands trembled.

"Let the local authorities handle his capture," she said. "Being right isn't going to make for a happy ending. We passed the point of happily-ever-afters long ago."

"Stopping him will make me happy enough."

"All he did was start the snowball rolling down the hill. The killing will continue as the snowball grows. Catching him won't solve anything. The only thing that will accomplish is we'll be able to punish him. And how can you adequately punish someone for millions of deaths? There is no winning or losing here. We've already lost."

Landau said, "This is not about victory. It's about putting that monster in prison. That's our job, and all we can do is uphold the law and do the best we can."

"Putting him away is not going to change the world. The evil was there, waiting for someone to unlock the cage. He knew that from the start, and he had the perfect key."

Landau turned his back on her. "If you want to quit, then go. I didn't want this job in the first place, but now I'm damn well going to see it through."

"Yes," Souad said, "be a hero to people who don't care if you catch him. All they want is their Big Macs, iPhones, 3-D TVs, and assault rifles. They just want to get by, enjoy a few beers on Saturday night with their buds, and go home to the wife and kids to watch *Duck Dynasty*."

Landau said, "Yes, we live in a country where stupidity is embraced and nurtured as if it were a virtue. But that doesn't mean I have to go along with it."

"Yes, Sal, you're one in a million. Bravo," Souad said.

"It's easy to shake your fist at the wrongs of the world and then expect someone else to fix it. And it takes a great deal of energy to keep ignoring the fact that you can do something positive about it. In my own way, I can help. If I don't do this, I'll be giving in to ignorance for the rest of my life. Ignorance isn't bliss. I don't want to become one of the masses. I want to know I did what I could, even if that's not enough."

"Even if it means sacrificing your life?" Rachael asked.

"Yes! Goddammit." Landau hunched over, holding his chest. He fished a bottle from his coat and shook two pills into his palm. He popped them into his mouth and swallowed them dry.

A tender smile passed over Rachael's face. "Whoever catches him, Sal, you or the Japanese authorities, it doesn't matter. You don't have to prove anything. Sal, come back tonight."

"For Christ's sake, I'm not trying to prove anything. I'm trying to do a job. And it's a job few people half my age can do as well." He turned and stomped out the front door.

Rachael turned to the others and apologized for creating a scene.

"Don't be sorry," Jessup said. "That's the best entertainment we've had since coming here."

Chapter Forty-nine

Diane worked at the Tel Hashomer hospital for four straight days with only a few hours of sleep per day. She dressed wounds, stitched up cuts, gave blood transfusions, and helped cook meals. She organized others with minor injuries to help clean up the puddles of vomit and excrement. The hospital ran short of food, sedatives, antiseptics, bandages, and blood, so she led searches through neighborhoods to collect food, bed linens, and bottles of any kind of alcohol.

On the second day of work, while in the process of washing the burns of a six-year-old boy in saline solution, she ran her hand through her hair to brush it away from her face and came away with a handful of hair. She did it again with the same result. She avoided touching her hair after that, but it was no use. Over the next few days her hair fell out in clumps until she was bald.

On the fifth day, the International Red Cross arrived by ship with a team of twenty doctors, a hundred nurses, and a shipload of supplies, including untainted blood. Still, that made for only a few hundred doctors for a hundred thousand patients. But that afternoon, exhausted from her foul work, Diane became obsessed with the idea of getting word to Declan that she survived. She arranged to board the hospital ship and use the satellite communications equipment to call Golden Eagle corporate offices. After an hour of trying to contact Declan, she was told he was en route to Tel Aviv. She gave them the address of the hospital and told them to get a message to him.

She returned to the hospital and found some amount of order restored, which is to say that tents were erected on the lawns and parking lots around the hospital, patients who had been sleeping in the corridors were moved to cots in the tents, and the dead bodies removed. Also, supplies had been restored so doctors and nurses could adequately treat patients. She tracked down Dr. Hersey, who she had been working with in the days following the blast. He took one look at her and hustled her into an examining room. Her white blood count was under two thousand (five to seven thousand is normal), she was seriously anemic, and her temperature was 104.

Dr. Hersey diagnosed her symptoms as serious radiation disease and prescribed a blood transfusion, hyperalimentation, and copious bed rest. They moved her to a room, and every three hours forced eggs, leafy vegetables, and beef into her. They also fed her all the sugar she could stand, along with vitamins and iron pills and shots of vitamin B1.

THREE DAYS later, two more hospital ships arrived, and a thousand patients were taken aboard. One man, however, came ashore—Declan Hughes. He had received a message from Liam Cullen that Diane was alive, and he had the address of the Tel Hashomer hospital. He procured a driver and car among the military personnel combing the wreckage.

At the hospital, he found the chief surgeon, Dr. Hersey. "We've been expecting you," Dr. Hersey said, "although we'll be sad to see our angel of mercy leave us. Come, I'll take you to her. I believe she's in the maternity ward feeding the infants."

Dr. Hersey led Declan down a corridor, and they ascended a flight of stairs. "Sorry to make you climb, but we only have power from emergency generators, and they don't operate the elevators."

"How is she, Doctor?"

"She's made it into stage two, but if she doesn't pace herself, she may never see stage three. Unfortunately, we can't keep her in bed for more than a few hours at a time."

"Explain to me what stage two and three are."

"With radiation sickness, stage one is the reaction to the bombardment of the body with neutrons, beta particles, and gamma rays at the moment the bomb exploded. We estimate 95 percent of the people within a five-mile radius of the blast absorbed enough radiation to kill them within the first week. The rays destroy body cells. Many people in this stage lingered on for several days while experiencing nausea, headaches, diarrhea, and fever."

Declan said, "Diane is part of that 5 percent?"

"She suffered all of those symptoms, but her strong will helped her survive."

"Strong-willed puts it mildly, Doctor."

Dr. Hersey smiled as they reached the second floor and began to scale the third. "Stage two normally sets in ten to fifteen days after the blast. Loss of hair, diarrhea and fever, and blood disorders appear. In her case, the white-blood-cell count dropped sharply, making her susceptible to opportunistic infections. During this stage, many patients die of respiratory system complications. She needs rest and an ample diet of protein and vegetables high in vitamin B1."

"What are her chances, Doctor?"

"She was lucky because she was trapped under a mound of books for days, which kept her immobile. The ones who lay quietly for days after the blast were less likely to get seriously sick. The ones who were active became the sickest. We don't know why, but that's what we're seeing in case after case." He sighed deeply. "Given her iron will, I see no reason why she won't live a normal lifespan. This sickness could keep her down another week, or it could linger for months. But I'm confident she'll overcome it."

They reached the third floor, and Dr. Hersey led him into a maternity ward. Declan's heart thumped, and not from climbing the stairs. Diane sat beside a bed with a baby held in one arm, pressing a bottle to its mouth. She looked impossibly frail, wearing green scrubs with an orange wool hat covering her bald head. He saw her profile, turning briefly, unconsciously, to full face, and then dropping her head to the baby again. Recognition held off for a moment longer. He couldn't believe those grayish skin tones and gaunt facial features belonged to her, but a glow in his chest told him it was, in fact, her.

Dr. Hersey rattled on about the effects in stage three, which were long-term complications they needed to be concerned with, but Declan was hardly listening.

She looked up, and their eyes met. She smiled, and he rushed to her and dropped to his knees beside her, burying his face in her lap. They stayed like that a long time, him holding her while she fed the baby.

"Well, I'll leave you to it," Dr. Hersey said.

"A moment, Doctor," Diane said. "Please tell Declan what you told me about radiation sickness and bone marrow."

Declan lifted his head from her lap. "Sweetheart, it can wait."

She kissed his forehead, and when he lifted his face, she kissed his lips. "What he has to say is my present to you. A most wonderful present. Trust me."

Dr. Hersey said, "I can't think how it's in any way wonderful. One of the seeds of the delayed sickness, in stage three, is caused by gamma rays entering the body at the time of the explosion, making the phosphorus in the victim's bones radioactive. The bones in turn emit beta particles, which, though they can't penetrate far through flesh, does enter the bone marrow, where blood is manufactured. That affects blood production and also alters the victim's DNA in the blood cells."

Declan's mouth fell open as he glanced back at her. Her face glowed.

"Gamma rays," he whispered. "A specific low-dose frequency of gamma rays making the bones radioactive." He wrapped his arms about her and the baby, giving them a loving hug. When he pulled away he said, "I can't wait to get you home. Our research team will tap dance to the moon and back."

"I'm not leaving," she said.

"Sweetheart, I'm taking you to a safe place, away from all this death. How do you feel about sailing to Tasmania?"

"Yes, all this death, and in the midst of it, I've developed a gift for helping people die with their dignity intact. We built an empire by manufacturing war machines. I'll not go back to that, ever. I've found a new calling."

He knew that tone in her voice, that steel in her eye. And, of course, he had lost his stomach for that as well. Still, she had unlocked the secret. They had to do something.

He laid his head in her lap, content to be with her. "Okay, no hiding in a safe place."

"There is," she said, "a stone-hearted cunt I'd like to serve up a big slice of karma to."

"President Harrington?" He thought about telling her he beat her to the punch but was gratified just to nod. She pressed the baby into his arms and handed him the bottle.

"You finish this one," she said. "You feed while I change diapers."

He looked down at the chubby red face, and he slipped the nipple into its mouth. He glanced around the ward, taking a count of beds, each holding a hungry baby. He had a lot of work to do.

Part Three
Razor's Edge

Every light casts a shadow, and the closer you get to the light, the darker that shadow becomes.
—Plato, Critias

Chapter Fifty

Matt Reece had ample time to think about his upcoming death. He sat in his seat and watched his reflection in the window, which grew shadowy, more angled, to the point he didn't recognize himself. Then the overhead lights went off and his reflection disappeared. Outside the window lay nothing but the distant twinkle of stars.

He thought about Jessup's reaction to his death and pictured him at the breakfast table, writing Matt Reece's obituary. It would fall to his father to write a draft and deliver it to the newspapers. The media would rewrite it, sensationalizing it to spur sales.

The jet hit a jolt of turbulence as he thought about what Jessup would write:

Matt Reece was born on the Promesa Rota ranch and had lived there all his life until he lost his way. He loved the ranch, his horse, his dog, his family. He was a superb horseman and a pretty fair cook.

What else could he say? He had lived a solitary life until he rode away from the ranch for good, or as it turned out, for bad. He looked at Lilikoi, and his heart sank.

She caught his eye and must have read his mind because she said, "If I'd let Ted kill you, I'd be tending my animals, and Gran would be alive."

He nodded. "I'd rather be eaten by tigers than blown to bits over the Sea of Japan." He reached over and took her hand. "But being with you these last few weeks has been the most exciting time of my life. Patrick was crazy not to see how wonderful you are."

She guffawed a harsh laugh, but something in her eyes grew softer. "A decent man finally falls in love with me, and look what happens. Why can't I ever get an even break?" She leaned into him and kissed him.

"Not that it matters now, but I wish I was the kind of man you need," he said.

"Cowboy, you are exactly the kind of man I need. If only Patrick had been more like you…. My only regret is that we won't get to raise our baby."

"Then you really are pregnant?"

She nodded. "I think so. Hold me, or should I say hold us?"

He wrapped his arms around her and the life growing inside her. At least he had that.

DAWN OPENED a thin crack along the eastern horizon. Silver light chased them across the globe, but ahead lay only darkness.

The plane began to descend. The pilot's voice came over the intercom, "We are nearing our destination. We'll fly a hundred feet over the surface of the ocean for the next thirty minutes to sneak in under Japanese radar, and then we'll prepare for landing."

As Matt Reece's anxiety mounted, a question arose with it, a topic that he'd thought about often but never voiced. "Kenji," he said, more to break the silence than curiosity, "why did you bring me along, not only the first day when I exposed myself, but at every turn you refused to let me go. You kept me with you no matter what. Why?"

"You're my son. Do I need more of a reason than that?"

"From what I've seen, you don't care about anything but you. I really want to know why you've dragged me along, when it would have been so much easier to ditch me."

"Two hundred years from now, the world will be different, and almost everyone living now will be dead. I will be revered as the man who brought a new world order. But it's important to have someone close who remembers me for who I was before the culling."

Matt Reece was speechless. It confirmed that Kenji did, in fact, think only of himself, loved no one else, not even family. But it was shocking to hear it.

"You mean," Lilikoi said, "someone who remembers you when you were still a human being? That is, before you grew horns and a tail?"

"Name-calling accomplishes nothing. It certainly doesn't hurt my feelings."

"You have no feelings," she said.

"I will be esteemed throughout the world. Alexander the Great, Genghis Khan, Napoleon, Julius Caesar, Lincoln, and Obama will pale compared to me."

For the second time, Matt Reece looked into Kenji's near future and saw death, and he was glad, even if it meant his own demise too. A quick end was better than ages of miseries compounded by guilt, coming slow like leprosy. And although he was upset about Lilikoi and the baby being there, her presence gave him the strength to face what lay only minutes ahead. He said, "That's only if you survive the explosion."

The pilot made another announcement, ordering everyone to gather in the cockpit. Matt Reece followed Lilikoi forward. She strapped herself into the copilot's seat. Kenji and Matt Reece jammed into the narrow space behind the seats, and Lieutenant Kien crouched in the doorway to the cabin. Matt Reece saw the pilot for the first time. Rob McCann, a middle-aged man whose head seemed far too small for his body—so small Matt Reece decided it must be the result of a childhood hormone imbalance.

McCann said, "We're about to make a water landing. That way, we don't need to lower the landing gear. We'll skim over the surface until we stop; then, we'll begin to sink. As soon as we're stationary, I'll open this emergency door"—he pointed to a section of windshield—"and we'll get the hell out in a hurry. I'll get us as close to land as possible, without grounding us." He paused and then said, "Everyone can swim, right?"

Matt Reece shrugged. "You bet. I'm sure I can."

"Neither can I." McCann laughed. "There's a life vest under each seat in the passenger cabin. Hopefully they all still work." McCann raised his voice. "There's still the possibility that a turbulent water landing will jar the arming device and it will blow, but we don't have any choice since we don't carry parachutes."

"Why have us in the cockpit?" Lilikoi asked.

"It's the furthermost distance from the wheel wells. If that blows, we might make it."

Lilikoi closed her eyes. "If it's in the nose wheel well, then we're right above it."

Matt Reece's windpipe tightened. *Not now,* he prayed, but it grew worse. As he wheezed, he closed his eyes and willed himself to relax. He pictured his lungs expanding with ease, his windpipe opened wide. A moment later, he was no longer rasping.

Slowly, he became aware of a strange sound behind him. He turned to see Lieutenant Kien, still crouched by the cabin doorway, eyes closed and snoring.

THE THIN line of brown in front of them grew into an island. Matt Reece could make out a rocky beach, trees, and green hills with cattle grazing.

"Hold tight," McCann said. His face scrunched into a mask of panic. He said something else through clenched teeth, but it was lost in the thunder of a helicopter screaming close above them.

Only days ago Matt Reece thought he'd have thousands of years in order to sort out the meaning of his life. Now he had seconds, and in that recognition came an epiphany.

As the island rushed to meet them, he grasped that the tragedy of death lay not with what one did while living, but solely with what was left unfulfilled. The idea was so simple he was embarrassed it had only occurred to him now. What lay unfulfilled was raising Lilikoi's child.

Lilikoi stared straight ahead, as if confident everything would turn out jim-dandy. Kenji also seemed confident. He was shocked at himself when a flood of tender feelings for Kenji rose up in his heart. Kenji and Lilikoi and the baby. They were all about to die, and this grand adventure had only seconds to play out.

He was amazed that his mind was churning on details at a time like this. He felt intensely alive. He stared at the front windscreens and wondered what his skull would look like after striking it.

McCann pulled the wheel back and eased the throttles forward. The nose rose, and the engines went silent. An appalling second passed, and another. The plane touched water.

An elongated hiss sounded behind them, and then Matt Reece catapulted forward as a deafening sound rushed at him. The plane dove under the water at high speed and shuddered as if mortally wounded. Everyone screamed. He found himself plastered against the windscreens.

Abruptly the force of the plane's dive spent itself, and the fuselage, buoyed by the air trapped inside, jerked upward until it broke the surface. A moment later came a sound of gurgling behind him. His thoughts were clear and disconnected, and he knew from the pitch of the plane that it was sinking tail first. He laughed, not quite believing he was still alive. He felt giddy, his nerve endings thrumming with energy, but he understood the falseness of that feeling.

Lilikoi seemed dazed, but alive, as was McCann. Like Matt Reece, Kenji flew over the pilot and smashed into the windshield. Kien had also shot forward, crushing Kenji.

"Christ Almighty," McCann yelled, "we're alive! How's that for a three-point landing? We're only eighty yards from shore."

Kien seemed groggy, but he pulled himself back behind the pilot's seat. Kenji didn't move. He could be unconscious or dead.

McCann popped the cockpit's emergency exit and swung away a triangular section of windscreen. "Let's get the hell out of here." He unharnessed and stood on his seat with his head out the emergency exit. A moment later, he plunged into water and swam for shore. Kien was right behind him.

Water was ankle-deep and rising fast. Matt Reece helped Lilikoi out of her harness and guided her out the exit. She was fully conscious and swimming with long strokes.

He placed his fingers to Kenji's throat and felt a pulse. A moment passed as he considered leaving him there to drown. He could feel Kirby's growing excitement.

He slipped his hand into the pocket where Kenji had deposited the flash drive and recovered it. He tucked it into his own pocket. Then he heaved Kenji back and sat him in the copilot seat. He slapped him hard across the face, trying to wake him. No luck.

"Hasta la vista, asshole," he said, and climbed through the exit. Outside, a red helicopter hovered well above the wreckage. A wave quilted with froth smacked his face. He swallowed a mouthful of salt water and began coughing, which caused a pure animal panic. His heart rate doubled. The water was cold and seemed to drain the heat from his body, leaving him shivering.

Slow down, he told himself. *If you panic, you die.* He scissored his legs, but his shoes were sucking him down, so he reached to his feet and slipped them off.

He dogpaddled halfway to shore, and with each stroke, he felt his panic growing. He stopped to look back. Eruptions of air billowed from the cockpit. Without making a conscious decision, he swam back.

The cockpit overflowed, and Kenji was floating with his face in the water. It was relatively easy to pull his stepfather free of the wreckage.

He glanced ashore. Lilikoi was lying on a pebbly beach. There was no sign of McCann or Kien. He wrapped an arm around Kenji's neck and scissor kicked, all out.

"C'mon!" Lilikoi shouted. "It could blow any minute."

An explosion was the least of his worries. Enough time elapsed since the crash that he was convinced there was no danger. In fact, he now believed there was no bomb, because a landing that jarring would have set it off. Not being a natural swimmer, his only fear now was drowning. He was slow and clumsy, gagging on mouthfuls of salt water.

His feet touched ground. When Lilikoi didn't rush out and help drag Kenji in, he realized something was wrong. He hauled Kenji up a slope and came back for her.

"Took your sweet time," she said. "Did you stop for coffee and doughnuts?"

"We were never in any—"

A thrashing explosion interrupted him. White water and sections of fuselage rocketed into the air. A section of wing landed only a dozen feet from where they crouched. Water and debris rained down. A wave rushed to shore and spilled over them.

"You have to hand it to Songoree," she said. "He never did anything half-assed."

He wanted to laugh, but he noticed a fragment of metal lodged in her side, the shape and size of a hunting knife. It may have been part of the throttle controls in the cockpit, he thought, or it could have been a projectile from the explosion. He ripped open her shirt to expose the wound.

Her face took on the color of chalk. She drew in air, enough for life but not enough to fully expand her lungs. He knew then it had either punctured the lung or was pressing against it. Either way it was painful. She glanced down at it. "I guess I'm fucked."

"I'll get you to a doctor."

Her body went limp, as if in a faint; her lips parted and her eyes half closed.

"Pull it out," she whispered.

He looked around for someone who could help. The beach was empty. He waved his arms at the helicopter. It moved farther away, down the beach. "I've got to find help."

"Just pull the damned thing out," she said, her voice tinged in agony. She coughed, and blood came from her mouth. The shaft jerked in her side, and her face emptied of life. Her head fell back, unconscious.

Quick, he thought, *pull it out before she wakes up.*

He grasped the end of the projectile and tried to ease it out. It didn't budge. He braced himself against her, set his teeth, and pulled with all his strength. It came free with a gush of dark blood. The purple wound in the brown flesh opened and closed with her breath. He ripped the shirt off his back, folded it twice, and pressed it to the wound.

Her eyes opened. She glanced at the fragment lying beside her. "Thank you—" Then her head sagged, and she went still.

He pressed his finger to her throat and found a pulse. He exhaled, overcome with relief. He jerked his head up to see Kenji standing up the bank. "Help us!"

Kenji walked down and crouched beside them. Matt Reece used the sleeves of the shirt pressed to her wound to secure the bandage to her side. He looked around and nodded at the section of wing laying several feet away. "We'll use that as a litter."

Kenji rose to his feet, and Matt Reece assumed he was about to retrieve the wing, but as he looked up, he saw a handgun in Kenji's fist hurling toward his face. He was caught off guard with a solid blow to the side of his head. He jerked back, falling into an oncoming wave. He felt a kick to his ribs, causing coils of pain to shoot through his belly. Then he drifted in a sea of blackness.

CHAPTER FIFTY-ONE

A THOUSAND feet above the sea, Randall sat in the helicopter's copilot seat, while Souad, Landau, Jessup, Vishal, and Patrick clustered in the passenger compartment. On their way to Miyajima Island, they passed over three police boats converging on the isle. As they passed over the verdant landscape, they spotted a private jet coming in from the southeast, dangerously low over the water.

"That's got to be them," Landau said, pointing at the jet.

Randal argued into the microphone, using rifle-hot Japanese while gesticulating.

A few minutes later, Jessup's heart leaped into his throat as the plane crashed into the sea. The copter descended to a hundred yards over the crash site. He breathed easier as he watched people scramble from the cockpit and swim toward shore. They were too far away for a positive identification, but relief washed through him.

He yelled to Randall, "Land this damned thing," just as a tower of water and debris shot out of the sea, tumbling in on itself with a roar. The copter veered sharply to the left. It felt like riding a bucking bronco. But Jessup kept his eyes glued to the people on the beach. Now that they were on land, he identified his son. He was alive, attending to a girl who appeared to be injured. Jessup sat helpless as he watched Kenji attack Matt Reece. It looked like Kenji was trying to kill him.

When the copter regained control, they dropped to a cleared spot of beach less than a quarter mile from Matt Reece and Kenji. As the copter doors opened, Jessup saw the girl lift what looked like a knife and stab Kenji in the thigh.

Jessup sprang from the copter and ran, closing the distance between them. Vishal shot past him and reached Matt Reece moments after Kenji fled into the trees above the beach. Vishal fell to his knees beside Matt Reece and cradled the boy's head in his arms, trying to revive him. Jessup held his breath, waiting to see if his boy was still alive.

Patrick dropped beside the girl. "Lilikoi! What the hell are you doing here?"

"Maybe a more appropriate question is, am I all right? And the answer, in case you're interested, is fuck no! I'm bleeding from a hole in my side, and I'm probably going into shock from surviving a plane crash. So are you going to help me or just sit there with that stupid look on your face?"

Patrick didn't move. He seemed to be the one going into shock.

"Don't stare at me like that," she said. "You may be batshit crazy yourself someday."

He wrapped his arms around her and hugged her. "Christ, why did you leave me?"

"Only you would think about yourself in this situation. Seriously, you think this is the best time to discuss why I left?"

He simply stared at her.

"Okay, I left you because you get every girl you want, and I needed to be the exception to that rule."

He kissed her, briefly but firm. When he pulled back he waited, as if he assumed she would slap his face. But rather than a slap, she leaned her head to his shoulder. He lifted her in his arms, and he stood.

"We need to get Lilikoi to a hospital," Patrick said. "Is Matt Reece alive?"

HIS BODY was too traumatized to feel anything. As his awareness grew clearer, he realized that he lay in a fetal position, caught in a rhythmic wash of gushing liquid. His eyelids crept open, and light burned his eyes, blurring everything into a cold white haze. As his vision cleared, he realized that he lay in the surf under a morning sky, watching turquoise water lap over his limbs.

He glanced up into a brown face, surrounding benevolent-looking eyes. *This must be the face of God.* Through his numbness he could feel fear tweaking his vagus nerve.

The face lowered until those beautifully formed lips touched his. His mind, caught in a membrane freeze, struggled with the shock of being kissed by God. He glanced up at God's face again, noting his unblemished coppery skin and an expression of joy that seemed comical. God cradled his head like a newborn, smiling at him—a smile that warmed his chest and spread out to his limbs, as if he were suddenly firing on high octane.

Instincts took over, and he tested his body: legs stretched, back arched, fingers clenched into fists and relaxed. Every part of him obeyed his mental commands, yet he couldn't shake the feeling that all this was an illusion, that he must be dead.

And then came recognition. It was Vishal, not God, holding him. But Vishal was dead. So perhaps it was God, and how fitting it seemed that God would look identical to his true love.

"Hey, cowboy, are we gonna to go through this routine every time we meet? I mean, there are easier ways to get me to kiss you."

Matt Reece wanted more than anything to believe what was happening, but everything he'd known for the last several weeks was screaming against it, and that sound was Kirby's voice—a voice of outrage.

"We're dead."

Vishal curved his body around and rolled, bringing Matt Reece to rest on top of him. Vishal let out a tender, almost placating laugh before their lips met in a meaningful kiss. Kirby's voice silenced as Matt Reece's passion ignited, and he knew this was no dream.

Vishal withdrew, lips lingering and eyes gazing up at him.

"It's time I took you home, cowboy."

Matt Reece rested his head against his lover's chest. Through his feelings of numb shock, one thing became certain: he was ready to go anywhere with this man, even back to the ranch, especially back to the ranch.

He noticed other men standing over him, and one of them was his father. Jessup helped Vishal haul him to his feet and then half crushed the life out of him with a bear hug. Jessup was too choked up for words, but so was Matt Reece. He wanted so much to explain how sorry he was for everything. But it somehow seemed pointless.

They carried him and Lilikoi to a helicopter, and he was up in the clouds again, this time flying over a massive city.

Vishal held him, and across the aisle, Patrick held Lilikoi. The numbness of his body began to give way to pain, and he remembered being beaten by Kenji. He endured several kicks to the head and gut before blacking out. But why did Kenji turn on him? Then he knew. He reached into the pocket of his tweed pants and groped for the flash drive. It was still there. Whatever drove Kenji away did so before he could retrieve the formula.

Chapter Fifty-Two

Landau, Souad, Jessup, and Randall retrieved an equipment bag before the copter lifted into the air and rocketed toward the city. Randall assured them it would only be a ten-minute flight to the hospital's helipad. As soon as the bird was away, Landau pulled a Glock from the bag, checked it, and slipped it into the holster. Souad and Randall did the same. They clipped the holsters to their belts at their backs and slid back into their jackets. Much as Jessup wanted a weapon, they only had three. He wasn't sure he could shoot Kenji anyway, and at least this way he wouldn't need to find out.

"Expect anything," Landau said. "Kenji had a lot of time to plan this. If *Jurassic Park* dinosaurs fly out of his ass and eat us alive, I want you to have expected it."

Souad chuckled. "An attempt at humor? Praise Allah, I think you may be human after all."

"You're only warming up to me because you've been away from your wife for too long."

Souad howled. "Give me a hug, sweetheart."

Even Jessup could see Souad's excitement had grown to a dangerous level. Landau needed to calm him down, but he didn't wait for that. He said, "Cut the crap. We've got a job to do."

Randall said, "If the police see these weapons, our asses are hash. So only draw them in a life-threatening situation."

Landau said, "The girl confirmed Kenji is armed, and she stabbed him in the leg. A wounded animal is desperate and therefore more dangerous."

Landau pointed at Randall. "You're here as an interpreter. No heroics."

"No worries. I'm a coward at heart." As if to prove it, he fished a roll of antacids from his pocket and popped two in his mouth.

Jessup held out his hand, and Randall dropped two in his palm.

Landau led them into the woods. They had studied maps of the island the night before, and he knew where to find the temple they were sure Kenji was heading for. His suspicions were confirmed when he found a trail of blood any novice could follow.

They moved up a steep hill where age-old pines, elms, and maples were easily navigated because there was no underbrush. They stayed in a tight group and hiked a brisk two miles before they came to a wooden gate twenty feet tall with a shingled roof protecting two statues on either side. Beyond it, a stone staircase rose up the hillside. There were drops of fresh blood spattering the steps. They passed under the gate and climbed.

At the top of the stairs, they saw the Daisho-in temple grounds. The main temple stood at the center, a two-story wooden building covered by a sloping roof with the tiers built with the corners upswept in the Chinese style, and an expansive front entryway with thick, unadorned columns. The structure was light and elegant, a masterpiece of twelfth-century Zen architecture. Around this temple were several buildings, including a three-story pagoda, shrines, and a dormitory for the monks. The place, as Jessup expected, was immaculate and projected a feeling of harmony with nature. The simple beauty of the grounds made him, momentarily, yearn for the tranquility of his ranch.

The police arrived, flooding into the courtyard from the opposite end. Five cops gathered at the door of the dormitory, and each officer held an automatic rifle and wore a helmet with built-in goggles and a headset. They waited for a signal. Another six were about to storm the two-story prayer hall.

Landau panted from the climb. Souad was wild-eyed, juiced. Landau pointed to the officers at the dorm. "Souad and Randall, follow them. Jessup and I will take the temple."

Jessup and Landau rushed to the main building. As they ran up the stone steps, Jessup noted spots of red leading up to the double doors. He pointed them out to Landau, who nodded and then flashed his credentials at the officer in charge. The man, whose name tag read Sergeant Jingoro, nodded and then waved an arm at the other officers. The doors flung open, and the officers moved into the hall and spread out across a spacious room with their rifles at the ready. They quickly began to search the hall. Jessup and Landau followed.

A monk sat at a low table before a shrine where a statue of a bronze Buddha towered to the rafters. It was a smaller copy of the great Kamakura Buddha. A multitude of candles flickered around the platform. The man gave no sign of anything being abnormal.

A door at the back of the hall opened, and a head peeked out. One of the cops pointed his rifle at it, and the door slammed. Sergeant Jingoro led the group through the main hall, dropping a search warrant onto the table where the monk sat staring.

At the back of the hall, they found the door locked. One officer used his shoulder as a battering ram. The door smashed open with a splintering thud. Jessup hung back, following a few feet behind. The only thing he found odd was the calmness of the monk sitting at the table. He made a mental note to return and question this man.

He followed Landau and the cops into a warren of hallways and doorways leading into rooms. They split up into twos, opening doors and searching rooms. Jessup and Landau followed Jingoro, who shouted in rapid-fire Japanese. Jessup assumed he was telling everyone to come out with their hands above their heads.

Each room Jessup entered was a storage room, holding statues of stone and wood, mostly images of the Buddha but other men as well, as if the old heroes of Japan had gathered at this temple, frozen forever in their ceremonial postures. One room had a bed sitting against the far wall, and someone dressed in gray robes crouched under it. Landau laid a hand on the grip of his handgun. Jessup tensed. Jingoro trained his weapon on the body and shouted. A frightened monk, no more than fifteen years old, emerged with his hands in plain sight.

"I'm too old for this," Landau whispered, and Jessup had to agree. He walked into the hallway. At one end two cops were holding several monks in a tight group. A creak of wood turned his head in the other direction. A figure stood before a window at the rear of the building. He wore a gray suit and stood stock-still. Jessup squinted in order to see in the dim light. The figure reached into his coat pocket, lifted his arm, and pointed at Jessup.

"He's got a gun," Landau shouted from the doorway. Jessup threw himself down. *Bam!*—a bullet slammed into a doorpost not six inches from Jessup's head. There were more shots, bullets zinging in both directions.

Landau freed his Glock and aimed, but the figure ducked down another hallway.

With ringing in his ears, Jessup lumbered to his feet and followed Landau after the gunman. They burst through a doorway and bounded down steps that led into a Zen-style garden. A shadow moved through the trees, and they gave chase.

They were well into the forest when a shot fired from the trees in front of them. Jessup ducked behind a stone Buddha statue. He tried to count to ten, but the numbers became a tangle without sequence. He gave up and peeked around the granite. He caught a glimpse of Kenji bent low and moving down a steep grade. A smudged, lonely-looking figure. He also saw Landau giving chase. He jumped up and ran after them.

Somewhere from far behind him, Souad yelled Landau's name.

His breath now came in ragged gulps, and his head felt dizzy. He pushed himself to run all out, closing in on the crunch of gravel he heard ahead of him.

Once again, he saw a shadow moving in the foliage. Landau stopped and raised his weapon, but froze. He waited for a clear shot, but it faded. Another gunshot came from their left, followed by a woman's scream. They ran toward it.

People were shouting from several different directions. He saw movement ahead. Landau aimed his weapon and came to a halt, searching. Jessup stopped just behind Landau. Out of the brush came a woman herding two children. She saw the gun and screamed, grabbing up her offspring.

They took off running. The trees were thinning, and he saw Kenji running toward a residential area. He assumed it would be impossible to find him if he reached those houses. He tried to run faster but couldn't. He lost sight of Kenji but kept going.

They bounded over a bridge that spanned a pond. On the far side, Landau tripped and pitched forward. His body hit the gravel, and his gun flew out of his hand, clattering several feet ahead.

"Fuck!"

Jessup jumped to Landau's aid. He rolled Landau to one side and checked for injuries. Landau's lips were split open; his face was bloodied. He helped Landau crawl to his knees and reached for the gun, but it was no longer there.

Kenji stood over them, holding Landau's Glock. They both froze. Kenji inched the gun across Jessup's face and pressed the barrel to his forehead. Gooseflesh tickled Jessup's neck. He closed his eyes, and his bowels released some fluids, a shitting feeling, a draining of all the pretensions and trivial hopes for himself.

A shot burst, and his body lurched, but he realized the shot came from farther away. He was still alive.

The barrel withdrew. He crouched there gasping, watching Kenji make a beeline to the houses. It was too dangerous going after him without a weapon.

Souad ran up with a policeman on his heels. "Salman, what happened to your face?"

Landau tried to rub the blood off his cheek with his coat sleeve. "I'm okay."

"Like hell you are. What happened?"

"I fell."

"No, I mean with Kenji."

Jessup pointed downhill. "He's down there, somewhere in those houses."

"Shit."

"I think I already have," Jessup said.

Chapter Fifty-Three

By the time Jessup, Landau, and Souad met up with Randall at the temple, Jessup had pulled himself together. Laudau held a handkerchief to his mouth in an attempt to stem the bleeding. He told Randall to arrange an interview with the abbot.

Randall disappeared and came back minutes later to lead them through a gate that opened onto a path paved with square stones bending through a compact garden to the side of a house. Randal pulled open a sliding door. Beyond the door was a room with a traditional tatami mat floor, sparsely decorated with low-standing furniture.

In the center of the room, the monk Jessup saw at the temple altar sat on a cushion beside a table. His posture enhanced his elegance, and his face displayed an expression of consummate dignity. He wore a gray outer robe with white undergarments. Embroidered onto the gray fabric was a small yet exquisite golden phoenix.

There was a stern air about the monk's shaven head. It was as though all his energy was concentrated in that scalp. To Jessup, the abbot resembled Kenji—same age, same handsome face. They could be brothers, although he supposed the abbot was the statelier, and his face was grave almost to grief. *Yes*, Jessup thought, *the man radiates an aura of despair.*

The abbot bowed. He lifted his head, and their eyes met. He introduced himself as Abbot Saito, speaking Japanese. Randall interpreted.

If Saito was at all shocked by the violence that had occurred, or the injuries Landau suffered, it didn't show. He lifted an arm and pointed to pillows across the table. His long sleeve swayed beautifully as his arm made this graceful movement.

Landau and Jessup removed their shoes and stepped into the room. They walked to the table and lowered themselves onto the pillows, all the time staring at the abbot's features.

Randall and Souad removed their shoes and followed, both kneeling behind Landau.

Randall translated the abbot's words. "We are honored you have traveled all this way to see us." He lifted a porcelain pot, filled four teacups, and set the pot on the table. He presented tea to the men according to etiquette, bowed, and poured himself a cup.

Landau said, "The honor is mine. Thank you for seeing me."

They raised their cups and sipped. The tea was like nothing Jessup had ever tasted. Saito noticed his surprise and explained, "Chrysanthemum tea; very rare, even in Japan."

Randall proved indispensable, for he was a well-intentioned interpreter. He seemed to disappear, and Jessup felt as though he and Saito understood each other perfectly.

A handful of seconds tiptoed by, each one distinct, each one a burden. Saito picked up a plate of dumplings. Jessup set down his cup and accepted one. Landau refused.

The cell phone at the abbot's elbow buzzed. Saito picked up the phone. "Please to excuse me," he said, and pressed the phone to his ear. A moment later he extended his arm, passing the phone to Landau. "For you."

Landau pressed the phone to the side of his injured face. Jessup was sitting close enough that he clearly heard Kenji's voice. "Agent Landau, the FBI rose to new heights in my estimation."

Jessup should have been shocked, but at this point he was beyond any emotion.

Landau said, "The police are combing the island. There is no escape. Give yourself up."

"Who said I want to escape? I called to inform you that my son, Matt Reece, has something that belongs to me. I want it back. You will give it to Abbot Saito before you leave the island, or there will be dire consequences for all of you."

"We flew Matt Reece off the island. Whatever he has went with him."

"I'm a man of little patience, Agent Landau. I suggest you retrieve my property and hand it over to Saito before this hour is up."

"I don't negotiate with people who threaten me."

Kenji continued, "Even if you capture me, which now is an impossibility, what I've initiated is unstoppable. Handing over my property will not make the slightest difference to what will happen to the human species."

"You're lying. If we apprehend you, we will stop this horror."

"What the world is about to find out, Agent Landau, is that all horror comes down to this—that there is no horror. There is only what must be done to survive. You have one hour to save yourself."

The phone went dead, and Landau placed it on the table. He glanced at Saito. "He has your phone number, so I assume that you know each other well?"

An indescribable smile passed over the abbot's face. "We were both born on the day your country bombed Hiroshima. We grew up together," Saito said, "like brothers."

As Jessup absorb the abbot's words, the sliding door opened, and Sergeant Jingoro stood in the doorway with his hands on his hips.

Jessup glanced up. He felt hope rising in his throat, even though he knew better.

"I saw you with a handgun earlier," Jingoro said to Landau. "I need to see your permit."

Randall translated, and Landau said, "Fuck me."

"Do you want me to translate that?" Randall asked.

CHAPTER FIFTY-FOUR

MATT REECE was treated for his injuries—no broken bones, only minor contusions with deep bruising—and released. Leftover pain smoldered in the pit of his groin, so steady that he could force himself to ignore it. He ambled down a hall and into Lilikoi's room. The shades were drawn. She was asleep. Her side was bandaged, her ragged hair jutting out against the pillow. He slipped off his shoes and lay beside her.

He kissed her forehead, her cheek, her fingertips. He had no doubt Kenji would have killed him had she not stabbed his leg.

She stirred and came fully awake. "We survived, cowboy," she said. "Who'd have thought?"

He said, "That metal didn't puncture your lung. You only needed twenty stitches. Dr. Isushumi is releasing us both. My family is waiting downstairs."

"Patrick?"

"That a problem?"

She bit her lip. "At Berkeley, he wanted to have a baby. I flew back to the island to think it over without him pressuring me. Now I'm pregnant with our child."

"If you still love each other, he'll—"

"The thing is," she cut him off, "I don't know if I should have this baby. I mean, how can we raise a kid in the middle of a world at war?"

He glanced over her shoulder at the shaded windows.

"Will you despise me if I terminate?" she asked.

He sensed that what she really feared was Patrick hating her for sleeping with him.

"I mean, I want to have children. It's just…."

"I think we'll regret it every day of our lives," he said. "But if that's your decision."

He brought her hand back to his lips and kissed her fingers as a way to anchor himself. "If you do, never tell him you were pregnant. Never. He'll hate us for it."

She nodded, tears welling up. Matt Reece managed a weak smile.

"Let's get you dressed and face the family."

He swung off the bed and walked to the closet, wiping away his own tears. He opened the closet, and clothes dangled on hangers like ghosts.

He lifted a kimono from the hanger and turned to her. "Your old clothes were torn, so Patrick picked this out." It was teal blue, very light for summer wear. It came with two undergarments of the thinnest white silk. He laid them on the bed, and she fingered the fine material.

He held them out as she glided into them one by one. When she slipped into the outer garment, she experimented with the sheer lines of the cloth until she brought them into a pattern that became even more beautiful. She combed her hand through her choppy hair. Even sheared, she looked the picture of feminine grace.

She took so much care that he was sure it was all for Patrick's benefit.

AN HOUR later, Jessup trailed their small group, strolling along Rijo-dori Street, heading toward Peace Park. Patrick and Lilikoi led the group, she looking so feminine in her kimono, shuffling with tiny steps. Jessup could hardly believe this was the same tigress who savagely stabbed Kenji with a blade. A few paces back, Vishal walked with his arm over Matt Reece's shoulder in a protective hold. It was Saturday, so school was out, and a stream of kids traveling in groups of four or five passed them by and also families being led by fathers. Old men sat on park benches, women pushed baby carriages, and lovers strolled hand in hand. It was clear that the violence consuming the world had not touched this city yet.

Jessup could hardly believe he had both his sons back, and that this adventure was over. The Connors clan would need rebuilding, a lot of doing whatever it took to bring them together. But after all he had endured, he felt up for any challenge. He held no feelings for Kenji, which felt strange. He had loved that man, body and soul, for eleven years. Now he couldn't even picture Kenji's face, nor did he want to.

Randall contacted him at the hospital to say Landau had been arrested, and he and Souad and Rachael Laughton were at the police station trying to arrange Landau's release. Once that sticky problem was put to bed, they would all train back to Tokyo, and Jessup could fly his family home. They hoped to leave tomorrow.

Home, he thought. It was time to turn the page. The world was in an uproar, but he had his boys alive and safe. The afternoon sun on his face felt warm and comforting. A good sign for this new beginning, a beginning that included Vishal and perhaps even Lilikoi. It was clear from the adoring way Vishal and Matt Reece held each other that they were inseparable. Lilikoi and Patrick, however, had barely spoken a word to each other, yet there was an almost visible tenderness pulling them together.

Patrick turned his head. "Let's kick it into second gear, folks. We want to get there sometime this century."

"The museum is open until seven," Jessup said. "We've got all the time in the world."

Vishal leaned close to Matt Reece's ear and said, "Let's ditch Lilikoi and your brother and get off by ourselves."

"Is there some reason you won't call him Patrick? He's 'your brother' or 'him' with you."

Patrick turned his head again. "Christ, the snails are passing us by."

Vishal squeezed Matt Reece tighter. "What I know is, if there's shit within a mile of him, he's gonna stir it. He's been riding my ass since day one. And he thinks everyone should kiss his butthole because he wears those inscrutable facial expressions that suggest he's inaccessible and indestructible."

"Maybe he's not an asshole. Maybe he's an enigma, and you can't see his good side."

Vishal lasered into Matt Reece's eyes. "You've changed your tune since the day we saw him stealing a wallet."

"He's my brother. Mine. It's not cool to kick someone else's dog."

"I only want us to enjoy some alone time. Let's not spoil the day."

Matt Reece hugged him tighter, but there was stiffness to their show of intimacy.

Patrick glanced over his shoulder, as if wanting to say something but reluctant to bring it up within hearing distance of the others. He furrowed his brow, obviously gathering his courage. He gazed at Lilikoi and said, "It goes without saying I don't have any illusions about us getting back together, all right? You disappeared without a word, dropping me like a turd. So it's not like I'm planning our commitment ceremony. But I need to understand. For me it's been a real mind buster."

Lilikoi's laugh was strained. "You noticed I was gone?"

"I was worried sick. I started using. My life turned into one constant shitstorm."

"I don't believe you. You always land on your feet no matter who you roll off of."

"I never cheated on you."

"Oh please. Who do you think you're talking to? I'm not one of your brain-dead bimbos trying to mother you."

"Bimbos?" he said, raising his voice.

"Can I finish, please? Yes, as I remember, you only had sex with your friends. Trouble is, you don't have an enemy in the world."

He crossed and uncrossed his arms over his chest.

Jessup tried to ignore this conversation because it was none of his business. But he felt his son got lost somewhere along the way of becoming a man. Growing up, he was a courageous youth, a boy with true compassion and decency. Jessup needed to know that this boy he raised, this person he loved so dearly, still had those same fault lines running through his core. Jessup tried to digest this bizarre stream of… he wasn't sure what. "Excuse me, but were you two involved?"

Patrick looked back over his shoulder. "Can we get some privacy here?"

"If you want privacy," Jessup said, "I suggest you lower your voices."

"Involved?" Lilikoi said to Jessup. "These days we call it fucking."

"It was more than that. You were everything to me," Patrick said.

Lilikoi looked at the sidewalk. "I'm a big girl," she said. "I could handle you straying once in a while as long as I thought you loved me. But the way you treated me, I wasn't sure of anything."

"I loved you."

"You were in love with the idea of having a baby. But your real problem was that you hurt people. You used and then discarded anyone who cared for you, all to feed your ego. I didn't want to be used."

"I'm sorry if I gave you that impression, Miz Freud. I wanted kids with you because I thought a baby would tie us together. You know, so you wouldn't get bored with me and find someone else."

"The one kind thing I can say about you is that you were never boring."

Patrick's face lifted. "We did have some laughs."

She nodded.

"This FBI woman, Rachael Laughton, told us you and Matt Reece are wanted for the murder of your parents."

She waved a hand with an air of dismissal.

"Must be nice not to worry about a little thing like doing twenty to life," Patrick said.

"I'm counting on time off for good behavior. I'll be out in six years, tops."

"You couldn't behave yourself for that long if they handcuffed you to the warden."

She laughed, and it carried a sparkle of pleasure.

Patrick took her hand in his, and she let him. "If I promise not to pressure you about a baby, maybe we could have some laughs again?"

She stopped and turned to face him. They all halted. Jessup stared into a gift shop window, pretending he wasn't listening.

"I'm pregnant," she said.

Jessup turned back to see Patrick looking gut-shot.

"You want to talk about it?" His voice sounded gentle and deeply hurt, but he didn't let go of her hand.

"What good would that do?"

"I'm sorry. I just—"

She cocked her head to one side. "Christ… two sorrys in the same day. Somebody phone Guinness. I think we've got a world record here."

"Will you marry him?" Patrick's voice was hardly a whisper, his posture rigid, as if he were prepared for her to deliver another shattering blow.

She said, "He asked me to marry him, but I said no. So now it looks like he'll marry Vishal instead."

Jessup turned to Matt Reece. "What the hell's been going on?"

Matt Reece said, "Do I need to spell it out, I mean, about the birds and bees?"

Vishal hugged Matt Reece. "Oh my God, we're having a baby?"

Patrick's features smoothed, and his eyes softened. He took Lilikoi in his arms and cradled her. "A baby Connors?" He paused and added, "Yes… definitely." The sincerity in his voice left no doubt—a sincerity that was reflected in his eyes.

"You're not angry?" she asked. "You're not jealous of Matt Reece?"

Jessup could tell that Patrick's manic laugh was not the response Lilikoi expected. Even Matt Reece seemed offended by it.

Patrick said, "You slept with him to be closer to me. A blind man could see it. You do love me."

She touched the hummingbird tattoo on his neck. "When did you get this? It's beautiful."

"A week after you left me, to remind me of you."

They kissed, and she was the aggressor.

Watching them, Jessup became amazed at how much emotion could be transferred by the simple act of touching lips.

When they pulled apart, Patrick said, "If there were any others, never tell me. Lie to me all the way to our graves."

She wiped a tear from her eyes and nodded.

Patrick draped his arm around her waist and walked with a proud strut.

Jessup remembered a passage from some obscure work, something along the lines of: The law of passion is that we cannot begin to love again until we find a love greater than the last one. He knew now that Patrick had been looking all this time but found no one as passionate about life as Lilikoi. And he thought that the first law of narcissism must be that we cannot adore ourselves unless our display of love is more amazing than the last.

Patrick looked back over his shoulder, shooting a look at Jessup. "Come on, Grandpa. Let's find a burger joint for dinner tonight."

Jessup followed. Burgers sounded fine to him.

THEY CROSSED a bridge and entered the Peace Memorial Park, which had once been a busy commercial district but had been leveled by the bomb.

The park was verdant and beautiful, with numerous memorials and monuments. A black marble plaque with English words carved into the surface told Matt Reece the park was dedicated to the legacy of Hiroshima as the first city in the world to suffer a nuclear attack, and the legacy to honor the bomb's direct and indirect victims, whom there may have been as many as one hundred and forty thousand.

At the park's center stood a two-story, modern museum dedicated to the bombing. They walked to the Genbaku Dome, the skeletal ruins of the former Prefectural Industrial Promotion Hall. It was the closest building to the hypocenter of the bomb that fateful day, and part of the building remained standing. It gave Matt Reece a sense of sacredness, a tribute to humanity's collective shared heritage of that catastrophe.

It became his new symbol of revulsion, even though it meant to show Japan's pledge for peace.

Thinking about that devastation, he remembered something Kenji said. That war was caused by greed, and the only way to stop the killing was to give people what they desired. He slipped a hand into his pants pocket and fingered the flash drive.

They wandered to the Children's Peace Monument, a statue of a girl with outstretched arms and a folded paper crane rising above her. Hanging from the statue were thousands of paper cranes strung together on long threads. The statue, Lilikoi told him, was based on a true story of a girl who died from radiation sickness. She believed that if she folded a thousand paper cranes she would be cured. "To this day children around the world make cranes and send them here." She took a slip of paper from a stack at the statue's feet and folded it into a crane. She placed it beside the statue. "This is for us," she told Matt Reece, "a prayer for healing."

Matt Reece asked, "Patrick, if you had to share something earth-shattering with the entire world, how would you do it?"

"If it's a video, use YouTube. If it's documents, use WikiLeaks."

"WikiLeaks? Is it hard to do?"

"Piece of cake. I've done it a shitload of times."

Matt Reece held up the flash drive. "Can you WikiLeak the files on this?"

Patrick said, "Jessup had one, and the information on it was bogus."

"On the flight here, Kenji put a gun to Lilikoi's head and told me if I flushed this, he would kill her first, and then me."

Jessup took the drive and gave it a close inspection. "If Kenji was that serious, we should assume this one's the real McCoy. Agent Landau will know what to do with it."

Patrick snatched the drive from Jessup. "If we share this with the world, everyone will have it then, not just the super-rich scumbags who started the wars. It's the right thing to do. Besides, Landau might be locked up for years."

Patrick squeezed Lilikoi closer to him. "What do you say, momma. Are you down with taking this back to the room and posting it?"

"Sure. I'm dying to see you in action."

Patrick growled as he kissed her. He turned to Jessup. "I'll need a few hours to post this. Let's meet at the hotel at dinnertime. And keep your eye peeled for good burger joints."

Before Patrick could turn away, Vishal held out his hand. "We got off on the wrong foot. Now that we'll both be daddy-in-laws, perhaps you and I can start fresh?"

Patrick shook Vishal's outstretched hand. "Wrong foot? For the last few years I've had nothing but two left feet and butt-ugly shoes. But it's a new day."

"So we're good?" Vishal said.

"We're better than good," Patrick said, "we're brothers."

Patrick and Lilikoi hurried away through the lovely summer's dusk.

Matt Reece was sorry Jessup had not gone with them, because he wanted alone time with Vishal. But he knew Patrick needed that alone time as much as he did. It occurred to him that in the future, when they were all raising the baby, it might be hard to be accommodating, always giving Patrick and Lilikoi the lion's share of the baby's time, settling for scraps of moments here and there. On the other hand, he and Vishal would be fathers, and part of the responsibility to raise their child would fall on their shoulders.

They strolled to the children's exhibition. Vishal leaned close and said, "You know something, cowboy, I'm looking forward to seeing the ranch you were raised on."

"Don't be too anxious. It ain't much to look at for a city boy like you."

"Remember Food Not Guns?" Vishal said. "We could grow food and raise cattle and chickens to donate to needy people. We could organize a food commune like they have in Israel. That way, there'd be dozens of people helping with the work."

Matt Reece remembered the night they passed out food in San Francisco. He could still see those faces light up with gratitude. It had given him a sense of purpose.

"I guess it wouldn't be lonely with you there," Matt Reece said.

"The baby will love it. We can buy her a pony and teach her to ride."

"Sure, and we'll teach him how to fish too."

"Yep, she'll be a regular tomboy," Vishal said.

"Start praying for twins, city boy, because I'm set on raising a son."

"Twins are fine by me."

Matt Reece pressed his face against Vishal's shoulder. "Okay. We'll raise a whole pack of kids on the Promesa Rota Kibbutz."

Chapter Fifty-Five

THEY STOOD at the Peace flame for only a moment and moved on to a saddle-shaped monument that covered a cenotaph holding the names of the people killed that horrible day. The arch seemed to provide shelter for the victim's spirits. The engraved epitaph said: "Let all souls here rest in peace, for we shall not repeat the evil."

They hurried into the Peace Museum. It was a somber atmosphere. The East Wing showed the history of the city before the bombing, displaying pictures and belongings left by victims. In the center of the vast room stood a model showing the damage done to the city, and a huge red ball hanging from the ceiling showed how far above the city the bomb exploded. The room was blanketed by a humbling silence, even though it was crowded with visitors. The silence, like the stillness in Matt Reece's head, came from reverence for the dead and from the horror done by man.

They moved on to the West Wing, which concentrated on the harm done by the bomb. Displays included clothing, watches stopped at the time—8:15 a.m.—of the bombing, hair, and personal effects worn by the victims; pictures of damage done by heat rays on wood, stone, metal, glass and, of course, flesh; and included mutilation by the radiation, detailing the health effects suffered by people who survived the blast.

That time, 8:15 a.m., tickled Matt Reece's memory. And then it came to him, the time his grandfather's watch had stopped. Coincidence? What were the odds? He wanted out of there. He needed fresh air and sunlight.

He heard a commotion behind him, and he turned to see the room swimming with activity. People stampeded to form a wide trough between him and someone staggering toward him. The sudden chill in his heart told him it was Kenji an instant before he recognized his stepfather, who now stood like an exclamation mark against this museum to record human suffering. He held an aura of arrogance and certainty. Dressed in brown work boots, tan pants, and a long-sleeve shirt, Kenji looked like a janitor, except that his clothing was splattered with dark spots that looked like blood. He held a pistol in one hand. His diamond-hard eyes bored into Matt Reece.

Matt Reece's heart rate doubled, and he wanted to scream something, anything, but his inner voice seemed to solidify into a pulsing knot at the back of his esophagus. It burned as it lodged there, locking his throat shut. Now there was no border between his skin and the surrounding thick air. An emptiness settled in his chest, and then it seemed to rush through him, annihilating every thought, every feeling.

But then he felt something rousing within; Kirby had awakened. This time it felt different. His head slightly moved back and forth, and he felt something predatory and perverted extending about his skull, as a cobra's hood spreads. He felt this, felt a menace preparing to strike, and he knew it was evil.

People rushed to the exits.

Vishal wrapped an arm over his shoulders. "Let's get out of here." But Matt Reece couldn't move. Vishal used a louder voice directed at Kenji. "Do us a favor, asshole. Find someone else to fuck over."

Kenji waved dismissively. "Well, well, looks like the lovebirds have reunited. Ain't that a fan-fucking-tastic testament to love?" He rested his hand over his chest. When it moved back to his side, there was a hand-shaped bloodstain over the breast pocket.

Jessup moved to stand between the boys and Kenji. "I'm taking my family back to the ranch. Don't try to stop us."

Kenji raised his gun, pointing the barrel at Jessup. "Matt Reece betrayed me. And now it's reckoning time."

"Give yourself up," Jessup said. "Let it end now."

Kenji shot Jessup a slight smile. "That's what I'm doing: giving myself up. You have more cops trailing you than flies on shit. You think I'm stupid? I've had people watching you since you arrived, listening, monitoring your movements. I command a battalion of loyal followers."

The rush of noise blasting Matt Reece's head contrasted with the silent room. Then he realized that the noise was his own labored breathing, which turned into thick wheezing. *Another attack*, he thought. He fought for control, and in that battle, Kirby grew stronger.

As if by some stage cue, a uniformed Japanese SWAT officer stepped from behind a pillar with his rifle trained on Kenji. Two more appeared across the room. Then Landau walked into the open from behind an exhibit.

"Agent Landau," Kenji said, "the last time we met, you were staring down my gun barrel. Well, in fact, it was your gun barrel." He looked down at the Glock in his hand.

"Drop the weapon, Kenji," Landau said. "You can't escape."

"What the hell is going on here?" Jessup said, his voice weak.

Three more SWAT officers appeared behind Kenji, cutting off any retreat.

Kenji moved his neck and his shoulders as if loosening up for a race. "Agent Landau knew I wanted the flash drive that Matt Reece took from me. So he used you as bait to set up this pathetic little snare."

"I said drop the weapon. You get one chance, Kenji," Landau said. "Come along gentle or come along dead."

The SWAT team inched closer, but Kenji held the gun on Jessup.

Landau said, "I'm only saying this once more. Drop the gun, and lay on the floor, facedown."

Kenji sank to his knees, but he kept the gun trained on Jessup. "I'll make a deal with you, Landau. I'll give up the gun, but only if Matt Reece takes it from my hand."

Landau shook his head. "I'm calling the shots here, not you."

Matt Reece wrestled Kirby for dominance. Even though Kenji was cornered, he still pushed his buttons, manipulated him. And against his better judgment, he said, "I'll do it. I'll take the gun." As the words left his mouth, he knew Kirby had the upper hand.

Matt Reece stepped between his two fathers. Now Kenji's gun pointed at his heart. He eased forward, keeping his movements slow, trying to draw more air past the blockage in his throat.

"Be careful, Matt Reece. Don't get too close to him," Landau said.

Now that there was nothing between them, Kenji looked less like a superhuman serial killer and more like a down-and-out research veterinarian. He was not seething with anger or fear. His eyes bored into Matt Reece with a calm, almost lazy stare.

Agent Souad came out of the shadows and stood next to Landau. "Something's not right. He's pissing on us."

Landau nodded. "For the first time since our partnership began, you and I are in complete agreement."

"Then put a stop to it."

"You're wound too tight," Landau told him. "Loosen up. Be ready for anything."

Matt Reece reached out and clamped his fingers around Kenji's weapon. To his surprise, Kenji released his grip, and he backed away.

One of the SWAT team yelled in English, "Down! Face on floor, arms and legs spread." He came up from behind and struck Kenji between the shoulder blades with the butt of his rifle. Kenji sprawled facedown, obeying. The officer dropped to one knee, and with quick movements, handcuffed Kenji's hands behind his back.

Once Kenji was subdued, the officer grabbed his shoulders and heaved him back up to his knees. He frisked his prisoner, checking each pocket, each crevice.

Matt Reece stared at his stepfather. After all they endured, after the people Kenji killed, it seemed impossible that he would end like this.

"I gave the flash drive to Patrick," Matt Reece told Kenji. "He's posting it on WikiLeaks. Now the fighting will stop."

Kenji shook his head. "Didn't you hear me say I've had you followed?"

The officer frisking Kenji dug a flash drive from the front pants pocket. As he held it out, a chill spread over Matt Reece's shoulders and scalp. Kirby surged.

"You betrayed me, you and Patrick," Kenji said with a nonchalant voice, as if he had asked Matt Reece to pass the salt. But to Matt Reece it sounded deadly.

Landau stepped forward and took the flash drive from the officer's hand.

"I took that from Patrick not twenty minutes ago," Kenji said.

"You're lying," Matt Reece shouted. "You've lied about everything right from the beginning, and you're lying now." He backed away, wanting to put as much space as possible between him and this fiend. "You can buy these at any convenience store. This can't be the one I gave Patrick."

The cop frisking Kenji pulled something from the right shirt pocket. He said in English, "What the fuck…?"

It looked like a piece of colored crepe paper, as big around as a saucer. Landau took it and laid it over the palm of his left hand. His face flushed white, and his eyes filled with fear as he raised his free hand to his mouth. "Oh Lord."

Souad grabbed Landau by the coat sleeve. "What the hell is it?"

"Get everyone out of here. Quick, let's go," Landau said.

Matt Reece inched toward Landau. "What have you got?"

Landau turned on Matt Reece and said, "Give me that pistol."

Matt Reece glanced down at the Glock in his hand, somewhat surprised that he still had it. Absently, like counting off prayer beads, he fingered the safety catch on and off in rhythm, like a ticking bomb. When he stopped, the safety was off. He pulled his arm back, not wanting to surrender it. "Show me."

Landau straightened his posture, visibly pulling himself together. He swallowed and held his hand out to Matt Reece. "Give me that weapon." This time it was a command.

Matt Reece backed away. "Just tell me what the fuck is going on."

Landau moved toward him but stopped when Matt Reece pointed the gun at him.

"Show me, dammit." He was gasping for breath so hard he could hardly understand himself.

Landau opened his palm, and Matt Reece saw a patch of skin with a hummingbird tattoo imprinted on it. He whirled toward Kenji, the Glock still held shoulder high. "What did you do?"

Kenji bowed his head, as if paying homage to some deity. "Have you ever seen the sight of a human chest and abdomen laid open? No? Imagine the harmony of the heart peeking out from behind lungs, the liver and spleen caressing, the dome of the rib cage protected by muscle and cartilage, and twenty-three feet of glistening bowels compacted into such a tiny space. It's a marvel of engineering. Now imagine two sets of bowels artfully intertwined. The sheer beauty of it left me transfixed."

Matt Reece leveled the Glock at Kenji's head and stepped forward until the barrel touched Kenji's temple.

Landau said, "No. Drop that gun. Trust me, he'll pay for this."

Kenji lifted his head to stare into Matt Reece's eyes. "You've never been particularly religious, son, which I applaud. That means, of course, that there is no God to shield you from a vengeful and punitive force. And it doesn't mean there is no good or evil in the world. Good and evil exist. And so does punishment and atonement. I've shown you how fragile this world is, how delicate the balance between good and evil. You betrayed me, and that was evil. Now I will demonstrate the full weight of the meaning of punishment."

What Matt Reece couldn't bear was the feeling that something vital had been uprooted from his chest. He wanted to cling to Kenji, make him take it all back. Until moments ago, he assumed this nightmare was over, that he and Vishal would begin a new life. Now he had no hope of ever escaping. Nothing was left but Kirby's rage.

"I can't let you do this," Landau said.

Matt Reece's gun hand trembled.

The SWAT team supervisor said in English, "Step away from the prisoner, and lower your weapon, or we will shoot."

Jessup moved away from the others, showing himself in Matt Reece's line of vision. He was sobbing. "Go ahead, son, kill that son of a bitch. Kill him. End this now."

"No!" Landau yelled.

Vishal said, "If you shoot, you're no better than him. That's what he wants."

Kenji lowered his head and barked out a sentence in Japanese. One by one, each member of the SWAT team retrained his rifle from Kenji to Matt Reece.

Matt Reece pressed the gun more tightly to Kenji's head, undecided, furious.

Landau eased toward him. "I promise we'll make him pay. Give me the weapon."

It all came back to him, everything since leaving the Promesa Rota. He often wondered why Kenji kept dragging him along. Now he understood. Kenji had, inch by inch, created and then nurtured Kirby, pushing him toward something that would make him as crippled as Kenji. His stepfather was consumed with proving that everyone was as much a monster as himself.

"Landau," Matt Reece said, "I'll trade you this gun for that flash drive."

"What will you do with it?" Landau asked.

"Finish what Patrick started, so the bloodshed can end."

Landau hesitated only a second. He held out the drive.

Matt Reece nodded to Vishal. As soon as Vishal took the drive from Landau, he threw down the gun.

Jessup snatched it up at the same instant Vishal pulled Matt Reece away from Kenji.

"I'm so proud of you," Vishal said.

Jessup pointed the gun at Kenji's head and pulled the trigger.

Click. Click.

Rifle shots rang out as Landau leaped to tackle Jessup. A burst of bullets cut across Landau's back, stitching a pattern from left shoulder to right thigh. He and Jessup spun to the ground.

It took a moment for Matt Reece to understand. Kenji's gun was not loaded. His stepfather was never in any danger. Kenji planned for the police to kill him, but once he threw down the gun, they shot at Jessup instead. But even that backfired when Landau leaped between Jessup and the sharpshooters.

He rushed to Landau and slumped to his knees. Jessup was dazed. Landau had been shot four times, and blood was rapidly staining his clothing, but he was alive. Vishal pressed a handkerchief to one wound and a bare palm on another.

Kenji said, "If you post that information online, in fifty years overpopulation will consume every bit of land, every scrap of food, until there's nothing left but killing each other, which they will do. The few survivors will devour the dead until there is no one left to eat. At least with my plan, two or three billion will survive."

"We can change," Matt Reece said. "Man can overcome, because we have the ability to reevaluate our circumstances and adapt. The human spirit can prevail."

Kenji shook his head. "Knowing can't save us. What is constant throughout history is greed and recklessness and a lust for violence. That is the story of man. You and I are powerless to change that. That's why I was able to start this war so easily, simply by pitting man's two strongest emotions against each other."

"Nobody," Matt Reece said, "not me, and certainly not you, has a right to play God."

Kenji laughed. "But that's what I've done. I command life and death. Patrick begged me to spare the girl's life and the life of your baby inside her."

Matt Reece leaped to his feet, bounded over Jessup, and kicked Kenji in the face, dead center. Kenji fell back as Matt Reece kicked him again. Teeth and blood splattered across the floor.

Souad grabbed Matt Reece from behind and hauled him out of striking range. "That's enough. We have him now, and he'll pay."

Kenji jerked himself to his knees and spoke in rapid-fire Japanese. His voice shook with rage. The SWAT rifles trained on Souad and Matt Reece.

Kenji said through bloody lips, "Now I'll show you what true power can do."

"What's the meaning of this?" Souad asked the SWAT supervisor.

The supervisor trained his weapon on Souad.

"Allow me to translate," Kenji said. "I told them: 'Look around at these exhibits. This is what the West did to us. We lost whole generations. I'm offering you and your families immortality, and they want to rob us again. They want it only for themselves. Don't let them take it. Follow me, and we will live for the next ten thousand years. We will defeat them this time and become the leader of the world. Only I can give you this.'"

Matt Reece thought, *He walked into this trap knowing he could turn them against us.*

Kenji said, "This is proof that human greed trumps everything. Prepare to die."

Matt Reece took the flash drive from Vishal and held it up for all to see. "This holds the formula to make us all immortal. I'm making this a gift to the whole world. We can bring about peace. Isn't that what this memorial is about? The promise to end all wars? Help me stop the killing."

One by one, the rifles turned back on Kenji.

"He's lying," Kenji said in English. "Only I can give eternal life. Only I am God." There was fury in his voice, and madness.

Matt Reece asked Souad to call an ambulance, or better yet, get his helicopter to land out front and take Landau to the nearest hospital.

Souad lifted his phone and called Randall. Seconds later he said, "Ten minutes."

A shout sounded at the front of the building, followed by another, and then a chorus of yells erupted. A burst of gunfire silenced the cries for an instant. The SWAT leader's walkie-talkie emitted a spray of Japanese sentences, and the leader turned to Souad. "A mob has gathered in the park. Word got out Kenji is here, and his supporters are fighting those against him. They're all trying to break in here, but my men have created a barricade at the front door. We're trapped until help arrives."

Individual voices could be heard, some in Japanese and some in English. "Give us the cure! Surrender Kenji!"

Souad glanced up at the roof. "Like hell we are." He hit his phone's Redial button. "Randall, change of plans. Don't land out front. Hover over the museum roof, and we'll climb in."

Souad closed his phone. "Lead us to the roof," he told the SWAT leader.

Matt Reece and Vishal lifted Landau and carried him. The SWAT team herded everyone to a stairwell, and they climbed the two flights.

Kenji sobbed, "Give me to my people. They hunger for what only I can give them." He sounded like those homeless lunatics on street corners calling for the second coming.

The SWAT team hustled them onto the roof. Matt Reece got a good look at the mob below. Several hundred people pressed against the front of the museum, some carrying signs. The mood was angry and getting more so as the crowd continued to grow. They clearly wanted blood, but were they for or against Kenji?

The SWAT team led the group to a clear spot on the roof. Matt Reece and Vishal leaned Landau against a vent. Landau was obviously in great pain. Matt Reece scanned the sky for the copter. Nothing.

Kenji stood gazing over the crowd, and by the shocked look on his face, Matt Reece knew his stepfather had made a gross miscalculation. Kenji expected a hero's welcome in his homeland, the victorious general returning with garlands around his neck and captured slaves at his feet. But this throng overwhelmingly wanted to rip him to pieces.

"Fools!" he screamed. "I'm offering you the chance to rule the world for eternity!"

Matt Reece laid a hand on Kenji's shoulder. "They don't want to rule the world through bloodshed. They've already experienced the pain that brings."

Jessup pointed at the sky toward the north.

Even before Matt Reece turned his head to look, he heard the sound of the rotor blades thumping the air. He saw the red copter, coming fast.

A roar shot up from the crowd below them. A quick burst of automatic weapons fired, and the chanting stopped. Matt Reece peeked over the edge of the roof to see people streaming into the museum's front doors.

Matt Reece stared at Kenji and said, "Your motive, overpopulation, I don't buy it. You wanted to ignite violence. You only wanted to kill."

"My mother's death became the motivation for everything I've done in the last half-century. I was driven by a deep need for justice. Consuela thought it was the greatest boon to mankind, while I knew it would destroy much of the earth. But from her enthusiasm, I hatched a plan to destroy all the developed countries except Japan. The meek will soon inherit the earth."

Matt Reece had believed the man's motives were to save humanity. Now he realized the truth, and it sickened him.

Kenji lifted his head. "We're alike, you and I."

"Wouldn't you like to think so?" His last word was drowned by a roar from the mob, who were now inside the stairwell.

"We've got to get him out of here," Matt Reece said.

Kenji seemed not to hear. He stared at Matt Reece, his eyes pleading.

The copter swung above the roof and lowered until it was only a foot off the deck. As soon as the doors swung open, Matt Reece and Vishal snatched up Landau and hustled him into the bird. Next came the SWAT team with the prisoner. Kenji allowed himself to be led in a stumbling scramble into the passenger compartment. He squatted on the floor and hid his face against his knees. Jessup and Souad were the last to board.

The door on the stairwell burst open. People streamed onto the roof. The sound of the rotor blades was lost in another roar. Mob sounds became a rhythmic assault, hoarse and inarticulate noises—a gigantic snarl.

The copter lunged away. Matt Reece closed his eyes and hugged Vishal to him. He breathed in shallow gasps, not from a blockage in his throat but from relief.

Matt Reece asked Souad, "What will happen to him?"

Souad said, "He'll stand trial here for the murder of Patrick and Lilikoi, and then we'll extradite him to the States to stand trial for the murder of Consuela and Vishal's grandfather. My guess is that he'll get life in prison with no chance of parole."

"Even if life is ten thousand years?"

Landau glanced up at Souad and spoke in a weakened voice. "Congratulations, partner. We wrapped up our case, and what a humdinger."

Chapter Fifty-Six

THE SKY filled with a bittersweet dusky light, illuminating the trees with a golden shimmer. Matt Reece slouched on a park bench with the docility of fatigue. He wore a potato-colored overcoat that was too big for him. Vishal sat beside him, with one arm curling across his shoulders. In the distance stood the hospital where Landau had been recovering for the last two weeks. They stayed for Landau's release so they could all fly back to the States together. He and Vishal had waited on that bench for three hours. He didn't know what the holdup was, but he refused to walk into the gloomy hospital interior to find out. He needed fresh air and nothing over his head except the blue dome of heaven.

The world situation had changed since he'd posted the contents of the flash drive onto WikiLeaks: fighting had stopped, governments at the United Nations had agreed to establish a one-child policy to combat overpopulation; Jessup arranged for Patrick and Lilikoi's bodies to be shipped to the Promesa Rota for burial; Landau was getting out of the hospital at any moment. Yes, there was much to be thankful for. The freshly inaugurated US president had sent the new Air Force One and a five-star general to escort them back to the States. They planned a parade in Washington, DC, addresses to the joint session of Congress, medals, a banquet in the White House. The president himself prattled to him over the phone, "You're a hero, my boy, a true red-white-and-blue-blooded hero."

Yes, the fat cats got what they wanted without having to give up their guns and bombs and battleships. The world was jubilant, and Matt Reece helped bring that about.

He couldn't absorb it all. In his dreams he still heard Kenji's mad shrieks, the threat of total annihilation of the planet, and he wasn't sure if he had done something even more monstrous than his stepfather. Only time and human nature would tell, and even if it took hundreds of years to come about, he would be there to see it. He needed to put a higher level of faith in human ingenuity. That was easy to understand, but hard to do.

Vishal whispered something, but he didn't hear. He remained silent, his head cocked to one side. All he heard was birds chirping.

"Were you listening?" Vishal asked, poking him in the ribs. "I said, I don't know how Kenji could live with himself after all the death he caused, and for what? Revenge for something he can't change. I hope for his sake he doesn't have a shred of conscience."

"He was right about one thing." A pensive adult quality cut through Matt Reece's thin voice. "Guns and bombs mixed with human greed make for a crazy world. More than anything else, he proved that."

"I can't believe you're defending him."

"I'm not," Matt Reece said. "I'm defending an idea, and I'm wondering if we'll ever see a sane world, or are we too far beyond saving?"

They both grew quiet, and he listened to the breeze soughing through the trees around them. The trees swayed, and their shadows looked like monsters dancing over the grass and stone.

He looked up to see Jessup pushing Landau in a wheelchair. Rachael walked beside the chair, holding Landau's hand. On the other side, Randall walked beside Jessup. Landau was dressed in slacks, but a hospital gown covered his chest, which was wrapped in bandages. He looked years older.

Matt Reece said, "Hey there, Sal, how are you feeling?"

"I can breathe without pain now, as long as I take my meds. But boy these pills do a number on me. Being home will help."

Vishal lifted a shopping bag off the bench and handed it to Landau. "We all pitched in and got you something."

Landau sat the bag on his lap and opened it. Inside was a new fly-fishing rod and reel. Landau smiled. "It's perfect. But how did you know I love to fish?"

Matt Reece said, "Jessup told us you always wore a yellow fly hook on your jacket lapel, to remind you of better times."

"I don't know how to thank you."

"Invite us over for a fish fry every now and then," Jessup said.

"Will do," Landau said. "Are you all going back to the ranch after they finish jerking us off in Washington?"

Matt Reece squeezed closer to Vishal. "We're turning the ranch into a commune to raise food for the needy. I can't wait for my first sunrise over the prairie again."

Landau cocked his head to look at Jessup. "And you?"

Jessup slung an arm up over Randall's shoulders. "We're heading up to New York City. I've been contacted by a group of mothers who are set on keeping up the pressure to rid our country of assault weapons. They're planning a protest rally in Central Park. That was Patrick's vision, and I'm going to carry on his fight."

Randall pressed his lips to Jessup's cheek. "We, not I. Don't leave me out."

Rachael said, "Raising food for the needy? Fighting gun violence? You give me hope for the future."

"It's a changing world," Jessup said.

"Well, I'm too old to change," Landau said. "I'm taking this new rod and reel and going back to what I do best." He squeezed Rachael's hand. "I'm getting a chill thinking about that first cast at dawn. Shall we go?"

She smiled. "Let's get you to the hotel."

"I want to stay here a while longer," Matt Reece said. "We'll catch up with you for dinner before we head to the train station."

Jessup pushed the chair along the path, taking Landau and Rachael and Randall to the hotel.

Matt Reece heard the clacking of shoes on the stone walkway. He looked up to see a middle-aged man being led by an impatient flock of children, begging him to hurry. The man held a wooden bucket and a washrag, no doubt taking his kids to the nearest public bath. Matt Reece watched them pass. He turned to glance at Vishal and closed his eyelids on tears.

Vishal said, "Don't be sad, cowboy. Just focus on all the hungry kids we'll be feeding. We'll have a dozen helping us on the ranch."

Matt Reece snuggled closer while turning to face a nearby pond, on which the evening sun was shining. The sky was reflected on the surface, beneath fish moved in a slow cadence, and duckweed waved to and fro. This watery sky was different from the one above their heads. It was clear and filled with a serene light; from underneath and from within, it swallowed up the earth, and everything seemed to sink into it like a great anchor of pure gold that became dark with rust.

"Yes, at least a dozen. Let's go home," Matt Reece said.

They rose, and arm in arm they walked over the stone bridge that crossed the pond.

Afterword

Kenji Hiroshige died fourteen years after being imprisoned. His illness had something naked and abstract about it, and to which no name other than death could be attributed. It seemed that death found a way to enter the scene and finally take what it had waited so long for. As the end came, Kenji Hiroshige made little resistance to his approaching fate. He showed signs of an unutterable weariness and often remarked to his jailers that he was "dead sick of being confined, sick of the whole damned thing." Giving his own version of "Give me liberty or give me death." His brow furrowed, lines of arrogance and boredom eventually spreading to his entire face, morphing into an exaggerated, grotesque grimace, and continued to deepen and spread until death smoothed them out.

Toward the end, Kenji Hiroshige made a last request, which, though scarcely understood, was dutifully complied with, although the doctors knew it would do him no good. His wish, which would bring about Kenji Hiroshige's last act, was that Matt Reece Connors visit him before his death.

Matt Reece came to stand at the side of Kenji's prison hospital bed. He hadn't aged a day, still as young and fresh and beautiful as a spring morning. Vishal stood beside him, and no one could doubt the intimacy that passed between them. And while Kenji was in one of his more lucid moments, propped up with pillows, shading his eyes with his wax-colored hands—he couldn't bear the light after being kept in a dim cell for so many years—he composed his features into a malignant grimace and said he was sorry for the pain he had caused.

Matt Reece could see that his stepfather's soul was tugging at its moorings and would soon break free to drift along unknown currents. With Matt Reece's head bent to his right, pity forced him to try to comfort this sick, dying man. Thus it fell to Matt Reece Connors to administer the last bit of human kindness to Kenji Hiroshige, holding that yellowed hand to ease the final spasms and be his helper into death.

So died the man who thought he would live forever, uttering his last sigh on a bitter cold night. The prison hospital room was brightly lit, with three doctors in attendance. The stern furrows of his boredom smoothed over his face, and he was carried along, leaving his waxlike shell behind.

The body was cremated, and Matt Reece Connors took the ashes back to the Promesa Rota ranch. On the first day of spring, Matt Reece and Vishal rode west, as far as the foothills of the towering White Mountains, and spread Kenji Hiroshige's ashes over a windblown bluff. They watched them rise on the breeze and settle over the landscape. Dust to dust, as it should be.

ALAN CHIN enjoyed a twenty-year career working his way from computer programmer to Director of Software Engineering, but he lost interest in computer science when he began writing fiction. He walked away from corporate America in 1999 and never looked back. Since then he has traveled to over forty countries, scuba dived the Great Barrier Reef, tracked black rhino in the Serengeti, and dined in most of the capitals of Europe. Oh yes, and he's published several gay-themed novels and two screenplays.

In addition to writing, Alan is making a name for himself as a literary critic for several online publications which include Examiner.com GLBT Literature column, Queer Magazine Online, and the Lambda Literary website. In 2007, QBlissmagazine awarded their Pride In Literature award to Alan for his debut novel. In 2010, Alan's novel, *The Lonely War*, swept the Rainbow Literary Awards, taking top honors in four categories: Best Fiction, Best Historical, Best Characters, and Best Setting.

Alan currently spends half of the year traveling the globe and the other half writing at his home in Palm Springs, California.

Website: alanchin.net
Blog: alanchinwriter.blogspot.com
Email: alanhchin@aol.com

THE LONELY WAR

Alan Chin

The realities of war are brutal for any man, but for a Buddhist like Andrew Waters, they're unthinkable. And reconciling his serene nature with the savagery of World War II isn't the only challenge Andrew faces. First, he must overcome the deep prejudice his half-Chinese ancestry evokes from his shipmates, a feat he manages by providing them with the best meals any destroyer crew ever had. Then he falls in love with his superior officer, and the two men struggle to satisfy their growing passion within the confines of the military code of conduct. In a distracted moment, he reveals his sexuality to the crew, and his effort to serve his country seems doomed.

When the ship is destroyed, Andrew and the crew are interned in Changi, a notorious Japanese POW camp. In order to save the life of the man he loves, Andrew agrees to become the commandant's whore. He uses his influence with the commandant to help his crew survive the hideous conditions, but will they understand his sacrifice or condemn him as a traitor?

www.dsppublications.com